Where the
Heart Leads

ALSO BY JEANELL BOLTON

What the Heart Wants

Where the Heart Leads

JEANELL BOLTON

FOREVER
YOURS

New York   Boston

Copyright © 2015 by Jeanell Bolton
Excerpt from *What the Heart Wants* is copyright © 2014 by Jeanell Bolton
Cover design by Christine Foltzer
Cover photo of couple © peopleimages.com
Cover photo of sky © Andrey tiyk/Shutterstock
Cover copyright © 2015 by Hachette Book Group, Inc.

Forever Yours
Hachette Book Group
1290 Avenue of the Americas
New York, NY 10104
hachettebookgroup.com
twitter.com/foreverromance

First published as an ebook and as a print on demand edition: November 2015

Forever Yours is an imprint of Grand Central Publishing.
The Forever Yours name and logo are trademarks of Hachette Book Group, Inc.

The Hachette Speakers Bureau provides a wide range of authors for speaking events. To find out more, go to www.hachettespeakersbureau.com or call (866) 376-6591.

The publisher is not responsible for websites (or their content) that are not owned by the publisher.

ISBNs: 978-1-4555-5731-8 (ebook edition), 978-1-4555-5727-1 (print on demand edition)

*Dedicated to the memory of friends Nicole
Zuber Domingue, Jeannette Faurot, and
Karen Stolz, who encouraged my literary
endeavors and enriched my life.*

Acknowledgments

This book took more than a village to write. It took an army.

Thank you to my family—Chris, Kit, Jen, Lee, Lauren, and Lexa—who loved me through thick and thin, supplied valuable information in their areas of expertise, and fielded late-night phone calls when my laptop took off on its own.

And to my rancher friends—Joan Barton, Patricia Carando, Carol Fox, Denney Rodriguez, Gary Wofford, and Michelle Wyckoff. And to my civic theater friends—Carrie Marks Nelson and Judy Sink Scott. And my ACC friend, Sonia Stewart. All of your information was right on. Any errors in application are my own.

And to my sharp-eyed beta readers—Joan Barton, Patricia Carando, Suzy Gregory, Suzy Millar Miller, and Denney Rodriguez.

And to the Austin chapter of the Romance Writers of

America, especially Janece Hudson, Jane Myers Perrine, Jessica Scott, Liana LeFey, and Claire Ashby.

And to Far North, our boondocks critique group, which puts up with me every month.

And to friends Joann Gerbig, Sharon Kite, Paula Marks, Marion Mayfield, Evelyn Palfrey, and, Ashley Vining, who have supported me from the outset.

And to Mike Miller, who let me take notes on his office at Georgetown High School. And Clara Sue Arnsdorff, who suggested the American Girl doll. And to Sheralyn Swenson Browning, who told me about butter paper.

And to Click Computer, which has never failed me, and, of course, to Google—don't ever think that writing a contemporary romance doesn't involve research.

Special thanks to the two people who have made this book possible—the Divine Liza and my Editor Extraordinaire, aka literary agent Liza Dawson and Hachette Book Group's Michele Bidelspach—to whom I owe a double thank-you.

Postscript: Forgive me, Texas, for opening a fireworks stand in October, but I claim authorial privilege.

And I also ask forgiveness from anyone whom I've left out of my acknowledgments. I'm writing them by the midnight oil, which means my overtaxed brain is sure to be forgetting someone important. Whoever you are, I didn't mean to pass you by, so please, please contact me, and I'll catch up with you in my next book.

Where the
Heart Leads

Chapter One

Moira drove into the asphalt lot across the street from the yellow brick building and swung her six-year-old Toyota into a marked space.

Panic crawled up her spine.

It's just another audition, she told herself. *You know the routine—you've been auditioning since you were a kid. No big deal. You either get the part or you don't, and if you don't, there's always another audition around the corner.*

But this wasn't Hollywood or New York—it was small-town Texas—and she wasn't a kid trying out for a role as somebody's tagalong little sister anymore. She was an adult, twenty-six years old, and this would be the first day of a three-month trial to be herself, Moira Miranda Farrar, with no safety net this time around.

The Bosque Bend Theater Guild had signed her on to direct their upcoming production, and if she could pull it off, they'd keep her on permanently.

And if they didn't? No, that wasn't an option. She *had* to keep this job. Everything depended on her success, not only for her, but also for her family, just as it had since she was four years old when Gramp discovered she had a freakish memory and a gift for mimicry. With his disability pension stretched to the limit, she'd become the major support of the family.

She draped her arms on the steering wheel and stared at the building that was gleaming gold in the bright October sun. It looked like an old high school to her, but Pendleton Swaim, her contact with the theater group, had called it the town museum and told her the board met there.

Glancing at her stylishly oversized wristwatch, she realized she was early, which gave her time to get the lay of the land before she met with her new employers.

They'd hired her, sight unseen, on the recommendation of Johnny Blue, who'd starred in the last sitcom she'd worked in before she'd married Colin four years ago. Well, it wasn't entirely sight unseen. All of America had watched her grow up playing an assortment of third-banana little sisters on TV comedies, and later, when she was too old for the bangs-and-pigtails roles, clunking around as Johnny's robot assistant on his sci-fi series. Of course, now that he'd moved on to films, Johnny was on the showbiz A-list, while she didn't even rate a Z.

She rubbed the scar on the underside of her left arm and compressed her lips into a determined line, then opened the car door, stood up, and smoothed the skirt of her cloth-belted safari-style dress. Even now, a member of the theater board might be looking her over from one of those dark windows in the yellow building. She glanced down at her sensible black pumps. Was she dressed conservatively enough for small-town Texas?

Just in case, she adjusted the leather portfolio under her arm, segued into her no-nonsense persona, and, despite there being no traffic, waited for the light to turn before she marched across the street. As she walked up the wide front steps of the building and through the imposing front door, her heart pounded with fear and excitement, just like it always did before a performance.

She'd crossed not only a visible threshold, but also an invisible one. She was committed—no turning back. Now to locate the meeting room before anyone else arrived.

According to the directory on the wall beside the stairwell, she was on the second floor, and the Bosque Bend Theater Guild met on the third floor, Room 300. She hurried up the stairs, passing a trio of anxious-looking adults who were herding along a group of schoolchildren wearing cardboard cowboy hats and poking at each other with plastic branding irons.

Room 300 was locked, but rising up on her toes and looking through the window in the door, she could see it had an elevated stage on one side of it. She smiled. Room 300 was not only an appropriate place for a theater guild to meet, but it would also be a good place for special rehearsals too.

Now to kill a little time before the meeting. She walked back down to the second floor and looked around the hall, then wandered into a display room.

Grimy fossils dug out of the Bosque riverbank dominated most of the space, but the far wall provided an interactive history of the Indians who had been the area's first settlers. The next room featured rotting saddles, wicked-looking branding irons, and ambrotypes of squinty-eyed cowboys, all donated, according to the legend beside the display, by Rafe McAllister of the C Bar M Ranch.

Under a wall map of the ranch sat a machine that dispensed cardboard cowboy hats and plastic branding irons. Moira looked at the list of color choices and ran her hand over the buttons. Tempting, but she decided to leave that experience for the next time around—unless she wanted to look like a total dork when she walked into her first meeting with her new employers.

She checked her watch again.

Nine minutes till blastoff. A leisurely stroll back up to the third floor again and she'd arrive at five minutes before the hour, an appropriate time for a new hire who was ahead of the mark. She turned the corner toward the front of the building.

And collided with a fast-moving freight train.

A flame-haired man holding a little girl by the hand steadied her with a light touch on the arm.

"Didn't mean to mow you down, ma'am. We're makin' an emergency run for the ladies' room."

Ma'am? He'd called her *ma'am?* Like John Wayne and Gary Cooper in the old westerns Gramp was addicted to? Did small-town Texans really do that, address all unknown females as *ma'am?* Holy Hollywood! Did Red have a horse hitched up to a parking meter outside?

Moira tried to smile back, but Tall, Red, and Handsome

was halfway down the hall before her lip muscles could get themselves coordinated. She stared after him in awe and wonder. He had the most beautiful eyes she'd ever seen.

Maybe there was more to Bosque Bend than a last-ditch job and a history museum after all.

Big Red and the little girl had stopped in the middle of the hall. The child was dancing with distress, and the high pitch of her voice echoed off the hard walls.

"Come into the bathroom with me, Daddy. I don't want to go in there by myself. It's big and dark and honks like an angry elephant!"

Red bent down to her. "Delilah, Daddy can't go in there. It's only for girls."

"Then I'll go with you to the daddies' bathroom, like when I was little."

"That's not gonna fly, baby. Tell you what. Daddy will stand right here by the door, and if you yell, he'll come a-chargin' in and rescue you."

Moira approached them, making sure her smile was properly adjusted this time. "May I help? I was about to use the restroom myself." She turned to the child. "Delilah, my name is Moira."

The little girl gave her a hard stare, then bobbed her strawberry blonde curls and broke into her own smile. "Okay. I like you. You're pretty."

Delilah thought she was *pretty*? Moira's breath caught and her heart warmed.

Big Red's daughter was telling the truth as she saw it, but having grown up on the Hollywood scene, Moira knew what *pretty* really meant—tall and willowy, blond and busty, languid and lovely—none of which she was. On the other hand, while being five three, small-breasted, and hardworking might not win her a star on the Hollywood Walk of Fame, she was very good at opening restroom doors.

Delilah made for the nearest stall, talking the whole time.

"I have three aunts and three uncles. Sometimes Aunt Rocky comes to our house to take care of me, but mostly she stays with Uncle Travis in his house. Aunt TexAnn and Uncle Wayne live in Austin because she makes laws that tell people what to do. Aunt Alice and Uncle Chub don't talk to us 'cause they're mad at Daddy. Oh—I have Aunt Sissy too, but she's not a real aunt. She works for Daddy in his office except on Friday afternoons, when she stays home with Baby Zoey."

"Um. That's nice." Moira had no idea how many aunts or uncles—make that half aunts or half uncles—she herself had. The only siblings she knew of were her eighteen-year-old half sister and her twelve-year-old half brother, but there were probably plenty more in the woodpile. Her mother's exes did tend to get around, and she was sure her father was no exception.

Delilah flushed the toilet and scurried out of the stall as the pipes trumpeted, sounding, just as she had said, like an elephant on the rampage. Moira helped her wash her hands, then escorted her back to her father.

Big Red's smile was slow and sexy. "Thank you kindly, ma'am. Delilah's not happy with the restroom, but it came with the buildin'. This place used to be Bosque Bend High

School before Eisenhower Consolidated got built so it could pull in all the kids at this end of the county, and we could play in 5A."

Moira looked at him blankly. What was he talking about?

He laughed, a rumbling basso. "It's Interscholastic League, ma'am. Bosque Bend lives for high school football, like every other town in Texas."

His drawl was getting deeper. "Ma'am" was two syllables now, and the first syllable of "football" rhymed with *boot*. "Like" was pronounced *lahk*, and the *o* in "town" sounded like the *a* in *cat*. Her old vocal coach would have had a field day with Big Red.

Delilah wound her arms around his leg. "Daddy, I'm tired. Can we go home now?"

As Red lifted his daughter into his arms, the overhead light glinted off the wide gold wedding band on his left hand.

Moira recoiled. *Married*—he was *married!*

Red adjusted his daughter against his arm. "I've got to stay in town to handle some business, sugar, so I'll have to take you over to Aunt Sissy's. You can play with Baby Zoey."

Delilah pulled away from her father and pushed out her lower lip. "Don't wanna stay with Aunt Sissy and play with Baby Zoey! Wanna stay with the pretty lady!"

Red looked at Moira and raised an eyebrow for a second, like the reverse of a wink. His deep voice turned to velvet. "Honey, I'd like to stay with the pretty lady too, but I can't stay with either of you right now. Got some people to meet up with." His gorgeous eyes focused on Moira and his voice took on a seductive lilt. "Maybe the pretty lady could meet up with me later this evenin' over drinks, and we could get better acquainted."

She gave him her best arctic stare. "I don't think so." Pivoting on the heels of her sensible black pumps, she marched back down the hall.

What a creep! Making a pass at her in front of his child. Married men had hit on her before, but none of them had ever done it with a preschooler in his arms. God, she wouldn't want to be Big Red's wife!

Her step slowed as she rounded the corner and started up the stairs.

Cool it, Moira. It doesn't matter. According to Google, there are almost twelve thousand people in Bosque Bend, so the odds are that you'll never see Big Red again.

Anyway, the last thing you're interested in is another handsome man. Once burned, twice shy.

She glanced toward the auditorium doors across from Room 300. She'd like to check out the stage, but Pendleton Swaim had told her the theater was kept locked. It didn't matter. The stage wasn't going anywhere anytime soon, and Pen had written the show for this particular venue, which meant there shouldn't be any wicked surprises.

"The holiday season is our big moneymaker," he'd told her when he'd interviewed her by phone. "But we ran out of holiday musicals that we could afford, so I wrote a new one. Lots of singing and dancing. Lots of kiddos too. We try to get the whole community involved. Little actors grow up to be big contributors."

"What's the plot?"

"Well, I've always been partial to O. Henry so I decided to base the play on his most famous short story, 'Gift of the Magi,' the one about the husband pawning his watch to buy the wife a comb for her hair, and her selling her hair to buy him a fob for his watch. I'm an out-and-out Anglophile so I set the story in London, which also allowed me to use a lot of children in the play—guttersnipes, bootblacks, flower girls, and the like. Never did like the way the story ended, so I expanded it to two acts and gave it a happy, toe-tapping ending."

"Sounds good to me," she'd told him. Moira was all for happy endings. In fact, she was in search of one of her own. God knows, she'd seen enough of the other side of the coin.

* * *

Moira paused outside the door of the boardroom and listened. Room 300 was alive with conversation and movement. The board members had arrived while she was protecting Big Red's daughter against the angry elephant dwelling in the restroom pipes.

Showtime, Moira. She murmured a few calming *oms*, smoothed down the skirt of her dress again, and fluffed up her hair for good measure. She still wasn't used to having it this short.

More important, was she dressed right?

Costuming makes the character, as the wardrobe mistress of *The Clancy Family* had told her when she'd rebelled against the pink-and-white dresses Nancy Clancy always got stuck with, and now she wanted to look like a total and complete professional. No pink and white, no ragged jeans, no resemblance to scatterbrained Nancy Clancy, smart-mouthed Twinky Applejack, or any of the myriad other roles she'd played. That part of her life was over. She was herself now, and she'd be the one directing not only the show, but also her own life.

Setting her jaw, she turned the knob and walked in.

An awkward, white-haired Ichabod Crane of a man rose in old-fashioned courtesy and pulled out the chair next to him. "Come sit by me, Moira. I'm Pendleton Swaim."

Moira gave the assemblage a confident smile—*pretend you've done this a million times before*—then walked briskly to the table and took her seat.

Pen beamed at her. "So nice to meet you in person. I must confess that I never watched *The Clancy Family*, but I did catch a couple of episodes of Johnny Blue's sci-fi show." Johnny had been a teenage Martian doctor with comic-book-hero powers, and she'd clanked around in a tin suit and pretended to have a robotic crush on him. It was the nadir of her acting career, but she kept the smile pasted on her face and followed the usual script.

"I had a wonderful time as a child actor, but as an adult, I prefer being behind the scenes." What choice did she have? Sure, *The Clancy Family* was top of the rerun heap, but her family couldn't survive off residuals.

Pen nodded understandingly. "Johnny said you would be perfect for us. He told me that as well as your years of practical experience, you have a drama degree from UCLA."

"Yes, when *Quark Kent* folded, I decided to take a break

from acting and go to college. Theater seemed the logical choice." What else did she know?

A long-necked, long-beaked woman with over-rouged cheeks and unbelievably black hair leaned across the table. "I'm Xandra Fontaine, and we're so happy to have you with us, Mrs. Sanger."

Moira gritted her teeth and gave Xandra her best fake smile. "Farrar, please. I've reverted to my maiden name—for professional purposes, of course." She paused for a second, then softened her voice. "Besides, I don't want to trade on Colin's name."

In fact, she'd erase every vestige of Colin from her life if she could. If Robota hadn't finished off her acting career, Colin had. His insistence that she stay home had seemed romantic at the time—until she learned what he really wanted from her.

Xandra's black eyes glistened with interest. "I just adored Colin Sanger. And he was so right for the role of Rhett Butler in the remake of *Gone with the Wind*. Tall, dark, and handsome—and that voice! It sent shivers down me each time he opened his mouth."

Moira lowered her lashes as if hiding a secret sorrow. "Everyone tells me that."

Yeah, Colin was a heartthrob. The women wanted him, the men wanted him—she would have had to sweep a pile of adoring fans off the doorstep every morning if they'd lived in a normal house rather than Colin's massively built mansion with an eight-foot-tall wall around it. The wonder was that he hadn't dug a moat and stocked it with alligators.

But that wasn't what his fans needed to hear. To them,

Colin was every role he'd ever played—brave, noble, and upright. And she wasn't going to be the one to tell them otherwise.

Image was everything.

The short-necked, pug-nosed woman sitting next to Xandra, who seemed to have dyed her hair out of the same pot as her neighbor, moved her head forward like a hissing snake. "He died so young."

Moira struck one of her better grieving widow poses. "It's been two years, but I miss him still."

Xandra took over again. "Too bad there were never any children."

The twosome stared at Moira accusingly.

Moira sighed dramatically and gave the same crap answer she'd given countless tabloid reporters. "We were both busy with our careers and thought we had all the time in the world."

The door opened and the people seated around the table bobbed their heads up long enough to identify the newcomer, a plump, grandmotherly-looking woman in a peacock-blue squaw dress cinched with a copper medallion belt. Her flyaway hair looked like an abandoned bird nest.

Pen gestured toward her. "That's Vashti Atherton, our accompanist. Musical genius. She scored *Gift of the Magi*. Her younger daughter, Micaela, will play Della, the wife. Phil Schoenfeldt—the towhead at the end of the table who's waving his hands around—has been cast as the husband. And Travis McAllister will sing the part of the Dreamer. He's the one talking to Vashti right now."

"Pen, I really do need to see a script."

"As soon as our chairman gets here, my dear. He's bringing us all photocopies of the latest revision."

The door opened again, and a middle-aged woman with a graying Afro walked in, waved at Pen, then passed by to take a seat farther on down the table.

"Lucille Benton. She has two teenagers in the show," Pen commented.

Xandra leaned across the table again. "Her daughter has been taking classes with Sister and me since she was a toddler. Fleurette and I choreograph all the numbers and train all the dancers—even the ones who don't patronize our studio."

Pen beamed at the duo. "The Fontaine sisters have been very generous in contributing their talents and expertise to our theater productions."

Moira commented the only way she could. "Wonderful!"

Vashti Atherton, Phil Schoenfeldt, Travis McAllister, Xandra and Fleurette Fontaine, Lucille Benton. She repeated each name to herself and glued it to a face so she didn't accidentally snub anyone in the grocery store. After all, these people would determine whether she stayed in Bosque Bend in triumph or slunk back to Pasadena in disgrace.

A masculine voice rang out from the end of the table, where most of the men seemed to have congregated. "Hey, Pen, what's holding up our chairman? Did his photocopier break down again?"

The room roared with laughter. Apparently it was a running joke.

Pen gave him a quick comeback. "You know more than I do, Travis. He's your brother." He turned to Moira. "We're not very formal—no elections or anything—but Rafe McAllister runs the show. Great guy."

"Rafe McAllister? I saw some items in the museum that he'd donated on behalf of the C Bar M Ranch."

Pen nodded. "The Colbys—they're the *C* in C Bar M—established the ranch in 1855, but couldn't make a go of it until the McAllisters—they're the *M*—came on the scene. The Colbys have pretty much died out, but the current generation of the McAllisters is going strong and has been quite generous to Bosque Bend. Now that Rafe's got the museum up and running, he's arranged for us to buy the old Huaco Theater just off the square and restore it as a permanent home for the theater guild. He thinks we can get a historical marker for it too."

Moira's eyebrows went up. "That's quite an undertaking."

Pen shrugged. "Rafe's an architect so he knows what he's doing. He wants to get the theater guild on a more professional footing so we can draw audiences from Waco and some of the smaller towns around here. That's where you come in. Donna Sue Gomez-Sweeny, the Eisenhower Consolidated drama teacher who started us out five years ago, said that we've reached the point where we should hire somebody full-time."

Moira glanced around the table. "Which one is she?"

"She's not here." Pen retrieved a card from his shirt pocket and handed it to her. "Donna Sue's having to step back—a new baby—but she wanted you to know how to reach her."

The door opened again and all the heads bobbed up again, but this time, they stayed up. A smile spread across Pendleton Swaim's face. "Rafe!"

Moira turned to see a tall redhead with a cardboard box under his arm enter the room. He gave the group a familiar easy smile, and his eyes twinkled like summer sparklers.

Nooooo!

Big Red started passing scripts down the table. "Sorry to be late, folks. It was that dang copier again." Moira froze in place as his piercing gaze moved down the table, then traveled back up and settled on her. "Glad to see our new director made it."

She forced the corners of her mouth to curve up, but her blood ran cold.

* * *

Wet autumn leaves slushed under her tires as Moira backed out of her parking space. The mid-October temperatures in Central Texas seemed to be as mild as back home in Pasadena, but this intermittent rainfall was driving her crazy. Pray God it wouldn't get too cold later on. She and her sister didn't have a heavy coat between them.

Her fingers tightened on the steering wheel as she waited at the street for a break in the traffic. *Damn!* That was Rafe McAllister standing at the curb in front of the museum, and he was looking her way. She'd like to run the jerk down.

No, Moira, play the game. Your sister is depending on you. Your brother is depending on you. Gram and Gramp are depending on you.

She'd thought she was off the financial hook when she married Colin and he arranged for Gramp to receive a monthly allowance. But after Colin died, not only did the allowance come to a screeching halt, but she was also left high and dry—Colin had never changed his will in her favor, which meant his ex-wife was now enormously wealthy, the Screen Actors Guild's coffers were overflowing, and she needed a job.

She mulled over her meeting with the theater guild as she cut over to Austin Avenue, Bosque Bend's main drag. Apparently the major purpose of the get-together had been for everyone to look her over, so she'd done her best, keeping a smile on her face and making sure to shake everyone's hand, even Rafe McAllister's.

And his gorgeous, cheating eyes had sparkled at her the whole time.

* * *

Rafe waved his hand as Moira Farrar drove out onto the street, but she didn't respond. Probably didn't see him—or didn't want to.

What the fuck was going on with the woman? He'd felt an immediate connection with her in the museum and followed up on it, but she went cold on him. Maybe he shouldn't have made a move on her right off the bat, but that rasping voice, which had been used for comic effect in *The Clancy Family*, had sent a wave of heat down him to right where it mattered. And she was such a cute little thing too. The sitcom cameras had never caught those high cheekbones and exotic eyes, the eyebrows that looked like they'd been painted on with a feather, the fanlike lashes, the sweetness of her smile.

He watched her car turn the corner at the end of the block. Colin Sanger had died two years ago. According to the tabloids, he'd dived into a half-empty swimming pool at night when the lights were off. So, did Moira have a current boyfriend?

Boyfriend—a stupid term for an adult male. *Say it out, Rafe—does she have a lover?*

A red Mustang pulled over to the curb, and his brother lowered the passenger window. "Hey, bro. You gonna stand there all day holding down the sidewalk?"

Rafe leaned his arms on the ledge of the car's open window. "Tryin' to think what else I can do to fix that damn photocopier."

Although, as usual, Sissy had used her magic on the temperamental machine and gotten it working like a charm. The real reason he'd run late was that Delilah had pitched a fit when he'd tried to drop her off at Sissy's house before the board meeting. Only the promise that he would invite "the pretty lady" out to the ranch over the weekend had reconciled Delilah to stay with Baby Zoey, but he wasn't about to announce that devil's bargain.

Travis laughed. "Bro, give up and buy a new copier. You got the money—if you haven't driven yourself into bankruptcy paying for that little cutie-pie director to come to town."

"You noticed too, huh?"

"I'm married, not blind."

"Speakin' of bein' married, I hear tell Rocky's not too happy about the amount of time you been spendin' with Micaela Atherton lately."

Travis snorted. "Rocky's on my back if I so much as hold the door open for a little old lady."

"Rocky's your wife, Trav, and Micaela's not a little old lady. A whole roomful of people saw you cuddlin' up to her at Good Times last weekend."

"Lay off, Rafe. Micaela and I were singing a love song and had to make it look good. For God's sake, we had a spotlight on us and everyone in the damn honky-tonk was singing along."

"Just be careful. Rocky's a damn good shot."

Travis grimaced and ran a hand through his hair. "You don't know how it is, bro. Rocky's after me again to hang up the band. Hell, all I need is a decent break and I could hit the big-time, maybe make the Grand Ole Opry." His face lit up. "Hey, how about you corralling Miz Farrar and bring her out to Omar's Good Times tonight so she can hear me? That woman has showbiz connections out the wazoo, and I want to be in her address book."

"Don't think she likes me, Trav."

"Rafe, every woman on the face of the earth likes you. It's those damned eyes of yours. You hypnotize them." He glanced around as the light changed, and the traffic started moving behind him. "Gotta go before I get myself rammed up the ass."

Rafe stepped back from the curb. "Later, cowboy."

Good Times. It just might work for him as well as Travis. He'd tell Moira he needed to discuss her ideas for the show, and maybe Omar's beer and ribs would warm up Hollywood's ice princess for him.

Chapter Two

Moira picked up a late lunch at Hardy Joe's, a hamburger drive-in down the highway that sported a neon fisherman on its roof—she'd never seen *that* in Pasadena—and made the turn into Lynnwood, an upscale subdivision to the east of the Bosque River. Two streets down, one street over, and she'd be at the brick-fronted ranch-style house that had come with the job.

Johnny Blue may have left *Quark Kent* high and dry, but he'd continued to keep tabs on his little robot girl, checking on her from time to time when she was in college, and even after she married Colin. Then, when the Bosque Bend opportunity came up, he'd not only negotiated a nice salary for her, but also persuaded the board to throw in a three months' lease on a partially furnished house.

Located at the back of a cul-de-sac, the residence was about ten years old, in relatively good condition, and wired for Internet. The appliances weren't stainless steel and the floors weren't hardwood, but the living room had a couch and an armchair in it, and the family/dining area came equipped with a Formica table and four matching chairs. On the other side of the house were two full bathrooms, a laundry room, and three nice-sized bedrooms. And most amazing to Moira, who'd lived her whole life in Pasadena where land was at a premium, there was a huge fenced backyard.

She eased into the double-car garage and cast an evil eye on the pile of luggage and household items that she and her sister had unloaded from the U-Haul trailer when they drove in yesterday evening. God, now they'd have to schlep it all into the house. But maybe a little manual labor would help her clear a certain redheaded Texan out of her head.

Damn! Why couldn't she stop thinking about Rafe McAllister?

His eyes, of course—the irises looked like they'd been pieced together out of shards of sparkling glass—and the sweet way he interacted with his daughter, and not that she was in the market, but the man was a walking pheromone.

She got out of her car and slammed the door shut as hard as she could to end the matter.

A joyous fanfaronade of barking broke out in response.

God, no. She knew what that meant. Somehow, within twenty-four hours of their arrival, her sister had acquired a dog—probably a flea-bitten mongrel that would give them both the mange. The barks grew more frantic the nearer Moira got to the kitchen door, and she opened it to high-pitched yaps of canine excitement.

Astrid stood just inside, holding a large, golden-furred, black-faced dog on a bright pink leash.

"Ivanhoe! No! Don't bark at Moira! *Sit!*"

Ivanhoe sat. Of course, he did. Canines always obeyed Astrid. It was as if she were goddess of the hunt. And she certainly looked like it in those skinny pants and long leather vest. Tall, slender, and dark-haired, just like their mother, Astrid made anything she put on look good.

Moira deposited her portfolio on the kitchen counter and gave the dog a once-over. *Cripes*, he was big—and drooling out of both sides of his mouth. "Is he a mastiff?"

Astrid's ponytail brushed the floor as she bent down to throw her arms around the dog's neck. He washed her cheek with a swipe of his long pink tongue.

"Yes, and he's just a puppy—I'm guessing about a year old."

Moira sat down on one of the dining chairs and stared at her sister's darling. "Where'd he come from?"

"Ivanhoe's an orphan of the storm." The dog whimpered in ecstasy as Astrid's hand moved down his back to massage his flank. "I went out into the garage to get some bath towels, and he rose up out of the shadows like the Phantom of the Opera." She stroked the dog's head and scratched him behind the ears. "He hid under that workshop table thing when I screamed. It took half a box of your Shredded Wheat to lure him inside the house. Mrs. Fuller, that nice lady next door who met us in the yard when we drove in yesterday, lent me the collar and leash, and I used our breakfast bowls for his food and water." She glanced toward the delicate rice bowls set out on a towel in the kitchen. "By the way, Ivanhoe really likes Shredded Wheat. We'll have to restock."

"Maybe he belongs to someone in the neighborhood."

Astrid gave the dog a final pat on the rump and stood up. "Mrs. Fuller said he got pushed out of a Volkswagen a couple of days ago and has been hanging around here ever since. People do that, you know, dump dogs when they don't want them anymore."

"Yeah, I know, but I don't see how we can afford him."

Ivanhoe walked over to Moira and grinned at her.

Damn. She had to avoid looking into those dark, soulful eyes and be logical. "He looks like a growing boy, and we have to watch our budget. Remember, part of my pay goes back to Pasadena to pay our brother's tuition. I don't want Arne to have to change schools again."

"I'm out of high school now. I could get a job."

"Transportation, Astrid. We only have one car, and Bosque Bend's too small for bus service."

Astrid gestured at the sparsely furnished room. "But I can't just sit around the house all day! We don't even have a television, and it doesn't take *that* long to do my nails." She spread her fingers to display the smiling suns on their tips. "By the way, do you like them?"

"Very nice."

Astrid didn't seem to care what she wore, but she was totally hung up on nail art. When Moira had left this morning, those same fingernails had been sky blue accentuated with white polka dots.

"Maybe I could turn the extra bedroom into a nail salon," Astrid continued, glancing down the hall.

Moira shook her head. "I don't think that would work out. This is a residential neighborhood. And I bet you'd have to get some sort of state certification."

But what *could* Astrid do? This was a nice house, much nicer than she'd expected, but Astrid couldn't stay here all day twiddling her thumbs—or collecting more stray dogs. A job did seem to be the logical solution, and it would be nice if Astrid could add to the family coffers.

"Maybe…maybe I could work out something for you with the theater people. Painting sets or something, but let's worry about that later. Right now we've got to unload the garage. Just give me a minute to change into jeans."

Astrid sprang up. "Awesome. And I'll introduce sweetie dog to the backyard." She led Ivanhoe toward the sliding glass door, then turned back. "Let's bring my futon in first thing," she called out. "I don't want us to sleep in the same bed like we did last night. Do you have nightmares like that very often?"

Moira gave her a bright smile and tried to sound offhand. "I think that was because I was anxious about meeting the board today."

But more likely it was because she went to sleep without finding the night light that had been her constant companion since Colin died.

He had brought so much darkness into her life—darkness and pain.

* * *

After liberating Astrid's foam mattress from the pile in the garage, Moira took the lead and walked backward up the garage steps into the kitchen.

"So what's Bosque Bend like?" Astrid called out as they maneuvered the mattress through the door. "I didn't get much of a glimpse of it when we drove in yesterday evening."

"Not as sleepy as Johnny described it. The courthouse has a square of quaint old storefronts around it, but the rest of the town seems to be hustle-bustling to join the modern world. There's a nice park on this side of the river and a lineup of flashy restaurants across the bridge. According to a Chamber of Commerce brochure I picked up at the museum office, Bosque Bend now has all the necessities of modern living—Walmart, Office Depot, Home Depot, FedEx, Starbucks, a small hospital…doctors, lawyers, and Indian chiefs."

They dropped the mattress on the bedroom floor and went back to the garage for its frame.

Astrid gave her a questioning look. "The museum office? What were you doing in a museum?"

"It's a repurposed high school. The civic theater has been using its stage for its productions." Moira hefted one end of the frame and started walking it toward the steps. "I met with the board in a practice room across the hall from the auditorium."

"What did you find out? When do they want the show to open?"

"The first weekend of December. It'll be a three-week run, Thursday, Friday, Saturday only. No Sunday performance. This is a churchgoing town."

They turned the bed frame to fit through the kitchen door, then tottered it down the hall.

"Doesn't give you much time for auditions."

Moira shrugged. "No need. The parts have already been cast, and the accompanist will play through the score for me tomorrow morning. I have no idea who the costumers and scenery people are, but I'll call a meeting of the adult actors Monday evening. The play requires a large cast of children too so that means I'll have to set up a meeting with them—and their parents—probably on Tuesday evening. And I'll also have to deal with—never mind…"

Astrid lifted a suspicious eyebrow. "You didn't finish what you were saying, Moira. What else will you have to deal with?"

Crap. She hadn't meant to say anything about Big Red. Rafe McAllister was just a passing hormonal fancy that her good sense would soon convince her was bad news.

Or it damn well better. No way she was getting involved with a married man—or any man at this point.

She tried for careless flippancy. "The chairman of the board made a pass at me, and I think he's got me in his crosshairs."

"Killer!" Her sister gave her a wide smile as they pushed the frame into her bedroom. "You need to start dating. And don't try to tell me you're still in mourning for Colin. I don't know what happened between you two, but it wasn't good." They lifted the mattress into place, and Astrid took a sheet out of the stack of linens in the corner of the room and flapped it open. "What's this guy look like?"

"He's a redheaded cowboy with gorgeous eyes, but it doesn't matter. He's not available, and I'm not interested. End of story." Except for the sudden rush of heat she refused to ac-knowledge. *Damnit! Had her libido no sense of decency?*

Her cell phone buzzed, and she raced back to the kitchen, then stared at the caller ID.

Rafe McAllister.

"Moira?"

Every nerve in her body vibrated to the sound of his voice.

"We need to talk business, and I thought we might as well get somethin' to eat along with it. How about I drop by your place at six thirty and take you to Good Times. It's our local honky-tonk. Best ribs in Texas. That work for you?"

She could scarcely refuse the chairman of the board, and he knew it. Looked like she'd be going out for drinks with Red Rafe after all.

* * *

At six thirty sharp, Ivanhoe notified Moira that her gentleman caller had arrived.

The murmur of polite conversation drifted down the hall as she stared at herself in the long mirror on the inside of her bed-room door. God, she hoped Red wasn't putting the moves on her little sister, not that it would get him anywhere unless he owned a fifty-dog kennel.

She tucked her tee into her jeans to see how it looked, then pulled it out again. Astrid had wanted her to wear a V-necked sleeveless top with large sequin butterflies fluttering diagonally down from the shoulder to the waist, but she'd decided on a loose shirt advertising Roscoe's Chicken and Waffles. She didn't want to look like she was trying to entice the head hon-cho.

Besides, there wasn't any reason to dress up for a country honky-tonk. Red would probably have on the same jeans and long-sleeved white shirt he'd worn earlier in the day.

Her sister's voice fluted down the hall. "Moira? Rafe's here."

"Coming."

Big Red rose from the couch as she entered the room, earn-ing him a grunt from Ivanhoe, who'd been resting his huge head on Rafe's leg.

Moira stopped in mid-step and her jaw dropped in surprise. Those jeans may have been the same ones he'd been wearing this morning, but pings of light bounced off the big silver buckle on the belt that held them up, his boots looked like Picasso had had a bad day—or a very good one—and that ma-roon bib-type western shirt played like fire against his red hair.

Oh God—they were a classic pair. He was a strutting pea-cock, while she was a wimpy-looking peahen. She should have opted for the butterflies.

"Ma'am," he said, giving her an easy smile. "You look lovely." His eyes fastened on her shirt and lingered on her breasts. "And Roscoe is a lucky man."

Behind him, she could see Astrid give her a thumbs-up, then clutch herself dramatically in the area of her heart.

Okay, Rafe McAllister may have won her sister over, but Astrid was at a romantic age and still believed in knights in shining armor—and cowboys in boot-scootin' finery.

She smiled politely, picked up her bag, and threw a light sweater over her arm just in case the weather turned cool. All the time, her brain was going eighty miles an hour.

What did he mean by that crack about Roscoe? It had to do with her boobs, she knew. Was he making fun of her? She couldn't help it if Astrid had inherited Gram's sexy Japanese eyes while she'd gotten Gram's small Japanese breasts. And anyway, it was no business of his. He'd never see them.

Moira steeled herself as Rafe escorted her out and bade Astrid good-bye. This would be a very difficult evening.

Her eyes went wide. *Oh my God!*

Waiting at the curb was the biggest, baddest pickup she'd ever seen.

Rafe's truck looked like nothing so much as Cinderella's coach on steroids, and it was waaaay too much. It had a generous backseat, an extra-long truck bed, four wheels on the rear, and a big hook thing on the wraparound back bumper. COLBY-MCALLISTER RANCH was stenciled in gold on the door.

Her first impulse was to turn around, run back into the house, and lock the door behind her.

But an inner voice told her otherwise. *Behave yourself, Moira. Remember that Gram and Gramp are depending on you, that Astrid and Arne are depending on you. Even Ivanhoe is depending on you.*

She took a deep breath. "That's—uh—not like anything I ever saw on the streets of Pasadena."

"It's a dually. Good for hauling livestock and construction equipment." Rafe stepped back and regarded his vehicle with obvious pride. "I've been doing my own contracting here in Bosque Bend, and this baby saved the city a lot of money on the high school conversion."

He swung the passenger door open, and Moira looked up and up and up.

"It's—it's a Swiss alp!" she croaked. "There's no way I can climb up there!"

"No problem. I'll help you. I do it for my mother and sister all the time."

Moira stifled a gasp as his hands encircled her waist and hoisted her up to the seat—it was as if he'd touched her bare skin.

She fastened her seat belt and concentrated on breathing normally. Why was she getting all hot and bothered? A drawling cowboy with a shock of red hair—he wasn't her type, no matter what his eyes looked like.

Rafe opened the driver's side door, and she glimpsed the ring on his left hand as he hoisted himself into the truck.

Besides, he was *married, married, married!*

He started the truck and glanced across at her, but Moira folded her arms across each other and looked out the side window as he drove down the street.

Lynnwood was blurring into twilight. The autumn dark was coming earlier every evening, and Halloween was less than two weeks away. She and Astrid would have to pick up a pumpkin at the store tomorrow and some trick-or-treat candy too.

Rafe stopped for a red light before turning onto the highway and gave her a reassuring smile. "You're gonna enjoy yourself this evenin'. Friday nights at Omar's, everybody in the house is wearin' western. You'll see more drugstore cowboys tonight than you ever saw in Hollywood."

"I thought you said you wanted to discuss the upcoming show."

"That too, but you need to get a good whiff of Texas first."

"I've been to Texas before. One of the characters I played, Twinky Applejack, sneaked into the luggage when her brother packed up to go to a dude ranch. She ended up at Southfork and hobnobbed with the Ewings."

He laughed, that deep rumble that struck a resonance she didn't know she had.

"I mean *real* Texas, not TV Texas. Good Times is my Uncle Omar's place, and he cooks up the best pork ribs for twenty miles around."

"What if I'm a vegetarian?"

He gave her a cattleman's look of pure horror. "You're not, are you?"

She couldn't help but smile. "No, but I'm not much of a rib eater either. All that sloppy sauce."

"That's an easy fix." He turned onto the highway. "By the way, Friday is a band night, and Seward Gap—that's my brother's band—is gonna be playin'. They do a lot of covers, and sometimes, when everyone's drunk enough, Travis throws in his own stuff too. We used to do an Everly Brothers act together while we were in high school, but Travis has moved on to bigger and better, while I'm mostly singin' Delilah to sleep now."

His wedding ring caught the last beam of sunset as he made a quick turn onto a ranch-to-market road, and the words slipped out of her mouth before she could stop them.

"Does your wife sing too?"

Rafe paused before answering, and his voice was bleak. "My wife…passed…three years ago come New Year's Day."

* * *

He'd always known he loved Beth, but he'd never known just how much until he found her lying on the soft winter grass with a bullet through her head. Cradling her in his arms, he'd carried her inside and laid her on the couch, then called 911.

Police Chief Mervin Hruska and his guys arrived in record time. Mervin, who'd been a groomsman at their wedding, had gently berated him for "disturbing the—uh—body" and pretended not to see the tears coursing down his cheeks.

Beth, the joy of his life, was dead.

His grandmother used to sing a song about a lovely dancer who was one of twilight's fairy daughters, and that's how he always thought of Beth. She was someone sent from above the clouds, a sprite, a beautiful girl overflowing with love and laughter.

His life had been perfect—he had a wonderful wife, a good job with good prospects, and the sweetest baby in the world.

Then his father died much too soon, and his world wobbled on its axis.

And when Beth was killed less than a year later, it went hurling into deep space.

The coroner said the bullet probably came from the gun of one of the itinerant ranch hands who had been shooting into the air all day on the ranch across the road—celebratory gunfire. But by then, the vaqueros were long gone, and he was left alone with his sorrow, his memories, and his precious child.

Travis, of course, took over the ranch for a while, and his mother moved back into the house to help with Delilah, but he was on his own in regard to female companionship.

Some guys would have drowned themselves in the bottle, but he'd never been much of a drinking man. Sex was the only thing he could lose himself in, and the physical act was all he wanted—relief with no emotional commitment—nothing that would break his bond with Beth.

Lately, though, he'd gotten tired of the game. In fact, Moira Farrar was the first woman in months he'd felt even a quiver of interest in, probably because she was such a serious little soldier, far different from the Hollywood stereotype he'd expected. And then there was that voice of hers. His body tightened at the thought of it. He'd recognized her immediately when he ran her down in the hall of the museum, but it was that husky voice that made him wonder about possibilities.

The car veered as he hit a rut in the road.

Get your mind out of your trousers, cowboy, and pay attention to your driving.

He put on his brights and slowed down to thirty, then dropped another five as he continued down the narrow, poorly lit road. The whitetails were in rut now, and twilight was a prime time for courting couples. A deer could leap in front of a vehicle without a second's notice, and the last thing he wanted was for a sexed-up buck to splatter his entrails all across the windshield when Moira had hardly been in town a full day.

He risked a sideways glance at her.

But why had she asked about Beth? Had someone gotten

to her already and said something about him? Maybe Bertie Fuller? Not that he could do anything about it if she had. He'd known the Fullers lived next door when he set Moira and her sister up in the Lynnwood house, but there wasn't anywhere else available. The guild couldn't afford to shell out rent on top of her salary, half of which he was footing anyway

Moira had gasped out the standard "I'm so sorry," when he'd told her about Beth's death, then rolled her lips inward as if she were punishing them for asking the question.

Now she was staring out the side window again. Maybe she was thinking about her husband. According to news reports, nearly every woman in the country had gone into mourning when Colin Sanger died, so Moira must have been devastated.

Oh God, this was a fine way to establish a relationship—with both of them thinking about their lost loves. Of course, because of Delilah, he'd had to rejoin the living a lot sooner than he'd wanted too, but Moira's loss was still relatively fresh.

On the other hand, she'd moved halfway across the country and was reinventing herself as a theater director. That signaled new beginnings to him.

He gave her a quick once-over.

Maybe she'd feel better when they got to Omar's. Like his uncle always said, everybody has a good time at Good Times. And judging by the set of her jaw, Rafe would guess Moira hadn't had many good times lately.

But maybe he was playing his hand wrong. Maybe he shouldn't be taking Moira to Omar's place first off, before she'd gotten to know him.

Good Times was predominantly a male hangout, and he'd brought women here before, but they were locals—the guys were their fathers, uncles, bothers, cousins, and ex-husbands—so the high testosterone levels didn't bother them. Moira was different. She was a hothouse flower, accustomed to dining at expensive restaurants with a whole lineup of servers catering to her every whim.

But what the fuck was a hothouse flower doing in a Podunk town like Bosque Bend?

He narrowed his eyes. Whatever the reason, he was damn well going to take advantage of it. He'd been attracted to her from the second he ran into her in the hall—the way she squared her shoulders as if she was trying to seem taller, the way she looked straight at him without flinching or flirting, her economy of motion, her calm eyes, her high cheekbones, and cute bump of a nose, her porcelain skin and curved cupid lips...

Careful, cowboy. You're driving.

He scanned the side of the road for the turnoff to Good Times. There it was, right past the sign for the county line. Looked like some of the boys had been using it for target practice again.

Half a mile down the road, he pulled into the crowded parking lot, jolting the dually into a space at the back. They'd have to walk uphill to the building, but the rise wasn't steep. He'd keep Moira close beside him to make sure she didn't trip on something in the dark. And if she did, he'd hold her even closer.

She turned to him as soon as he cut off the ignition. "Before we go any further, I want to apologize for mentioning your wife. I'd noticed your ring and assumed—well…"

He breathed a sigh of relief. So that's why she'd been giving him the cold shoulder. Might as well let her have it straight.

"I'll always wear this ring." He flexed his left hand and looked at the token of his eternal commitment. "I'm thirty years old, and I've had my share of relationships since Beth died, but I'll never remarry."

This way, if he and Moira did hook up, she'd know the score. Love was off the table for him. It hurt too much.

* * *

Moira was surprised to realize that she liked the feel of Rafe's arm looped casually around her as he led her through the jungle of old cars, new cars, vans, pickups of all sizes, a couple of motorcycles, even a small RV.

Up ahead, a string of randomly blinking lights hung down from the front roof of a cinder-block building with two corrugated metal units attached to each side of it. It looked like a setting for yet another follow-up to *Texas Chainsaw Massacre*, which made her wonder whether Rafe was actually trying to keep her steady on the uneven terrain or trying to prevent her from escaping.

She stepped out of Rafe's embrace as they walked up onto the wood slat porch. Horseshoes and old Coca-Cola clocks hung on one side of the door, and a large, weathered poster was mounted on the other side. It advertised a snarling, beetle-browed wrestler billed as "The Meanest Man in Texas."

"Is that your uncle?"

"No, it's Growler Redlander. He got this place up and runnin' forty-some years ago. It's just across the county line from Bosque Bend, and back when the town was dry, folks used to drive over here for their liquor. Omar snapped the place up when ol' Growler died, tripled the size of it, and started hirin' bands and cookin' up ribs. Everybody and their dog comes here now."

He rested a hand on her shoulder, a heavy, possessive hand that seemed to mean a lot more than that casual shoulder hug. All her alarm bells went off.

She wasn't ready for this!

But if she wasn't ready, why did she have the urge to snuggle up against him and purr like a contented cat when his arm moved around her shoulder again?

Chapter Three

Rafe pushed open the door, and they walked into the room together.

Moira peered into the dark. Long trestle tables lined the back wall, and the right side of the room was crowded with four-person tables, all of them occupied.

"That area to the left of the stage—why aren't there any tables there?"

"That's the dance floor. And the door off to the right leads to the kitchen, where the crew chops up the ribs. And the guy who's makin' his way toward us, the one all in black with the ostrich father in his hat, is Omar himself. He cooks the ribs out back all afternoon till they're ripe and ready, then gets himself all gussied up for the evenin's fun."

Rafe gave his uncle a high five and a fist bump. "To good times, Omar."

"Glad you could make it, Rafe. Introduce me to the little lady."

Moira felt herself being nudged forward.

"Omar, meet Miz Moira Farrar. Moira is Bosque Bend's new theater guild director. Moira, this is the one and only Omar Schuler, rib chef extraordinaire."

She smiled and held out her hand.

Omar didn't seem to want to let go of it. "Thought you looked familiar, angel. I remember when you were Cliffie Clifford's surprise prom date on *Teen Time Hookups*. Whatever happened to him?"

"I'm not sure." Actually she knew exactly what had happened to Cliffie. After the series folded because Cliff was so drugged out that he couldn't remember his lines, he let fly with a couple of rounds of buckshot at the producer's house. The last she'd heard, Cliffie had grown a shaggy beard, had his face tattooed like a Maori warrior, and was peddling bead necklaces and low-grade crack on the Santa Monica boardwalk.

Rafe scanned the crowd. "Hey, Omar, I'd like to get us a table near the stage. You still keepin' a spare in the back room in case the King shows up?"

"Sure thing, Rafe. Y'all get on up there, and I'll get you set up."

"Thanks, Omar." They bumped fists again. "I owe you one."

Rafe took Moira's hand and worked his way toward the stage, clapping several backs in the process and introducing her to more people than even she could remember, partially because she was blinded by the glitter.

A Hollywood premiere had nothing on Omar's. The men looked like they had signed up for the Rose Bowl Parade, and every woman there, even the ones with gray hair and bifocals, seemed to be dressed as either a leather-fringed Annie Oakley or a this-side-of-slutty Miss Kitty.

Definitely, she should have worn the shirt with the butterflies on it—and added a sequined cowboy hat for good measure.

A teenager wrapped in a white apron came out of the kitchen and put a table down in front of the stage, then added two chairs.

Rafe slipped him a five. "Thanks, guy. Appreciate it. And how about getting us a good dozen ribs? And a pitcher of"—he gave Moira an assessing glance—"Bud Light?"

She nodded. She wasn't much of a drinker, but she preferred lite beer if she had a choice.

The teen pocketed the tip. "Thanks, Mr. McAllister. I'll see to it."

"One more thing, cowboy."

Rafe gave her a wink, and she wondered what was up.

"Hold the sauce."

* * *

Moira looked across the table at Rafe, really *looked* at him, something she hadn't allowed herself to do while she thought his wife still walked the earth. He wasn't as breathtakingly handsome as Colin, but his features were regular, he had a great smile, and oh—those eyes.

And she'd totally misread him—that's what Hollywood does to you—although that wedding ring had played its part. Now they had to begin all over again.

She searched for a safe conversation topic, something you'd talk about to a person whom you'd just met six hours ago. "Uh—Pen Swaim told me you're an architect as well as a rancher, so why do you live in Bosque Bend? I would think you'd find more business in a big city like Dallas."

"Beth and I did live in Dallas for couple of years after we graduated from University of Texas, but when my father died, I had to come home to take care of the ranch."

"You must have a lot of family here."

He laughed. "When I was a kid, it seemed like everyone in town was a cousin. The McAllisters run to small families, but my mother—she's a Schuler—had ten siblings, and most of them are all still around."

"Doesn't anyone ever leave Bosque Bend?"

"McAllisters usually stick, but a lot of the other kids, especially the ones who go off to college, leave for good. Bosque Bend's been makin' up for it population-wise, though. Floravista—that's a community for active adults—has attracted lots of retirees. My mother moved there last year."

Moira nodded. "Retirees are good for community theater—they're usually big donors." She paused as their waiter deposited a pitcher of beer and two glass mugs on the table. "There's a guy coming up behind you who's lugging a big music case. I guess that means the band's about to set up."

Rafe twisted around. "That's the double bass. Right behind him are the fiddle and backup guitar. Travis is coming through the door now. He's lead guitar and vocals." His eyes narrowed. "And the woman with him is Micaela Atherton."

Moira studied the striking-looking brunette tagging along

behind Travis McAllister. What a wonderful Della she'd make. "I know she's singing the female lead in the *Gift of the Magi*, but she's also in your brother's band?"

"Sometimes." He poured more beer into her mug, then refilled his own. "Micaela's a pianist and usually plays classical, but Travis gets her to cut loose every now and then." He took a long swallow of the brew. "Rocky—that's Travis's wife—won't be too happy about Micaela bein' here tonight."

Their waiter reappeared with a tray piled full of ribs, placed it on the table along with a half roll of paper towels, then cast a confused glance in Moira's direction. "Omar says it's on the house because you're a big star."

Rafe grinned as he watched the teenager head back toward the kitchen. "I guess he doesn't watch reruns."

Moira laughed and picked up a rib between her thumb and forefinger. "Poor Nancy. How soon she is forgot."

Rafe took a couple of more swallows of beer and watched as Moira nibbled at the tender pork. *Not only pretty, but has a sense of humor.* He liked a woman who knew how to laugh. Maybe he'd get her out on the dance floor with him later on in the evening, when everything got mellow, and find out what else she knew how to do.

* * *

The background noise died down as the band members talked among themselves, tuned their instruments against the tinny piano, and ventured a few experimental riffs.

Moira watched the action on the stage as she polished off

her second rib and sipped at her mug. She could see why Rafe was concerned about the relationship between Micaela and Travis—the pianist's dark eyes followed his brother's every move, and the smiles Travis was giving her were a lot more than friendly.

Travis walked over to the microphone and strummed a chord for attention, although the glittering rhinestones embedded on the front yoke of his teal-blue, silver-fringed shirt should have done the job already. "Howdy there, folks!"

The crowd roared a howdy back at him. Apparently Seward Gap was a local favorite.

"Glad to see so many of y'all out here at Good Times tonight. Coming in, I spotted Mayor Traylor and his lovely wife—take a bow, you two—and I see that our new theater guild director, Moira Farrar, is here too, getting acquainted with my brother and the local scene—stand up, Moira!"

Oh God, no! She shrank against the back of her chair. Everyone else was sparkling in their cowboy best, and she was wearing a dumb chicken-and-waffles T-shirt.

Rafe leaned across the table. "Stand up and get it over with," he hissed, "or he'll come down here and lift up your hand like you've won a prizefight."

Moira scrambled to her feet and the room applauded a welcome.

Travis grinned. "Moira, this first song is for you—and your date." He flashed Rafe a wicked grin, gave the band the downbeat, and launched into Willie Nelson's "Red-Headed Stranger." The audience joined in on the choruses.

Rafe rocked his head in his hands. "I hope Rocky gives him holy hell when he gets home tonight."

"Is Travis's wife really named *Rocky*—R-O-C-K-Y?"

"It's Marcy Ann, but her father always called her Rocky." He finished the last of his beer in one big gulp. "Her mother is a Colby, as in Colby-McAllister Ranch."

Moira nodded and reached for another rib. Everyone around here seemed to have a history. That must be how it worked in small towns.

Couples began to move onto the dance floor as Travis switched gears to a soulful Ernest Tubb classic.

Moira took a swallow of beer to wash down the tender pork and concentrated on Travis's performance. His voice was good, and he knew how to use it. A vibrant baritone, it could dig down low and dirty, then soar up to the rafters for angelically sweet high notes. But what really grabbed her was that sexy edge, that cutting little whisper.

She understood why Travis had been cast for the dream sequence in which the penniless husband imagines what it would be like to be as rich as John D. Rockefeller. Rafe's brother had versatility, voice, and stage presence, not to mention good looks. He wasn't as tall as Rafe, but his features were sharper—maybe too sharp—and his auburn hair—darker than Rafe's—was better behaved.

Moira finished off her beer and crossed her arms, considering. Not everyone yearns for bright lights, but it was a wonder Travis hadn't left town for Nashville or New York by now.

* * *

Rafe smiled when Moira held her mug out for a refill. She'd charmed Omar, hadn't made any snide observations about the dress code, gone along—after a little urging—with Travis's introducing her, and right now she was tapping her fingers to the fast one-two beat of "The Devil Went Down to Georgia."

Yeah, Moira was mellow—relaxed, smiling, and lazing back in her chair. It was a beginning, but he wanted more than that.

He wanted her to be as hot for him as he was for her.

Now was the right time to get started, when half the tables were line dancing to "Watermelon Crawl."

Get her on the floor for the fast ones, and she'd be in his arms for the slow ones.

The music paused as the band tuned up for the next number, and he leaned toward her. "How about we—"

Travis called out his name. "Hey, Rafe, I've had a request for a blast from the past—the Everly Brothers. You got your pipes tuned up?"

The crowd, pretty well oiled by now, started pounding on the tables. *Shit, what choice did he have?* Throwing Moira a look of apology, he hopped up onto the low stage. Travis stuck an extra guitar in his hands, and Rafe strummed an experimental chord to make sure he still remembered how to play.

Travis edged over to him. "How about 'All I Have to Do Is Dream'? It might help your case." He nodded toward Moira.

"Trav, I haven't touched a guitar in months."

"Give it your best, bro. The mayor's wife is the one who wants to hear us, and I'm not about to turn that woman down." He returned to the microphone. "Back by special request from Missus Mayor—the McAllister Brothers!"

Rafe stepped forward to share the mike. He usually got a charge out of revisiting the old act, but not right now. He had other things on his mind—like a California girl with a restaurant advertisement hugging her breasts.

He looked over at her. She gave him an amused grin and toasted him with her mug, so what the fuck. He signaled Travis, and they hit their guitars at the exact same moment, then began to sing.

Moira took a swallow of beer and closed her eyes to savor the blend of the brothers' voices. As usually happened when close relatives sing together, their timbres rubbed against each other, contradicting and complementing. The sound of Rafe's deep bass against his brother's baritone made her tingle all over, and the overt sexuality of the song didn't hurt either.

She took a final sip from her mug, then pushed it aside half-full. No more for her. She didn't want to get all warm and cuddly and do something stupid, like have sex with Rafe McAllister in the palatial backseat of his truck.

She took sex much too seriously to let that happen. That was one thing she'd learned from Colin—that sex is serious business.

May his soul rot in hell.

* * *

Three songs later, Ernest Tubb was walking the floor over his lost girlfriend, and Moira had relaxed enough that Rafe could hold her against him from shoulder to knee.

He leaned down to nuzzle her neck.

Her scent was in his nostrils, the feathery softness of her short-cropped hair brushed against his jaw, and her arms were clinging to his shoulders. It had been months since he'd been this attracted to a woman. Maybe he could take her somewhere tonight where they could be alone, somewhere that had at least a couch in it.

But no, it was way too soon. He wanted Moira for more than a one-night stand.

Besides, he was sort of her boss, and he didn't want her to think the job came with strings. He'd better clear the air on that score on the drive back to town—which meant they should leave now, while he was more glow than flames.

He made a production out of looking at his watch. "Time to call it a day. Your sister said y'all had a lot to do tomorrow, and I have a blacksmith comin' tomorrow so I'll have to get up early."

Moira opened her eyes and moved out of his arms, then gave him that soft, fuzzy look women get when they've just been awakened.

He took a deep breath, picked up his hat, and waved at Omar, who was standing at the back of the room with a couple of black-clad bouncers, then caught up with Moira as she collected her purse and sweater.

Ten minutes and far too many handshakes later, they were out the door and into the sudden silence of the night. A cool breeze rattled through the live oaks, and Moira pulled the sweater around herself like a shawl.

No need for that—he put an arm around her shoulders and drew her against his side. God, he was so hot that she should have felt branded. Not that he hadn't already branded her in another way—by tomorrow morning, everyone in Bosque Bend would know he'd cut her out of the herd.

When they got back to the truck, she circled an arm around his neck to be lifted up into the truck. Her eyes half closed and her sweet breasts rested against his chest.

Poor baby. She must be exhausted—within twenty-four hours, she'd moved into a new house, met the board, been yanked out to a honky-tonk by a guy she hardly knew, and slow danced against him like she meant it.

He drove slowly down the rough road to minimize the bumps and jolts, picked up speed when he turned onto the highway, then dropped it again when he spotted the BUY-1-GET-5-FREE fireworks stand. A protective steel wire with flags hanging from it blocked access to the stall itself, but left enough room in the lot to accommodate the truck. Exactly the sort of setup he'd been looking for.

He crossed the road and pulled into the clearing.

Moira's eyes went wide as he jerked to a stop. She glanced at the darkness out the side window, then backed as far away from him as the seat belt would allow. Her hand moved to the door handle, and her voice became a frightened whisper.

"What are you doing? Why are you parking here?"

Rafe slipped into the same slow, easy cadence he used to calm a spooked horse. "Just wanted to talk, Moira. Thought it was a good place to sort out a couple of things without Mrs. Fuller countin' the minutes we stayed in the truck before I walked you up to the door."

Her eyes switched back and forth from window to window

as if she were searching out an escape route. "I don't like being locked in."

He flipped open the latch and leaned back into his door to put a few more inches between them. Pretty good bet she wouldn't hop out into a cedar thicket in the middle of the night.

"First of all, I want to say thanks for going with me to Good Times, and second, I'd sure appreciate it if you and your sister would consider comin' out to the ranch Sunday afternoon." He gave her a lopsided smile. "The only way I could get Delilah to stay with Sissy this mornin' during our board meeting was to promise her the pretty lady would visit us this weekend, and I figure two pretty ladies would make her even happier."

And that having her sister along would make Moira more comfortable.

Her voice was tight and brittle. "I don't see a problem with that, but I get the feeling the other shoe is about to drop."

He ran his hand through his hair. How could he say what he wanted to say without her becoming one with the truck door?

"Okay, here goes—number three." He took a deep breath. "You know I'm attracted to you—I made that pretty clear while we were dancin'."

He glanced at his wedding ring, then looked back at Moira. "I'm committed to Delilah's mother in eternity, but down here on earth, I think we could have a good time together."

Moira glued herself to the door again, and his redheaded temper flared.

"For God's sake, stop lookin' at me like I'm goin' to have my wicked way with you! Yes, I want you in my bed! Yes, I'd like to roll you under me right now, but what I'm tryin' to say is that whatever relationship we have and how long it lasts is up to you!" He switched on the ignition and shoved the truck into gear. "And whatever you decide won't affect your job! You have an iron-clad contract, and I'm not in it!"

Goddamnit, she'd grown up in Sodom and Gomorrah. Everybody knew what it was like in Hollywood. She'd probably had twice the number of lovers he'd had.

* * *

Moira awoke the next morning to the screech of her Darth Vader alarm clock, Arne's birthday present to her last year, followed immediately by Ivanhoe leaping onto the bed and licking at her face like a sponge mop.

She squawked, and Astrid came running in, grabbed Ivanhoe by the collar, and hauled him off the bed, then commanded him to lie down, which, judging by the steady beat of his tail on the carpet, he did.

Moira wanted to draw the sheet up over her head and get a few minutes more sleep, but she felt the mattress dip and knew her sister had sat herself down on the side of the bed.

Astrid wanted to talk.

"Oh, Moira—I'm so excited about Rafe inviting us to visit his ranch tomorrow afternoon. It's totally awesome—a real live Texas cattle ranch! And he's such a sweetheart. That vet he recommended for Ivanhoe—I called as soon as the office opened this morning and made an appointment for eleven.

We'll have to work out the transportation, though. You're supposed to meet Mrs. Atherton at ten thirty, aren't you?"

Moira rolled over and tried to clear her head. She'd set Darth Vader for later than usual, then hadn't slept well, even though she'd found her night light last night when she rummaged through her underwear. Maybe it was because she was in a strange bed in a strange house. Maybe it was because she was still haunted by demons of the past. Or maybe because whenever she shut her eyes, a certain redheaded Texan was looking at her with way too much interest.

Happy Times had been an experience in itself—Omar and Seward Gap and the cowboy costumes. Then there was Rafe and what he'd suggested—an affair, a sexual relationship, which she could opt out of at any time. No romance, no commitment. Their joining would be strictly physical, a gratification of her female parts and his male parts.

It sounded so...so heartless—but it also sounded safe. No strings attached, which might suit her just fine. At least in theory.

She'd loved Colin so much, and for the first couple of months, everything had been great—until she learned what he really wanted from her. So maybe the sort of relationship Rafe was proposing, one that was based on sexual attraction rather than love, was the way to go.

And she certainly was attracted to him.

But could she risk it? She'd never made the Hollywood party circuit and didn't know the ropes. What if she fell in love with him—or he fell in love with her?

She swung her legs to the side of the bed.

"I've reconsidered. Maybe we should put off visiting Rafe's ranch. Maybe next weekend instead of tomorrow."

Astrid gave her a look of disbelief. "Come on now. You don't want to let the cowboy's little girl down. Besides, it was pretty obvious last night that he's got the hots for you."

"I'm not sure whether I feel the same way about him." *Liar. You want him, but you're afraid of getting involved.*

Astrid waved her hands in the air. Her nails were painted with red-and-gold scallops today. "What's not to like? He's good-looking and rich and nice—and oh, those eyes! Besides, he didn't give you any grief about your Roscoe tee, did he? In fact, he complimented you on it—and what was under it."

"It's just that he—he…"

"He what?"

"I-I'm not sure I'm ready for a relationship yet. Colin—"

"Colin's dead. Moira, get on with your life. I like Rafe. He brought you home safe and sound, he gave me the name of a good vet, and he didn't stare at my boobs like he was trying to figure out my cup size."

"I'll think about it." She stood up and headed for the bathroom. "Give me a few more minutes to wake up."

It's just a visit to a ranch, nothing more, she told herself as she brushed her teeth. Rafe won't try anything with Astrid and Delilah on the premises. And when you come right down to it, he'd done the gentlemanly thing in an ungentlemanly situation—proposed they have an affair but keep it light.

She washed her mouth out, combed her hair back off her face, and swiped her mouth with lip gloss. No need to dress up today and no need to make pretty.

And Astrid was right. It was time for her to start dating again. Colin was dead, and she wasn't going to let him control her from the grave. Maybe this sex-only thing would be just what she needed to get a new start, a new life.

Her mind made up, she grabbed some underwear, a fresh pair of jeans, and her old UCLA sweatshirt from the closet off the bathroom and finished dressing.

Astrid was pulling up her sheet and coverlet as she emerged from the bathroom.

What else do you say to a little sister sweet enough to make your bed? "Okay, Astrid. Sunday's a go. But don't leave me alone with Rafe."

"Sure thing. I'll stick to you like glue." She shot her sister a coy glance. "Unless you want me to unstick."

* * *

Rafe dismounted, gave Sarge a pat on the flank, then led the big pinto into the corral. Sometimes he drove one of the lighter pickups around the ranch, but as Dad always said, you have a lot better view from a horse's back than you do from inside a truck. Besides, Sarge needed the exercise.

Rafe tilted his hat back to take a long last look around. He'd been in the saddle since dawn and would have liked to stay outside a while longer, but Saturday was when he worked on the books.

Damn. Sometimes he felt like nothing more than a glorified accountant, but he had to keep tight rein on expenses for the ranch to pay for itself plus make enough profit to provide the

McAllister bloodline with spending money. But along with his fifty percent of the take, he got one hundred percent of the problems.

He replaced the bridle with a rope halter, then draped the sweat-soaked saddle pad across the fence to dry.

And why shouldn't he be the one to handle the problems? Problem solving was his business. Want a house built across a stream? He knew how to do it. Need an old high school to be repurposed as a town museum? He was the go-to guy.

Yeah, the go-to guy. But his father had died with a raging gut, and Beth had been killed by random gunfire. And he couldn't do a damn thing about either one of them.

His cell phone rang as he heaved the saddle over his shoulder.

Shit! Hope that didn't mean that Travis had found another dead calf.

He pulled the phone out of his jacket.

"Rafe, this is Moira." Of course it was. Every cell in his body recognized her voice. "How do Astrid and I get to your ranch?"

He couldn't help but grin. After the scene at the fireworks stand, he hadn't been sure she'd take him up on his invitation. In fact, he'd had the distinct impression that she was going to turn him down.

"Just go north on the highway and then east on Colby Road. A ways down, there's a turn off to C Bar M—that's our brand. Drive past the one-story house at the entrance—Travis and Rocky live there—and come on back past the trees to the big house."

Sarge wiped spittle on his sleeve to remind him that he was waiting to be brushed.

"I forgot to ask—do you and your sister ride?"

"We can manage."

Rafe dodged an impatient switch of Sarge's tail, switched the cell to his left hand, and started brushing the big horse with his right.

"I'll saddle up a couple of horses for y'all, then. Use plenty of sunblock and wear hats."

Sarge nudged him hard, almost knocking him off his feet.

"Better go. Got a thousand pounds of horseflesh demanding my attention right now."

He stuffed the phone into his shirt pocket and set to work for real. Sarge shivered with equine ecstasy and made gurgling rumbles deep in his throat.

Rafe snorted to himself.

Wished he could have that kind of effect on Moira Miranda Farrar.

* * *

Moira picked up the *Gift of the Magi* music score and dropped it in her portfolio. "I'll drive us over to Mrs. Atherton's. Then you can take Ivanhoe to the vet and stock us up on groceries. I'll call you when it's time to pick me up, probably midafternoon."

She slid into the driver's seat and watched as Astrid tried to convince Ivanhoe he wanted to get in the car. Understandably nervous, considering how his last ride had turned out, Ivanhoe had to be lured into the backseat with the last of the Shredded Wheat.

After giving a quick wave to Mrs. Fuller, who was erecting blood-spattered Halloween tombstones in her front yard, Moira backed out onto the street and took the appropriate jogs and turns to get to the highway.

She took advantage of a red light as they neared the heart of town to review the directions Pendleton Swaim had scribbled down for her, then wound her way through a tangle of old-fashioned streets and ended up in front of a happy-looking yellow cottage surrounded by a pleasant confusion of flower beds and concrete nymphs. Its metal roof peaked up into a central point above a sweet dormer that looked like a half-opened eye, while pink roses weighed down a trellis on the right side of the house.

Moira handed the keys over to Astrid, grabbed her portfolio, and mounted the steps from the sidewalk to the ground level of the house. Up another set of stairs and she was on the white-railed porch that circled halfway around the left side of the house. A child-sized bicycle was parked under a window beside a painted box overflowing with boy-type toys.

Mrs. Atherton, her long silver earrings flashing in the morning light, opened the salmon-colored door before Moira had a chance to knock. "Come in, my dear. I've been watching out the front window for you."

Chapter Four

Moira looked around as Mrs. Atherton escorted her past an ornate umbrella stand and a wall of gilt-framed photographs into a large room papered in soft yellow. A large painting of a half-dressed maiden carrying a water jar hung on the near wall, and an open violin case lay on the seat of the baby grand piano that dominated the far wall.

The room was joyous with color. Underfoot was an intricately patterned Persian carpet, and the Victorian sofa and chairs had been freshened up with pink-and-orange chintz and topped with brightly colored throw pillows. Mrs. Atherton's long purple skirt, scarlet cummerbund, and beaded blouse completed the extravaganza.

And here she was in jeans and a college sweatshirt, just as out of place in Vashti Atherton's house as she was at Good Times last night.

Her hostess gestured toward the sofa. A brass tray containing a steaming Chinese teapot and a pair of tiny cups sat on the low table in front of it.

"Let's get acquainted a little before we look at the score, dear. I hope you like jasmine."

"It's my favorite," Moira said, settling into the comfortable cushions. "And thank you for inviting me over, Mrs. Atherton. I've studied the score, but I really do need to hear what it sounds like. The music is what tells the story."

"So glad to hear you say that, dear, but please call me Vashti." Her hostess poured the tea and handed a cup to Moira. "After all, you are our director, and we're all calling you by your first name." She lifted the cup to her lips for a long sip. "But from what you say, I assume you have a musical background?"

"Sort of ragtag, but I've got a good ear."

Vashti replaced her cup on the tray. "Let's get right to it, then. I can't sing all the parts at the same time, but you'll get the idea. Did you bring a digital recorder?"

"I get more out of listening to music on the scene. A recorder misses the nuances."

Vashti beamed at her and stood up. "So true, my dear." She crossed to the piano and closed the violin case, then placed it on top of a large music cabinet. "Oh, by the way, my older daughter, Carmen, will handle the violin parts and spell me at the piano. Her little boy is in the cast, so it should work out."

"I'm sure it will."

Moira put her cup down and moved a spindle-back chair over beside the piano bench. Now to open her ears and turn on her magic memory machine.

Vashti flexed her hands and began playing through the score, backing up occasionally to explain a standout moment she seemed particularly pleased with.

Pen was right—this woman was a genius. Her music defined the story arc—first there was status quo, then hope, then a minor success, then the real downer, and finally, the miracle of the happy ending. The audience would leave the theater feeling drained but satisfied, just like she felt right now. This show could make it a lot further than Bosque Bend.

"Vashti, this knocks me over."

"Thank you, my dear." Her voice took on a bite. "I just hope the Fontaine sisters' choreography won't detract from the music. Sometimes they get carried away, like last summer, when we did *You're a Good Man, Charlie Brown* and…never mind." She turned back several pages. "Let's look at the last couple of measures of 'Della's Prayer' again."

It was after three when Moira called Astrid to come pick her up.

Mrs. Atherton walked her out onto the porch and patted her arm. "One more thing, dear. Micaela told me that you and Rafe McAllister were at Good Times last night, and I just wanted to say that Rafe's a dear boy. You can ignore anything Bertie Fuller tells you."

With a benedictory smile, she turned and walked back into the house.

Moira stared at the closed door.

Now what the hell was that supposed to mean?

* * *

Ivanhoe barked joyously as Moira opened the car door. She gave her sister a tired hello, stuffed her portfolio under the seat, and looked in the back at Astrid's foundling. His eyes were bright with welcome, and his tail wagged like a fan set at too high a speed.

"Hi, doggie. Where'd you get that new collar and leash?"

Astrid checked behind herself for traffic and pulled out from the curb. "I thought navy blue was more appropriate for an alpha male like him, so I picked them up while I was at the supermarket, and…" She paused.

"And?" Moira prompted.

The words rushed out of Astrid as if she'd been holding her breath. "It's also in celebration of my new job!"

"Job?"

"Moira, it's rockin'! I'm going to be working part-time for Ivanhoe's vet! The minute we walked into the office, a German shepherd challenged Ivanhoe to a testosterone contest, and Dr. Sjoberg liked the way I handled the boys. Hired me on the spot. It'll be on a trial basis, just like your job, but I start Monday." She turned onto Austin Avenue. "And transportation comes along with the deal, so you needn't worry about carting me back and forth."

Moira's chest tightened. Her eighteen-year-old, drop-dead gorgeous sister had been hired on the spot? The vet was providing transportation?

"How…how old is Dr. Sjoberg?" She hadn't brought her baby sister all the way to Texas to be seduced by some hot-to-trot middle-aged veterinarian with a yen for teenage girls.

Astrid shrugged. "Maybe about fifty. She lives in the ritzy part of Lynnwood, up on the hill."

Moira released her breath slowly—and silently. *She.* Astrid's employer was a woman. *Thank God!*

"I got everything on the grocery list too, including all the Halloween stuff," Astrid continued. "Bats, flying witches, a pumpkin, and half a dozen bags of those little Milky Ways we both like." She slowed to a smooth stop for a traffic light, then upped speed as Austin Avenue became a highway. "How'd it go with Mrs. Atherton. She looks kind of like a combination of a Mother Goose and a deranged fairy godmother."

Moira laughed. "Vashti has her own style, all right, but she knows her music."

Her portfolio began to buzz. Maybe it was Pen Swaim or…Rafe McAllister.

But it was Donna Sue Gomez-Sweeny.

The drama teacher spoke in energetic rushes and interrupted sentences. "Welcome to Bosque Bend, Ms. Farrar! I'm Donna Sue. You've probably heard about me—and I wondered if—maybe about six thirty—or later, if it works for you—I could drop by this evening—you're in the Lynnwood house, aren't you?—to give you lists of the cast and crew."

Moira nodded into the phone. Those lists were exactly what she needed, and the sooner, the better. "Six thirty will be perfect."

* * *

Moira has just cleared the supper table when the doorbell chimed.

Donna Sue proved to be the same whirlwind of overactivity in person that she'd been on the phone. Her dimples flashed in and out, her hands fluttered, her brown eyes sparkled, and her head bobbed to dramatize her every word.

Her belly did too.

"Hi! I'm Donna Sue, and here's the list—cell numbers, landlines, e-mail addresses, and all. Just wanted to get them to you—and meet you too—while I'm still mobile." She wagged a manila folder in Moira's direction. "I hope you don't mind my having cast the roles already."

After taking one look at her guest, Moira was glad she'd asked Astrid to take Ivanhoe for an evening walk. He would have been all over Donna Sue, and the drama teacher, who appeared to be about twelve months gone, was in no condition to ward off a determinedly friendly canine.

"On the contrary, I'm grateful. Saved me a lot of time, and you know what everyone can do. Come in and talk to me, if you have the time." Moira pushed the door open all the way to accommodate her visitor's girth.

Donna Sue grinned and patted her baby bump—which was actually more of a baby basketball. "Babes, I have two weeks to spare before my little girl arrives—at least that's what the doctor says I have—but what does he know—and then it's off to the races."

Moira led her guest into the front room, at the same time trying to remember what her character in that after-school special had done when her "mother" went into labor on the kitchen floor.

After edging her bulk down carefully onto the couch,

Donna Sue opened the folder and withdrew a sheet of paper. "Everybody's thrilled about you taking the job, babes, especially with *Gift of the Magi* in the works. I'm okay with the tried and true—you should have seen my *Sound of Music*—but Pen's play has never been staged before." She waved the page around. "One thing you got going for you—and I'm not kidding—is that Bosque Bend has some real talent."

Donna Sue moved her finger farther down the list. "You've already seen Micaela Atherton, and you heard Travis McAllister sing—he's playing the Dreamer—when Rafe took you to Good Times last night." She gave Moira a sly look and her dimples twitched.

Moira jerked and her eyes opened wide. "How did you—?"

"Babes, you gotta understand. Everybody in Bosque Bend—and I mean *everybody*—is into everybody else's business. It's like a soap opera around here." Her brows drew together as she regarded the list again. "A word of warning, though—Travis will drop you in a second if he gets a good gig—you can't blame him—and also, he's made some emergency visits to the hospital a couple of times lately—God only knows what he's got. You should probably back him up with an understudy—I recommend the Benton kid, Sergio."

Donna Sue examined the list again and stabbed the page so hard it rattled.

"Billie Joe Semple plays the milliner—that's the second female lead. And then there's Rafe. He's the policeman—a London bobby complete with helmet, truncheon, and mustache. He begins and ends the show sort of like—you know—the Street Singer in *Threepenny Opera*."

"Rafe's in the cast?"

Donna Sue's dimples deepened, and she patted Moira's arm. "Babes, Rafe's *always* in the cast. He's sort of a good-luck charm. Plus he's the only basso—at least the only *real* one—for miles around, and—wow—does he deliver! The audience loves him. Of course, half the town's related to him."

Donna Sue looked at another page.

"I've printed out a list of the kids too—complete with phone numbers and e-mail addresses." She cocked an eyebrow. "A word to the wise, learn from my mistake and don't rehearse them too often in the auditorium—they get used to it and run wild. Let Xandra and Fleurette—they're a little weird, but you can trust them—handle everything in their studio for as long as you can."

Donna Sue shuffled her pages and pulled out a final sheet of paper.

"This is the list of the crew. Rafe's on it too, of course. Just tell him what you need—scenery, props—well, no, everyone in the cast pitches in on props—you'd be surprised what people have stowed away in their closets and back rooms." She handed the folder to Moira. "And if Vashti and the Fontaine sisters have at it again like they did this summer, the best thing is to get Rafe—he's a rock—to step in. All the women—it's those sexy eyes of his—adore him."

Moira stared at the page. "I didn't realize he was so involved."

"Babes, Rafe McAllister's the one who put the Bosque Bend Theater Guild on the map. I got it up and running, but we weren't going anywhere—I mean, nooowheeere—till he joined us. That was after Beth—she was his wife—died. I think he did it to honor her memory—she had the most beautiful soprano—really luscious—I've ever heard. Sang Marian in my *Music Man*."

Donna Sue handed the folder over to Moira, then heaved herself up. "I'd better head off. My husband gets anxious—he'll even call the police—if I run late. He's says he's afraid—and I think he really means it—the baby will drop out in the middle of the produce section at H-E-B." Her dimples appeared again. "Get it—the *produce* section?"

Moira walked the drama teacher to the curb and watched as she maneuvered herself into a fire-engine red smart car.

Beth—so now she had a name for Rafe's late wife. Probably tall, blond, busty, and beautiful—a Hollywood-beautiful woman for a Hollywood-handsome man.

* * *

Today was Beth's birthday, and he'd almost forgotten. How could he do that when he missed her every minute of his life?

The Sunday morning strains of "God Be with You Till We Meet Again" drifted across the cemetery as Rafe knelt to place a bouquet of fragrant lilacs in Beth's grave vase. Ever since he and Travis were kids, Mom had brought them here in season to decorate the family sites. So many McAllisters and Schulers were buried in this cemetery that the place looked like a flower garden by the time she'd hustled them back in the car. But the only grave he was visiting today was in the new section of the cemetery, the one with the headstone inscribed

Bethany Mary Hansson McAllister
Beloved Wife and Mother
She sings with the angels

He stood up, brushed the grass off his knees, and glanced around at the church he'd grown up in, the church in which he and Beth were married the week after they graduated from Eisenhower Consolidated.

They'd met when the high school students from the Bosque Bend end of the county had been transferred over to the newly constructed consolidated school. It had been a hard adjustment for him, especially since he'd had the flu and started a week late. His first day back, he'd been standing in the center of the front hall and trying to make sense out of the list the office secretary had given him when a beautiful girl smiled at him and asked if she could help.

She'd guided him to his classroom, then hurried off down the hall with a smile and wave of her hand. He saw her later that day in the cafeteria. She'd smiled at him again, and he knew he was in love.

He'd walked Beth out of class that day, and the next, and next. The fourth day, she'd actually waited for him when he was a few minutes late getting out of class. That weekend, he'd taken her out to the ranch. After dinner, while everyone was watching television, he'd drawn a pencil portrait of her.

That sketch hung over Delilah's bed now, like a guardian angel. He didn't want Delilah to ever forget who her mother was. Especially since she had just turned one when Beth was killed.

He picked up a blade of grass and twisted it between his fingers, remembering the happy times.

Within a month of meeting, Beth and he were a couple. They spent a lot of time in the backseat of his car, but held off on doing the deed because Beth had taken a church pledge to wait till she was married, an abstention which they more than made up for during their summerlong honeymoon in the C Bar M foreman's house.

Come fall, they'd packed their bags and set up housekeeping in Austin to attend University of Texas. Beth majored in vocal performance while he crammed a six-year architecture degree into five. When he graduated, Uncle Al hired him into his Dallas architecture firm.

A shaft of slanted sunlight played across the close-mowed lawn, and Rafe heard footsteps approaching. He slapped his Stetson on his head and stood up.

Better get outa here. Didn't want to run into any of Bertie Fuller's cronies and set them to talking again—although he doubted they'd ever stopped. Damn, he wished there had been another house available for Moira.

He glanced around.

It was Travis. He must have driven up when the organ swelled on that last chorus.

Travis nodded toward the lavender blossoms in the grave vase. "Thought this was where I'd find you. You had a good woman, bro. I was almost as much in love with her as you were."

Rafe gave his brother a searching look as they started walking toward their vehicles together.

"You've got a good woman yourself, Trav." He'd never forget how Rocky had sat up with him the night after Beth was buried, when he finally had to acknowledge she was really dead. It must have been hard on Rocky—she'd known Beth since high school—but she'd plied him with hot tea and let him talk it out.

So what was Travis's problem?

"What's going on with you and Rocky?"

"I dunno. Maybe it's that we're hitting the four-year mark. Maybe it's that all she talks about is the ranch."

"Rocky and her mother are the last of the blood Colbys. Part of the C Bar M is hers."

Travis snorted out a laugh and paused beside his car. "Maybe half an acre. You've been overpaying them ever since Rocky's mother moved her kids to town after her old man met up with a rattler that was meaner than he was, but you know as well as I do that her great-granddaddy screwed up big time. Every time he gambled away a parcel of acreage, our great-granddaddy bought it up." Travis gave his brother a knowing glance. "And while we're talking about women, what's going on with you and Moira Farrar? You were all over her while I was singing 'Good Night, Irene' at Omar's on Friday night."

Rafe shrugged and leaned against the side of the Mustang. "I like her."

"Careful there, bro. You're treading on sacred Hollywood turf. Remember she was married to Colin Sanger, every woman's dream lover. Even Xandra and Fleurette are nuts about him, and that's saying a lot."

"Yeah, I know." He scuffed the soft ground with the toe of

his boot. "I've invited Moira and her sister out to the ranch this afternoon. You gonna be there?"

"I'm off to Waco. Seward Gap has a gig at the Tenth Street Primitive Baptist Church fiftieth reunion."

The music swelled again and Rafe looked back at the church. Carmen Atherton was really laying into the pipe organ today. Maybe she was thinking about Beth too. She and Beth had been best friends all through school. It had been a twosome at first—Beth and Carmen—then became a threesome when Rocky joined the crew. He frowned in thought. Odd—he never heard Rocky talk about Carmen anymore. Beth must have been the glue that bound the other two together.

Oh God, Beth had been the glue that held him together too. She had a grace about her. It wasn't just that she was beautiful, but that she was kind and good and caring. Beth glowed with happiness. She was his delight.

He looked up at the clear, cloudless sky.

Was she still in existence somewhere in the universe? Did she know what a joy her daughter was? That Delilah was four now and getting taller and prettier and smarter every day? Did she know how lonely he was? Did she know he had his eye on Moira Farrar? Little Moira Farrar, who was all grown up now and sexy as hell?

He looked at Beth's flowers, and a wave of guilt rolled through him. Three years ago, if he could have, he'd have walled himself into a monastery, alone with his memories of Beth, but Delilah had needed him, his family had needed him, the ranch had needed him.

And now he needed Moira Farrar.

Travis lifted himself off the side of the truck. "One more refrain, a final resounding chord, and everyone will be pouring out of the church. Time for both of us to get out of here."

* * *

As Moira eased down the driveway, she looked up at the string of green-eyed bats and hunchbacked witches hanging from the eaves of their front porch. "You did a great job getting the Halloween decorations up, Astrid. And it was nice of Mrs. Fuller to lend us her ladder."

"Yeah, she's cool—and I've got to remember to take the ladder back to her when we get home this afternoon. I'll take the pink leash and collar back too." She glanced toward the backyard as Ivanhoe leaped against the chain-link fence and voiced his protest of their departure. "Poor baby. I hate leaving him all alone while we're at the ranch."

"He'll survive."

Moira drove up to intersection, caught a green light for once, and turned right.

Halfway up the highway, the car in front of her slowed down as it approached a break in the evergreen thicket, then turned into BUY-1-GET-5-FREE.

Moira did a double take.

In the dark of night, when Rafe had parked in the clearing to state his case, the scene had looked like a Maurice Sendak jungle, but in the bright afternoon sunlight, it looked more like a Norman Rockwell slice of Americana. A string of lights outlined the lot, two RVs and a Porta-Potty were parked under the trees in the back of the lot, and several customers were lined up at the sales counter. Apparently Bosque Bend celebrated Halloween with a big bang.

Astrid wove her hair into a long braid and tossed it over her shoulder.

"How much farther?

"Just a couple more miles. Watch for Colby Road on the left. It may be hard to spot."

Actually, the road was clearly marked, and after another mile, Moira turned into the entrance to the C Bar M Ranch.

Every bit of moisture in her mouth dried up.

Calm down, Moira. This is just a courtesy visit. Yes, a courtesy visit to your boss's home. Well, also to the home of a guy who'd propositioned her the first day they met. A guy who made her blood run hot and her mouth go dry whenever she thought of him, which was way too often.

She drove past the single-story house at the gate and continued up the narrow tarmac road bordered by barbed wire on either side. Beyond the fences, black cattle built like tanks lifted their heads as the car passed, as if to check them out.

The lane angled around a stand of tall trees, then broadened into a wide concrete circular driveway in front of a flat-roofed, two-story mansion.

The outside of the house was faced with a hard-surfaced material that had the look of sunbaked adobe, while large, dark windows and long, iron-railed balconies punctuated its smooth lines and rounded corners. Four wide steps led up to the covered porch that stretched the width of the house, and several outsized urns of purple caladiums sat on either side of the giant front door.

And Rafe, Mr. Cool, was sitting out front, waiting for them.

Chapter Five

Rafe unfolded himself from the wicker lawn chair and waited for Moira and her sister to come up the walk.

Don't rush it, cowboy. She's got her sister with her. Pretend you've come out to sit out on the patio and enjoy the cool weather. Don't let on you've been wearing out your watch looking to see how many more minutes it would be till they arrived.

A wave of heat swept through him as he watched Moira come up the flagstone walk. She and her sister were both carrying broad-brimmed hats, but while Astrid was dressed in jeans and something that looked like an old hoodie, Moira had on a rose-colored, figure-hugging western-style shirt and jeans that were tight enough to show off her pert little bottom.

Rafe smiled. No Roscoe's Chicken and Waffles this time around.

God, he wanted her. He hadn't been this fixated on a woman since…well, since Beth died. For the past three years, he'd been in some kind of sexual limbo, taking what was offered and moving on just as casually, but Moira—he'd like to keep her around for a while.

"Really appreciate y'all comin' out this afternoon," he said, trying to inject a light tone into his voice as he escorted his guests toward the house. "Mom just phoned that she and Delilah are runnin' a little late, so I thought we could go inside and visit a little before the tour."

He pushed open the center-balanced revolving door, and Moira looked up at the two-story skylight in the middle of the hexagonal foyer, then turned around slowly to see the rooms and the ascending staircase radiating out from it.

He tensed, waiting for her reaction.

God, he wanted her to like his house. He wanted her to like *him*.

"This is beautiful, Rafe! I expected a ranch house like in the movies, maybe one story and spread out, or maybe a King Ranch–style Victorian, but this is so beautiful."

Relief flooded through him.

"Actually, the original *was* a Victorian. Great-grand-daddy Gilbert built it in the late 1800s, but termites took it down when I was in college. Dad hired one of my mother's brothers—Uncle Al's an architect—to build us a bug-proof house, and since I was pretty far into my degree by then, he took me under his wing, and we worked on the design together."

He moved up a step into the family room and swept his arm around, indicating the thick Navajo-style rug in front of the tall brick fireplace, plush furniture, grandfather clock, and old Baldwin upright. "My mother did the room. She used what we could salvage from the old house, then added some new couches and chairs."

An interior decorator friend of his had taken care of the rest of the house. She'd had taken care of him too for a while, until she realized Delilah would always come first.

Moira wandered over to examine the yard-wide arrangement of photographs on the near side of the fireplace while Astrid looked out of the floor-to-ceiling window wall. He moved as close behind Moira as he could without violating her space.

"Mom put that together. It's a collage of the three of us kids—TexAnn, Travis, and me. Mom did the one on the other side of the fireplace too. Used pictures of Schulers and McAllisters back as far as she could find them. The Schulers are musical and artistic. The McAllisters are hardheaded wheeler-dealers."

Shit! Why the hell did he say that? Was he warning Moira that he could be a hard-assed son of a bitch? Why? Was he considering a long-term relationship?

He touched Beth's ring, his forever ring, to remind himself of his commitment.

Moira stepped back to take in the total composition. "This is so original. How did your mother get the idea? Most people would have stuffed the pictures away in a shoebox."

"Probably from a 4-H bulletin."

Astrid gave him a questioning look. "4-H? Isn't that when kids raise pigs and stuff?"

"Pigs, goats, cows—all sort of animals, but it has other programs too. Art, sewing, music—that sort of thing. We were homeschooled until we reached high school, so Mom signed us up with 4-H so we could meet other kids. Of course, with us being in 4-H, she had to teach some of the cl—"

A car door slammed out front, and Astrid waved a hand at him. "If your mother drives a maroon Mercedes hatchback, she's here."

Delilah's high-pitched voice cut through the adult murmur at the door. "Daddy—Daddy—Daddy—Daddy—Daddy! I saw a car outside! Is the pretty lady here?"

Moira moved forward as Rafe, holding Delilah on his hip, stepped up into the family room, followed by a tall, trim woman in a stylish dark print dress. Her smile was easy, her hair was auburn, and her eyes sparkled like diamonds. No need to ask who she was.

Delilah wiggled out of her father's embrace and hurled herself at Moira, who barely had time to brace against what felt like a launched cannonball.

"Pretty lady! You *did* come to see me! Just like Daddy promised!"

Moira lifted Delilah in her arms, and her heart melted. If she ever had a daughter, she'd want her to be just like Delilah.

"And my sister is here too," she said, turning to Astrid so Delilah could meet her.

Astrid reached out to touch the white collar of Delilah's navy-and-red plaid skater dress. "I like your outfit. Very stylish."

"I chose the 'terial and Nana made it for me. Nana's teaching me to sew. She can do anything."

"Not quite, honey, but I try." Mrs. McAllister held out her

arms to take Delilah, whose four-year-old weight Moira wasn't used to hefting, and set her on the floor, then smiled at her son's visitors.

"I'm Enid McAllister, Rafe's mother. Welcome to Bosque Bend, Moira. We're so glad you're here. And, Astrid, are you a thespian like your sister?"

Astrid's eyes widened in alarm, and she held up her hands in protest. "No way! I'm better off in the audience."

Mrs. McAllister laughed. "I'm with you, Astrid. We'll have to reserve seats for *Gift of the Magi* next to each other."

Rafe wrapped an arm around his mother's shoulders. "Mom, I'm gonna give Moira and Astrid a tour of the ranch. You want to come along? I could saddle up Lady for you. Got the blankets and the pads all laid out, and the horses are brushed up and ready for action."

"Thanks, honey, but I'm scheduled to teach some ladies at Floravista how to chain stitch in about thirty minutes. I would like to visit with Lady for a minute, though. Y'all go ahead and start walking. I'll catch up. It'll just take me a minute to change Delilah into jeans."

Rafe escorted his guests through the house, then down the back steps to the tarmac road. The well-stocked library and large gleaming kitchen had been impressive, Moira thought, but the covered flagstone patio and pool went above and beyond. This was the kind of house Johnny Blue had grown up in.

Tires whooshed on the tarmac, and an open-topped Jeep turned the corner of the house, jerking to a stop in front of them. The door opened, and a smiling woman with corkscrew curls the color of butterscotch taffy leaped out.

She laughed, a joyous, bell-like sound, and her hand, tipped by gold-painted fingernails brushed a jiggling curl back from her face.

Her voice had a childlike sweetness. "Sorry, Rafe, I didn't realize you had company. I'm heading to H-E-B and wondered if you needed me to pick up anything for you while I'm there."

"I think I'm okay for now." Rafe gave her an easy grin and put his arm around her shoulder. "Y'all, this is Rocky, my favorite sister-in-law."

Moira was entranced. Travis's wife looked as slim and fit as a Hollywood stuntwoman, and she had a camera-friendly face too—china blue eyes, rosebud lips, and a pointed chin. Any wardrobe mistress worth her salt would have considered that Mexican-style embroidered blouse, the fawn-colored pants, and those high-heeled riding boots to be the perfect costume for a heroine out of the Old West. All Rafe's visitor needed was a guitar in one hand and a six-shooter in the other.

"Rocky, meet Moira Farrar and her sister, Astrid Birdsong. Moira's signed on as our new theater guild director."

His arm stayed around his sister-in-law as he walked her over to meet Moira and Astrid. It was a signal, Moira realized, a message that Rocky was under his protection. But why did he think Rocky needed protecting? Because Travis was flirting with the pianist?

"Moira Farrar?" The blue eyes widened. "*The* Moira Farrar? Ma and I used to watch *The Clancy Family* all the time when I was a kid."

Moira smiled graciously, as she'd been taught to do when dealing with fans. "I'm glad you enjoyed it." What else could she say? Rocky didn't know that *The Clancy Family* was just another day on the job to her. Gramp didn't force her to work, but she was always aware of how much the household depended on her.

The kitchen door opened, and Moira watched as Mrs. McAllister, holding Delilah by the hand, paused for the briefest of moments before putting a welcoming smile on her face and coming down the steps to greet her daughter-in-law. "How nice to see you, Rocky."

Rocky turned around, and Rafe dropped his arm.

"Enid! Love your dress! Another exclusive from Paris?"

Mrs. McAllister laughed lightly. "Don't lay it on too thick, Rocky. You know I make all my own clothes."

Moira looked from one woman to the other. What was that all about?

Cut it out, Moira, you're making something out of nothing. This isn't a suspense thriller with a motive behind every action. Mrs. McAllister paused because she didn't realize Rocky had come on the scene, and Rocky's reference to her mother-in-law's dress was simply an over-the-top compliment.

Delilah wrapped her arms around her father's leg. "Can Auntie Rocky go riding with us? Can she, Daddy? Can she?"

Rafe didn't hesitate. "Of course, she can, sweetheart. Auntie Rocky's always welcome."

He'd take advantage of any opportunity he could get to be supportive of Rocky. Travis may not be sleeping with Micaela now, but everyone in town knew it wouldn't be long. Rafe had always liked Micaela and been surprised when Travis dumped her to marry Rocky, but once Trav had done the till-death-do-we-part, that was the end of the story as far as he was concerned.

Rocky laughed, "If that's an invitation, I'm accepting."

"Then let's hightail it down to the barn. I'm puttin' Moira on Star and Astrid on Dakota, so you have your choice of Lady, Blackie, or Bella—Mom's not goin' with us."

Rocky's coming along was to his advantage. It meant they'd ride two by two instead of three across. He'd partner up with Moira, of course.

"Gotta tell you, though, Bella's in a nasty mood today. Up to her old tricks. Tried to nip me this mornin' when I brought her in from the pasture." He snorted to himself, knowing his warning was in vain. As if Rocky would let anything stop her from riding her favorite horse.

His mother consulted her watch and gave him the look. "Rafe, I can't stretch this any longer than ten minutes."

He lifted Delilah to his shoulders and clutched her legs to hold her in place. "Then let's get a-goin', folks!"

Mom led the parade, with Rocky and Astrid not far behind. He and Moira brought up the rear, which was exactly the way he wanted it.

With his hands otherwise occupied, there was no way he could even reach out to Moira, but he got a buzz on just from being near her. If they were alone, he'd have chanced backing her up against one of those cedar elms lining the road. Instead, he was walking along with his daughter on his shoulders and his tongue stuck to the top of his mouth.

Talk, you idiot. Say something, anything, so she knows your vocal chords are still working.

"Uh, how does the C Bar M compare to Southfork?" *God, that was a dumb thing to say. Apples and oranges.* The C Bar M's six thousand acres dwarfed Southfork's two hundred, but the Southfork mansion overshot the C Bar M's ranch house by almost two thousand square feet.

Moira laughed. "I don't know. The interiors of *Dallas* were all on soundstages by the time my character visited, so I never saw anything but backdrops."

The barn came into view as they rounded the last stand of trees. What would Moira think of it? She'd liked the house, but Uncle Al had designed most of it. The barn, on the other hand, was entirely his baby, a gift of love to his father.

He lifted Delilah to the ground as he waited for Moira's reaction.

She stopped in her tracks and inhaled as if she had come up from a deep dive, then turned to him. "This is a—a barn? It looks more like a palace!"

"That's what my dad called it—a horse palace. The stalls, tack room, and hay storage are on the ground floor, the bailer and mowers in one wing, with ranch vehicles, flatbed and horse trailers in the other. And there's an office suite upstairs. *Ranch and Range* ran a feature on it, and I got some nice commissions off of it too, which helped a lot when Delilah came along."

"You designed it?"

"Every square inch of it."

"It's…it's…I can't find the words…"

She didn't have to find the words. The expression on her face and the wonder in her voice were enough to satisfy him.

* * *

He stopped at the barn door to breathe in the aroma of sweet hay, then walked in and looked around to see where everyone was. Mom stood by Lady's stall, feeding her a carrot she'd swiped from the tack room refrigerator, and Astrid was hanging back and watching as Rocky fought Bella to get a bridle on her.

Rocky won, of course—she always did. God, she knew horses. And cows. In fact, she could outride, outrope, and outshoot any man on the place, including him. So what the fuck was Travis's problem? Micaela burned up the piano keys, and she could sing the daylights out of any music ever written, but Rocky, who'd grown up with a hard-ass father on a hard-luck spread, was the ideal ranch wife.

Rafe set Delilah down and touched Moira's arm to get her attention. She jerked as if he'd been wiping his feet on a nylon carpet.

Goddamn! If she was that sensitive when he barely touched her, how would she react when he kissed her? When he held her close against him again like he had at Omar's honky-tonk, but this time, without everyone in Bosque Bend looking on?

Save that till later, cowboy. Right now you've got to take care of the horses.

"Moira, I'd appreciate it if you'd stay with Delilah while I saddle everyone up."

Moira nodded and took Delilah's hand while he walked over to Dakota's stall and led the tall gelding out, being careful to avoid Bella, who was rolling her eyes at the sight of the saddle Rocky had lifted from the rail.

The next time Rafe looked up, Rocky was riding Bella out of the barn.

He couldn't help but smile. Rocky and Bella—those two were a lot alike—both fair-haired and both spirited. But the beautiful Bella was dangerous. He'd have gotten rid of her by now if it weren't for Rocky. She didn't need to have her favorite horse sold out from under her at the same time her husband was playing footsie with his old flame.

He walked Dakota over to Astrid, and she swung herself into the saddle like a pro.

"How do the stirrups feel?"

"Spot on. You guessed right." She picked up the reins. "I'll go on out and get acquainted with Rocky." She clucked at Dakota and walked him out of the barn.

Rafe led Star out of her stall, trailing a hand along the side of Moira's waist as he passed by, which was all he could manage with Delilah pulling at him again.

"Can I ride Star, Daddy? I want to ride Star."

"Sorry, Sugar. Miss Moira's our guest so we'll let her ride Star." He hung the mare's halter on a hook outside her stall, and like the sweetheart she was, Star dipped her nose for the bridle. "You can sit in front of me on Sarge."

Delilah looked like he'd promised her a second Christmas. "On *Sarge*? I get to ride *Sarge*?"

"Sure thing, but let's get Miss Moira into the saddle first."

Star was bombproof, but he'd stay close to Moira anyway—as if he hadn't planned to do that already.

Moira swallowed hard as she looked at the dark brown horse with the splotch of white on its forehead that Rafe had saddled for her. Astrid had won horsemanship awards in summer camp, but her own equestrian experience was limited to that week she'd spent at Southfork and a month of playing an Indian girl in a really rotten movie, which thank goodness, no one ever saw.

Sending up a little prayer, she hooked her toe in the stirrup and threw her leg over the horse's back.

As soon as she picked up the reins, Rafe left her to lay a pad across the back of a big pinto who looked like he'd been splashed with war paint, added a blanket and saddle, then lifted Delilah up on top of the stack. The four-year-old grasped the pommel as if she'd been riding since she was born, which she probably had.

Then, with single fluid movement, Rafe lifted himself onto the horse behind his daughter.

Moira gasped. Rafe McAllister was cowboy incarnate.

And he was for real.

A strident whinny came from outside the barn, and Moira caught flashes out the door of Bella rearing up, her mane and flowing tail whipping to and fro as she tried to toss Rocky off into the dust. But no matter what twists and turns Bella maneuvered, Rocky stayed on board.

Suddenly the white horse dropped her head, accepting her fate, and Rocky walked her over to Astrid. The two of them started talking as if nothing had happened.

* * *

Moira waited as Rafe closed the pasture gate and swung back up on his horse.

"We'll go at a walk most of the way," he explained to her. You can see more, and there's less chance of your horse ending up with a broken leg."

She could hear Astrid and Rocky talking back and forth behind them. From what few words she could make out, they were comparing their fingernails—an interesting way to bond—but she and Rafe rode in an easy silence.

Moira looked around automatically to check the position of a camera crew, but all she saw was an endless sweep of land and a gathering of puffy white clouds in a pale sky. No traffic noise, nothing needing her immediate attention, no reason to hurry, hurry, hurry. Everything was at its own pace.

She could get used to this.

She cast a quick glance at Rafe and was jolted back to reality.

Was that a gun stock sticking out of the leather scabbard hanging from his saddle?

"What is that—a rifle?"

He patted the scabbard. "Heavy-duty shotgun."

A shotgun? For a pleasure ride on his own property? She tried for corny humor. "You expectin' to run into rustlers, podnuh?"

Rafe's face turned to granite and his voice hardened. "We do have rustlers from time to time—usually penny ante—but right now I'm on the lookout for feral hogs. Coyotes and rattlesnakes too. The hogs tear up the land, and we lose a couple of calves a year to coyotes and rattlers." He squinted up at the thick canopy of trees they were passing under. "Lately, we've been having trouble with panthers." He gave the landscape a narrow-eyed 180-degree survey.

"Panthers?"

"Panthers, cougars, mountain lions, pumas—whatever you want to call them. They'll go after anything they can get, us included." He scanned the horizon again. "This is raw land. You have to respect its danger."

Rafe looked back as he heard Rocky's laugh—he'd know it anywhere. She and Astrid had been talking pretty much the whole ride. Good—the way things were going with Micaela and Travis, Rocky would need all the friends she could get.

He settled back in the saddle and moved Sarge a little closer to Moira. "You'll be seein' some cows as soon as we cross the rise. We got a river that cuts through all the pastures, and they like to spend the afternoon in the shade down in the wallows."

Moira looked around at the close-cropped winter grass and rocky terrain. "A river?"

"Not really a river. It's a tributary of the Bosque. Doesn't even have a name."

"Why do you have multiple pastures?"

He paused and looked around himself as if counting acreage. "We have to keep the herds movin' to avoid over-grazin'. In good years, we need about three acres per cow-calf unit, four acres if we haven't had enough rain. Also, we keep the bulls in a separate pasture and rotate them to be sure we don't have inbreeding—it weakens the stock."

The foursome descended into a scattered herd of cows, which gave them questioning looks, then totally ignored them.

Delilah, who'd been slumped against her father with her eyes half-closed, suddenly leaned forward and pointed toward the herd. "Look, Daddy—deer!"

Moira followed her finger and saw a trio of delicate heads lift themselves above the grazing cattle and twitch their over-large ears. She turned to Rafe. "Why are deer in with the cattle?"

"Mom says the deer are tryin' to protect themselves from hunters, but Uncle Omar's theory is that the cows are so dumb they think the deer are cattle, and the deer are so dumb they think the cattle are deer."

Moira laughed. "I like your Uncle Omar. It must be nice to have so many members of your family nearby."

Colin rarely visited his mother and father, she remembered. She'd met them only once—two ordinary ducks totally in awe of the swan they'd somehow managed to produce. She'd always wondered if something about the way they'd raised him had caused him to turn out the way he did, or maybe it had been whatever he'd experienced when he first hit Hollywood. Rumor had it that his first wife, a screen siren about fifteen years older than he was, had dabbled in "exotic" sex. But maybe Colin had just plain been born with a screw loose.

Whatever, he shouldn't have imposed his hang-ups on her.

The old guilt nagged at her. *And she shouldn't have let him.*

She watched as Rafe maneuvered Sarge to avoid a big cow who saw no reason to give way to a mere horse before he answered.

"Yeah, I think the McAllisters stick around because they want to make sure I'm doin' right by them. The C Bar M has been passed down from oldest son to oldest son for four generations, and everyone who's in the bloodline gets a share of the profits." He glanced behind them. "When Travis and Rocky have kids, the Colby bloodline will disappear into ours."

Moira heard another bell-like peal of laughter behind her and looked back. Why in the world was Travis straying when he had such a magical creature as Rocky at home? Dear God, she hoped whatever was going on with Travis and Micaela didn't hit the fan until after the show closed.

Which reminded her, she'd better check with Rafe about the rehearsal schedule.

"Will you be able to attend the adult cast meeting tomorrow night?"

"I'll be there this time, but I can't guarantee every Monday—it depends on whether Rocky or Mrs. Goodrich—she comes twice a week to clean up the house—can stay with Delilah. Tuesday through Thursday are out, but I can usually be there Friday and Saturdays. My mother kidnaps Delilah for weekends."

They moved away from the herd, and he gave her a speculative glance. "When you gonna be in town tomorrow?"

"All day. I'm talking to the Fontaines at nine—they set up the appointment, but I would have contacted them soon enough anyway—and after that, I'll go over to the museum to see what the theater rooms are like."

A pickup drove up to the other side of the river and turned around, then started honking and tossing out loose hay.

"That's Jimbo Crane, our neighbor's son. Works for us part-time. He's luring the cows into another pasture."

"By blowing the horn?"

"Cows are curious. They'll follow an interesting sound any-where it leads them, especially if they associate food with it."

And sure enough, the cattle began lumbering across the shallow stream after the truck.

"Jimbo left a leg in Iraq so he's got a prosthetic, but you'd never guess it. We have a couple of other hands on the payroll too—local guys who go home at night. The place is too big for Travis and me to handle by ourselves."

Moira squinted at the cattle. "What are those yellow things hanging down from the calves' noses?"

"We're testing a Canadian method of weanin' for A&M. The plastic flap lets a calf drink water and eat and get plenty of socializin', but keeps it from nursin'. That way we don't have to separate the cow and calf till we take the calf to market—and by then neither one of them cares. We used to use a shock treatment—separating the calves and the cows by a fence line, and they'd spend the next week runnin' up and down the fence, tryin' to break through to each other, bawlin' like lost souls. Sometimes a cow—they can weigh over a thousand pounds—would smash through the fence and we'd have to start all over again."

"A mother trying to reach her child."

Rafe nodded. "I grew up with the racket and didn't think much about it, but it made Beth cry so she and Delilah moved in with her mother when it was weanin' time." He looked at the herd again. "Far as I can tell, those little plastic flaps are a godsend."

The sky murmured behind them and Rafe looked back,

then reined in his horse and waited for Rocky and Astrid to catch up.

"Y'all, we need to head on back to the house. Sounds like we've got a storm on the way."

The thunder rolled again, louder, and Rocky rode up beside Rafe. "Gotta go. Left the top down on the Jeep." Without waiting for a reply, she slapped Bella on the flank and galloped across the field, jumped a fallen log, and disappeared behind a stand of trees.

"Me too!" Astrid called out as she dug her heels into Dakota's ribs.

Moira wished she actually *did* have a camera crew with her. First, the white horse running across the meadow with the fair-haired woman on her back, then Astrid, her black braid flying behind her. It looked like a scene Fellini might have staged.

Rafe gave Moira a reassuring smile. "No need to join the speed demons. A slow trot will get us to the barn before the rain comes, and it's a lot safer. Rocky would dare the devil."

Chapter Six

Moira followed Sarge through the barn door. No rain had fallen yet, but navy blue clouds had gathered at the edge of the sky and the air smelled of ozone. She looked around the barn. Rocky was nowhere in sight, but Astrid was leaning against Dakota's stall, waiting for them.

She pushed off the stall and walked over to them. "Rocky had to take care of her car, so I rubbed down both horses and put them in their stalls. Rafe, that Bella horse tried to bite me. I've never had a horse do that before."

Rafe shook his head. "Bella's vicious—bad to the bone. I'm surprised you could handle her at all."

He swung off his horse and reached up for Delilah. As he lowered her to the ground, a thunderclap shook the barn, and she buried her face against his leg.

Astrid stepped forward. "Rafe, how about I run Delilah into the house right quick before the rain starts while you take care of Star?"

"Good idea." Rafe knelt down to his daughter's level. "Miss Astrid is going to get you to the house before the rain starts, sugar. She'll take care of you till the pretty lady and I come in."

As Astrid and Delilah started up the road, Moira swung her leg over Star's back to dismount, but before she could reach the ground, Rafe's arms were at her waist and he was turning her to face him.

Her heart pounded, and she grasped his shoulders. She wasn't expecting this. *And she didn't want it—or maybe she did.*

He slid her slowly down his body, tight against his hardness, and she felt the heat rise in her cheeks. Her breathing turned to a soft pant and the barn was suddenly much too warm.

Oh God, she did want it.

He kissed her—softly, gently, lingeringly.

She felt faint. She felt happy. Her ears rang. She could live in this moment forever.

His voice was a whisper in her ear. "Have lunch with me tomorrow in town."

Moira nodded, so full of wonder she could hardly speak. One syllable was all she could get out, but it was enough.

"Yes."

* * *

The rain came in spits and spatters, first a polite pitter-patter, and the next minute, a windshield-blinding maelstrom, then back to the droplets again. Moira gazed out the window of the car at the sodden landscape, but didn't really see a thing.

Good thing Astrid had volunteered to drive. She'd have run them off into a ditch.

What had Rafe McAllister done to her? Her pulse was thumping and her nerves humming, and she felt like she was floating on air. God help her, that was exactly what it had been like when Colin kissed her the first time.

Remember that, Moira, and don't let yourself get caught in another spiderweb. Forget about love. The windshield wipers backed her up with each swish—*sex only, sex only, sex only.*

Astrid shot her a quick look. "Okay—spill. What happened with you and the cowboy? You've been in another universe ever since I left you two alone in the barn."

Moira couldn't help but smile. "He kissed me, and I'm meeting him for lunch tomorrow."

"Cool. Rafe sends out good vibes. And that Rocky—she's a riot. If everyone in Bosque Bend is like those two, I think I'll hang around a while."

* * *

Moira heated up the skillet to make pancakes for supper while Astrid took an old beach towel outside to dry off Ivanhoe, who apparently didn't know what a covered back porch was for. Through the sliding glass door, she could see him bark with joy, spin around like a top, then knock into Mrs. Fuller's aluminum ladder. It went down with a loud crash that set off another round of barking.

Astrid folded the ladder, leaned it against the porch, and ushered Ivanhoe into the house.

"You'd think we've been gone a week," she grumbled as she grabbed the pink leash and collar. "I'd better return this stuff to Mrs. Fuller while the rain is letting up. I'll take the ladder too."

Moira waved her spatula at her. "Don't be too long, I'm starting to cook."

The first stack of pancakes was on the table when Astrid came bursting through the door. "You won't believe it, but when I told Mrs. Fuller that we'd just come back from a tour of the C Bar M, she stiffened up like I'd just blessed the devil and said to tell you that Rafe McAllister's never shown up in church since his wife was killed. Has he said anything about that to you?"

Moira shrugged. "No, and I'm not going to ask him. He's still wearing her ring."

* * *

Rafe sang Delilah's nighttime prayer with her, then walked over to the window and stared out at the stand of trees in front of the house.

The bright moon illuminated the profile of the tree house his father had built for him and Travis when they were kids. It wasn't anything fancy, just a sturdy platform up in the branches of a big live oak—looked more like the beginnings of a deer blind than anything else.

He hadn't thought about it for years. He and Travis had lost interest in tree houses when they'd discovered girls. No one had kept the thing up, and the platform must have rotted out by now.

Maybe he'd rebuild it for Delilah when she got older, but with girl-type embellishments. No—the tree was in a straight line to where he'd found Beth's body, and lightning might strike twice.

But right now his plate was full up with other projects—the theater guild, the play, the Waco project…Moira.

He sat down in his chair, crossed his arms behind his head, leaned back, and smiled.

All in all, it had been a good day. He'd gotten Moira out to the ranch, which had been a biggie, and she'd liked his house and the barn. She also seemed to enjoy the ride around the ranch. And she hadn't shied from that kiss that was more than a kiss in the barn.

He closed his eyes.

Moira was different from the other women he'd dated since Beth was killed.

And face it, cowboy—you're a lot more attracted to her than she is to you—or than she wants to be to you. On the other hand, she'd loosened up in Good Times after a couple of beers and hadn't objected when he held her so close on the dance floor that she must have known he was aroused. But the second he stopped at the fireworks stand, she went batshit crazy on him.

He frowned. Moira had grown up on soundstages, so who knows what might have happened to her along the way. Whatever it was, being married to Colin Sanger must have made up for it. So why was she playing him hot and cold?

He'd known he was risking getting his face slapped for the way he slid her off her horse today, but wonder of wonders, she not only accepted the kiss, but also accepted his invitation to lunch.

All systems seemed go. He took one last glance at the tree house and closed the shade.

* * *

Moira searched through her wardrobe for just the right dress—cute, casual, and a little flirty. How about that Zulily number she had hiding somewhere in the back? The charcoal, ginger, and tangerine one with the off-center zigzag design that folded from left to right across the front? And she'd wear heels too, not the I-mean-business pumps she'd worn to her meeting with the board, but slingbacks with delicate leather butterflies lightly affixed to the vamp, shoes that whispered, "Catch me if you can."

She paused.

What did she really know about Rafe McAllister? That he had a nice family and a big ranch? That he was involved with theater? That just thinking about him made her tingle all over?

But appearances could be deceiving and so could her hormones. What was he like in the darkest dark of night when no one else was around?

A cold shudder raced through her, and she returned the Zulily and the fanciful butterfly shoes to her closet. A skirt and short jacket over a linen blouse would be safer, and she'd wear her sensible black pumps again. After all, she needed to look professional—and not just for Mr. McAllister. Before toddling off to lunch with him, she was meeting with the Fontaine sisters. then and driving over to the museum to get acquainted with its head docent and pick up the keys to the theater rooms.

The woman had sounded like a martinet on the phone and would probably require a picture ID, fingerprints, and DNA swab before she handed them over.

* * *

Moira parked her car in the concrete parking lot, squared her shoulders, and walked around to the front entrance of Xandra and Fleurette's studio. Their choice, their territory, their advantage. What in the heck could they want to talk to her about that was so important and so private that they'd asked her to come to see them as soon as possible?

Two storefronts wide, the Fontaine School of Dance reigned like a queen over a side street across from the seen-better-days Spanish-style Bosque Bend Public Library. Beige draperies threaded with gold hung behind the display windows, which featured portraits of Xandra and Fleurette in their younger days—she'd guess they were in their early fifties now—as well as photos of students in recital costumes. A professionally printed poster advertised upcoming classes in ballroom, swing, and line dancing for teens and adults. Another poster listed opportunities for preschoolers on up—creative movement, tap, ballet, pointe, jazz, and hip-hop.

Moira turned the old-fashioned pressed brass doorknob and entered the lions' den—the *lionesses'* den—then stopped to look around. Gymnastic equipment, floor mats and a pair of trampolines occupied a far corner, and each of the other corners held an electronic spinet. Her eyebrows went up as she noticed tracks for folding doors that partitioned the room into four equal sections, which would allow several activities to go on at once. Apparently business was doing well enough that Xandra and Fleurette had additional teachers on staff.

She ran her hand down the ballet barre as she walked along a side wall toward the door in the corner labeled OFFICE. The click of her heels on the hardwood floor echoed like rifle shots. The overheads were on, but the emptiness and silence of the high-ceilinged room was intimidating.

This is the scene where the heroine discovers the dead body and screams her lungs out. *But no, Moira—you've already done that in real life, and it wasn't a shadowy practice room, but a beautifully decorated bedroom with the morning sun shining through the window. And you didn't scream.*

She knocked on the door.

Xandra and Fleurette—she never thought of them as Fleurette and Xandra—were sitting close together on a spindly settee crammed beneath a clerestory window. The sun shone on their heads and shoulders, but left their bodies in shadow. Moira felt her chest tighten. In those black full-body leotards, the Fontaines looked like a pair of spiders waiting for her to fall into their trap.

Xandra leaned forward and pierced her with gimlet eyes. "Thank you for coming, Ms. Farrar. Please sit down." She indicated a desk chair with caster feet. "We need to talk to you about something very serious." The sisters exchanged looks. "First of all, we want you to understand that *dance* is our passion. We are professionals who have appeared—as *primas*—on many stages. She waved her hand toward the collection of framed photographs on the wall behind her. "We are also businesswomen with tight schedules. Nevertheless, we have been active in the theater guild since its inception. However, *some people*"—Xandra's face went grim—"do not seem to appreciate our contributions." Her mouth tightened to a thin line. "We've talked it over and have decided that we cannot continue associating ourselves with the guild if this situation persists."

Moira pressed her hand against her chest and let her face show disbelief and shock, which was pretty much real. She'd checked the Internet and the Fontaines were the only dance teachers in town.

"Xandra…" She schooled her voice to a comforting coo. "I know there are always problems when true *artistes* work together, but please give me a chance. Mrs. Gomez-Sweeny told me that you and your sister are vital to the guild." *Well, not exactly, but near enough.* "In fact, she suggested that I have the children rehearse in your studio for as long as possible before they join the adult cast."

She glanced from one woman to the other, her expression as sincere and caring as she could make it. And she truly did feel a sympathy for the two women. From what she'd heard, Xandra and Fleurette had given generously of their time, training, and talent, although she would bet their participation in the guild was good advertising too—*but hey, we all have to eat.*

The sisters' eyes brightened, and they both started talking at once, though Xandra quickly dominated. "We just knew that you—"

"I told Xandra that surely Colin Sanger's wife—"

"He was such a gentleman, so debonair—"

"And you were so darling as Twinky Applejack, whom I liked much better than that silly—"

"Although of course you were wonderful in both roles," Xandra interrupted, casting her sister a shut-up look.

Moira lowered her head modestly. "Thank you. And I know Colin would want me to thank you for your good opinion of him too." Which was true. Colin respected and valued his fans. Unlike lesser stars, he understood that his career depended on maintaining a spotless public image. "Now, I'd love for you to show me around your studio, if you have the time."

Those were the magic words. The sisters sprang up off their settee and walked her into each quarter of the room, explaining in meticulous detail who taught what and where. Apparently, Xandra, tall and spindly, specialized in classical dance—ballet, pointe, ballroom—while Fleurette, short and muscular, preferred the more robust styles—tap, jazz, hip-hop.

Moira noticed a shadowed staircase on the side wall in the shadow of the stacked mats. "And do you have another practice room upstairs?

The sisters froze, and an aura of discomfort strained the atmosphere. Moira was puzzled. What boundary had she crossed?

Xandra forced a smile. "Sister and I live upstairs. We have a kitchen, a bathroom, and separate bedrooms." She started walking toward a tall showcase at the front of the room. "Let me show you some of the trophies our students have won."

It was an obvious distraction, but Moira let herself be herded over to the glass display case.

She opened her eyes wide and waved her hands to express her admiration and awe. "Impressive!"

For whatever reason, the women seemed to breathe easier, and Moira was able to leave on a high note. She walked out into the sunshine and congratulated herself on a job well done. Now to face the martinet at the museum. Maybe the sensible pumps would carry the day.

As it turned out, she could have walked into the docent's office dancing hip-hop in her Zulily dress and butterfly shoes and still been given the keys. The martinet was a fan.

"Oh, Ms. Farrar, you don't need to show us any identification! We all know who you are! We've been expecting you! I've got the keys all ready for you—color coded and labeled. The red one is for the greenroom—that's what you call the room where the cast gathers during the performance, isn't it?"

She handed over a jangly key ring.

"Oh, and would you mind autographing this Post-it note for my granddaughter? She's been watching reruns of *The Clancy Family* with me and just loves Nancy! You're such a funny little thing—always getting yourself in such crazy predicaments! We laugh at you all the time!"

Moira mustered up the standard gracious smile, signed her name, and drew a quick happy face, then grabbed the keys before the docent had second thoughts about entrusting them to a lamebrain like Nancy Clancy.

She jingled them in her hand as she walked out of the museum office, her back soldier straight. She wasn't Nancy or

Twinky or Robota or any of the other roles she'd played—she was Moira Miranda Farrar, director, and she was going to inspect her realm, then be off to meet her knight gallant for lunch.

She'd better keep a close eye on her watch. This was one appointment she did not want to be late for. They'd set the time for eleven thirty, and Rafe had told her his office was above the jewelry store on the square.

* * *

With every step up the stairs, Moira devised another "what-if."

What if Rafe had meant this morning to be a business meeting? What if he thought she was easy pickings because she slow danced with him at Omar's? What if she'd dreamed it all? What if she hadn't remembered the time correctly—or the location of his office?

Now that last one was ridiculous because she was quite good at remembering things—unless her pulse was beating like a tom-tom and her ears were ringing with siren calls.

Cool it, Moira. You've had crushes on guys since you were a kid, and Colin was the only one you truly fell in love with. Rafe McAllister is just a passing fancy of your sex-starved female hormones, and you've got it bad.

But maybe the best way to get rid of an itch is to scratch it. Maybe a relationship like Rafe proposed, sex only, is the way to go.

Being head over heels in love with a guy gives him too much power.

She reached the landing at the top of the stairs.

Yeah, sex for the sake of sex—that would be her modus operandi from now on. Or was she just rationalizing? Trying to justify the heat she felt every time she was near Big Red—every time she thought of him?

A wide-open door loomed at the top of the stairs, and she could hear people talking inside.

She stopped at the threshold. Rafe was bending over the shoulder of a dark-haired woman and looking at a computer screen. A lineup of machines and horizontal filing cabinets covered the counter behind her desk, and a child's play space was on the far wall.

Delilah had everything she'd ever need when she put in her time at Daddy's office. A chalkboard hung behind the little table and chair set, and bright pink shelves overflowed with toys, storybooks, coloring books, crayons, dollies, and a family of stuffed animals. And if she ran out of steam, a lime-green nap futon was available.

Moira knocked on the doorframe to announce herself, and Rafe looked up, then crossed the room to meet her.

The dark-haired woman stood up. "Hi! I'm Sissy Nieto, Rafe's assistant. You two are going for lunch, right?" The corners of her mouth twitched in amusement, and she put a teasing emphasis on *lunch*.

Rafe shot her a killing glare. "It's *lunch*, Sissy. Moira gets her choice of Calico Cat, Fish Daddy's, or Six-Shooter Junction."

"Whatever you say, Rafe. I'm leaving now. I assume you won't need me back this afternoon?" Sissy opened a drawer for her purse and gave him a wide-eyed, too-innocent stare.

As soon as the door closed, Moira stepped away from Rafe and lifted her chin in defiance. Her pulse might be jumping sixty, but if he had plans to lay her out on that lime-green futon, he had another thing coming.

"I choose Six-Shooter Junction."

Without missing a beat, Rafe grabbed his Stetson from the counter. "Six-Shooter Junction it is, milady. Your carriage awaits out back."

* * *

Everything looked neat and orderly in Rafe's office as he took her through it except for the wall across from his desk, which was covered with layers of architectural drawings on sheets of pale yellow paper.

She had her doubts when he'd said they would go down a fire escape, but the cast-iron stairs had been charmingly renovated—someone, probably Rafe, had painted it a bright blue and placed a pot of purple flowers in each turn. And the alley was so well kept that, at first, she'd thought it was a side street. And, contrary to Sissy's insinuations, Rafe acted like a perfect gentleman when he helped her into the truck.

He stopped at a traffic light on one corner of the square, and Moira watched as a workman climbed up a tall ladder and slipped a smiling pumpkin face over one of the streetlights surrounding the courthouse. Farther down, the square was blocked off with sawhorses.

"What's going on over there?"

Rafe didn't even look. "They're decorating for the big Halloween celebration. We do the same thing at Christmas, but with plastic snowmen and plywood angels."

"No wonder I had to park six blocks down from your office." Her sensible heels had turned out to be the right choice after all.

Rafe stepped on the accelerator and merged into traffic.

"It's a fall festival sort of thing. The arts and craft show starts on Wednesday. The talent shows and the beauty contests are added in next week, and then, on Halloween, we have the Pumpkin Party for the young'uns. Lots of country kids come in for it—they live too far apart for trick-or-treating. All the civic groups participate, and there are games, carnival rides, a fortune-teller—all sorts of things. Everyone wants to make sure the kids have a good time." He slowed down to let a horse van turn in front of him.

"Delilah's preschool is sponsoring a fishing booth this year. The kids drop a weighted string over the side of the counter, and a mother who's hiding under the counter clips a little toy on it."

"So that's how that works."

Rafe turned onto a street paralleling a green expanse. "Bosque Bend's pretty good about community projects. This park, the Shallows, is a good example. The river used to slop over its bank whenever a good rain came along, and the shore was an eyesore—and could be dangerous. Now look at it."

Moira nodded. "It's lovely." A trail circled the large fountain and branched out to the east and west along the river. It would be nice to walk down one of those paths sometime. Maybe even with Rafe. They could bring a picnic hamper and spread a blanket under the shadow of the low-branching trees, and…who knows what might happen…

Don't get ahead of yourself, Moira. Hold back, hold back. You don't know if you can trust this man. People aren't always what they seem.

Rafe crossed the bridge and turned onto the street that ran parallel to the river on the other side, the side lined with restaurants. No need to guess which one was Six-Shooter Junction. The animated marquee sign that featured two electronically smoking pistols framing a list of the specials of the day was a dead giveaway.

Rafe parked the truck and came around to lift her out. To anyone watching them, he was a tall man courteously helping a height-challenged woman out of a big truck. They wouldn't know that he skimmed his hands lightly—just enough that she knew they were there—along the outline of her hips. They wouldn't know that he brushed her breasts against himself, causing her nipples to send her signals she was trying to ignore.

And they wouldn't know that when she reached the ground, his sparkling eyes looked deep into hers.

Those eyes—just when she thought she'd become immune to them, they worked their magic all over again.

Chapter Seven

Six-Shoooter Junction was as cowboy kitsch inside as it had been outside. Intertwined cattle horns hung over the doorway, and the walls were covered with huge reproductions of 1800s "Wanted" posters intermingled with leather chaps, ten-gallon hats, canteens, spurs, holsters, collections of old guns, and even a couple of wicked-looking bullwhips.

The thirtyish woman behind the host stand was costumed accordingly—unless she usually wore a low-cut salmon-orange gown, a collar of assorted glittering necklaces, and earrings so heavy that they sagged her earlobes.

Moira felt the hostess's eyes slide right over her and settle on Rafe. The woman shifted her hips and gave him a studiously sexy smile.

"Howdy there, cowboy. Haven't seen you around these parts lately. Want your usual table?"

Rafe tugged politely at the brim of his hat and broadened his drawl. "Sure thing, Miz Liz. Got a little California gal with me and want to show her some good ol' Texas hospitality."

Liz raised a sardonic eyebrow and she tossed her hair. "Hospitality—is that what you're calling it now, Rafe?"

For a second there, Moira thought Miz Liz was going to slither up to Rafe and rub herself against him like a cat in heat, but instead, she turned to a younger woman who was wearing a purple version of what was apparently Six-Shooter Junction's version of the classic saloon gown. "The Quanah Parker table."

Moira checked out the restaurant as the hostess's understudy led them past tables named for Annie Oakley, Bat Masterson, Deadeye Dick, Pawnee Bill, Calamity Jane, Stagecoach Mary, and Will Rogers. The place was half-full, which meant it must be overflowing in the evening, which also meant the cuisine would be pretty good. Not that she was a connoisseur. Pretty much, she ate whatever was put in front of her.

The assistant hostess seated them in an alcove decorated with an Indian blanket and enlarged photos of Indians, teepees, and warhorses. As Moira slid around to the back of the bench, she peered up at the blowup of a stone-faced warrior hanging at the back of the nook. She'd seen that picture somewhere before.

Rafe followed her around the padded bench and placed his hat between them, establishing enough of a boundary that Moira didn't feel the urge to scoot away from him.

But why was she being so skittish? After all, she'd been playing around with the idea of having an affair with him. And she'd been thrilled to the core when he ran her down his body in the barn, then kissed her.

God, she was at war with herself. She wanted to move closer to him, but she also wanted to play it safe.

A waiter in full western regalia sauntered up to their table. His name tag identified him as Marshal Wyatt Earp, and he was dressed for his character, complete with an obviously plastic pistol and what looked like a genuine handlebar mustache. After depositing two glasses of ice water and a basket of rolls on the table, he adjusted his gun belt and flashed his badge.

"Howdy, ma'am, Mr. McAllister. Sorry I didn't get here earlier. Got held up by a fracas down at the O.K. Corral."

Moira knew a cue when she heard it. "Them Clantons always was low-down varmints."

Six-Shooter Junction was theater-in-the-round, and the actor in her couldn't help but play along.

* * *

Rafe didn't bother with the menu—he knew it by heart—which gave him a few extra minutes to study Moira as she read through hers, page by page by page.

His little soldier was game. She was enjoying the outrageous ambience of the restaurant just as she'd accepted dress-up night at Omar's. Texans knew what their image was to the world, and they enjoyed pushing it to the limit—and Moira was getting a kick out of playing along. She'd fit right in. Maybe he could convince her to stay around a while—like permanently.

He glanced down at Beth's ring and took that last thought back.

Well, he might not be in the market for a wife, but there was no getting around it that he wanted Moira in his bed—although a mound of sweet-smelling hay would work just as well.

He liked the outer package—the steady hazel gaze, the angles of her face, the soft, sweet mouth, the supple slenderness of her body—but it was her intensity, her inner strength that had attracted him from the moment he nearly mowed her down at the museum. She threw her whole self into everything she did—escorting Delilah to the ladies' room, meeting the board, riding a horse, even choosing her meal. What would it be like to have all that intensity directed at him?

He shifted uncomfortably on the padded bench, then cast a sidelong glance at Moira, who was still studying the menu like it was the script for the rest of her life.

Did he have a chance?

"See anything you like?"

What would she order? Chicken salad? That seemed to be the favorite lunch of the women he'd brought here before. He always wondered if they made a beeline for the refrigerator when they got home and ate half a ham to compensate for starving themselves when they were with him.

She closed the menu. "The six-ounce filet. Rare. Sautéed spinach. Fried sweet potatoes."

It figured. That intensity of hers must burn up a lot of calories. He grinned to himself and signaled the waiter.

Moira unfolded her napkin and looked around the room again. A giant chandelier made of deer antlers hung over what was apparently the restaurant's party table, which was currently occupied by several well-dressed women wearing pastel cowboy hats like those dispensed in the museum.

She looked around in wonder. "This place is way over the top. Nothing is real. It's like a stage setting."

Rafe laughed. "Speaking of stages—have you had a chance to check out the theater rooms yet?"

Moira nodded. "Just this morning. I started with the dressing rooms. They're huge. I guess they used to be classrooms?"

"Yeah. We needed rooms on the second floor so that they'd be at the bottom of the theater." He paused to reach for a roll. "What about the stage itself?"

Moira took a strengthening breath. "It's good-sized, but the backstage area is crowded, especially with the light booth in the wing. I'd like to move it, maybe into the balcony, and we need to get all the curtains on a motorized system rather than relying on a strong arm standing in the wings." She paused—he might not like what she would say—then decided to let it all hang out. After all, the theater guild had hired her to bring them up to snuff. "There are plenty of gels and lamps, of course, but the lights need to be...brought up to date too. I'd like to get a new board and dimmers. And some automated lights that can be controlled by the board."

Rafe shook his head. "No go. We've got a light crew that knows how to operate the equipment as it is, and I don't want us to drain donors and the city arts coffers for a stage we're not goin' to use for very much longer. We'll get state of the art when we're in our own venue."

The Bosque Bend Theater Guild would have its own stage? Pendleton hadn't mentioned that to her. "When will that be?"

"Sooner rather than later. We've finalized the deal to buy out the current owner of the old Huaco movie theater, and she's signed the papers." He finished off his roll. "Josie Apodaca has been runnin' a used furniture store out of the theater lobby for the past fifteen years, and she told me she's havin' a big sale this week before she moves out—doesn't want to take anythin' with her when she sets up in Floravista. It might be a good chance for you and your sister to pick up whatever furniture you need."

"Sounds like a good idea." It would be nice to have a couch in the family room and maybe a few more chairs, just to fill up the space. The rooms were so empty now that they echoed. "By the way, I've been meaning to tell you that how much Astrid and I appreciate the theater guild arranging for us to have a house. I was expecting to have to do a lot of cleaning, but it's in great condition too. How long since it's been occupied?"

"Just a couple of months." His eyebrows twitched. "Rocky's mother met a guy online and went off to Florida to marry him."

"You're saying that Rocky's mother lived there?"

Rafe nodded, "Theda Eagan moved her kids into town after the rattler took Rocky's father down. Dad helped her buy the house."

"So Rocky lived there too?"

He nodded. "Until she married Travis."

"That's double good luck for me, then. I like Rocky."

Rafe gave her a big smile. "Everybody likes Rocky. She can be sorta crazy, but she's a lot of fun. Always laughing. Travis was lucky to get her." His eyebrows twitched again. "I just hope he can keep her after all this business with Micaela runs its course."

Moira took a sip of water and looked at Rafe over the rim of her glass.

Rafe McAllister was one good-looking man, and it wasn't just the sparkling eyes.

Damn. *Why had she ordered such a big meal?* She didn't care about food. Lunch with Rafe wasn't about eating. A hamburger at that drive-in with the neon fisherman on its roof would have been just as good. And a lot more private.

Rafe's voice snapped her back to Six-Shooter Junction. "You must miss California. Do your parents still live there?"

She rattled off her standard reply. "My mother has lived abroad for several years. I don't see her very often."

"What about your father?"

She gave him a bright smile, the same smile she'd given entertainment reporters who asked about her so-called home life, and the same nonanswer. "Our mother's parents raised Astrid and me—and our brother." She tossed her head as if everyone in California had absentee parents. "Actually. The three of us are half siblings—same mother, different fathers. That's why Astrid and I don't look alike."

His forehead knit in disagreement. "But y'all *do* look alike. She's taller than you, but there's something about your eyes and the shape of your faces."

Moira shrugged her shoulders. "That's the Japanese in us. Our grandmother's parents emigrated from Osaka two months before she was born."

"Well, you've got me beat. The most I can claim is one-sixteenth Comanche." Rafe glanced up at the enlarged photo behind him. "Quanah Parker was my grandmother Schuler's great-grandfather."

Moira looked at the picture again. So that's where she'd seen that stone face before—worked into Enid McAllister's family collage. And that was the exact same expression Rafe had on his face when he'd told her about the panther.

Maybe she'd better change the subject.

"I'm going to have to start thinking about costumes soon. Donna Sue told me to get in touch with a woman named Marilyn Bridges."

"Her ladies will sew up stuff for us, but we store the old costumes too. Maybe you can use some of those."

"What about wigs and stage makeup?"

"A local salon, Ooh La La, takes care of our hairstyling and supplies us with wigs when we need them. Billie Joe keeps the makeup in a refrigerator at her restaurant—Calico Cat—and orders whatever else is needed."

Moira went into concentration mode. "Billie Joe Semple. The milliner, makeup, restaurant."

Rafe could almost hear her brain filing the new information in its proper drawer. He gave her a sidelong glance. "Do you have us all memorized already?"

She shrugged. "It's sort of a trick."

And he'd bet it was a survival mechanism too, a way to bring order to her own personal universe. He'd read a thumbnail sketch of Moira Miranda Farrar on the Internet yesterday evening after she and Astrid left, and her background had sounded damn sketchy to him. Her mother had been a model he'd never heard of who was now embarked on a career of se-rial matrimony all across Europe, and her father had been a big-wig French industrialist he'd never heard of who'd been involved in some sort of price-fixing scandal. And three half siblings being raised by their grandparents wouldn't have been the ideal home life. Neither did playing the youngest orphan in a TV revival of *Annie* when she was just four years old.

The age Delilah was now, for God's sake!

His little soldier hadn't been the lackadaisical Nancy Clancy she'd played on television. She'd been a working adult in child-sized clothing.

* * *

Moira smiled as Rafe parked the dually in the empty spot be-side her Toyota. Their vehicles looked like David and Goliath.

The street, which had been parked up tight this morning, she noticed, had entirely cleared out. They were alone. This could be interesting. Would he slide her down against him again? Or drift his mouth across her face or down her throat, maybe nibble at her ear?

He came around to her side of the truck, and her heart thumped with anticipation.

But all he did was lift her to the ground, kiss her gently, then step back. "See you tonight at the rehearsal."

She stared after him as he walked to his truck, then fumbled with her key lock and slid into her car.

That was all? A granny kiss and "See you tonight at the re-hearsal?"

After all the drama she'd put herself through?

It was as if an inviting swimming pool had gone empty the very second she'd decided to dive in—just like the stupid story she'd given out about Colin.

But that had been the best she could think of at the time.

* * *

Rafe reviewed his lunch date with Moira as he drove back to the office. Six-Shooter Junction had been fun. And dropping her off at her car afterward had been even better. He could still taste her sweet lips.

He'd wanted more, a lot more, but flattening her against the side of the truck for a tongue twister on a city street under a bright noonday sun wasn't his style. He preferred more privacy—and more possibility.

He parked the truck and climbed the fire escape into his office.

The door to Sissy's office was closed, so maybe he could take a couple of minutes off to kick back and relax a little.

But before he could even pull out his chair, his phone buzzed, and Sissy—who'd apparently returned from lunch after all—announced that Chief Hruska was waiting to see him.

Rafe pushed away from his desk. What was going on? This sounded serious. Cousin Merv usually got in touch with him by phone.

He opened the door to the outer office. Mervin was standing by Sissy's desk.

"Let's go inside," he said, swiveling a meaningful look at

Sissy, who was well known for passing along whatever she heard. "This is confidential police business."

What the hell? Rafe's mind raced through every deal he'd been involved in lately. Had Josie Apodaca's damn tarot cards told her to back out of their agreement?

He ushered his cousin into his office and closed the door firmly, then leaned back against the edge of his desk.

Mervin grabbed the extra chair and sat down on it backward.

"Keep this under your hat for now, but Rick Cabot, who's handled our pathology for the past hundred years, is retiring, and the city council is hiring a woman out of Houston, a real live forensic pathologist, to replace him. I interviewed her, and she told me the first thing she wanted to do was to go over old cases, especially those I've had second thoughts about." Mervin cleared his throat. "You know I've never been happy with Cabot's ruling on Beth's death, so I'm going to hand the file over to the new gal on the block."

Rafe couldn't remember how to breathe. It was like all the air had been sucked out of the room.

This was even worse than he'd imagined. His ears were ringing so loudly that if Mervin was saying anything else, he couldn't hear it. He reached out to the edge of the desk behind him to keep from falling down.

"I understand."

But he didn't. He'd finally made his peace with God about Beth's death. It had been an accident, a crazy freak accident, and neither he nor anyone else could have prevented it. And now...

Mervin stood up to go. "It'll probably be a while before we know anything, but I wanted to keep you in the loop. It might be that nothing will come of it, but you're my cousin, and I wanted to let you know what was happening before anything hits the grapevine."

Mervin closed the door behind him as he left, and Rafe didn't open it again till it was time to pick Delilah up from her Monday afternoon playdate with Cousin Sharon's twins.

His heart broke as he listened to Delilah, buckled into her car seat behind him, talk about finger painting in preschool this morning, then playing dollies with Sharon's girls in the afternoon. She was so happy, so innocent. He'd told her that Mommy was in heaven, but never gone into details. What could a four-year-old understand?

And now the whole town would be talking about how Beth had died, and Delilah was bound to hear some of it. There was no way he could protect her from all the grisly details, from learning that her mother hadn't just one day floated to a heaven of unending sunshine, but been killed in her own front yard while she was tending her winter flowers.

* * *

Rafe walked into the auditorium a few minutes after the appointed time and took a seat in the back row against the wall.

A painful chapter in his life had cracked open, and the theater was his choice of sanctuary. It was a place of true love and happily ever after, where problems were solved with a song and a dance and no one ever reopened a case that had been long closed—or a wound that had begun to heal.

He looked down toward the stage and noticed that Moira was having an intense conversation with the Fontaines. Whatever she was talking about with the sisters, they were happy about it, bobbing their heads like fishing corks. *Smart girl.* Xandra and Fleurette had a major case of paranoia, but they were damn good at their jobs.

Suddenly she looked up, gave him a quick nod, then turned her attention back to the black-clad danseuses

Fire flashed through him.

He dropped his eyes and checked out what was going on down front. There was no escaping the fact that the battle lines had already been drawn. The Athertons had claimed the left side of the auditorium, with Vashti sitting on the piano bench while Carmen, holding her violin bow like an unsheathed rapier, stood guard beside her. The Fontaines' forces had taken possession of the front row seats on the right side of the auditorium. Fleurette was on one side of Xandra, and Desdemona Benton, Xandra's prize student, sat on the other side, with Desdemona's brother and Buck Overton, her muscular boyfriend, completing the row.

Rafe steepled his fingers and speculated about Desdemona's romance.

Following in the footsteps of his older brother, Buck Overton had been a star halfback for Eisenhower Consolidated last year and was now taking courses at the community college in Waco. Dolph Sr. had spread it round that Buck was dating an interior design major who'd been a Cotton Palace debutante, but everyone in Bosque Bend knew he was hanging after Desdemona Benton. Maybe because she was as graceful as a doe and looked like a young Diana Ross. Maybe to irritate his father, who'd walked out on First Baptist years ago when it started welcoming nonwhites into the fold.

Rafe turned his head as his brother scooted down the row toward him.

"Hiya, bro. You look down. Bad day?"

"A lot of things happening."

Travis folded down a seat. "I'm with ya, bro. Rocky's mother called me this evening before I left the house. She wants us to give her a lump-sum payment for the house, which I told her she's not gonna get. Theda doesn't realize she's gonna need a place to come back to if—*when*—loverboy dumps her for the next fat chicken to cross the road."

"What's she want it for?"

"Boyfriend wants to buy a boat, supposedly so they can sail off into the sunset together." Travis shrugged. "I can't out and out tell Rocky that I think boyfriend knows a sucker when he sees one."

Micaela Atherton hurried down the far aisle to join her mother and sister at the piano, and Travis leapt to his feet. "Gotta go. See you later."

Rafe watched in disbelief as his brother followed Micaela down to the Atherton stronghold. If Travis was going to run around on Rocky, at least he could be more subtle about it.

There was a stir down front as Moira picked up a list and started calling roll. Her dark voice carried to every corner of the cavernous auditorium as she repeated names, checked them off, then repeated them again, enunciating carefully.

After passing out the updated version of the script, she took her place behind the lectern. Her eyes flitted to the back of the auditorium, as if making sure he was still there.

God, she was as aware of him as he was of her.

As soon as the audience flutter quieted down, Moira introduced herself with a brief personal biography that Rafe thought was more interesting in what it didn't say than what it did.

She touched on Nancy Clancy, Twinky Applejack, and her robotic life with Johnny Blue, then mentioned UCLA, but totally omitted any mention of her life with Colin Sanger. Instead, she lowered her eyes and said in a soft tone that she was a widow.

Rafe raised a sardonic eyebrow.

All in all, it was a charming, modest presentation. But his gut told him it was also an act. But maybe his gut was wrong. Maybe he was just imagining things. After all, as Colin Sanger's wife, Moira must have lived the kind of life every woman dreams of—hobnobbing with statesmen and celebrities, visiting exotic locales, being on the arm of *People* magazine's most handsome man three years running, being in his bed...

God, maybe that was why she went hot and cold on him. Sanger must have been the consummate lover, and there was no way a Texas cowboy could compare to him.

On the other hand, he reminded himself, Sanger was no longer in the competition.

Moira called on the cast members individually and asked

them to tell her a little about themselves, their theatrical experience, and what their dream role would be.

Finally, it was his turn. Moira's lips curved with humor. "And you, sir, you at the back, will you please introduce yourself?"

The room rolled with laughter. Everyone in the auditorium knew he'd taken her to Good Times the day after she came to town. Probably half of them also knew they'd had lunch together at Six-Shooter Junction today and—judging by the murmur—were busy telling the other half.

He stood up and twitched an eyebrow at her. "My name's Rafe McAllister, I've got a ranch outside of town, and I've been active in the theater guild for three years now. My dream role would be Billy Bigelow in *Carousel*, but"—he growled down to his lowest register—"I can't reach the high notes."

The laughter was even louder this time, and Moira joined in, then stepped forward and let her voice take on an authoritative edge.

"First of all, I want all of you to turn off any handheld devices you have and pack them away."

One of the teenagers, Stu Schlossnagel, Rafe thought, raised his hand. "But Ms. Farrar—I need my tablet to take notes on what you're saying."

Moira gave him a beatific smile. "Stu, you'll *remember* what I say. You are an *actor*." Rafe gave her points. Stu was testing her, but she'd reinforced her authority without humiliating him. And she'd given everyone else something to think about too—in fact, she'd made playacting sound like a divine calling.

"The ban on cell phones, tablets, or any other handheld

devices applies to all rehearsals and performances—backstage and also in the greenroom. You don't want to miss a cue or"—she smiled to indicate a one-liner was coming—"have any annoying beeps or buzzes interrupting tender love scenes."

Her audience tittered knowingly.

"I myself, however, will always be carrying a cell phone, so when you get home, please give my number to your family. Tell them to text me if there is an emergency. I promise I will contact you immediately. Every single one of you is vital to the performance, and it will be the poorer for your absence, but you and your family are more important than any show."

Rafe was impressed. Moira understood that her community theater actors were volunteers, real people with real lives.

"Also, there will be no alcoholic beverages, no smoking of any kind, and no drugs anywhere on the premises. No excuses, no second chances. Filming can be held up while a Hollywood star recovers from an injury or goes through rehab, but a stage show doesn't have that latitude. Once that curtain opens"—she made a sweeping gesture toward the new grand drape that he'd moved heaven and earth to persuade the museum board to invest in—"the show must go on."

There was a moment of awed silence, then thunderous applause, even from Stu. Rafe grinned. His little soldier had them in the palm of her hand. She was that good.

Moira dipped her head in modest acknowledgment and settled into a conversational tone. "Each of you has received a copy of the new script. Pen Swaim has sharpened some of the dialogue, and I asked Vashti to extend the children's dance numbers. Which reminds me—if you have kids in the show, we need to see them here in the auditorium at six thirty tomorrow. Miss Xandra and Miss Fleurette"—a nod and a smile in their direction—"have graciously agreed to rehearse the children in their studio on Tuesday and Friday evenings.

"Mrs. Atherton and I will attend these sessions, which means the adult rehearsals on those nights will not begin until eight. Later on, of course, we will need to integrate the children into the rest of the show."

Moira looked at her notes again.

"We have just five weeks to shape up this play, but I want us to learn the songs and get the concept down pat before we add in the choreography. So let's get started. Everyone up onstage! We'll be starting with 'Street Song.'"

She gave her audience a blinding smile. "I'll just sit back and enjoy."

Chapter Eight

Moira took a deep breath and sank back into her chair. The performance pressure was off her. Vashti could handle the next hour or so.

She looked at the cast list again and identified each person by name and vocal parts. The altos and basses stayed with Vashti while the sopranos and tenors off to the boardroom with Carmen and Micaela. An hour later, Vashti asked Billie Joe to bring everyone back into the auditorium so she could hear the full chorus. The fourth time through, Moira called it a day.

Vashti would have kept the chorus there all night if it had been up to her.

Several cast members came over before they left to give Moira a personal welcome to Bosque Bend, take selfies with her, and express belated condolences regarding Colin's death. As always, she told herself they meant well, fixed a sad smile on her face, and said, "Thank you. I miss him still."

And, as always, her throat caught on the lie.

She hated being such a hypocrite, but there wasn't any other choice.

Rafe eased himself off the apron of the stage. "Tired?"

"Drained." She always was after a performance, and this had been an important one.

"You did great—kept your cool with Stu, turned the Fontaines up sweet, and gave Vashti the rein she needed without letting her take over the show."

"Thanks." Moira gathered up the leftover scripts and reached for her portfolio. "Once I started talking, I really got into the swing of it. It was like an opening night—the Moira Miranda Farrar show." She let her shoulders slump. "But now I feel like a deflated balloon."

Rafe put a supportive arm around her as they walked up the aisle. "Lean on me."

She moved closer to him. She wished she could lean on him in other ways too. She wished she could tell him about Colin. But no, that was her one allegiance left to the king of Hollywood—that she would never tell. Anyone. She pushed the self-locking door closed, and they walked down the stairs, out of the museum, and across the street. A floodlight illuminated the other end of the parking lot, where two male figures lounged against the light pole.

Moira clicked her car door, but before she could open it, Rafe's arms enfolded her. Day and night disappeared. Her good sense flew out the window, and she molded herself to him all the way down.

His tongue traced the outline of her lips, and her heart

skipped a beat. Then he kissed her, gently, as if she were something rare and wonderful. His kiss deepened and she melted into his arms. This could go somewhere, and she was ready for it.

Kissy squeals emanated from the other end of the parking lot, and Rafe pulled away from her. "Stay here. I think I know one of those guys."

He walked toward the floodlight. The shorter one seemed jumpy, ready to run, but the tall, muscular one took a drag on his cigarette, looked in their direction, and held his ground.

Rafe's hair blazed fire as he stepped into the bright light, and his deep, vibrant voice rang out like a death knell. "Sammy Schuler, isn't it? Grady's son?"

The kid's head jerked in recognition, his bravado disappeared, and he couldn't talk fast enough. "Yes, sir, Cousin Rafe, sir. Didn't mean nothin', sir. Just funnin'. Didn't realize it was you, sir." Moira moved in closer. She had to be in on this.

Rafe's voice softened. "Sammy, you out here every night?"

"Yes, sir. Me and some of the guys—we sorta hang here." He shrugged. "Nothin' else to do."

Rafe took Moira's hand and drew her forward. "Sammy, Ms. Farrar here is my friend, but I can't be at the museum midweek so I want you to keep an eye on her. If she ever comes out of that door alone, you walk her to her car. Agreed?"

The teen's chest swelled with relief and responsibility. "You can depend on me, Cousin Rafe."

* * *

Moira had turned Darth Vader off so she could sleep late in the morning, but she hadn't thought to turn off her cell, and it was buzzing like a hive of angry bees.

She reached out to grab it from her bed stand, hit Talk, then lost her grip on the phone and knocked it off onto the floor. Scooting to the edge of her bed, she picked it up and stared at the caller ID.

The number was local—Rafe? The phone buzzed again.

"Hello?"

A lilting voice answered her. "Oh my God, hon—you sound awful. Are you sick? This is Rocky, and I just called a second ago, and it sounded like something terrible had happened. Do you need help? Do you need me to come over to the house and take care of you?"

Take care of her? How sweet can you get. Is this what Texans were like?

"Thanks, Rocky, but I always sound like a frog right when I wake up in the morning, and that crashing sound was me fumbling for the phone."

"I woke you up? Oh, hon—I'm so sorry!"

Moira swallowed to clear her throat. "No problem. Uh—everyone okay at the ranch?"

Is Rafe okay?

Rocky laughed. "As far as I know—and believe me, I know more than anyone else. After all, I'm the only live-in hand. Listen, hon, the reason I called was that I wanted to see if I could take you and Astrid out to lunch at Calico Cat today. I've got to go into town to pick up a load of salt blocks at the feed store so I thought it would be a chance for the three of us to get together."

"I'd love to, and I know Astrid would too, but she won't be home till about one thirty. Could we do Starbucks instead, maybe two o'clock?"

"No prob, hon. In fact, that will work better for me too. Gives me time to check out the bulls before I drive in to town. We've added in a new boy, and I want to be sure he's not giving the older guys any lip."

"Uh—okay." Too much information when she was still half asleep. "I'll wake up for real now and see you at Starbucks this afternoon."

Two lunch invitations in two days. Either Bosque Bend was a very friendly town or she was a very welcome commodity. She hoped it was a little of each.

* * *

Rocky stood up when Moira and Astrid came in the door and waved them to the table. Apparently she'd finished her ranch shopping early because she already had an orange plastic cup and a glazed doughnut in front of her.

She was dressed for her role again, Moira noticed, in a yoked shirt, Dale Evans divided skirt, and turquoise-colored cowboy boots. A soft suede jacket with fringed sleeves hung on the back of her chair.

Moira and Astrid placed their orders, waited at the counter for them to be prepared, then walked over to join Rocky. Astrid seized Rocky's hand as soon as they sat down and examined her nails. "Purple and blue with a football across the middle. What's it all about?"

Rocky laughed. "It's the Generals, the Eisenhower Consolidated Generals—my high school team. We're replaying Waco in bi-district this year." Rocky laughed. "Waco and Eisenhower Consolidated are traditional enemies, so everyone in town is excited about it." She raised her hand like she was shaking a pom-pom. "Go, Generals!"

Rocky laughed again and took a sip of what Moira recognized as Starbucks' featured Halloween concoction, then made a sour face at the cup. "Guess I'm the reckless type," she said. "I'll try anything once—or even twice."

She laughed and took another sip, then glanced around impishly and dropped her voice to a semi-whisper. "And not just Halloween drinks. I tried a lot of things in high school. I was really naughty. All the boys in Eisenhower Consolidated were after me, and I liked them too." She twiddled the plastic stick in the lid of her drink and sighed. "High school. Those were fun times." She gave her guests a sly-faced look. "Y'all know what I mean."

Moira nodded and smiled, but no, she really had no idea what Rocky meant. Astrid might—she'd gone to public school, although Moira knew her sister hadn't made many friends and rarely dated—but she herself had never been to a brick-and-mortar school. Instead, she'd been educated between takes by a series of earnest, conscientious studio tutors who spent most of the class time marveling at her total recall.

Big deal. Memorization had been her job.

What she'd yearned for—hungered for—was contact with kids her own age—real kids, not underage actors. For better or worse, she wished she'd had Rocky's kind of experience. What would it be like to be part of a classroom? To go out to recess rather than out to auditions? To have a best friend that she shared all her secrets with? To have a crush on the cutest boy in class rather than an actor who'd been cast as your boyfriend, but who broke your heart by ignoring you off set?

God, Rocky must have been the live wire of her group—wickedly funny, always laughing. A real entertainer.

Rocky took a third swallow of her drink and stuck out her tongue. "Three strikes and it's out. I don't think I'm gonna try this one any time soon. It tastes like Enid McAllister's eggnog." She pushed the cup away and laughed, a musical trill up the scale. "You've never lived till you've had to make a toast with it on Christmas Eve. Enid's a dear and I adore her, but I wish she'd destroy whatever 4-H bulletin she got that recipe from."

Rocky laughed again, and Moira couldn't help but laugh along with her.

She's madcap. Way too young, of course, but I'd love to cast her as Auntie Mame.

Astrid finished off her scone and wiped her fingers on a napkin. "Were you in 4-H like Rafe and Travis?"

Rocky backed off in mock dismay. "Me? No way. I was too busy on the ranch. Pa had me herding cattle. Besides, I've never had a yearning to make my own clothes or paste old photos onto cardboard and hang them in my living room."

She laughed again, and Moira laughed too. Rocky was so wicked.

She gave Moira a mischievous smile. "Well, enough about me. Tell me, little Nancy Clancy, how are you adjusting to life in the sticks? I hear that Rafe took you to Six-Shooter Junction yesterday and that last night you two stayed late in the dark museum after everyone else had left."

Moira took an extra second swallowing a bite of croissant. She could say something out of left field, like that she and Rafe had reenacted the love scene from *Pretty Woman* on the back of the baby grand piano, but she smiled and played it safe. "Rafe's been very charming."

Rocky's expression turned serious, and her blue eyes clouded with concern.

"Be careful, hon. Rafe's my brother-in-law, and I love him to death—but I have to tell you that Rafe's been tomcatting all over town for the past three years and the relationships never last more than a couple of months. He's still hung up on Beth, may she rest in peace."

"Did you know her?"

"She was my best friend."

"What was she like?"

Rocky looked into space as if searching through the past. "Beth was one of those golden girls—she had everything. Her parents lived in a big house in the new section of Lynnwood, up on the hill—three-car garage, swimming pool, hot tub, the works. She was smart in school too and had a beautiful singing voice, and of course, she married Rafe."

"Did she have many friends?"

Rocky nodded and her golden-brown curls shimmered in the overhead light. "Beth was the most popular girl in Eisenhower Consolidated. If she had ever run for cheerleader—which she didn't because her preacher disapproved of the short skirts the cheerleaders wore—she would have been elected by a landslide." Rocky's voice broke. "I miss her. I really wish she hadn't gone and gotten herself killed." She managed an apologetic half smile. "Sorry to be such a downer, y'all. I didn't mean to talk about all that."

It was an awkward moment. Moira painted a smile on her face and searched for a happier topic. "What about you, Rocky? Have you and Travis been married long?"

"Four years." Rocky looked out from under her lashes and grinned coyly. "We eloped to Waco one weekend. Ma was our only witness."

"And you've lived at the ranch ever since?"

She nodded. "Yeah, in the foreman's house." She leaned across the table, and her voice dropped to a dramatic whisper. "I'll tell y'all a secret—I'd be a lot better foreman than Travis is. Rafe should have hired me. I could take care of that panther that's been hanging around in a second."

Her thumb and forefinger mimicked shooting a pistol. "Yippee-kay-yay-kay-yo! *Pow!*" The women at the next table looked around as Rocky pretended she was blowing smoke off the muzzle of a gun.

"That's how Pa brought me up, to do whatever needed doing. Me and my cousin—he lives in San Saba now—were the only ranch hands Pa had. Herd them, brand them, worm them, cut them—I can do it all." She laughed. "Yeah, I was a real tomboy till I discovered how much fun boys were." She winked knowingly. "Boy, howdy, I can tell you I sure was glad when Ma moved into town and I started at Eisenhower Consolidated. A whole school full of hot boys!"

Astrid waved her hand—probably to draw attention to her

manicure—tiny pink roses edging one side of a leaf-green background—and broke into the conversation. "Moira said we're living in your old house."

Rocky nodded. "Yep. Rafe bought it back from Ma when she moved to Florida, and I've still got an extra key somewhere, if you need it."

"Florida? She's retired?"

Rocky smiled. "Better than that. Ma moved there to be with her soul mate. They're gonna start a boat tour business." She laughed and held her nose. "No more stinky cowboys for her!

"That reminds me, y'all. I'll tell you a good one on Rafe and Travis when they were in high school." Her blue eyes sparkled with amusement.

"They were doing the 4-H thing, of course, and each of them had a steer in the stock show. Their pens were across from each other, and they got to feeling way too good while they were mucking the pens out and started swishing cow pat at each other across the aisle. Splattered wet poop all over each other and anyone else who was passing through. Oh my God, they were sliding and rolling around in the stuff and laughing like crazy!"

She fastened her eyes on Moira as if gauging her reaction to the story, then squinched her nose and turned the sides of her mouth down in a clownish look of disgust.

"Men are such pigs."

Moira laughed and finished off her tea.

Rocky knew how to tell a story, even one she probably shouldn't have.

"Thanks for the coffee and goodies, Rocky, but we'd better

leave now. Rafe said a used furniture store is having a going-out-of-business sale, and Astrid and I wanted to hit it this afternoon."

Rocky's eyes opened wide. "Josie's?"

"Yeah. Do you know where it is?"

"Sure do. Tell you what." Rocky stood up and pulled on her jacket. "I'll go with you. That old gypsy will give y'all a better deal if I'm along."

* * *

Moira parked the Toyota in the middle of the block and looked around. The area was questionable at best.

A trio of grubby-looking men standing in front of Ulrich's Drive-in Beer and Grocery across the street gave them a once-over as they got out of the car. A fourth man sat on the curb in front of the store, taking long pulls from a bottle in a paper bag as he gazed into space.

After double-locking her doors, Moira followed Rocky and Astrid back down the broken sidewalk, past an empty building, to a corner storefront with MUEBLERIA USADA spelled out on the old theater marquee above the door. SALE was scrawled across the front window in what looked like red poster paint.

Rocky opened the door for Moira and Astrid, then followed them in. The store, which must have been the theater lobby, was wide, shallow, and had a slight incline toward the back.

At the back of the room stood a tall, gaunt woman with

frizzy, iron-gray hair. Her arms were folded like an Indian chief, and her expression was grim.

Rocky gave her a lighthearted wave. "Hi, Josie. I'm Rocky McAllister. You remember me."

The woman's expression didn't change. "Mahogany armoire. Brass candelabra."

Rocky laughed. "That's right. You bought them from my mother when she moved to Florida." She gestured toward Moira and Astrid and smiled broadly. "My friends have just moved into Bosque Bend and need a few things. I told them you're the best furniture place in town."

The woman focused her black eyes on Moira. "You the director lady for Mr. Rafe's theater?"

"Yes. I'm Moira Farrar and this is my sister, Astrid Birdsong." She extracted a credit card from the purse in her portfolio. "We've got a budget of three hundred fifty. What will that buy us?"

Josie motioned toward the furniture lining the walls and shrugged her shoulders. "Whatever you need. Don't want nothin' left when I move outa here this weekend." She glanced out the side window at the convenience store across the street. "Shoulda got outa here a while back. Used to be respectable around here, but with that long-distance bus stop on the side of the buildin' and Ulrich's across the street, it's gone bad. Mr. Rafe, he say he gonna take over the whole block 'n make it respectable again, but I dunno."

* * *

It had taken almost two hours and a pounding headache, but finally their furniture selections had been made, bought, and paid for. When Moira asked about delivery, Josie shrugged and went enigmatic on her. "Mr. Rafe, he said you don' worry about it."

Whatever that meant.

Moira breathed a sigh of relief as she, Astrid, and Rocky returned to her car, which, thank God, was still there and still intact. After she gave Astrid the keys, she climbed into the back, eased down into the seat, and closed her eyes. Once they got home, she'd take an aspirin and lie down for a while before she had to head off to the children's get-acquainted meeting.

Astrid put the car in gear and headed over to Starbucks to drop Rocky off at her car. Determined to be gracious, Moira opened her eyes as Rocky unlocked the door to get out.

"This was great, Rocky. Thanks for inviting us. We've got to do this again sometime."

"And thanks for helping us at Josie's too," Astrid chimed in.

Rocky laughed. "Y'all are a lot of fun. Call me anytime." She reached into her purse and handed a pen and piece of pink stationery across the console at Moira. "I almost forgot. Would you mind writing a little note to my mother and signing it? I want to give it to Ma for Christmas. She's crazy about *The Clancy Family*."

Moira put her portfolio on her lap to use as a desk.

"What's your mother's full name?"

"Theda Kay Colby Eagan."

Moira used her purse as a desk so her handwriting was a little wobbly, but she doubted if Rocky's mother would give her a hard time about it.

To my friend Theda Kay Colby Eagan—

Best wishes for a happy future and may you find love forevermore.

> *Your friend,*
> *Moira Miranda Farrar*
> *(aka Nancy Clancy)*

After adding the usual happy face, she handed the pink page back to Rocky. Fans were fans, but it made her feel a little uncomfortable to autograph a note for a friend, even though it would be used as a gift to her mother.

* * *

Moira pushed open the front door of the museum, surprised it was unlocked, and hurried upstairs. The auditorium door was flung open, the lights were on, and two black-dyed heads turned around and watched her as she came down the aisle.

Crap. She'd deliberately come early, but Xandra and Fleurette had beaten her here.

Fixing a smile on her face, she walked down to the front, trying to figure out who the woman in the parka sitting beside the sisters was. Five children, all bundled into padded jackets, were strung out beside her.

The Fontaines and their friend rose from their seats as Moira approached, and Xandra's mouth tightened as if she expected Moira to accuse her of jimmying a window to get in.

"The night custodian opened up the museum before you got here because it's so cold outside," she announced. "His granddaughter takes tap from Fleurette, and he recognized her from the recital last spring."

"How nice of him," Moira returned in her most pleasant voice, then held out her hand to the woman sitting beside them. "Hi. I'm Moira Farrar."

The woman looked tired, but her handshake was firm. "I'm Kathleen Loughlin, and these are my kids." She glanced toward the children—an older girl, two boys, and a pair of bright-eyed little girls. "They've all signed up for the show. My oldest is in Xandra's advanced ballet class, the boys have already told me they want to shine shoes, and my two little girls are more interested in dressing up than anything else."

Xandra attempted a smile. "Mrs. Loughlin is our full-time accompanist. We'd like to save Vashti the trouble of coming over to our studio twice a week and instead have Kathleen rehearse the songs with the children."

Moira took a quick breath. "Wonderful!"

Wonderful? It was fantastic! If Vashti didn't have to show up at the dance studio every Tuesday and Friday, the opportunities for the Athertons and Fontaines to engage in a battle royal would be cut in half.

Moira walked up to the lectern. The familiar jitters coursed through her as she looked out at her audience of parents, and she couldn't help but glance toward the back of the auditorium for a reassuring flame of red hair, but Rafe wasn't there.

She felt his absence even more than she'd felt his presence.

* * *

The Fontaines had barely cleared the auditorium when the Athertons arrived for the adult rehearsal and established command center at the piano.

Moira approached Vashti immediately and told her about Xandra's offer to have their accompanist work with the children at the dance studio, then waited for the pianist's blistering reply.

To her surprise, Vashti went for it. "My dear, I'm not only okay with Mrs. Loughlin teaching the songs to the children, but I'm relieved. To tell the truth, I was not looking forward to working with Xandra and Fleurette in such close quarters. And I know Kathleen. She subbed for me at First Baptist a couple of times."

After everyone had settled in, Vashti ran the principal actors through "Street Song" again, then sent Carmen off to work with Billie Joe in the boardroom while she rehearsed Phil, Sergio, Travis, and Micaela on their solos.

Moira sat back to listen and take notes

Phil's ringing tenor filled the auditorium, but he seemed wooden—more like he was singing an oratorio than a love song. Oh well, maybe he'd loosen up after a couple of rehearsals. Sergio was a little stiff too, but he was just eighteen and understandably nervous. In contrast, Travis was Mr. Suave himself, probably because his main focus was Micaela.

Moira didn't know whether to laugh or cry. Good thing Donna Sue hadn't cast Travis as the husband. The stage would have gone up in flames.

Micaela, on the other hand, was Della personified, the vulnerable, hopeful, sweet, innocent, starry-eyed wife, who loved her husband with her whole heart. Moira put down her pen and leaned back to absorb the beauty of the lyrics and the music.

> *Who would I be if I weren't me?*
> *Maybe a pirate sailing the sea?*
> *Maybe a princess, maybe a queen,*
> *Maybe an actress on the silver screen.*
> *Or maybe I'd be like Nellie Bly*
> *And amuse, amaze, and edify…*
> *Maybe I'd dance, maybe I'd sing.*
> *Oh, I could do most anything.*

Who would she have been if Gramp hadn't spotted her imitating characters on cartoon shows, if she hadn't spent her childhood on sets and stages, if she'd lived a normal life—like Rocky?

Sometimes, as she waited for a cue backstage, she'd daydream about living in a storybook cottage in a storybook neighborhood with a storybook mom who baked cookies and a storybook dad who read her stories before she went to sleep each night.

Micaela's voice warmed, and Moira knew what was coming next. She closed her eyes to sample the sweetness of the moment and hide her own pain.

But whatever happens, whatever may be,
I have you, Jim, so I'm glad I'm me.

* * *

As soon as the practice was over, the Athertons hurried up an aisle and out the door, with Phil and Sergio right after them, but Travis remained behind, his legs dangling off the edge of the stage.

Moira picked up her portfolio and gave him a questioning look. She was surprised he hadn't left with Micaela.

He eased himself onto the floor. "Com'on, little doggie. We're a-leavin' Cheyenne, and I'm your cowboy bodyguard for the evening. Rafe asked me to make sure you got to your car safely."

Moira rammed her notepad into her portfolio like it was a punching bag. How many people was Rafe going to make responsible for her protection? First Sammy and now Travis—and neither of them was necessary. She'd survived the worst Hollywood had to offer, and she could damn well survive callow teenagers hanging around a floodlight and inhaling lung cancer.

On the other hand, she was deathly afraid of darkness, so maybe it wasn't such a bad idea to have some company as she moved through the creaky old building, turning off lights and locking doors.

They stepped out onto the sidewalk. Travis looked around at the lonely lampposts and empty street. "Damn, I want out of this nowhere town."

So, Travis *did* recognize his own potential. "Have you tried getting solo gigs in some of the bigger cities in Texas—Dallas or Houston?"

His face took on a bitter cast. "Rocky doesn't like me to do overnight gigs"

Moira didn't reply. *Not going to get in the middle of that one.*

They walked across the street and into the parking lot. A familiar figure stepped away from the threesome under the floodlight and came toward them, challenge in his stride.

Travis waved and kept on walking. "Hiya, Sammy. I'm Travis, Rafe's brother. He told me you'd be here."

The teenager nodded solemnly and, mission fulfilled, lit a fresh cigarette and returned to his friends.

* * *

Rafe tossed and turned in his bed. It wasn't the bed he'd shared with Beth, of course. That bed had left the house the day after her funeral. And it wasn't a bed he'd shared with anyone when he was on the town. Those beds had been safe distances away from the ranch, often in homes he entered through a side door so the neighbors wouldn't talk.

He threw an arm back over his head and stared at the ceiling.

Moira. God, he ached for her. And she hadn't turned him down so far. But where did they go from here? And where could they meet? Not along the highway, no matter how upscale the motel. Moira was better than that.

He was more attracted to her than he'd been to any woman

since Beth died. She had an inner strength that drew him like a magnet, and that neat little shape and sweet, kissable lips didn't hurt.

He stared out the window at the barn light down the road. But would she want to stay around as long as he wanted her to? Sure, she had the job, but Colin Sanger's widow didn't need the money.

He yawned and rolled over, winding the sheet around him.

But if she didn't need the money, why the fuck had she taken the job?

Chapter Nine

Moira went to bed tired. The two rehearsals had taken a lot out of her, and she needed a good night's sleep.

But as soon as she closed her eyes, she was enveloped in the familiar darkness.

Total darkness, as if she'd been buried in the center of the earth.

Tears trickled down her face.

She tilted her head to maneuver them close to her mouth so she could lick up their moisture because she didn't know how or when the darkness would end.

If ever.

There was nothing to do but sit back on her haunches.

And wait…

Something cold touched her cheek, something cold and wet.

She screamed, and Astrid, dressed for the morning, came running into her room, grabbed Ivanhoe by his collar, and hauled him off the bed.

"For shame, Ivanhoe! You frightened Moira!"

Moira sat up. *Crap*. She'd had the nightmare again, and the big dog had tried to comfort her.

"That's okay. He did me a favor. I needed a cold nose in my face right about then," she said, untangling herself from the bedcovers. Apparently she'd been kicking around for half the night.

Astrid was instantly alert. "That dream again? Are you okay now? Dr. Sjoberg will be here right about now, but I could stay with you for a few minutes. She'd understand."

Moira moved to the side of the bed and wiped her face with the edge of her hand. "Yeah, it was the dream, but you go on to work. I'm awake now, and I have Ivanhoe here to take care of me."

She patted his majestic head, and he let his tongue hang out in a panting smile.

A horn sounded in the street, and Astrid looked out the window, then back at Moira. "You sure you're okay?"

Moira pointed her arm toward the door. "Go!"

Ivanhoe followed his mistress to the door, then returned to Moira with his tail drooping.

She smoothed his thick fur. "I know I'm only second-best, doggie, but I'll try to give you what comfort I can. And you can comfort me."

Still in her sleep shirt, she wandered into the family room, picked up the control of the big-butted television that Josie had thrown into the deal, and ran through the channels for a rerun of an innocuous sitcom that could clear the shadows of night from her brain.

Ivanhoe curled up against her leg.

Damn. What had triggered the dream this time?

Maybe it was the show. Everything seemed to be going well, but this was her first time working with community theater, and every day was a new challenge. Vashti and the Fontaines were spoiling for a fight, Travis and Micaela were burning up the stage, and she'd caught one of the mothers coaching her little girl from the back of the auditorium as if the show were a child beauty pageant.

She glanced around the room. When she and Astrid had moved in, it had seemed so barren. Now, with a couple of shelving units against one wall, a buffet against the adjoining one, and an upholstered couch and chair in place, the place looked downright homey.

The next time she saw Rafe, she'd have to be sure and thank him for bringing everything by yesterday evening and then helping Astrid move it into place.

She clicked the television off again and made herself stand up and walk over to the sliding glass door to look at drizzling rain. *Damn.* Not only was the nightmare still hanging over her, but Astrid has made off with their only umbrella, which meant she'd get soaked to the bone when she stopped by H-E-B to buy a baby present for Donna Sue.

The doorbell chimed, and Ivanhoe raced to the door to protect her from what must be nothing less than a zombie invasion. Glancing out the living room window as she passed through to the hall, Moira saw a panel truck parked at her curb with ROSEMARY'S FLOWERS stenciled on its side.

With Ivanhoe still barking like a maniac, she walked to the

door and opened it to a man in a heavy jacket holding a vase of yellow flowers. He looked at the little envelope attached to the vase.

"You Ms. Farrar?"

"Yes."

"Flowers for you." He thrust the vase at her, stepped off the porch, and hustled back to his truck before Moira could even say thank you, and who could blame him? The cold was biting, and Ivanhoe sounded like he would too.

She closed the door and locked it carefully, then carried the bouquet to the kitchen, with Ivanhoe parading in front of her, his ruff still up.

Doggie settled on the throw rug as she opened the envelope and pulled out the note inside.

Thinking of you.

Rafe.

Suddenly the dreary, sodden day seemed brighter, and the nightmare receded into the new day.

* * *

Donna Sue was sitting up in the bed and staring at her mobile phone when Moira entered the hospital room.

"Babes! Come in! You've got to see this. It's a terrific—I mean a really *super*—picture!" She thrust the cell phone at Moira. "Genevieve Valentina—we're going to call her Ginny—

she's so photogenic! Wait till you see her. The nurse should have her back in the room any minute. They're weighing her—regulations, you know—to make sure she's thriving, though Lord only knows why. She weighed eight pounds, two ounces—can you believe it?—when she was born. Of course, Leonard was photogenic too—Ginny's brother—but in a more masculine way!"

Moira's eyes stung unexpectedly as she looked at the photo. "She's perfect," she whispered.

Genevieve Valentina Gomez was indeed a charmer, but then, Moira had never met a baby who wasn't. In fact, she adored babies and everything about them—their cuddliness, their soft skins and chubby pink cheeks, their solemn eyes, their sweet cupid lips, their cooing cries. When she and Colin were first married, she'd assumed they'd have children right off. After all, he was in his late thirties.

But Colin had opted for a vasectomy early in his career, when he was enjoying everything Hollywood had to offer and didn't want any evidence left behind.

She handed over her pink gift bag from H-E-B, then took the visitor's chair beside the bed. She hoped Donna Sue would like her choice. She'd looked up and down the rack in the baby aisle before finding exactly what she wanted—little pink slippers with red ribbon roses on their toes. Sweet baby shoes for sweet baby feet.

Donna Sue lifted the shoes out of their bag and held them up to admire, then gave Moira a dimpled smile. "How darling! I love them—absolutely adore them." She leaned over to give Moira a light hug. "They'll be so perfect for Ginny."

She laid the shoes down carefully on her bedside table, then turned to Moira, her brown eyes snapping with curiosity. "Now, tell me—I'm dying to hear—what's going on with the rehearsals. Are Travis and Micaela still doing their star-crossed lovers act?"

Moira rolled her eyes. "Oh God, Donna. Even when they don't say a word to each other, it's so obvious—and distracting. I'm worried that the audience will be watching the two of them instead of the play."

"Not much you can do, babes." Donna Sue shrugged. "Travis and Micaela were a steady couple—from high school on—and they can't help but sizzle whenever you get them together." She scooted back on the bed and winced. "Damn episiotomy. I'm never having sex again."

Moira laughed. It felt good to laugh. She hadn't been doing enough of that lately. Bubbly Donna Sue and wicked Rocky—her new friends. Both of them made her laugh. Rafe was a friend too, but he was in an entirely different category. Humor wasn't his primary attraction.

Donna Sue filled a cup from her bedside water pitcher, then looked at Moira again. "What about the kids' get-together yesterday evening? Have you met Kimberly Nixon yet?"

"She gave me her daughter's pageant resume—all three single-spaced pages of it. And she had Wendy rigged out in a pink-and-white dress like Nancy Clancy used to wear."

Donna Sue took a swig of water. "Just don't let her get away with any crap, babes. You gotta call her on it right off the bat —Kimberly, not Wendy—Wendy's just doing what her mother tells her to—or it'll drive you crazy." She replaced the cup on her bedside table. "Oh, and speaking of crazy, my classes are a total mess because Ginny—she's so precocious—came early, and I wondered—don't feel you have to say yes—if you could possibly go in Friday morning and talk to the kiddos. My first class is at nine, and I can call Fred Hurst, our principal—he's a great guy even though none of his teams ever got to state when he was coaching—and he'll show you around like you're Elizabeth Taylor reincarnated. I mean, babes, I've got a lot of substitutes scheduled, but you'd be the big cheese!"

"No problem," Moira assured her. "I have most of Friday free." She'd been planning on dropping by the library to look at costume books, but that could wait. Besides, she wanted to know what a high school was like—a real high school, Rocky's kind of high school, not the ones on television and in the movies where all the students' complexions were clear, they broke into song and dance at the slightest opportunity, and vampires lurked around every corner.

The door opened, and a nurse wheeled in a Plexiglas cradle on top of a metal cabinet, then transferred a blanket-wrapped bundle into Donna Sue's eager arms.

She nuzzled her baby's face and cooed sweet nothings to her baby.

Moira felt a sweet pang of longing in her breast. Would she ever be a mother? Ever hold her own sweet little baby in her arms? Maybe a little boy with a shock of bright red hair?

Close that door right now, girl! Any relationship you have with Rafe will be on the terms he originally proposed—sex only—body satisfying body.

* * *

Rafe rolled up the original blueprints for the Huaco Theater that he'd been studying all morning and stuck them back in their slot. Why in the hell had he decided to take on an entire block? Restoring the old movie theater would have been enough in itself, but the rest of the damn block too? God, he must have been out of his mind. Still, for the renovated Huaco to be successful, theatergoers had to have a reasonable expectation of not getting their tires slashed while they were tapping their toes to *Thoroughly Modern Millie*.

He ran his hand up his forehead and through his hair. He had too much going on at the same time—the renovation, the theater guild, the new pathologist, Rocky's mother, Moira…

He walked over to the window and tried to sort things out. The drizzle had passed, and the sky had turned the striking blue that usually follows a hard norther.

Taking a couple of deep breaths, he leaned on the window frame and watched as Rosemary's driver turned into the wide alley and angled the delivery truck into its parking space behind the flower shop. Judging by the way the driver scooted into the back door of the building, the temperature must still be down in the forties.

Had Moira liked his flowers? Rosemary had put together a simple arrangement of daffodils, then backed it with foliage—charming, he thought, but not enough to scare Moira off.

He returned to his desk, picked up a pencil, and started drawing circles and attaching them to each other with straight lines. The last thing he'd expected when Johnny Blue recommended Moira Farrar was that he'd be giving her the rush. Sure, he'd enjoyed her characters on TV, but he'd never been what one would call a rabid fan. Nancy Clancy and Twinky Applejack had been two-dimensional cartoonlike creations to him, and Robota—well, it was hard to relate to a tin suit with lightbulb eyes.

But he'd related to the living, breathing Moira the instant he set eyes on her. And the more he was around her, the more he wanted to relate to her.

He glanced at his watch and reached for his bomber jacket.

It was almost time for Delilah's preschool let out. She'd never had to wait for him yet, and she was never going to.

* * *

Moira arrived at Eisenhower Consolidated early in the morning, passed under a large pale blue banner with GENERALS RULE! printed on it in purple, and waited at the security desk for clearance by a goggle-eyed clerk, who got an autograph out of her in the process.

Mr. Hurst was fiftyish, combed his thinning hair forward, wore red-framed glasses, and had just put a phone to his ear. He closed the laptop on his desk and reraised a forefinger in apology, then nodded her toward the chair in front of his capacious desk—the penitent's chair, Moira figured.

She down and looked around. So this was what a real principal's office looked like. Another large purple-and-blue banner, this one reading GO, GENERALS! was tacked on the wall above a display of diplomas, certifications, and commendations from community organizations. Framed photos of Eisenhower Consolidated football teams hung above the bookcase, and two upholstered chairs lined up with a metal filing cabinet against the far wall. A coffeemaker, a microwave, and the burnt-orange neon outline of a steer's head sat on top of a long table against the opposite wall, with cardboard boxes stacked underneath it.

"I have Moira Farrar in my office now, and I—yes, Nancy Clancy." He shuffled through the mess of documents that obscured the large calendar on his busy desk, nearly knocking over a trifold iPad, a cup full of pens and pencils, and a vase containing a bouquet of purple-and-blue papier-mâché flowers. "Anyway, I'll—"

Moira could hear an explosion of excitement on the other end of the line, but Mr. Hurst interrupted ruthlessly. "She's subbing for Donna Sue, so I've got to take her to class now. Call me later." He replaced the phone in its cradle, gave Moira a welcoming smile, and came around the side of his desk.

"We're honored to have you here at Eisenhower Consolidated High School today, Ms. Farrar," he said, shaking her hand. "Our students don't get to meet a person of your stature every day, and it will mean a lot to them. It's about time for classes to change, so I'll take you to Donna Sue's room and get you settled. She's got three theater classes in a row; a speech class; thirty minutes for lunch; a class prep period, which I suggest you spend in the teacher's lounge because everyone will want to talk to you; then two advanced theater classes."

A loud electronic horn blared as they emerged from the office, and Moira quailed as a tsunami of students burst into the hall, high-fiving each other, yelling back and forth, and banging locker doors. It was like a crowd scene from *Ben-Hur*.

Maybe real high school wasn't so great after all. She could never have survived in this melee. The sound was ear shattering, and there were just plain too many people moving around. She'd probably have ended up trampled on the floor if she were on her own, but Mr. Hurst led with his shoulder and cleared a way for her, then cut smartly into a side hall, hung a quick left, and walked her into a classroom.

Moira followed in his wake, totally confused by the voyage, but relieved that they'd finally reached land.

* * *

The rest was a piece of cake, as she reported to Astrid at dinner. "Mr. Hurst stayed in the room for about fifteen minutes, then left me on my own. The classes all went well, as far as I could tell. Donna Sue is putting on *Hedda Gabler* this spring—more power to her—and some of the students tried to impress me with their deep understanding of Ibsen's motivations and themes. A few others wanted to let me know they were destined for much better things than *The Clancy Family*, but no one gave me any real trouble. I tried to talk to them about preparing for a career in entertainment, but no one seemed interested, so I switched to funny stories about my own career. They loved the one about how I was all set to play George Clooney's daughter until the director decided he should have a son instead."

Her only real hitch had come at the end of the day when she was running out of steam and a purple-haired girl at the back of the class asked her what it was like to be married to Colin Sanger.

"That part of my life is over," she'd said, pasting a strained smile on her face to indicate fortitude in the face of tragic adversity. "That door has closed."

But there was always the possibility that it might open again when she least expected it. And that's another reason she couldn't get seriously involved with Rafe. He was too good a person to get pulled down into her sewer.

* * *

Moira hummed the happy version of "Street Song" as she drove into town for the evening rehearsals.

The midweek practices had gone well. The leads had their songs down pat and were interacting in character on-stage—except for Phillip Schoenfeldt, of course. What was wrong with him? He was still as standoffish as ever in his scenes with Micaela, and it wasn't as if they had to roll about naked on the floor. All he had to do was give her a couple of hugs and one brief close-mouthed kiss. But the way Phil was keeping his distance from Micaela, no one was going to believe he even liked her, much less be willing to sacrifice his most valued possession to buy her a Christmas present.

Moira parked her car in the dance studio's side lot and hurried inside to get warm. Her thin T-shirt and blue jean jacket weren't cutting it—she had to get herself a real live winter coat.

The first thing she noticed when she came through the door was that the Fontaines had taped a grid on the floor of one of their front areas. Her eyes opened wide.

"Those are the museum stage measurements you've taped off!"

Fleurette hunched in on herself as if she'd been beaten, and Xandra's voice snapped with venom. "The grid will help the children learn the choreography in relation to the auditorium, and we're *not* going to pull the tape up!"

Moira's mouth dropped open. Why did Xandra think she'd want them to pull up the tape? She schooled her own voice to a level tone. "I like the grid. It's a wonderful idea."

Xandra rewarded her with a quick, nervous smile and a jerky nod while Fleurette positively beamed.

What was going on with those two?

Whatever, she'd have to figure it out later.

Moira looked around. Everyone seemed to have arrived so she'd better take roll. There were already three dropouts, bringing them down to eighteen children, but ten were all she really needed for the show—if they were the right ten, like the five Loughlin kids and—well—Wendy.

Wendy Nixon, who had stage presence, an unnatural poise, and took directions far too well. Moira felt sorry for her, but she also had to foil all of her mother's attempts to teach her how to steal the show.

As soon as the kids' rehearsal ended, Moira was on her way to the museum for the adult rehearsal. Her teeth chattered like the proverbial castanets as she waited for the car heater to warm up. Who would guess it ever got this cold in Central

Texas? Bosque Bend was just a few miles north of Waco, which didn't exactly put it in the arctic zone.

She parked as near as she could get to the museum's front door and dashed across the street like a ground squirrel. It was either that or freeze to death.

Thank goodness the night custodian was at the door so she didn't have to pause and fumble with her ice-cold keys. She hurried up the stairs and into the auditorium, which was almost too warm.

The principals began arriving. First Billie Joe, then Phil and Sergio. A few minutes later Micaela, wrapped in a warm-looking wool coat, walked in with her mother. Next came Rafe, who gave her a smile that was more than a greeting. She dug her fingernails into her palms. She'd gone four whole days without seeing him.

Vashti called Rafe up front, and Moira watched him saunter down the aisle. That loose cowboy lope was an automatic turn on.

He's just another cast member, she told herself. *Just another cast member.* But the heat slithering through her told her otherwise.

Taking a ballpoint from behind her ear, she turned to a new page in her notepad and tried to be objective as Vashti ran Rafe through a vocal warm-up and then made sure he had "Street Song" down.

Now it was Billie Joe's turn. The big woman shifted her weight from foot to foot as she walked slowly and carefully up the steps. Definitely, Billie Joe should not be dancing down the stage steps in the aisle scene in the second act.

Moira looked up as someone edged down her row. *Rafe.*

He took a seat beside her, and his hand moved across the arm separating their seats so the tips of his fingers rested, as if by accident, on her thigh.

Every cell in her body caught fire.

He knew what he was doing, and it wasn't fair when she was trying to concentrate on Billie Joe's performance. She dropped her notepad in her portfolio as an excuse to move her leg away from his hand.

Sergio took his turn in the hot seat. Next up was Phil, then Micaela. Sergio was singing into the role now, Phil's delivery was musically impeccable and emotionally unbelievable, and Micaela floated effortlessly through every one of her songs.

Halfway through "Della's Prayer," Moira felt Rafe drape his hand on her leg again, but this time, she didn't drop her notebook in her portfolio. There was no use denying it—she liked him to touch her.

It's a normal physical phenomenon, she told herself. *He's a hunk and you're hungry. Maybe it's a sign of sexual healing. Maybe you'll even be normal one of these days—whatever "normal" is.*

Sergio lifted his hand in the direction of the door, and Moira looked around to see Desdemona and her beau coming into the auditorium. The ballerina was carrying a dripping umbrella, and Buck's longish hair was slick with rainwater.

What was it with autumn in Texas? The sky had been cold but clear when she'd driven into town.

She glanced at Buck and Desdemona as they took seats side by side in the front row. Odd, she'd never seen the two of them hold hands or even exchange more than a few words with each other. In fact, she'd wondered if Buck *could* talk. He certainly couldn't sing. After Vashti had tried him out, she'd taken Moira aside and suggested the football hero be given a nonsinging role, maybe as a silent bobby strolling in the background behind Rafe.

Sergio hopped down from the stage, raised his hand at Moira in silent farewell, and walked out between his sister and her boyfriend. Apparently they'd dropped by just to give him a ride home.

That was it for the evening. Moira snapped her portfolio shut, and Vashti packed up her music. "I have a few things I need to talk to you about, but I'll leave it till tomorrow. Micaela and I have to get home as quick as we can to take care of Carmen's little boy," she explained. "She's playing at the Bosque Club tonight."

Moira glanced around the empty auditorium to make sure no one had left anything behind, then walked up the aisle with Rafe and turned out the lights. They went down the dark stairs and stopped at the front door for her to adjust the automatic lock. She licked her lips and gave him a shy smile.

"Thank you for the flowers. I've always liked daffodils."

His arms slipped around her, and he drew her gently toward himself, then kissed her forehead and the tip of her nose.

"I've missed you, darlin.'"

The hard walls and the empty hall gave his voice a familiar echo. He sounded like Colin.

Moira stopped breathing, then wiped her hand down the side of his denim jeans and slumped against his shoulder in relief.

She was with Rafe, Big Red, Rafe of the sparkling eyes, not with Colin, who preferred leather.

An oversized belt buckle jabbed her in the ribs and she suppressed a nervous giggle. *Yeah, for sure, she was with Rafe.*

His lips explored her eyelids, the shape of her ear, and the curve of her cheek, slowly, as if learning her inch by inch, and she arched herself up against him. Her pulse fluttered. *Damn, she was a goner.*

She'd thought she'd never come alive again, had guarded herself against it. But this long, tall, drawling cowboy had stirred a spark in her the first time she met him. A spark that had become a flame.

Rising up on her toes, she cradled his jaw in her hands, brought his head down to her level, and kissed his lips. Her palms were excited by the stubble of his nighttime beard, and she closed her eyes to intensify the sensation.

He flitted a thousand baby kisses on her mouth, then moved down her throat. His hand stroked her arm up and down, and she melted against him.

Rafe. Big Red.

The darkness around them was inhabited by malevolent spirits, but she knew she was safe with this good man.

His tongue teased her lips, and she opened them to him. He explored the sensitive skins above her teeth, and the flame inside her turned into a blazing fire. That did it. She couldn't help it—she was his for the taking.

Rafe sent a hand up under the back of her T-shirt and unhooked her bra. He'd been wanting to get hold of these sweet little mounds ever since she walked into the front room of the Lynnwood house with Roscoe's Chicken and Waffles stretched across them. He turned her in his arms to caress their baby-soft undersides and play with her tightening nipples.

Her breath came faster, and she moved her butt against him.

Damn. His little soldier was a firecracker.

He lifted the loose shirt off over her head and tossed it onto the concrete bench beside the door, then pulled her against him so she would feel his hardness against the small of her back as his mouth explored the tender skin behind her ears, then down the side of her throat.

Moira arched and moaned as Rafe's fingers returned to her burning nipples again, buffing them into full erection. She was panting for air, her skin was burning, and her body had gone weightless. She was heading toward oblivion and didn't know how to stop herself.

Suddenly her knees buckled, and she backed against the museum door for support. Rafe held her as she shook like a leaf and gasped for air.

The heat rose in her cheeks, and she crossed her arms to cover her breasts. Her head moved back and forth in apology.

"I'm sorry, I'm so sorry. I didn't mean to."

For a second, Rafe didn't understand. Then he did. Moira had ignited and taken off all by herself. He was in awe.

He gathered her against himself and smoothed her hair. "You're beautiful, so beautiful."

Chapter Ten

As they crossed the street, the full moon mirrored itself in the puddles and wet pavement, lighting their way.

Moira kept her distance from Rafe. Her shirt was back on her now—not inside out, she hoped—and she was down to earth again, but she wasn't sure she could control herself if he touched her again.

God, she had really done it—spontaneous combustion—a female premature climax.

Why? Maybe because she was drained, operating on empty, that Rafe caught her in a weak moment. But more likely because something deep inside her had responded to him from the moment he nearly ran her down in the hall.

Rafe had been very gentlemanly about the situation, holding her until she could stand on her own, helping her get her shirt back on, even complimenting her on her response, but she was still embarrassed.

They reached her car, and she glanced across the parking lot toward the floodlight. Apparently the tobacco brotherhood had packed it in for the night, so she and Rafe were all alone.

He took her in his arms as she pressed the control to unlock her car door and gave her one of his patented sweetheart kisses, then exhaled roughly in frustration and backed away.

His voice was gruff.

"I'd ask you out to the ranch again, but Delilah and I are gonna be gone all weekend. My sister is havin' a gatherin' of the clan in Austin to announce she's runnin' for the state Senate, and when TexAnn cracks the whip, we all jump."

He kissed the tip of her nose, which seemed to be his thing.

"But I'll be back on Monday—would you be free for lunch? Tuesday, Wednesday, and Thursday are Daddy time, but I'd sure like it if you'd join Delilah and me on Friday for the Pumpkin Party on the square. She's goin' to a sleepover at her second cousin's house afterward, so I thought maybe you and I could round out the evenin' with an hour or two at Good Times. You'll get to see Omar dressed like Dracula and singin' Elvis."

Her voice was a breathless croak. "Sounds great."

Maybe they could ignore what had happened in the museum lobby and start the relationship over again. The Pumpkin Party would be a wholesome, family-type outing, and Good Times would be a lot of fun. Omar rigged out in a black cape and fly-away collar was a sight she didn't want to miss.

Rafe kissed her again and, keeping an arm around her, ran a finger down the slope of her breast, then looked at her.

"Any reaction?"

She managed to laugh. "It was difficult, but I kept myself under control."

His voice deepened into a harsh whisper that sent her senses spinning.

"I like it better when you let go."

* * *

Saturday morning, Moira got up bright and early; threw on a shirt, a sweater, and her blue jean jacket; then drove to the museum to rehearse the adult chorus and block out the "Street Song" scene. Xandra and Fleurette were there to explain the choreography, and they gave her exactly what she'd asked for—a fast-paced opening, like the first scene of *Guys and Dolls*, that would slow down when Phil and Micaela entered the scene.

After lunch, she paid bills, washed clothes, and attended a dog-training seminar with Astrid, then, as supper cooked, called Gram to catch up on the news, none of which was particularly earth shaking. The neighbors had bought a hybrid car, her brother was getting along well in his new school, and his tuition installment was due. But, as she'd told Gram, there was nothing she could do about the tuition until she got her first paycheck.

Astrid took Ivanhoe for a stroll around the cul-de-sac while Moira turned on the television and tried to watch a rerun of *Dr. Who* saving the world again, but couldn't make herself follow the plot. All she'd been able to think about since Friday was Rafe.

Damnit. Not being able to see him all weekend had thrown her own personal universe for a loop. In just one week, Big Red had become far too important to her life.

No question about it—she and Big Red were going to wind up in bed together. He was still in love with Beth, of course, and she—well, she was still in hate with Colin, but they could enjoy each other for a while. That way he could keep his wife's memory alive, and she could keep her husband's secrets dead and buried.

Her phone rang. It was Johnny Blue. She frowned and checked her watch. The last she'd heard, Johnny was on location in England. If it was seven fifteen in the evening here, that meant it was one fifteen in the morning over there.

"Hey, Moira, how ya d-doing? Those Texans treating you all right? Need ol' Uncle Johnny to c-come to town and set them sh-straight?"

Oh God. Johnny was either drunk or high. Maybe a couple of six-packs, maybe a toke or two—or more. He'd never been into the hard stuff, but there was always a first time.

She put a smile in her voice. "I'll take a rain check on your visit, Johnny." *Please don't come to Bosque Bend and screw everything up for me.* "You know how it is—I'm trying to put a show together and you'd be a total distraction. The women would be following you around like a pack of bloodhounds."

She had a special bond with Johnny Blue, probably because she was the only actress he'd ever worked with who hadn't fallen for him, or maybe because they'd been fellow travelers, kids who'd raised themselves in the showbiz jungle. She'd spent most of her childhood on sets, using Pasadena as a crash pad, while he'd lived in the Beverly Hills mansion of his producer father and his succession of wives and mistresses. Both of them had a hunger for permanence and stability.

But he was the last person she needed to show up while she was trying to put together a show. To put together a relationship with Rafe. Trying to put together her life.

Johnny laughed. "That's the n-nicest turndown I've ever gotten, girl. Hey, the McAllister guy that Pen Swaim had me talk to—is he taking c-care of you and your sister? That house t-turn out okay?"

"The house is great, Johnny. It even has indoor plumbing."

She'd thought she'd found her permanence and stability with Colin, but the price was more than she'd bargained for. Johnny had thought he'd found his when he cracked the glass ceiling of his father's world, first on television, then in movies, but it had plunged him into a lifestyle that wasn't going to have a happy ending.

Johnny snorted out a laugh. "I'll put off my trip then, but g-gotta come down to Texas sometime, maybe after this gig wraps up. Just inherited a house from m-my aunt and uncle in Austin. Thought maybe I'd hibernate in it for a while and g-get my head on s-straight."

Yeah, she'd heard that one before. She loved John Keller Blue like a brother, but he was a lost cause.

* * *

Monday, at last. Rafe would be back in town.

Moira lay in bed drowsing and making up stories in her

head. This time around, *she* wanted to be the heroine, the girl who got the guy.

A car honked in front of the house and Astrid called out a good-bye as she flew through the door. Moira slid reluctantly out of bed, put on a warm robe, and went into the kitchen to make breakfast so Ivanhoe, who didn't seem to understand about daydreaming, wouldn't come in to fetch her.

She had two whole hours to get ready for her lunch date with Rafe. Predictions were that the cold weather would lift today, which meant she could wear that Zulily zigzag dress.

After finishing her cereal and putting the bowl down for Ivanhoe to lap up the remaining milk, she took a leisurely bath, washed her hair, and set out her clothes. Oops, she'd forgotten how short the skirt was—the butterfly shoes wouldn't work. She'd have to wear high-heeled boots instead, and she'd better dig a pair of tights out of her drawer or a playful breeze would give the citizens of Bosque Bend a show that the theater guild wasn't paying her for.

She held the dress up in front of herself in the mirror.

Was it too hippy-dippy for her for the rehearsal tonight? She didn't want to have to come home and change after lunch.

She was feeling adventurous today, and Bosque Bend would have to take her as she was.

She picked up her portfolio and hit the road.

The temperature was in the seventies, the sky was studded with happy-looking clouds, the hum of the road was as relaxing as a good yoga session, and the refrain of "Della's Prayer" echoed in the corridors of her mind.

If I sing enough, if I pray enough
If I am very, very good
Maybe everything will turn out
As I hope it will, as it should.
As it should.

* * *

It was truly her lucky day—there was a parking space available in front of the jewelry store. Moira's heart pounded as she walked up the narrow flight of stairs to Rafe's office. She was excited and apprehensive at the same time. He'd played it off, but what happened in the museum lobby was downright freaky.

She walked through the open door of the office. It was Friday afternoon so Sissy wasn't there, but where was Rafe?

Something clanged in the inner office, and Rafe's voice cracked with anger. "Cut it out, you jerk-ass motherfucking piece of shit!"

Moira walked to the door of Rafe's private sanctum.

"Uh, having problems?"

Rafe turned around.

* * *

Take a deep breath, cowboy. Smile and pretend to be calm and in control of yourself, even though those black tights and tall boots are making you feel anything but.

He made a gesture of apology. "Sorry about that, darlin'. You're safe. I'm not psychotic—but the photocopier is." He switched the system off. "We always give cast members twenty advertising flyers to pass on to their friends and relatives, and I wanted to have a stack of copies ready to show you, but I can't get the damn machine to work." He lifted the master from the tray and handed it to her. "It's probably better that you see the thing first anyway, before I print it out. Let me know if there's anything I should change."

Moira put her portfolio down on his desk and studied the page.

She curled her lower lip in.

"I like the colors, the deep green and deep red against the snow-white background. Christmas colors for a Christmas play, of course, but they show against each other too. And when they overlap, like where you have the red lettering out-lined in green, they get darker."

"That's the color wheel at work. Red and green make brown."

She lifted her eyes, those almond-shaped eyes, and he could feel himself hardening. Damn—he wished he'd worn boxers.

"The comb you put in the girl's hair is charming, *But...*"

A bucket of cold water splashed over him.

Moira pointed to the large font across the top of the page. "But I'm uncomfortable with my name being in such a promi-nent position. What about Pen and Vashti?"

"Pen and Vashti are home folks. Everyone's accustomed to them pulling rabbits out of hats, but you're the new girl in town, the big attraction. Anyway, from what I've heard, Judy Schoenfeldt is writing the two of them up in the playbill like Shakespeare and Mozart."

Although he damn well knew that no matter what Judy

said, Bosque Bend would still think of Pen as the weird guy who had a telescope in his tower room to keep track of his neighbors, and of Vashti as that crazy woman who looked like she'd just dropped in from Oz.

Moira laughed and handed the flyer back to him, then indicated the wall opposite his desk, the one layered with sheets of butter-yellow paper. "Tell me what's going on here." A smile hovered at the corners of her lips.

Those sweet, kissable lips.

He moved closer, not quite touching her. "My projects. My plans aren't very far along on the rest of the block, so I'll show you what I'm working on for the interior of the Huaco." His arm brushed the side of her breast as he reached up to lift one of the larger pieces of tracing paper off the wall, but she didn't move away.

So far, so good.

He laid the sketch out on his desk and let his leg nudge her hip as she leaned over to look at his plans.

"Josie's already moved out so I grabbed a sledgehammer this mornin' and broke through the back door—it had been Sheetrocked over for years—to get a good look at the theater itself. It's in a lot better shape than I thought. The curtain is in shreds, of course, and the buildin's infested with rats, but the roof looks like it's in good shape, and there's some nice art deco work on top of the proscenium."

He put an arm loosely around her waist, as if positioning her so she could see the plan better.

"But I've got to find out what kind of room there is backstage. Not much, as I remember—Travis and I used to perform at the Huaco's kiddie talent shows every Saturday morning, and we got to know the place pretty well."

He drew her a little closer to his side.

"I'll probably get rid of a couple of rows of seats and build an apron out to extend the stage forward."

"How many seats would that leave us?" Moira's voice came out a little breathless, as if he was getting to her.

"About three hundred, including the balcony. Of course, they'll all have to be refurbished."

"Three hundred? That's a lot smaller than the museum auditorium—only half the size."

"The museum auditorium has never worked that well for us—Bosque Bend doesn't have enough theatergoers to fill up anything but the center block, so we've been ropin' off the seats outside aisles to compact the audience."

He moved his hand up her back and stroked her arm.

Slowly.

Then he turned her toward him. Her pupils were dilated, and she was sending out sparks. She'd exploded for him like a powder keg last Friday, and he wanted more of the same, but this time, he wanted in on it.

He took her into his arms, and she moved her head against his shoulder and closed her eyes.

Electricity shimmered in the air between them.

Moira gloried in the feel of him—his warmth, his solidity. This was what she wanted, what she'd come here for. Lunch didn't matter, the poster didn't matter, the play didn't matter. All she wanted was Rafe.

He kissed her until she was dizzy, playing with her lips and exploring her mouth, at the same time holding her against himself with one hand and caressing her hip with the other. He was moving her toward the daybed in the corner of the room, she knew. Her knees bent by reflex against the edge of the cushion.

They sank down together on the soft cushions. The smell of sex was in the air. She was going to do it, do it with Big Red, and Colin be damned. She covered Rafe's face with fierce, defiant kisses, then threw her head back in ecstasy as his lips moved down past her throat.

He unlatched the top of her dress and unclasped her bra. His tongue wet her nipples with moisture and his mouth worried them into tight nubs of sensation.

Yes! This was what she wanted! Don't stop, don't stop, don't stop, don't stop!

A lightning bolt of desire shot through her, and she let her legs fall open. He ran a hand up under her too-short skirt and pulled down her tights. She arched and squeezed her inner thighs in anticipation.

His other hand went up inside the loose sleeve of her dress and stroked her arm up and down. Everywhere he touched, she caught fire. She was in a haze of sensation. A haze she wanted to stay in forever.

He moved his hand around to the tender underside of her arm, up past her elbow, and paused, then circled her scar with a light finger.

She froze. *No, no, no!*

The hazy heat evaporated. She turned away and pushed down her skirt.

Rafe sat up. "What's wrong? Did I hurt you?

She shook her head. Her voice wasn't working right, but she had to say something. "You didn't hurt me. It's that, just that…I'm sorry…I can't do it."

She hiked her tights back up, didn't even try to rehook her bra, and latched her dress closed.

"What was that I touched? A scar?"

"Yes, yes. It's a scar, and it still hurts." But it was more than a scar, and he would never know how much it hurt. "I have to go now."

She reached for her portfolio and headed for the door, grabbed onto the banister, and went down the steps as fast as she could.

Pausing at the street door, she ran her hand through her hair and stretched her mouth into a confident smile. Maybe then no one would notice that her lipstick was long gone and her bra was hanging loose. She'd go home and change into something else—a nice suit of armor would do.

And she'd have to remember to tell Astrid that she'd be staying home for Halloween after all.

Chapter Eleven

Rafe leaned back into the couch, spread his arms, and threw his head back.

Good job, cowboy. She bolted on you before you got your belt unbuckled. He ran his hand through his hair, then massaged his face.

What the hell happened? She'd been as hot as he was, then suddenly, she was running out the door. Was it a tease, some kind of sick Hollywood game? Everything had been moving along until he touched that scar, the one on her underarm. Damn thing was just a slight ridge about the size of a half-dollar, but he'd been surprised to find it on skin as baby smooth as hers.

Was that what had spooked her, him touching the scar? Was it an alarm button? *Danger, danger*—redheaded cowboy getting too close for comfort?

Anger rushed through him.

Goddamn if he was gonna let a fucking scar stop him.

He walked into the outer office and slammed the door shut, then filed the master flyer for *Gift of the Magi* till Sissy got back on Monday.

There'd be other days. And Moira wasn't going to get rid of him as easily as she seemed to think she would. There was no way he was gonna write her off. In fact, he wanted her more than ever.

He needed her.

* * *

The children's rehearsal ran over so Moira made it to the auditorium for the adult rehearsal a little late. A quick glance around told her that Rafe hadn't arrived yet.

Phil, Travis, and Sergio were sitting down front, and Billie Joe stood beside the piano, talking to Vashti. The Fontaines were up onstage, chalking a grid on the floor similar to the one they'd taped on the floor of their studio, but with different references and guides.

This was another choreography night. Xandra and Fleurette would work out the Dreamer's big number, Billie Joe's mirror scene, and Rafe's march. And when the chorus showed up about eight thirty, she'd run them through the entire street scene—song, choreography, and action.

And if Rafe didn't appear, she'd give his time slot to Billie Joe, who was not a natural dancer.

Taking her usual seat in the middle of the auditorium, she watched as Xandra led Travis, then Sergio, through what was basically a solo waltz. Travis's performance had a sexy edge, just like his voice, while Sergio's movements were as clean and graceful as his ballerina sister's.

Next came Billie Joe.

Halfway through her number, there was a murmur of interest from the chorus members who were sitting in the back of the auditorium and Moira knew without looking that Rafe had walked in.

The blood rushed to her head and her brain went blank. *Escape, escape!*

She scrambled out of her row and hurried up to the area below the stage as though she wanted a close-up view of the rehearsal.

Focus on Billie Joe and pretend you don't know Rafe's coming down the aisle.

And Billie Joe did need help. The Milliner's dance was simple—two-steps and twirls as she took hats on and off—but no matter how many times Vashti rehearsed her, Billie Joe got her feet mixed up and couldn't keep up with the beat.

Moira jerked around as Xandra, schedule in hand, sidled over to her. "Make Vashti quit hounding Billie Joe," Xandra hissed. "Fleurette and I will work with her at our studio. She needs to start slowly and build up." She tapped the page. "And besides, we're supposed to have started on the street scene by now. Fleurette and I have classes to teach tomorrow morning and need to get home at a decent time tonight."

Moira arranged her face to register chagrin and sympathy. "I'm so sorry we're running late, Xandra, and I can't tell you how much appreciate your willingness to work with Billie Joe privately. By the way, I love the way you've choreographed the mirror sequence—it will probably be the hit of the show."

Xandra gave her another one of her tight smiles and returned to her seat.

Moira gritted her teeth. The Fontaines would never be in her corner, she'd probably pissed Vashti off, and she'd run out on Rafe. Was there any way she could have made a bigger wreck of the day? She might as well pack up her bags and move back to Pasadena.

* * *

Rafe wasn't surprised when the second he arrived, Moira ran as far away from him as she could get. Judging by her costume change, she was really spooked. But if she thought razor-pleated slacks, a tailored shirt, and a man-cut jacket would put him off, she had another think coming. A butch outfit on a very feminine female of the heterosexual persuasion was more of a come-on than a put-off.

The room went silent as he walked up onto the stage and waited for Fleurette to show him the tap-step march she'd devised.

This was a moment of high drama, and the actor in him was enjoying every minute of it. The chorus was frozen in place, the Fontaines were leaning forward like hungry vultures, and Vashti was looking back and forth from him to Moira like she was watching a tennis match.

He narrowed his eyes.

Moira's move down front had been a tactical error because

now he was standing center stage, and she was on the floor directly below him. The only thing she could do was retreat back to her usual chair and call for the street scene.

* * *

Moira stuffed her script in her portfolio and stood up. The rehearsal was finally over and she could go home.

The chorus came off the stage without the usual murmur of small talk and joined Phil, Sergio, Vashti, and the Fontaines as they hurried up the aisle for a swift exit. Travis lingered behind for an extra second, then gave his brother a salute and walked out the door.

Rafe was still here, on the floor.

And they were alone.

He gave her one of his easy smiles and started toward her, as if expecting her to walk out with him, but she ran up the steps at the other side of the stage and tried for a bright, sunny voice.

"Don't wait for me tonight. I'll be here a while longer yet."

Rafe looked up at her one long second, then shrugged as if it didn't matter, lifted his hand, and gave her another one of those damn smiles of his. "See you later."

Moira watched him leave, allowed him five minutes by her watch to clear the museum, then, her heart beating in her ears, peeked out the auditorium door to be sure the coast was clear.

As she stepped out into the hall, the old building heaved a groan like Dracula's tomb cracking open.

The dim overhead cast a dismal pall down the hall that left the corners in shadow, and she palmed her keys so they stuck out between her fingers like claws. Her heart thudding in the silence, she hurried down the stairs, then out the front door.

The knot in her chest dissolved. The sidewalk was shining wet under the blessed full moon.

Across the street, she saw Sammy Schuler leaning against the floodlight, alone.

He threw his cigarette into a puddle, sauntered across the street, and met her at the curb. Neither of them spoke. *Fine.* Moira didn't want to talk. She didn't even want to think.

A light breeze rattled the trees, and Sammy shivered, then coughed.

Moira looked him over.

Good grief—and she thought she had troubles. That felt jacket of his was soaked through and through. The whole time she'd been cozy and dry inside the museum, Sammy had been waiting outside in the rain in case she didn't have an escort.

"You know, you can come into the auditorium on nights like this. The door is unlocked while we're rehearsing. We don't allow smoking, but you'd be warm and dry."

Sammy shivered again.

"Maybe."

* * *

Moira closed her iPad. She'd spent all afternoon in the library across from the Fontaines' dance studio, leafing through period fashion books, jotting down costume ideas, and working up a color palette.

Now to grab a bite to eat across the river and drive back here for the children's rehearsal.

She glanced toward the Fontaine sisters' lair as she walked to her car, putting a pleasant smile on her face in case any of the cast members were hanging around. And that smile was damn well going to stay on her face all during the adult rehearsal tonight too. The cast didn't need the distraction of her soap-opera life.

Backing out of her parking space, she headed toward G&G Chicken across the river. Not that she felt much like eating, but she didn't want to faint dead away from hunger and have everyone think it was because she was heartsick about the breakup with Rafe.

Her smile faded as she stopped at a red light.

Oh, crap. She *was* heartsick about it.

She missed his cowboy drawl, his easy smile, those stupid sparkling eyes. She missed talking to him and laughing with him. She missed his arm around her shoulders. She missed his lips on hers. And, yes, she missed his hands going wherever they wanted to go.

But it was all for the best, she reminded herself, reasserting her smile. She was in Bosque Bend to direct the theater guild, not to have a love affair with the chairman of the board.

Correction—a *sexual* affair. No *love* involved.

As if to put an exclamation point on the end of her pronouncement, a spate of fat raindrops splashed onto her windshield. She glowered at the sky and turned on her wipers. The weather would not give her a break, although it wasn't as if she was wearing anything perishable. Her jeans and turtleneck pullover were comfort clothes she'd had since college.

At least she didn't have on a man-suit this evening. And why in the hell did she think dressing like George Clooney would put Rafe off? Every time she'd sneaked a glance in his direction—which was far too often—he was watching her, studying her, maybe trying to figure out what made her tick.

But she had news for him. She wasn't going to let Rafe McAllister or anyone else root around in her psyche. Her past was a closed door.

The light changed and she drove a couple more blocks, then turned in at the sign of the crowing rooster and ordered at the drive-thru window.

Mrs. Loughlin would take care of everything with the children's chorus tonight, but the adult rehearsal was another matter. She may have screwed herself. After all, Rafe was a son of Bosque Bend, and she was the new girl on the block. Would the other actors give her a hard time because she'd publicly rejected him? Maybe sabotage the play?

* * *

Most of the chorus members had already arrived and taken their places onstage when she arrived. They didn't seem as upbeat as usual, but nobody hissed or threw rotten fruit in her direction so she guessed she'd survive.

After reviewing the initial "Street Song," Vashti introduced the minor key version, which ended the first act. Then the Fontaines, who'd driven over with Billie Joe, choreographed the mob scene in the milliner's shop when the customers ended up having a melee while they were trying on hats, which the cast seemed to have a lot of fun with.

All in all, it was turning out to be the best chorus rehearsals yet. Everyone paid close attention and the horseplay was kept at a minimum. Apparently her personal drama had a sobering effect on them.

Now for the principals. She'd work Travis and Sergio into Phil's dream sequence first, then look at Desdemona's ballet. Let's hope Xandra's request to slow down the tempo of "Della's Prayer" didn't set Vashti off. Xandra was right. The dream sequence should be—well—dreamy.

She stood up to get a better view of the stage as Travis and Sergio mounted the steps, then turned as she heard Desdemona greet someone who had just come in.

It was Sammy, and he was taking a seat by the ballerina and her beau.

Moira smiled.

Good. They were all about the same age. Maybe Buck and Desdemona could convince Sammy to come in out of the rain on a regular basis.

Moira turned back to the stage, where Travis and Phil waited for her direction while Sergio, as the understudy, observed from the wings.

"What I'm after is a weaving in and out of Jim and the Dreamer. Phil, you start out in the spotlight, then retreat as the Dreamer comes forward and takes the spotlight from you. At the same time, your voice will get softer, and Travis's will gain strength. Play with it, guys—but Travis, remember, when you get to the song's climax, Phil's voice must predominate, even though he'll be a couple of yards behind you. Got it?"

Travis saluted, and Phil gave her a thumbs-up as the soft, open chords that introduced the Dreamer sequence filled the auditorium.

> *If I were as rich as Rockefeller, John D.*
> *Whenever I walked down the street*
> *The gents would tip their hats at me*
> *And I'd give dimes to all I'd meet*
>
> *If I were rich, I'd buy Della those hats*
> *And beautiful dresses for her to wear*
> *And beautiful shoes with stylish spats*
> *And beautiful combs for her beautiful hair*

Moira's eyebrows went up—Phil was really into the song. So why was he such a cucumber with Micaela?

The second time through, Travis echoed the last couple of words of each line in falsetto, then moved forward as he took over the song, with Phil providing the echoes.

> *If I were rich, I'd buy a car*
> *An electric one, just for Sunday*
> *A horseless carriage for travels afar*
> *And a second one for M…*

Vashti stopped playing and looked up at the stage, her forehead knit with concern.

Travis shook his head. "Sorry. Let's take it from the top."

He began again, flubbed a line, then frogged out.

Moira stood up.

Travis cleared his throat, put his hands on his knees, and took several loud breaths, like he couldn't get any air.

Oh God! He'd turned pale, and there were sweat circles under his arms. Moira hurried out of her row and made for the stage as he groaned and clutched at his belly.

Sammy's voice rang out from the back of the auditorium. "It's the same thing his father had! Get him to the hospital! Quick!"

* * *

Moira walked through the double doors of the Bosque Bend Hospital waiting room, then winced at the overbright fluorescent lights.

To make it worse, the long, windowless walls were covered with a repeated design of floor-to-ceiling blowups of children swinging into the air, teenagers frolicking at the seashore, and an elderly couple strolling along a blue-flowered pathway—all spaced between wide diagonal stripes of pink and cream.

Enid McAllister sat on one end of a sick pink vinyl couch. A tote bag lay on the floor beside her, and a skein of green yarn was in her lap. She looked up, tried for a smile, and patted the space beside her.

"Come sit with me, Moira. It would be nice to have some company."

Moira settled herself on the couch and asked the question she was afraid of hearing the answer to. "How's Travis?"

He'd become more than a cast member to her. He was Rafe's brother.

"They're running tests. The doctors don't know yet whether or not they'll check him in. It could be something minor, but with our family history, they want to be sure. I'm camping out here for now." Her mouth twisted. "I know the drill."

"How…how many times has Travis had this kind of attack?"

Enid looked down at her hands as if they could provide an answer. Moira wanted to put a comforting arm around her shoulders, but held back. After all, she'd only met Rafe's mother once, and Enid probably knew that she and her son were on the outs.

"I don't know. He doesn't tell me these things—doesn't want to worry me."

"Has—has anyone contacted Rocky?

Enid's face froze for a semi-second, and her eyebrows lifted. "No one can reach her."

Moira blinked. So, she hadn't imagined it—there was bad blood between Enid and her daughter-in-law, but it wasn't fair for Enid to hold it against Rocky that she hadn't shown up at the hospital yet. There could be all sorts of legitimate reasons why she wasn't here, none of which Moira could think of at the moment. But she glued her mouth shut. Enid didn't need to hear a spirited defense of Rocky when her son might be at death's door.

Enid reached for her knitting needles. "How did the rest of the practice go?"

"Sergio Benton, Travis's understudy, finished the scene with Phil that we were working on."

Moira watched Enid's needles guide the yarn in and out of itself. "I—I hope you're not offended that I continued with the rehearsal."

Enid looked up from her knitting. "Moira, if there's one thing I've learned in my life, it's to keep on going. We may find out that all Travis is suffering from is an addiction to my brother's pork ribs. And you did the right thing—arranged for him to get to the hospital immediately."

"Actually, it wasn't me—I didn't understand was happening. Your nephew, Sammy Schuler, was the one who said to take Travis to the hospital. Before I knew it, Buck Overton had walked Travis off the stage and out the door. I never imagined he could be so decisive."

She'd have to completely revamp her image of Desdemona's boyfriend. Apparently he was the strong, silent type.

Enid rested her knitting again. "I've always had a fondness for Buck. It was hard for him to grow up in the shadow of his brother, and Dolph Junior is as ignorant and boorish as his father."

Moira's eyebrows went up. Apparently Enid McAllister wasn't one to mince words.

The doors to the waiting room swung open, and Enid looked up with hope on her face, but the newcomer was an anxious-looking middle-aged woman escorting a teenage boy whose arm was hanging at a painful angle. They went up to the intake window at the rear of the room, and a nurse opened the door to the treatment area.

Who was Enid expecting? *Rafe?* Moira bit her lip. If Rafe did walk in, what would he think of her sitting here with his mother?

The doors opened again, and Micaela Atherton burst through. Her cheeks were flushed; the orchid pinned on her elegant lace dress was hanging dangerously loose; and her hair, usually disciplined into a sleek twist, was almost as disarranged as her mother's.

Enid rose from the couch and embraced her like she was a long-lost daughter.

Moira's mouth fell open. Why were Enid and her son's paramour so chummy? Sure, Enid would have become friendly with Micaela when Travis was dating her, but Micaela was the "other woman" now. Did Enid approve of her son fooling around on his wife? The situation was getting more Hollywood by the moment.

Micaela drew a chair over to the couch and laid her sequined evening bag on the floor beside her. "What happened? I was singing at the Nyquist wedding, and Mom called to tell me Travis was in the hospital, that it was his stomach again. Is there a definite diagnosis?"

Enid shook her head. "They're calling it gastritis, just like with his father."

Micaela buried her face in her hands. "Oh God, I pray. I pray for so much."

Enid laid a comforting hand on her shoulder. "I know, dear. So do I."

There was a commotion at the door and Rocky pushed through them. Her jeans were a shiny dark blue, with copper-colored conchos down the sides, and her pale blue denim shirt complemented the tight taffy ringlets bouncing against her shoulders.

Micaela rose from the chair and picked up her evening bag, obviously preparing to leave.

Rocky's eyes were hard, but her voice was syrupy with concern. "Oh, do you have someone in the hospital too, Micaela? Did your dear mother have a stroke?"

Micaela gave her back smile for smile. "You're so kind, Rocky, but Mother is just fine." She turned to Enid. "It was nice visiting with you, Mrs. McAllister, and I do hope your son will recover quickly."

The doors closed behind her, and Rocky took the chair Micaela had vacated.

"I'm so sorry I wasn't here, Enid. I drove down to San Saba to help my cousin's wife with her PTA coat drive—those poor little tykes were so grateful—and didn't realize my cell had run out of juice. I got Billie Joe's message on my landline as soon as I got home." She laid her hand on Enid's arm, and her voice lowered to a sepulchral whisper. "How's Travis doing?"

Enid shook her head. "No news yet."

"Is Rafe in with him?"

"He's trying to find someone to stay with Delilah."

A male nurse came back in and walked over to them.

Rocky stood up. "What's the word?"

"Still nothing yet, ma'am. But just to be on the safe side, we're admitting Mr. McAllister to the hospital for the night. He can have visitors now, but relatives only, and no more than two at a time." His gaze swept the three women.

Moira edged back on the couch. "I'll wait here for you and Rocky."

She'd flip through the stack of *People* on the table beside the couch. Maybe somebody she used to work with had scored a feature story.

But half a dozen reports on Johnny Blue's outrageous escapades and one croupy baby later, Moira was still alone in the waiting room. She looked at the clock on the wall. Almost eleven, and she was coming on sleepy. Maybe she should leave while she could still drive, but she didn't want to run out on Enid and Rocky.

The intake doors banged open, and her head snapped up.

Rafe.

His hair was a mass of rumpled flames, and his shirt was hanging out of his jeans.

Moira rose from the couch. "I'll go on now. Rocky and your mother are in with Travis. They should be back soon."

His voice was raw with pain. "Don't leave. Please."

He sat down beside her and rubbed his face as if he was in pain, then sat silent and unmoving, a hand spread across his forehead and eyes.

Moira clenched her hands, wanting to help, to comfort him, but not sure of what to do. She tried to rise again. "I'll...I'll see if the admittance clerk will let you—"

He grasped her wrist and pulled her back the couch. "No. Stay with me. I've been through this before. There's nothing anyone can do. Nothing."

He ran his hand through his hair, then speared her with his eyes. His voice was low and guttural, almost a growl.

"I need to talk."

Chapter Twelve

He'd just put Delilah to bed when Billie Joe's call came in. Then he'd spent what seemed like an eternity tracing down Mrs. Goodrich, who, as it turned out, was playing Bunco at her daughter-in-law's house just down the road from the C Bar M.

God, he was tired—tired, frustrated, and angry, an explosive combination. He glared at the wall art, which he hated. Those pictures—childhood, adulthood, and old age. The three stages of life—all that damn thing needed to finish it off was an open coffin.

He had to make Moira understand.

"I spent hours in this room each time Dad had another attack, and then later, when he was dying. And I was here for Travis last spring and again, a month ago, just before you came to town." He grimaced as he looked at the photos on the wall again. "They've tried to perk the place up, but there might as well be prayer stalls and incense here—no one is in this room unless something really serious is happening on the other side of those damn doors."

He didn't know if Moira understood what he was saying or not, but at least she was looking him in the face now, which was a big improvement over the rehearsal, when she'd reverted to ice princess again.

Curiosity had been written all over the other cast members' faces, but he'd put on one of the greatest shows of his life, laughing and exchanging clever quips, pretending he wasn't at all concerned that Moira had frozen up on him.

But apparently the ice dam was broken because she was listening to him now too.

"Sammy said something about your father having the same thing."

He nodded. "Dad's first bout was four years ago, just after Travis and Rocky were married." He ran his hand through his hair again. It helped him think. "He was in and out of the hospital for six months. I was still living in Dallas and came down on weekends. Travis had his hands full with the ranch so it was mainly Mom and Rocky taking care of Dad."

"What was the diagnosis?"

Rafe snorted his derision. "Gastritis, always gastritis. But it didn't matter what he ate or how many pills he took, the pain always came back."

He sprang up and moved around the room, then stopped to glare at that damned white-haired couple on the wall, each of them bursting with health and vitality.

The rage grew in him—maybe it had never left him—and he smacked his fist into his hand.

"Sixty-two is too young to die! Hell, my great-grandfather Gilbert lived till he was ninety-five, and that was back in the day! And my grandfather made it to eighty-three before he got careless walking a horse into a travel van!"

Moira came over and put her arm around his back. "I'm so sorry. It's hard to lose people you love." Her voice was soft and calming.

Goddamn! Didn't anything unnerve her but that goddamn scar? Didn't she understand what he was goddamn saying?

He turned on her. "My father died on my watch! And now my brother is dying! And I can't do a fucking thing about it!"

She dropped her arm and stepped back a pace.

For the first time, she understood Rafe McAllister. He was a lot more than a sexy, easy-living, howdy-ma'am guy who had the wherewithal to dabble in theater. A lot more than the talented architect who designed horse barns and renovated old schools, more than the tough rancher who guarded his herd against snakes, hogs, coyotes, and panthers. Rafe was driven, just like the people she'd grown up around. The actors, the directors, the producers, the cameramen, the makeup artists, even the script girl—everyone on the lot—they had that same fire within them, and they crashed through impassible barriers every day to reach impossible goals.

But what Rafe had taken on was the total responsibility for his chunk of the world. He'd designed a prize-winning barn for his father, repurposed Bosque Bend's old high school, and was laying down plans to gentrify the whole block around the Huaco Theater.

And now he wanted to stave off death.

She locked eyes with him. "Rafe, if I knew a magic word, I'd heal Travis for you." She reached out to him. "And I apologize about…yesterday. I wanted to…be with you, but I…panicked."

He gave her a searching look, then crushed her in his embrace and claimed her lips. The overbright room dimmed to a haze, and she looped her arms around his neck.

Rafe was a good man, a caring man. He loved his family and supported his community.

He was also the man she had danced close and slow with, the man in whose arms she'd come alive, a man whose fire had lit her like a torch from the first moment she saw him.

Whatever he wanted from her, she would give.

Chapter Thirteen

The sky was overcast on Thursday morning, and the air was still, its silence broken only by a few reluctant birdcalls.

After Astrid left, Moira put on her denim jacket and took Ivanhoe out for a walk to show off his extra-extra-large Batman outfit and look at the cul-de-sac's Halloween decorations. Ghosts and skeletons danced from trees, gleeful witches rode their broomsticks across windows, and zombies stalked the yards.

She shivered as a gust of wind swooped down the street, tumbling autumn leaves across the pavement and reminding her that she didn't live in Pasadena anymore. Ivanhoe seemed to be enjoying the weather, but he had a thick fur coat on. She, on the other hand, was freezing her tail off.

Which meant she couldn't put getting winter coats off any longer, especially since Astrid was off at eleven today. They'd drive into town and do some shopping. She'd throw lunch at Billie Joe's Calico Cat into the bargain.

The minute Dr. Sjoberg dropped Astrid off, Moira hustled her sister into the Toyota.

"Happy day before Halloween. It's coat-buying day."

As she backed out of the driveway, Mrs. Fuller glanced up from the vicious-looking, red-eyed spiders she was affixing to her tombstones and yelled hello.

Astrid waved back, then tilted her head in thought and turned to Moira.

"I don't get it. Mrs. Fuller's been really sweet, but she talks smack about the McAllisters all the time. Yesterday evening, when I was walking Ivanhoe, she told me that everybody in Bosque Bend knows that Rafe's great-grandfather stole the C Bar M from the Colbys, that the ranch really belongs to Rocky and her mother."

Moira gave Astrid a quick glance. "Any idea where Mrs. Fuller is getting this from?"

"She keeps talking about Alice and Chub. I think Alice is her daughter."

"Alice and Chub—Delilah said they were her aunt and uncle so Chub must be Beth's brother. Delilah also said they were mad at her daddy." Moira sighed. "Families get messed up sometimes."

Astrid raised an eyebrow. "Don't we know it."

* * *

An hour later, bundled up in their new coats, Moira and Astrid braved the elements and walked down the street to the Calico Cat, which was located in a century-old bakery just off the square. Billie Joe herself met them at the door, seated them at a corner table, then bustled off to greet Mayor Traylor and his wife as they came in.

Astrid hung her quilted A-line coat on the back of her chair and looked around at the sea of white tablecloths, the hardwood slat floor, and the glistening brass rails of the balcony.

"This place is awesome. I love the border thing all around the wall—those calico cats tumbling all over one another. And the balcony looks so glamorous, like something out of cowboy times."

Moira nodded. "Billie Joe really has something going on here."

The woman might not be able to tell her left foot from her right, but she sure knew how to set up a restaurant.

Astrid laid her menu down and looked across the table at her sister. "Hey, we really made a hit at Overton's Department Store with that Dolph guy. I thought he'd start salivating any minute. And the reductions he gave us on our coats! I think he would have ended up giving them to us free if we'd really pushed."

"That was Dolph Junior. His father, Dolph Senior, owns the store. There's a younger son too—Buck's in the cast, but he's shy around women."

Billie Joe came back to take their orders. "I'm really glad you came by today, Moira. The most wonderful thing has happened. A Hollywood reporter came by this morning and said he wants to write about the show—well, he asked about you mostly. Xandra and Fleurette—they always eat breakfast here—wouldn't talk to him, but I told him how much we all like you. He said he had to leave right away to cover some kind of story in Houston, but he'd be back before our opening night because the story had to be in by then or he'd lose the assignment. Isn't that great? Hollywood is interested in our *Gift of the Magi*!"

"What's his name?"

"Boyd Yancey—do you know him?"

"Not that I can remember."

"I'll bring you his card. He wants you to contact him."

She gave Billie Joe a practiced smile. "Thanks, Billie Joe. I'll see if I can work him in."

Like hell she would. The second anniversary of Colin's death had just passed, and she had a pretty good idea what Boyd Yancey really wanted to interview her about.

She rolled her lips in. But he wasn't going to get a word out of her, now or ever.

* * *

Rafe's voice called out to Moira as she crossed the street to the museum, and she stayed at the curb to wait for him.

Her heart beat faster as he came closer.

Yeah, she was stuck on this guy.

He took her arm.

"But it's Thursday, Rafe. What about Delilah?"

"Mom is staying at the house tonight to finish Delilah's Halloween costume—she wants to be a fairy so she can have a magic wand to hit boys over the head and turn them into frogs—so I thought I'd drive in and practice with the chorus for a few minutes, then visit Travis in the hospital. Will that work out?"

"Fine. How's Travis doing?"

"If nothing else happens, they're sending him home tomorrow. Rocky's got a truckload of Jell-O waiting for him."

They entered the building and started up the steps.

"Hey, I've been wonderin'—what are you wearin' for the Pumpkin Party?"

What was she wearing? She gave him questioning glance. "You mean long sleeves or short sleeves? I guess it depends on the weather."

"No, I mean, what kind of *costume* will you be wearin'? Angel, devil, French maid?" He gave her a theatrical leer and twirled a nonexistent mustache.

She still didn't understand. "I wasn't planning on one. I haven't worn a Halloween costume since I was a child." And even then, it had been as an extra in *A Nightmare on Elm Street* knockoff. "Are—are you dressing up for Halloween?"

"Of course. We all do. Why should the kids have all the fun?"

"What are you going to be?"

His eyes sparkled at her. "Let's make it a surprise."

They reached the top of the stairs and walked into the auditorium together. Every head in the house turned. By the time they got halfway down the aisle, the applause had started.

Moira gave everyone a smile of appreciation, then got down to business and called the whole cast to come up onstage so Vashti could run them through both versions of "Street Song."

With Halloween being on Friday, they only had one more day to rehearse this week, and she wanted to shore up the first act as much as possible.

Everything sounded good. Rafe's strong bass wove in and out of the chorus, and when the children's high-pitched voices were added, it would be perfect.

Not that she was really aware of anything but Rafe.

He stayed halfway through the rest of the scene as Phil and Micaela went through the "Walking Along with You, Down the Avenue" sequence, in which they enjoy a window-shopping stroll down the street. It set up the story. First Micaela admired a particular hat in the milliner's window and sang "Ribbons, Feathers, and Flowers." Then Phil, after checking out his pocket watch, came back at her with "Lovely Locks," insisting that he didn't want her to wear anything that covered up her beautiful hair.

The scene was going well for a first run-through, Moira thought, but it would be better if Phil could bring himself to act more like he was attracted to Micaela.

Next, she called Sergio up for the major Dreamer scene so he would feel comfortable if—*when* he needed to step in.

Her antennae went up. She hadn't realized how good Sergio was. If she'd been the one doing the casting, he'd have gotten the role over Travis. No matter what he sang, Travis's baritone had a country-western delivery, while Sergio's tenor was pure musical theater. And he could sing the high notes without resorting to falsetto.

"Nice work!" she called up to him.

Sergio ducked his head in her direction, then hopped offstage and joined Buck, Desdemona, and Sammy in the back of the auditorium.

Moira nodded toward the ballerina. "Okay, let's see what 'Della's Dream' looks like again, and then I'll let everyone go for the evening."

Desdemona hurried down the aisle, holding her dance shoes by their ribbons, then sat on a prop chair to change out of her tennies and clomped over, flat-footed, to stand beside Micaela. The combination of stylishly ragged jeans, an over-large Eisenhower Consolidated T-shirt, and stiffened shoes was a picture Moira would not easily forget.

Moira signaled Vashti to begin. This scene was tricky—Desdemona was supposed to reflect Micaela the same way that the Dreamer reflected Phil, but this time the reflection was expressed in dance. Moira watched as Micaela looked into a mirror that wasn't there, faced the audience that wasn't there, and began to sing, confiding her heart's desires.

Three measures in, Carmen lifted her violin, cuing Desdemona, who'd been frozen like a statue in the background, to begin her slow, graceful, wake-up movements.

Moira relaxed back in her seat. So far, so good. Later she'd have to bring in the other ballerinas—the older Loughlin girl and two chorus members. Like every other chorus member, the three girls were double cast, which meant their costume change before the next scene was going to have to be lightning fast.

Desdemona had the stage now, with Micaela providing a soft, wordless melody in the background. The two women related to each other, blending into one. There was chemistry between them, as if they cared for each other, which was exactly what Phil's scenes with Micaela did not have.

Moira applauded loudly and wished everyone a happy Halloween.

Oh God, she still didn't have a costume

* * *

Ivanhoe yipped a welcome from the backyard as the doorbell rang. Rafe was here, but Moira wasn't sure she was ready yet.

She'd tried for Mexican senorita, an easy costume for a couple of California girls. Her spangled fiesta skirt and the flamenco shoes were authentic, but Astrid's short-sleeved, heavily embroidered peasant blouse was a leftover from high school, and the red sash she'd knotted around her waist had started life as a fashion scarf. The little black velvet purse with the gold chain was just something that had shown up in their luggage.

She looped her neck with a couple of yards of red wooden beads from H-E-B's Christmas aisle and looked in the mirror again. Then just for kicks, she pushed the blouse off her shoulders—after all, adult Halloween costumes were usually outrageously sexy. But no, that was too obvious.

Besides, Rafe would have Delilah with him.

The doorbell rang and she shrugged the blouse back into place. Damn—part of her wanted to run for the hills, and another part of her wanted to throw herself into Rafe's arms and beg him to carry her away to his knightly castle on his white horse—preferably not Bella—and make wild, passionate love to her.

Personally, she was rooting for the knightly castle scenario.

As she walked down the hall, she could hear Rafe trying to convince Astrid to come along with them again. He'd called earlier in the day to be sure Astrid knew she was invited, but she'd insisted that she'd rather stay at the house with Ivanhoe.

Moira slung the little purse over her arm and picked up the rose-patterned shawl Astrid had contributed, then made her grand entry into the living room.

A charming strawberry-blonde fairy awaited her. Enid had done a top-notch job. Delilah's costume came complete with delicately tinted gauze wings, a cape in iridescent pastels, shoes that twinkled on and off, and a wand made of tinsel strung through a narrow plastic tube—not exactly the sort of thing that could cause a preschool boy any damage, Moira noted.

The fairy was accompanied by the sexiest-looking pirate Moira had ever seen. Cowboy Rafe was a turn-on, but Pirate Rafe raised the bar with his knee-high stage boots, black-and-red striped pants that looked like they were painted on, and a black frock coat over a white shirt unlaced enough to reveal a spread of russet chest hair.

He swept the tricornered hat off his head and bent his knee to execute the perfect pirate bow.

"Cap'n Hook McAllister at your service, ma'am."

Delilah giggled and grabbed at his leg. "Dad-dee."

Rafe picked his daughter up in his arms and gave her a quick kiss. "And here's my Tinkerbell."

Moira fluttered her eyelashes and played along. "Alas, Cap'n. I know naught of the high seas. I am but an innocent senorita on her way to a Halloween party in Texas."

"We'll give you a lift in our galleon, then. It's parked at the curb." He looked at his watch, not exactly regulation equipment for a seventeenth-century pirate. "And we better get a move on. The gates to Wonderland have already opened."

Astrid walked out with them to light the jolly-faced jack-o'-lantern on the front porch, and Rafe made one last try at including her in the outing. "Are you sure you want to stay at the house? The carnival is a lot of fun, and costumes aren't mandatory."

"Thanks, but not this year." She stood up and looked at the canine face staring at her through the screen door. "Ivanhoe needs me. This is his first Halloween."

Moira waved her sister good-bye, then watched as Rafe lifted Delilah into the backseat and strapped her in.

Now it was her turn. His breath whispered in her ear as his palms slid up under her breasts and his thumbs found her nipples.

"All hands on deck."

* * *

Rafe parked behind his office, which was the nearest he was going to be able to get to the square tonight. The night wind was brisk, but once they got inside the grounds, the crowd would cut the wind and generate enough heat to warm them up.

He ushered his ladies across the street and stopped at the ticket booth set up under the light of a pumpkin-clad street-light, ran his credit card, and received a couple of treat bags and a thick roll of tickets, then walked into the carnival with Delilah on one side of him and Moira the other. He'd never invited any of his other girlfriends along on an outing with Delilah—it hadn't seemed right—but he hadn't had a second thought about inviting Moira.

She leaned into him. "What are all the tickets for? I thought you said the Pumpkin Party is free."

Rafe took her arm again, and a shiver of heat coiled through her. Maybe there was a spark of something else too, but she didn't want to identify it. Sex would be the beginning and end of their relationship. They'd both agreed on that.

"The booths are free, but the tickets are for things like the carnival rides and the fortune-teller. We also use them to vote on the costume contest. A Schuler usually wins that one—the family votes as a bloc."

A bloc? His family was large enough and were enough in agreement with one another that they would vote as a bloc? Her family couldn't even stay married.

She turned her head from side to side as they walked down the crowded aisles. The setup seemed to be like every other community fair she'd been to—a village of tarpaulin tents sheltering tables and upright display panels. Three rows of tents marched down the south sidewalk and onto the lawn of the courthouse. To the east, she could see the top of a small Ferris wheel over the trees.

A voice boomed out in front of them. "Rafe! Long time, no see!"

Moira stood back as a large, balding man holding a little boy by the hand stopped in the middle of the aisle to give Rafe a smacking high five, then motioned to his entourage to join him.

Rafe introduced everyone rapid-fire. "Moira, meet Great-uncle Tiny, Uncle Tom and Aunt Miriam, Cousin Miriam, Cousin Julie, Cousin Helen, Cousin Tom, and Cousin John. The young-un is Cousin Ryan." Moira nodded and smiled, but for once, her magic memory machine fizzled out on her. There was no way she could process so many names and faces at once, especially since each and every one of them was dressed as a vampire.

Delilah focused on the little boy, raised her magic fairy wand, and yelled "Frog!" but her father caught her arm before it could descend on the boy's bat-eared hood. Swooping his daughter up in his arms, Rafe apologized profusely to his great-uncle's family and moved quickly down the row.

Five minutes later, after dodging a group of screaming teenagers carrying pillowcases full of loot, Rafe was hailed by another group of relatives.

Moira was caught somewhere between wonder and horror. How could anyone have such a big a family? All she had, besides Astrid and her brother, were Gram, Gramp, and Kimiko. Gramp's extended family was still in Norway, and Gram was an only child who had produced an only child, while her mother, Kimiko, was missing in action—and God only knows what had become of her father.

By the time they reached the end of the row, Delilah's first treat bag was almost full and Moira had been greeted by the museum docent, a teacher she'd met at Eisenhower Consolidated, the newspaper delivery boy, the grocery store clerk she'd bought Donna Sue's gift from, several cast members, and a number of people she'd swear she'd never seen before in her life.

So, this was how it felt to be on the A-list, to be recognized by everyone at every turn.

They made the turn into the next row and Rafe plowed on ahead.

"I want to see how the fishin' booth is workin' out. Cousin Sharon's husband and I put the thing together this mornin', and I need to make sure those struts are still holdin'."

As they approached the stall, the supervising mothers rose from their lawn chairs to greet Rafe. He introduced them to Moira, then disappeared behind the booth.

"We think the world of Rafe," the lead mother told her. "He's so good about helping us when we need something for the preschool. Are—you two—uh—a couple?"

Rafe reappeared before she could answer, thank goodness, and reported that the booth would last another hundred years, then called out to a man coming down the aisle who was dressed in knee britches, neck ruffles, and a long jacket.

"Hey, Merv! You're wearin' my costume from *1776*!"

The man grinned. "Back up there, Rafe! I rented this outfit fair and square from the theater guild booth!"

Theater guild booth? Moira gave Rafe a questioning look, but he just took her arm and pulled her forward.

"Moira, this is my cousin Mervin Hruska—well, actually he's a second cousin on the McAllister side. In real life, Mervin is Bosque Bend's police chief, but we'll have to let him off duty long enough tonight to go fly a kite and discover electricity."

Moira smiled and nodded—she'd been doing that a lot tonight—that was about all she could do with loudspeakers on both sides of her.

Mervin motioned toward Delilah, who had her thumb in her mouth and was clinging to Rafe's leg. "Looks to me like the fairy princess is getting sleepy."

Rafe picked his daughter up and she leaned into his shoulder. "Yeah, we'd better move along. She's about to get her second wind, and you don't want to be anywhere around when that happens."

Moira grabbed Rafe's arm as they continued down the aisle. "What was your cousin talking about? What theater guild booth?"

"Donna Sue established it a couple of years ago. We rent out our old costumes for Halloween. It generates a few bucks and a lot of publicity. My pirate costume is a combination of *1776* and *The Sound of Music*." He made the turn into the third row and picked up his pace. "The booth's not far down. We usually keep it open as long as we can in case someone needs a last-minute costume, but at this time of night, Carmen Atherton and Billie Joe Semple will be packin' everything away."

After fist bumping another contingent of cousins, Rafe stopped at a double booth, pushed aside a metal clothes rack blocking the front of it, and called out into the dimly lit tent.

"Hey there, Carmen. How are things goin'?"

A piano introduction Moira recognized came out of a loudspeaker down the row, and she looked around as a light soprano began singing "Sixteen Going on Seventeen" from *The Sound of Music*.

"What a sweet voice," she commented. *Perfect for a production of* Cinderella.

Carmen emerged from the booth. "That's Desdemona Benton. Her brother did a number from *Gift of the Magi* earlier, and after that—sorry, Rafe—Percy Washington absolutely butchered your solo from *1776*. Billie Joe is backstage now, waiting in line to belt out 'St. Louis Blues.'"

She took a dog costume down from the rack, folded it, and laid it in a large storage box. "I think Phil's performing after her, and then Micaela and I are doing a duet to finish off the show. There's been a good crowd all evening."

As they turned down the last leg of the carnival, just as Rafe had predicted, Delilah woke up and insisted on being put down. After running down the row ahead of them to collect another bagful of treats, she headed toward the rides and got in line behind Kathleen Loughlin and her two little girls.

Moira moved forward to visit with the accompanist. She liked her and wanted to get to know her better. Besides, Kathleen might be able to tell her what was going on with the Fontaine sisters, who still couldn't seem to decide whether she was for real or not.

"This is really a community celebration—treats, games, rides. But what's in that tent over there with the stars and crescent moon on it?"

Kathleen's face lit up. "That's Madame Drabarni. You've got to visit her. She's sweet to the kids, and tells adults what she thinks they need to know. It's five tickets, but the money goes to the county food pantry." She moved closer to Moira so her daughters wouldn't hear. "It's Josie Apodaca. She does it every year."

"I don't know if…"

Rafe laughed and ripped five tickets off his roll. "Take these and go say hello to Josie for me. I'll be over here with the bumper cars for a while. Delilah's a demon behind the wheel."

Moira walked over to the closed tent and handed the tickets to the turbaned attendant. He lifted a flap and bowed from the waist.

"Enter. Madame Drabarni awaits you."

Chapter Fourteen

In the dim light of a brass lamp, Josie looked like a Babylonian empress. Her purple robe was embroidered with astrological signs, her head was wrapped in a gold cloth, and long, barbaric earrings brushed against her shoulders. She sat behind a round table covered by a green damask drape, on which rested a small handbell and a pack of tarot cards.

As far as dramatic settings go, Josie was right on.

Moira sat down across from her and waited for a spark of recognition, but Josie, her expression impassive, stayed in character. With a slow, deliberate movement, she picked up Moira's hand and studied her palm, then dealt the cards, then swept them aside. Her voice was deep and drawn out, as if from a great distance.

"I see a man who burns with the fire of righteousness. I see a woman who endures. He is the flame, an' she is the earth. She will anchor him, an' his fire will cleanse her."

Wow! Okay—she got it. Rafe was the flame and she was

the earth, but what the heck did the rest of it mean? That they were somehow destined to be together? That they would complete each other? Not that she believed in seers, of course, especially one she'd bought used furniture from.

Besides, she had no idea how to "anchor" Rafe—he seemed to be able to take care of himself—and doubted that anyone could "cleanse" her. She was a lost cause.

Josie rang the bell. "Next customer."

The first thing Moira saw when she emerged from the tent was Rafe's head flaming under the artificial lights. *How the hell had Madame Drabarni set that up?*

He took her hand. "How'd your séance go?"

Moira managed a light laugh. "Josie put on a good show." No way she would repeat a single word of Josie's pronouncement.

Thinking it over, she decided that "burns with the fire of righteousness" could apply to a minister or a policeman, even to Bosque Bend's newspaper editor. And women were frequently described as being "of the earth."

Maybe it was Madame Drabarni's standard line.

The crowd had thinned and the wind was kicking up. Rafe opened the flaps on Delilah's cape and pulled it around her for warmth while Moira shifted her shawl up on her shoulders. He glanced toward the dark side of the square.

"The fireworks show is about to start, but Delilah's worn herself out rammin' that little car around so I think we better call it a day."

Moira fell into step beside him as they walked toward the street.

"You should have seen her go after the other kids' cars. If they hadn't been padded all over, I'd be facin' a couple of lawsuits. I think she's gonna be another TexAnn."

"What's your sister like?"

"TexAnn liked to keep Travis and me in line when we were kids, and now that she's a state representative, she's keeping all of Texas in line."

Moira heard the *pow-pow-pow* of Roman candles and looked back to see a brilliant series of starbursts lit the dark sky. The Pumpkin Party was coming to an end.

Next, they'd deliver Delilah to his cousin's house for a sleepover, and then the two of them would go out to Omar's for a beer. Then he'd take her home, and she and Astrid could gorge themselves on leftover Milky Ways—a satisfying end to a satisfying evening, but there was a restlessness in her that wanted more.

She rested her eyes as Rafe drove down a couple of streets to an older neighborhood near the square.

He parked in front of a Craftsman-style house with a happy-looking scarecrow and a parade of child-friendly plastic pumpkins decorating the front porch, then lifted Delilah and her little pink suitcase out of the truck and walked her up to the door, which had just been opened by a smiling woman with hair almost as red as his.

Moira's heart lurched as he bent down to hug and kiss his daughter good night.

How wonderful to be a beloved child, to have a warm, caring father like Rafe. She wouldn't recognize her own father if she met him on the street.

* * *

Rafe was amused by the way that Cousin Sharon's eyes kept flitting to the dually the whole time she was welcoming Delilah, obviously trying to figure out the identity of his date. With a pair of active twins on her hands, Sharon didn't get out much. She must be the only person in Bosque Bend who didn't know he was seeing Moira Farrar.

He headed back to the truck, pulled himself into the cab, and looked over at Moira. The night shadows emphasized her high cheekbones, the sensuous curve of her lips, the clean line of her throat. And that Mexican costume of hers was sexy as hell. He liked the way the skirt swung and twisted with her every move, and he'd swear that blouse had elastic in the neckline.

His body stirred with interest, and he played with the idea of suggesting she move over into the seat beside him.

No, Rafe. Baby steps. Let her be. Didn't risk setting her off again.

He worked his way back to Austin Avenue, and ten minutes later, they were on the highway. Rafe adjusted his cruise control to an easy fifty miles per hour. Away from the city lights, the night was pitch-black—great for Halloween, but dangerous for whitetails trying to cross the road. And for the drivers who encountered them.

Moira's hoop earrings gleamed with reflected light as she turned her head to look at BUY-1-GET-5-FREE as they drove by. It was all lit up and doing a land-office business.

"Looks like a lot of people are buying fireworks."

Was she really thinking about fireworks or about when he stopped there when she first came to town and he'd suggested they have an affair? They'd come a long way since then. Maybe he could even get her to move over to the center seat when he took her home.

"Yeah. People around here like to celebrate Halloween big. I saw some of Josie's kinfolks parking their RVs in the back of the lot last week. They always come down a couple of days early to stock the shelves."

He turned off onto the ranch-to-market road and put on his brights so he wouldn't miss the cutoff to Omar's. Pranksters usually made off with the sign about this time every year.

He wasn't happy about having to park on the road, but Good Times was overflowing. Omar would probably sell enough beer and ribs this evening to carry him through to next Halloween.

He lifted Moira out of the car. She pulled her shawl around herself and moved closer to him. "I didn't realize how dark it was."

She was shivering, even under that shawl. He'd better get her inside right quick.

The bouncer stationed on the porch nodded recognition as they walked in. Apparently Uncle Omar had his muscle wearing glow-in-the-dark skeleton outfits again this year.

Rafe looked around. Good Times was crowded all the way up to the stage, probably violating every fire regulation on the book. And, as usual, the noise was at jet-takeoff level. He and Moira would have to talk mouth to ear to communicate.

No problem there. Maybe if he whispered in her ear, she'd follow him anywhere.

Now to make his way through the happy horde of superheroes, witches, vampires, and popular TV characters to get to the long tables against the wall. He took Moira's hand, straightening his elbow so her hip would brush against him with every step.

Damn, the place was even more crowded than last year.

Which table had the theater guild ended up with? Omar made a killing renting those tables out on nights like this, what with everyone from the Floravista Socialights the teachers' union to the city council vying for reservations.

Hey, was that Phil Schoenfeldt standing up and waving at him?

He took a firm grip on Moira's hand and maneuvered her toward the table.

Phil, who'd obviously rented the George Washington costume from *1776*, stood up to greet them as they reached the table, while his wife raised her palm and said "How!" in accordance with her Indian costume. Faux fringed buckskin decorated every seam, and the band around her forehead sported what looked like one of Omar's ostrich feathers.

After some seat switching involving Billie Joe and Deborah Washington, Rafe managed to get Moira both across from him and sitting next to Judy Schoenfeldt. He wanted to keep her within reach, but he also wanted her to have the opportunity to get acquainted with the woman who wrote up the playbill.

Moira took a sip of the mug of beer that Rafe had passed to her and squeezed her eyes shut. Definitely not a lite beer.

She pushed the mug away and greeted Phil's wife with an easy smile. "*Hola!* I'm Moira Farrar, and I'm a Mexican senorita. You're an Indian maiden. Right?"

"Spot on. I'm Judy Schoenfeldt, and I rented Pocahontas from the guild booth but have no idea what play it's from."

"Rafe told me you're putting together the playbill." Thank God she didn't have to shout. The table being against the wall meant that most of the crowd noise stayed out in front of them.

"It's my thing. I was a journalism major, and I write features for some of the area newspapers." Judy leaned toward her as if to get a scoop. "How's it going with *Gift of the Magi*?"

"Terrific! The story is perfect for Christmas—so heart-warming—and the cast is great! Everyone's going to love it!" Which was what she would tell anybody who asked, even if she was tearing her hair out after a bad rehearsal—or was gritting her teeth about a tenor who treated his leading lady like she had a communicable disease.

"Phil is really impressed by how you're pulling it all together. He says you're just what we needed—a real pro."

Moira stifled her intimations of inadequacy in favor of insipid modesty. "I just hope I can do the play justice." And she did want to make *Gift of the Magi* everything it could be and should be, but she also wanted to keep her job.

Judy glanced toward her husband, who was having a heated conversation with a man sitting at the next table. "Phil loves to sing, but he's not the *best* actor in the world."

"He has a gorgeous voice. It's a joy to work with him." She could scarcely tell his wife that Phil was pretty near the *worst* actor in the world.

Phil interrupted to ask Judy about their children's babysitter, and Moira looked around at Omar's Halloween decor. Strings of orange lights were looped across the walls, hollow-eyed gauze ghosts hung from the rafters, and plastic skulls lit up every table. Nothing to write home about, but it got the idea across.

Suddenly Judy raised up in her chair, and Moira realized something was going on up front. She looked at the stage area, then at the stage, then caught Rafe's attention across the table.

"They're setting up a microphone. Is a band playing tonight?"

Rafe turned around to look. "No band, but there's an open mike, and the karaoke machine is fully loaded. Omar's spreadin' his vampire cape like he's gettin' ready to sing, which means it's time for us to hit the dance floor."

Moira left her shawl draped on the chair. With so many people crowded into the building, she was almost too warm. And Rafe, she knew, would warm her up even more.

The saccharine strains of "Love Me Tender" filled the room as Rafe took her in his arms. She laid her head on his chest and closed her eyes as they swayed to the music.

She didn't want to leave the dance floor—ever. She and Rafe were as close as they could get with clothes on. Her breasts rubbed against his chest, his leg nudged against a very sensitive part of her, and his erection pressed into her belly.

Someone yelled, something crashed, and the music stopped.

A trio of bouncers in skeleton suits cut through the crowd to get to the fight that had broken out around the karaoke machine, apparently over who was next in line. Beer bottles flew through the air and women started screaming.

Rafe hustled Moira back to their table.

"It's the annual Halloween riot," he said, putting the shawl around her shoulders. "Time for us to be getting' out of here."

The cold night wind bit into Moira as they walked out the door. Rafe kept an arm around her shoulders while they walked down the parking lot to the road, but she couldn't stop her teeth from chattering. Dear God, the shawl wasn't enough. She was freezing!

He lifted her into the dually, and she scrambled over to the center seat, as far away from the cold as she could get, then snuggled against him when he climbed into the truck. He turned on the heater and took her into his arms.

Everything that was female in her responded to him. To Rafe the Red, Rafe of the sparkling eyes, Rafe the rancher, the architect, the music man, the father, the brother, the son. She lifted her face to him. To face Rafe, the lover.

His finger drifted across her ripening lips. Then his mouth found hers, and he kissed her, rolling his face from side to side to massage her lips. She didn't know a kiss could be so fulfilling and so devastating at the same time. Her head was spinning.

She sank against his chest, and he moved his hand down from her throat to caress her arm—stroking, lightly stroking—and occasionally leaned down to kiss her cheek. She closed her eyes to maintain the bliss that was overwhelming her like a warm mantle.

It was like the forever moment on the dance floor—herself

cuddled against Rafe's warmth, inside the closed cab, with all the world locked out.

His hand touched her breast, and she sucked in a deep breath.

She wanted him so much it hurt, but was *this* where it was going to happen? In the front-seat cab of a truck parked on the road below a honky-tonk?

She didn't care where it happened. She could trust Big Red. It was as if Colin had never existed.

His hand moved up and down her arm in an ever-changing pattern, then touched the tender underside of her arm.

He was testing her, searching for her scar. She willed herself not to react.

His finger located the ridge and gently traced a circle around the scar. Then he stopped and looked at her. His eyes sparkled in the darkness. The car was quiet except for the light hum of the car heater.

He drew in a rough breath. His voice was a whisper.

"Come home with me, darlin'. Stay the night."

No, I can't, I can't! Colin…

But Colin was dead and she was alive. And going home with Rafe wouldn't really mean anything. It wouldn't be the sort of relationship she'd had with Colin. There wouldn't be any emotional commitment. It would be sex only—body pleasing body.

She made the same decision she'd made in the horse barn, but this time she was committing herself to a lot more than lunch.

"Yes."

Chapter Fifteen

Rafe ditched his scabbard and pirate hat in the truck and walked Moira quickly into the warm house.

He hadn't started out the evening with the idea of bringing her home, but the heat they'd built up on the dance floor, then in the truck, had made it the only option—unless they slid down on the seat of the dually and that sexy skirt got tossed up then and there.

The foyer light came on automatically, and he flung his pirate coat over the newel post.

"My room is upstairs."

She wound her arms around his neck, and her voice dropped to a husky whisper. "Show me the way."

A forest fire raced through him. He lifted her off her feet, swung her around, and rained pinprick kisses on her closed eyelids, down her small, perfectly shaped nose, and across to her exotic cheekbones. He wanted to get her up the stairs *muy pronto*, but first he needed a taste of her.

Just one taste.

His lips wandered along the edge of her hairline and explored the tender skin in back of her ear. She whimpered and her eyes closed.

One taste wasn't enough.

He traced a silky eyebrow and kissed her eyelid and the curve of her cheeks, then her sweet, sweet lips. She opened her mouth to him, and he played with her tongue and, without breaking the kiss, boosted her two steps up the stairs so their faces would be on the same level.

She dropped her arms down and her hands pressed against his buttocks so his erection prodded the juncture of her legs.

Wow! They'd better make it up the stairs fast before he lost it. He managed to move her up a couple more steps. Then his hands rested on her shoulders to hold her still as his mouth moved down her throat to the neckline of her blouse, nipping and kissing all along the way.

She moaned and rotated her pelvis against him.

It was going to be a miracle if they made it to the landing.

The beads were the first thing to go. He lifted them off her neck, and they rattled down to the foyer floor. Next was the blouse, which—the hell—he couldn't get out from under that damn red sash. Growling in frustration, he pulled the elastic neck of her blouse down over her shoulders, then past her strapless bra so it rode around her waist.

A couple of deft movements later and the bra tumbled down the stairs to join the beads in the foyer.

He paused to look at her, at those sweet, soft mounds that had sent a wave of heat through him every time he thought about that evening in the museum. God, they were so per-fect—vanilla cupcakes topped by ruby cherries rigid with de-sire.

He dipped his head to taste one, then the other as she clung to him, arching her back as if in offering. She shuddered and began taking high-pitched gasps of breath.

Damn—he still couldn't get that sash undone. The hell with it. He leaned down to tease her nipples again as his hands moved up and down her back.

She switched her head back and forth, then suddenly grasped the laces of his pirate shirt, ripped it open, and ground her breasts against his bared chest.

To hell with foreplay!

He lifted her farther up the steps, but had to stop to run his fingers over her satin-smooth shoulders and give her a hard, thorough kiss, darting his tongue into her mouth in promise of what was to come.

Her hand caressed the bulge in his pirate pants, which he suspected were made of pure spandex and would be murder to get out of.

Coming up for air to keep himself from exploding, he moved her up a few more steps and took a quick look up at the landing. Only a couple more to go. He wasn't about to try any-thing on the stairs without an ambulance crew standing by.

He dug his hand up under the red sash to work on the knot of the sash again, but it held, so he tried to pull the skirt out from under it. Then, when he tugged on it, the waistband stayed under the sash, parting company with the rest of the skirt. The thing was too damn fragile to live.

Only one more step to go. Moira looked around and moved up on her own.

Rafe breathed a sigh of relief and brought her against himself. They were skin on skin now. Things were getting real.

God, she was hungry. His little soldier was as hot as they get. And she wanted to run her own show.

Her hazel eyes were dark, her cheeks were painted with color, and her lips were swollen and red. He yanked once more at the sash, and finally it came free.

Now all she had on were big hoop earrings and skimpy purple panties.

He peeled down his pirate pants and got rid of his stocking boots.

She reached for his throbbing erection, but he grabbed her wrist. No way this was gonna be a solo flight. One touch and he'd be gone.

He took her down to the thick designer rug, and they came together in a frenzy, kissing and stroking and panting as if they were trying use up every breath of air in the house. Moira was a wild woman, and when he tried to hold back on her, it seemed to arouse her even more.

She pulled off her panties, spread her legs, and bumped up against him. "Now, now, now!"

He slid himself all the way into her body. She was slick and ready. Her eyes closed and her head rolled back in ecstasy.

He began a rhythmic pump, and he knew this first time wouldn't last long. He also knew there was going to be a second time tonight. Maybe a third.

Her nails raked his back, urging him to move faster.

Forget finesse. Forget timing. This was a jungle mating, hard and fast, and she was driving it. Her hips pushed up to meet his every thrust, and her inner muscles clutched at him as she raced toward her zenith. Then she stiffened, let out a thin, keening cry, and rammed herself up against him as if to join them together for eternity.

Two hard strokes more and he spiraled through the universe, then gradually came back to earth and closed his eyes. Moira was by his side and all was right with the world.

Now he knew what it was like to have his little soldier's intensity focused on him and him alone—and he liked it.

* * *

Moira opened her eyes to morning and studied the patterns of light on the ceiling.

Last night had been unbelievable. She'd been beyond talking or even thinking. All she could do was want, and all she'd wanted was for Rafe to keep his hands on her, his hard body against her, his length inside her.

She looked across the bed. He wasn't there, but a nightwatch plaid robe was. She yawned and moved her shoulders, rotated her hips, and stretched her arms and legs to make sure they still worked, then looked around the room. The only information she had processed last night was that it was large and contained a king-sized bed. Now she could see that the window wall beside the bed had a wrought iron balcony hanging off it, and there was a small sitting room in an L on the other side of the room.

Three sliding doors covered the wall opposite the bed. The doors had been closed last night, but two of them were open now—the bathroom and what looked like an office. The third one was probably a clothes closet.

She sat up and started to push down the covers, then realized that her great view of the back of the ranch down to the barn through the big window meant that anyone on the tarmac would have a great view of her too.

Sticking her arms through the sleeves of the robe, she padded into the bathroom to see if she looked any different this morning. The mirror over the sink—the second sink, the one nearest to the big double shower—told her that her lips were puffy and her hair looked like she'd spent the night rolling around in the upper hall with a man who turned her into a woman she never knew she had in her.

A woman who would be so eager for him that she'd tear his shirt off him and couldn't even wait till they made it up the stairs., She closed her eyes for a second as a wave of heat suffused her, then smiled.

Rafe knew what he was doing, and he did it well.

But today was the morning after, and look at her, wearing a robe that was way too long for her and brushing her teeth with her finger.

She lapped the robe over its cloth belt to keep from tripping as she wandered back into the bedroom to look for anything—*anything*—she could wear.

Too bad there weren't any lightweight curtains around she could take off their rods and pleat into a sexy sari. But maybe she could make a toga for herself out of the sheet. Damn. If she'd known last night was going to be *the* night, she would've packed a suitcase.

"Good mornin' glory!"

Rafe came into the room with a broad smile on his face and the remains of her clothes on his arm. The skirt and her panties would be goners she knew, but Astrid's blouse, her bra, and the flamenco shoes seemed to have survived. He deposited everything on a chair across the room and came over to kiss her forehead.

He hadn't shaved yet, and he hadn't bothered with a shirt or shoes either. His jeans rode low on his hips, and he was looking at her like she was breakfast.

Excitement percolated under her skin. Even on the morning after in the bright light of day, when she should be recovering her right mind, she still wanted him. Rafe McAllister was, plain and simple, the sexiest man alive.

He leaned over and kissed the back of her neck as his hands moved around to cup her breasts. This wouldn't last, but she could enjoy it for now.

She arched back against him.

* * *

It was noon when she awakened again. Oh, damn—she hadn't contacted Astrid to tell her where she was. For all she knew, Astrid had put out a missing persons alert out on her.

She nudged Rafe awake. "I need to tell my sister I'll be home this afternoon, but my cell is in that little black purse I was carrying. Do you know if it's in that pile of clothes you brought up?"

Rafe reached out to his bed stand and handed her a phone. His voice was gravelly with sleep. "Use the landline—and I want you to stay here till Delilah comes home on Sunday."

Moira took in a quick breath and closed her eyes for a second as the familiar spiral of heat wound through her. *Better and better.* "I'll—I'll ask Astrid to bring me some clothes."

His mouth traced the rim of her ear. "Don't dress up on my account, darlin'." He skimmed his hand down her shoulder and along her hip. "I like you just the way you are."

She pulled the sheet around herself as if Astrid could see her over the phone and punched in her sister's number.

"Astrid, I know I should have called you earlier, but I'm at the ranch with Rafe."

"Cool. I figured as much."

"And I—I'm going to be staying another night. Could you bring me some clothes? Jeans, shirts, that sort of thing? The Mexicana outfit isn't going to cut it."

"Sure thing. See you in about thirty minutes. Oh, and before I forget, Billie Joe Semple called this morning and asked if you had heard from Boyd Yancey, whoever he is."

Moira's heart froze.

"He's nobody."

* * *

Rafe turned on the dishwasher. Bacon sandwiches probably weren't Moira's idea of a nourishing breakfast, but it was actually afternoon now.

He'd take her for a tour of the house while their pork grease and white bread settled. She'd seen the master bedroom, of course, and the kitchen and family room, plus she'd had a quick glance at the library the first time she was here, but she hadn't seen the other side of the house.

She hitched up the robe again as he led her through the kitchen door into the large dining room with a long table in it, then reared back in amazement.

"Rafe, it's big enough to seat the entire road show cast of *Wicked*.

He couldn't help but grin. "Mom says it's for the inevitable day when every McAllister and Schuler in America comes to visit at the same time."

She laughed and her eyes swept the walls. "And I like the landscapes. Are they of the ranch?"

He nodded. "One of my aunts did them. She's had a couple of New York shows."

So far, so good. Next came the real show.

He ushered her through the wide doorway into the living room. It was a twin to the family room on the other side of the foyer, but on a lower level. And the mood of the room was unrelentingly modern, with floating-sphere standing lamps and a red leather semicircular sectional.

Then there was the mural stretched across the long wall of the room.

Moira walked along its length, as if trying to comprehend the paintings, the collages, the needlework, small sculptures, and carvings, all mounted on the stark white wall to form a cacophony of style and color. The art would have been daunting if it had been hung in a disciplined row, like in a museum, so instead, he'd crowded the individual pieces up, down, and sideways so that the wall itself became a giant work.

She backed up, bumping into the sectional, then turned to him.

He steeled himself for her reaction.

Was she going to give him some polite crap about it being unique and challenging?

She closed her eyes and shook her head, then took a deep breath.

"This is so strong, Rafe—a gift that keeps on giving. It's like finding a treasure trove—I don't know what to look at first, but I want to examine everything. Where did you get all of the artwork?" She moved up closer to peer at the painting of a woman wearing a mobcap. "Some of it looks quite old."

He rubbed his arms in satisfaction and smiled. His little soldier had not only good taste in men, but also a good eye for art.

"Everything on that wall was created by a Schuler, back to Mom's way-back grandfather who was a travelin' portrait painter during the Revolutionary War."

She indicated a large portrait of a guitarist he'd used to anchor one corner of the mural. "That's Travis, isn't it? Did you do it?"

"Yeah, back in my semiabstract days. I don't do portraits much anymore."

The doorbell gonged, and Moira pulled the collar of the robe around herself. "It's probably Astrid with my clothes."

She gave him a glance that meant she wanted him to make

himself scarce. He understood. Astrid knew they hadn't spent the night playing checkers, but Moira didn't want to throw their relationship in her sister's face.

Yeah, he understood, but it rubbed him the wrong way. There was a back-alley implication that left a bad taste in his mouth. Moira was better than that, and he was too.

* * *

Moira took the drawstring bag of clothes Astrid had dropped off upstairs and opened it on the unmade bed with Rafe looking on.

Jeans, shirts, a heavy sweater, underwear, tennies, boots, toiletries. Exactly what a girl needed who was spending the weekend with her lover.

She reached for a long-sleeved, blue-checked shirt, then hesitated. "Which should I wear, Rafe? Shorts or jeans?"

He picked up a lacy nightie and ran it through his fingers "This for tonight, darlin', but jeans for now. I thought we'd go down to the barn and I could show you the office suite, and then we could take a ride. I need to check on a couple of things." He dropped the nightie on top of her pile. "Travis has only been able to work half days, so we're all tryin' to do a little more. Jimbo Crane is actin' foreman, and the other guys are taking on extra hours. I've sorta shut down my day job for the time being."

He looked out the window as she dressed—as if she had any modesty left after last night.

"Don't get me wrong," he continued. "I'm not givin' up on

architecture. That's the Schuler in me. But the other half of me is McAllister, and I'll live on this land till the day I die."

She zipped her jeans, buttoned her shirt, tied on one tennis shoe, then rummaged through the clothes pile for the other one.

"I can understand that." *Ah—there it was, snagged on her red bra.* She shoved her foot in it and tied the lace. "There's a peace out here, like you're making a connection with something beyond yourself."

"Yep. There's nothing like it."

He offered her his arm, and they walked downstairs, grabbed hats off the mudroom pegs, and went out the kitchen door across the patio to the tarmac road.

Acorns crunched under their feet as they strolled down the tree-lined lane toward the barn.

Moira breathed deep. It was a beautiful day to be outside. The sun was warm, the sky was blue, and here and there, heaps of small gold leaves dotted the road.

Rafe paused as a deer came up to the barbed-wire fence, leapt over it with the grace of a ballerina, bounded across the road, and leapt into the next pasture, followed by three more deer in an evenly spaced line. At the same time, a tree in front of them let loose its leaves and they floated aimlessly to the ground.

Moira looked up in wonder.

Oh God—the showers of gold, the graceful deer—it was like a Disney movie. She could almost hear the symphony in the background.

"What kind of tree is this?"

Rafe hugged her a little closer. "Cedar elms. They shed their leaves every year about this time."

As if on signal, two more trees showered their pathway with gold.

Moira caught her breath. "It's beautiful, so beautiful."

And to think, if Colin hadn't died and left her high and dry, she would never have come to Texas, never have met Rafe, never have walked down this enchanted lane with him.

Suddenly she and Rafe were caught in a shimmer of shining gold.

Moira leaned her head against his shoulder and shut her eyes to absorb the beauty of the moment.

It would be so easy to fall in love with him.

But if she did, she'd have to end their relationship. Rafe was a good man, and she was…not a good woman.

* * *

Rafe took a break from accounts for a second to check on Moira.

She was still looking out the window.

He frowned. She'd been quieter this afternoon ever since the cedar elms unloaded on them—almost sad, like she was thinking about something. About last night? Was she comparing him to Colin Sanger?

He glanced at the gold band on his finger. In the three years since Beth's death, he'd never brought a woman home till now. Because of Delilah, of course, and—well—because of Beth.

But somehow, with Moira it seemed right. Like it had been

right to take her to the Pumpkin Party. Like it had been right to bring her up to his ranch office.

Both he and Travis had fully equipped offices so they could keep track of sales and communicate with auction houses and livestock businesses all over the nation. The bloodlines of every cow, bull, and calf on the C Bar M were on record, as were all their tax records and contracts, although the older ones were still in the filing cabinets against the wall.

Right now he was checking up on expenditures. The ranch was big enough that it always turned a profit, but the size of it depended on his management.

Moira turned away from the window. "I understand that you own the ranch because you're the oldest son, but what about Travis and Rocky—and Delilah?"

"Travis will always get a percentage of the profits—less, if he isn't acting as foreman. As a Colby, Rocky will too. Delilah will get her percentage when she comes of age because she's a blood McAllister, but she won't inherit. Travis is my heir, and unless I have a son, the third person in line is my father's younger brother."

"That's complicated." Moira paused for a second, then came out with it. "Is there any way the Colbys can get a foothold on the ranch again?"

"Why are you asking?"

"It seems old-fashioned that the female line can't inherit."

Rafe shrugged. "In this case it doesn't matter. The Colbys own so little of the ranch that the only way they could get any control would be through marriage—and I'm not plannin' on proposing to Rocky anytime soon." He closed down his computer. "Tell you what. How about we go downstairs and I'll show you how to make Star so happy that she'll gurgle at you."

* * *

Moira watched as Rafe saddled the horses. Step-by-step, she realized, he was introducing her to his world. He'd already shown her the business office and coached her on brushing down Star, and now he was teaching how to saddle Star. Not that she'd be hefting a forty-pound saddle like Rocky did. That woman must be built of muscles.

After making sure her stirrups were okay, Rafe swung onto Sarge's back.

"I want to see what's happenin' in the three-eighteen," he said as they started down the tarmac. "It's at the end of the road."

She tilted her hat against the sun. "What's the three-eighteen?"

"We call our pastures by their acreage. Easier to keep track of them."

"So, referring to the three-eighteen would mean you have three hundred eighteen acres in that particular pasture?"

"You got it. We lease some of neighbors' land too, the Johanssons', the Bartons', the Rodriguezes'. It takes a lot of grass to feed the number of cows we run, especially in this part of the country."

They rode in silence for a while. It was an easy silence, Moira realized. Rafe was a comfortable person to be with.

At the end of the road, he opened the gate for her to ride through.

She looked around the pasture as he got back in the saddle again. He was right—the land was rough. The grass was sparse, the prickly pears were plentiful, and gnarly oaks grew in clumps, forming dense overhead canopies. To complete the scene, the other side of the river was bordered by jagged, sinister-looking cliffs.

She shivered. The place had a bad feel to it, and they were all alone.

Not quite alone. A white horse was galloping toward them at breakneck speed.

Rafe stood up in his saddle. "Damnit! I've told Rocky not to run Bella like that!"

Moira felt an urge to hide her face as Rocky approached. Now Rocky would know she'd spent the night.

But what was there for her to do—pull the saddle blanket over her head? And it wasn't as if the channels of communication in Bosque Bend hadn't already spread the word far and wide that Moira Farrar had gone home with Rafe McAllister last night.

So what? She was an adult—a *consenting* adult—and she could sleep with King Kong if she had the hankering to. Still, it bothered her that people would be talking about her, maybe even speculating on exactly what sexcapades had gone on in Rafe's bedroom—thank God that no one would know about the stairs.

The situation had been different with her and Colin. They'd been married. People expected them to have sex. But her relationship with Rafe was an affair—by definition, a temporary, shallow physical relationship that wouldn't last.

And for his sake, she wouldn't let it become anything more than that.

Rocky slowed Bella down to a trot as she drew nearer, then turned Bella to ride next to Rafe. Star nickered a greeting to her stablemate as Rocky gave Rafe the news.

"There's a dead calf under the live oaks up there, Rafe. Pretty well eaten up—looks like the panther got to him. I've called Travis to bring a truck in and pick up what's left."

* * *

Rafe looked over at Moira, sleeping by his side. He must have exhausted her. God, he'd been on her night and day. Like they were honeymooners.

Crossing his arms behind his head, he lay back. For once, he hadn't dozed off afterward. Maybe it was that the house was too warm right now—he'd turned the thermostat up this morning when it was cooler, and the heat had risen into the second floor while they'd been out on the range. Or maybe it was that he had a lot to think about.

He liked Moira in his bed. He liked her in his house. He liked riding around the ranch with her. But Delilah had to come first, which meant there was no way Moira could move in with him. He'd have to get her back to the Lynnwood house tomorrow afternoon, before his mother dropped Delilah off.

They'd have lunch at Six-Shooter on Monday, of course, and he'd see her at rehearsal. After that, there would be the long wait till Friday, when Mom claimed her grandmotherly rights again.

Friday. It seemed a long time off. He studied her as she slept, his eyes tracing the lines of her brow, her closed eyes, her cheek and jaw. Then, careful not to wake her, he slid out of bed, pulled on his jeans, zipped them without buttoning them, and walked into his office to get a sketch pad.

* * *

Moira snuffled in her sleep, then blinked. It was dark outside—how long had she slept? And where was Rafe?

She cleared her eyes and looked around the room and saw him sitting in a bedroom chair with a drawing tablet propped up on his knee and a pencil in his hand.

She shivered and pulled the covers up around her. The room was cold and she was totally naked—again. "What are you doing?"

He closed the tablet. "Drawin' you. I'll bring it over so you can see."

She watched him approach. His shoulders were broad, his hips were narrow, the muscles on his arms and chest were well-defined without looking bulky.

No doubt about it—Rafe was a hunk.

He sat down beside her and opened the tablet. It was a portrait, a three-quarters close-up of her face with her head resting against the pillow. The sketch was almost poetic in its simplicity, a study in a minimalism that expresses everything.

Was this what she looked like to Rafe—a woman with soft,

almost smiling lips and feathered eyelashes? A woman happy with herself and her lover?

"I love the way you've drawn me. You made me look like someone I've always wished I could be."

Rafe laid the tablet down on the bed, then looked at her, his face more serious than she had ever seen it before.

"You are that woman, Moira. That's how I see you, and art sees true."

Chapter Sixteen

They slept late Sunday, and after breakfast, Rafe took her out with him again. The day was cold and the wind was blowing from the north, so he bundled her up in her UCLA sweatshirt, his bomber jacket, and an extra scarf before they went out. Maybe he should have gone alone, but she was leaving today, and he wanted to keep her with him as long as he could.

They rode back to the three-eighteen again.

"The panther's probably got a den in the cliffs," he said, as he moved into the lead. "If I can spot it, Travis and I might be able to smoke it out next week when he's feeling better."

He looked back and watched as Moira guided Star around a nasty stand of prickly pear.

She had a good seat on her and was handling the reins like she'd been doing it all her life. He could shape her up into a neat little horsewoman in no time. But would she want to come out to the ranch on a regular basis? Could she deal with being isolated with him every weekend? And then there was his cooking, which even his mother had told him wasn't fit for a dog.

He pulled back on his reins, laid them on Sarge's neck, and looked out over the rock-strewn pasture. "You should see this place in springtime. It's covered with bluebonnets."

Moira rode up beside him. "Bluebonnets?"

"The state flower of Texas. They grow wild. Not that easy to propagate, but Beth got them to grow in those big pots around the front door in the spring. She had borders of flowers around the walk every season of the year—salvia and pansies mostly. She'd put Delilah on a blanket on the grass and explain what she was doin'—waterin' the plants, loosenin' the soil around them, then singin' to them so they would grow."

"Donna Sue told me she had a beautiful voice."

Rafe squinted his eyes and looked at the cliffs. "Beth qualified for the Metropolitan Opera tryouts, but decided not to follow up—said she didn't want to spend her life in a practice room."

Moira nodded. "I can understand that. It's the same thing with an actor. There's no way to lead a normal life. Does her family still live in Bosque Bend?"

"Her parents died in a car accident the year after Beth died. Her brother is the only one left."

"Chub?"

Rafe jerked his head in surprise. "You've met him?"

"Delilah recited a list of her aunts and uncles when I was guarding her from elephants in the restroom. She said Aunt Alice and Uncle Chub were mad at you."

"Chub was always a little squirrely, and after Beth died, he started tellin' people I was the one responsible for...what happened to her, that I'd set it up somehow. God only knows where he came up with that, but Chub also thinks the moon landing was staged in an Arizona desert. Anyway, Bertie Fuller, your neighbor, bought into it."

He moved Sarge down toward the river and looked at the cliffs again.

His voice came out soft and slow. "I would have given my life to save Beth. I'd gone to the barn, checkin' on a sick horse, and when I got back, she was lyin' on the ground in front of the house. It was New Year's Eve and there'd been a lot of gunfire all day so the coroner said it was celebratory gunfire—you know, aerial firing, when vaqueros shoot into the air to celebrate a holiday. Sometimes a bullet arcs and comes down on top of someone."

Moira nodded. It happened every now and then in California too. But to have it happen to a woman who'd gone out to tend her flowers in her very own yard—that was cruel. Beth should be the one out riding with Rafe today, not her. Rafe didn't deserve to lose his wife, and Delilah didn't deserve to lose her mother.

He looked over at her.

"It must have been hard for you when Colin died. Y'all had only been married—what—two years?"

Her voice went flat. "Two years, one month, and one day."

He frowned. Had he heard her right? Where had the grieving widow gone, the bowed head, the fluttering hands, and the whispery voice? What was going on? Was she angry at Colin because he'd died on her? Because he hadn't checked the water level before diving into the pool for that nighttime swim?

He tried again. "What did you do after you were married? TV? The stage? That Johnny Blue sci-fi thing was the last one I remember you on."

"I stayed home. I don't want to talk about it."

C'mon! He'd spilled his guts to her—it had wrenched his soul to tell Moira about Beth, but he'd wanted her to know what happened because he wanted her to know about *him*. Well, also because he wanted to start the ball rolling so she'd tell him more about herself.

It was like every damn time he thought they had some real communication going, she backed out on him. Sure, the sex was hot, but he wanted more than sex. He wanted to get to know her, for her to tell him things about herself, like why that damn scar was so important to her.

She didn't need to tell him about her love life with Colin. In fact, he'd prefer the King of Hollywood be left out of it. But she could at least tell him about her family and how she grew up. He didn't even know what her favorite color was.

He clucked at Sarge to get him moving a little faster. Was he just another stud to her? Was that the Hollywood way of life—any bed in a storm, wham-bam-thank-you-sir?

He looked over at her. Moira, her jaw set, was sitting up in the saddle like she had a board down her back and staring straight ahead.

No. There was something else going on. And it was tearing her to pieces.

* * *

Moira looked at Rafe across the kitchen table.

Her wonderful weekend was almost over. And it was ending on a sour note. Why did he want to know about her marriage? Had he heard something?

She took a bite of one of the less charred slices of pizza he'd burned in the microwave and washed it down with water.

"It's time for me to pack up so you can take me home. Didn't you say your mother will be bringing Delilah back about two o'clock?"

He gave her his usual easy smile. "Usually. Sometimes she's late, like when you and Astrid—" He fished his cell phone out of his pocket.

"Travis! What's up?…What?…Damn that horse! I'll be right there."

He grabbed his jacket. "I need to get down to the barn *muy pronto* to help Travis control Bella. She's thrown a shoe and won't let the blacksmith fix her up."

Moira pushed back her chair. "I'll go pack."

Climbing the stairs was like rereading an erotic novel. Had she really been so hot that she'd torn Rafe's pirate shirt off him? That she'd screamed "Now, now, now!" at the top of her lungs?

She ran her hand along the antique crazy quilt, which was back in place after Rafe had pulled it off the railing to cover them as they drowsed on the landing Friday night. Rafe may not be much of a cook, but he did keep a neat house. He'd even given her space in his closet for her clothes.

But she was clearing it out now and throwing everything pell-mell into the laundry bag Astrid had used for the delivery—probably because a suitcase would have set off Mrs. Fuller's radar. One last look around and she was ready to go.

Her eyes fell on Rafe's art tablet, and she picked it up to take one more look at the sketch he had made of her. His portrait of the herself of her dreams.

She stared at the page to commit it to memory before replacing the tablet on Rafe's bed stand.

Time to go. Hefting the laundry bag, she headed down the stairs to the foyer. Rafe wasn't back yet so she stepped up to the family room to look at the photos of him on his mother's collage.

She couldn't tell which baby he was because all of them were bald, but his red hair stood out in older pictures of him. One picture showed him and Travis performing in what looked like a country fair. Another was of him, his brother, and sister all dressed up for Christmas. And then there was the wedding picture, which she hadn't singled out before. Beth was radiant with happiness, and Rafe looked like he'd just won the lottery.

Moira studied the photo. Beth was tall and had light hair, just as she'd imagined, but surprisingly, her build was lanky rather than voluptuous, and although she had a wonderful smile, she wasn't Hollywood beautiful. In fact, her nose was long and, technically speaking, her jaw was a little wide. But her face glowed with happiness.

Moira whipped around to face the window. *Was that a car stopping out front?*

A maroon Mercedes was parked at the curb, and Enid

McAllister was walking up the sidewalk with Delilah skipping beside her.

Enid had brought Delilah home early.

And now she was working the front door.

Moira went cold. There wasn't time for her to scoot herself upstairs and lock herself in a bathroom, and hiding wasn't in her nature anyway. She'd have to brazen it out. Delilah wouldn't question her presence, but Enid would know damn well why she was standing there with a laundry bag at her feet and no car at the curb. Not that she would say anything with her granddaughter on the scene.

The door swung open, and Moira put a welcoming smile on her face and stepped down into the foyer.

Enid froze on the threshold, but Delilah shrieked with joy and rushed inside. "Pretty lady!"

Moira opened her arms and braced herself for the usual assault. Over Delilah's head, she could see a warm smile spreading across Rafe's mother's face.

A warm smile? What was going on? In the hospital, Enid had obviously preferred Travis's girlfriend to his wife, and now she was smiling at the woman who had spent the weekend in her older son's bed, as if welcoming her to the family.

* * *

Rafe could hear Bella's stomping and crashing from halfway down the path.

What had set her off this time? That is, besides the blacksmith being impertinent enough to lift her queenship's foot.

Bella let out a bloodcurdling scream, and Rafe started running. That horse had been born mean.

The blue heeler in the blacksmith's pickup started barking as he approached, and Bella went off into another fit of whinnies. She did not like dogs. In fact, she'd trampled the bejeezus out of the last one they'd had on the place.

Rafe walked into the barn and took stock of the situation. Bella had worked herself into a lather, her eyes were rolling, and she was snorting—if she were a dragon, the barn would be in flames.

Travis had managed to get a rope around her neck and secure it to the posts on either side of the stall so Bella couldn't rear up and scream anymore, but she was still taking angry bites at the air.

"She won't let the blacksmith get to her," Travis said. "Nothing to do but sedate her."

Rafe nodded and headed for the tack room refrigerator. "I'll take care of that."

He filled a syringe with the sedative, squeezed a drop out of the tip, then walked toward Bella's stall with the needle behind his leg. Bella might be mean, but she wasn't dumb. She knew what the syringe meant, and she didn't like it.

She eyed him suspiciously as he entered the stall. Travis started a meaningless conversation with the blacksmith to divert her attention while Rafe leaned casually against the wall on the other side of her. Without looking at Bella, Travis moved half a step closer to her, a challenge she couldn't refuse.

She lifted her head, narrowed her eyes, and bared her teeth.

That was his opening. Rafe went in for a quick shot, then

backed away as she screamed her outrage and flailed at the rope.

She began to wilt. Her eyes glazed over and she wobbled on her feet.

The blacksmith took it from there.

* * *

Rafe ran his hand around the cold steering wheel as he drove Moira back to the Lynnwood house. The afternoon sky had covered itself with low-hanging clouds, and a freeze was being predicted for tomorrow. That was Texas weather for you—seventy degrees one day, freezing the next.

He looked over at her. Her head was slumped on her shoulder and her eyes were closed. He smiled and his loins stirred with memory. She hadn't gotten that much sleep at the ranch, and he hadn't either.

That had been an interesting scene he'd walked in on when he returned to the house—Moira, holding Delilah on her hip, was standing in front of the collage of him and his siblings while his mother was pointing out his baby picture to her. He had to hand it to both of them—they were acting like it was the most natural thing in the world, but just to be on the safe side, he'd asked his mother to stay with Delilah, then hustled Moira into the truck to take her back to the Lynnwood house.

Damn, he wished she could stay another night—or two—or a couple of months. Lunches and rehearsals on Monday, then Friday nights and Saturday nights at the ranch were not enough. Friday night through Sunday morning—it was the same calendar he'd set his other girlfriends—but sex on schedule wasn't what he wanted from Moira.

What *did* he want from her? Why *had* he brought her out to the house instead of taking her to a ritzy hotel in Waco? Maybe because Moira was different from the casual girls he'd hung out with.

She was different from Beth too.

Both of them were beautiful, he thought, but Beth was light itself, totally transparent, a butterfly, while Moira was an old soul, opaque with mystery and passion.

He turned the corner into Lynnwood, and Moira began to stir. She was fully awake and gathering together her things by the time he parked in the driveway.

He helped her down to the ground, then kissed her in front of God, man, and Bertie Fuller, who was unearthing the last of her Halloween tombstones, before he walked her up the sidewalk.

He could feel Bertie's eyes drilling a hole through him all the way back to the dually. Whatever someone had said that had turned that woman against him, it had worked. He wouldn't be surprised if flying monkeys followed him all the way home.

* * *

Moira wiped her forehead and prayed for strength.

The first day of the week, and the adult rehearsal was a bummer.

It figured. She'd been headachy and depressed most of the day. Maybe it was the letdown from her weekend with Rafe. Maybe it was the autumn time change that had messed up her internal clock. Maybe it was that Rafe had called and canceled their lunch date.

"It's Delilah," he'd explained. "She took her fairy wand to pre-school and hit one of the little boys with it so she has to stay home for three days. I've got her in the office with me for the morning, but Cousin Sharon can't take her till two this afternoon." His voice softened. "I'm sorry, Moira, but I probably won't be able to make the rehearsal either. I'm supposed to meet with a prospective client in Waco at three."

Rafe. She would miss him. Her mind kept replaying the weekend. He'd made her feel like she was the most beautiful woman in the world. If he called her back right now, she'd hop in the car and drive out to the ranch like she'd been offered the lead in a Joss Whedon epic.

But instead, he had canceled on her all the way around.

And if he was canceling out on her already, how long would their relationship last? Rocky, who should be a reliable source, had said Rafe's affairs were short run. Well, she'd better make the best of it. But what would she do when it was over?

Rafe had made it clear from the outset that her job was safe, but would she want to stick around after they broke up? If she missed him this much after just two days, how would she feel after they'd been together for two months?

To counter her malaise, she'd thrown herself into a frenzy of activity, but when she stopped to drop fabric swatches off with Mrs. Bridges, the ever-threatening rain had cut loose and she'd been soaked so thoroughly that Marilyn insisted on wrapping her in bathroom towels and wouldn't let her leave till she was dry.

Damnit, how can a state supposedly parched by drought have so much rain?

And now, the rehearsal too was a total loser. The light crew hadn't shown up, the chorus seemed to have a Halloween hangover, somebody had played around with the controls so the curtain got stuck half open, Phil was acting more distant from Micaela than ever, and Vashti and Xandra, still fighting the battle of Micaela's dream ballet, were giving each other looks that would have killed lesser women.

To top it off, Billie Joe, still under the impression that *Gift of the Magi* was teetering on the edge of Hollywood stardom, had asked her about Boyd Yancey again.

And just when she thought it couldn't get any worse, the storm hit its zenith and the auditorium lights started flickering. She gritted her teeth and put in another request for fortitude, then edged back into her seat, bent her head, and covered her face with her hands.

Someone came down her row, and a gentle hand touched her arm. Moira looked up. It was Carmen Atherton.

"Everything will work out, Moira. You're doing a good job." She nodded toward the piano, where her mother and Xandra Fontaine were stiff-necking each other. "Mom and Xandra always have at it. They're each other's favorite enemies. But it's all for the good of the play. You'll see."

Moira looked at Carmen. With the vibrant Micaela around, it was easy to look past her, but she was really quite pretty—fairer than her sister, pale really, with calm gray eyes and a Madonna face.

There was a stir onstage and everyone was looking at the door. Moira turned around. Rafe and Travis were coming down the aisle, grinning like chessy cats and dripping with water.

Rafe waved at her. "I made it, Moira! And look at who I found wandering around the ranch with nothing to do. Thought, I'd bring him with me so we could have an appreciative audience!"

Laughter filled the auditorium, and the two men strode down front.

Moira felt herself relax. Big Red was here. Her world was in kilter again.

* * *

The rain was down to a dribble as Rafe walked Moira out of the museum and across the street. Backing her against her car, he went as far as he could go without being arrested for public indecency. God, he missed her. Missed her so much he couldn't sleep last night.

He knew every inch of her now, but she was so much more than beautiful. He liked talking with her, laughing with her, watching her learn how to ride, listening to her silence. He'd done everything he could to get out of that appointment in Waco, but the Baylor gig was on the line.

God, he was horny. Maybe he and Moira could get together tomorrow.

He kissed her on the tip of her nose. "What are you doin' in the mornin', darlin'? Tuesday is Art Day in Taylor so Sissy's drivin' down there to help her mother set up her display so that daybed in my office is just waitin' for company."

Moira opened her car door and stepped behind it. "Sorry. Donna Sue's home now and I told her I'd come visit."

He heard the rest of the sentence loud and clear. *And she wasn't going to be available at his convenience.*

He'd known it was a mistake as soon as the words came out of his mouth. They sounded crass even to him. Besides, he wanted more from this woman than a noontime quickie.

* * *

Moira searched the side of the road for her turnoff. There it was, Cedar Hollow Road. The Gomez-Sweeny family lived even farther down the highway than Rafe did.

Donna Sue met her at the door with Genevieve Valentina in her arms. Her dimples flashed in welcome.

"You got here at the right time—my kettle just whistled hot cocoa." Moira followed her hostess through the house into a warm, cozy kitchen. "How about you pulling out a chair and holding Ginny for a sec—she's wearing your adorable little shoes—while I mix the cocoa. Or would you prefer tea? I could fix that too."

"Anything hot. It's cold and wet out there."

Moira's heart quickened as Donna Sue handed her the baby. Ginny made a sucking sound, and her hand crept out from under the blanket. Five perfect little fingers grasped at her thumb.

Donna Sue put a mug and a napkin down in front of her. "Did you have any problem—some people do—finding us out here in the boondocks? Bosque Branch is what they call a rural subdivision. Everyone on the street has about five acres and our neighbors to the north—the Fishers are totally super—have a couple of horses, and they let Xavier and me—he's my husband—ride them whenever we want."

Ginny squirmed and began to make fretful little noises, and Donna Sue reclaimed her. "Oh, babes, let me put her in her crib. She can get cranky."

Moira crossed her arms over each other in self-comfort. Would she ever hold a baby she didn't have to give back?

Donna Sue returned to the room and sat down across from her. "Xavier—he's a saint from heaven—took Leonard off to visit his great-grandmother in Little River-Academy—so it'll be just us girls this morning." She took a sip from her mug. "Now, tell me—how did my classes go? You were so good to go talk to them—I think Mr. Hurst will give me Teacher of the Year for this—and I hope they behaved themselves. Did they ask about anything—I mean about *anything*—other than Johnny Blue?"

Moira laughed. Donna Sue knew her classes well. "Not really."

Donna Sue took another sip of cocoa and hunched in closer across the table. "I've heard some really bad things about him lately and not just in the scandal sheets."

"He's self-destructive." Moira breathed deep and exhaled softly. "He's been good to me, but I wish he'd be better to himself."

Ginny cut loose with a wail that would melt a snowman's heart, and Donna Sue made a quick trip to the nursery and back. "She lost her binky," she explained as she sat down again. "But Mommy found it for her."

She flashed her eyes at Moira. "Okay, now—spill. How are things going—I mean really and truly—with the show?"

Moira laughed. "Well, I should have the entire first act shaped up by Saturday, which will give us two weeks to pull the second act together and a week to polish."

"Sounds great! What about Phil Schoenfeldt? I wasn't sure about him in a romantic role, but he's got such a great voice."

Moira paused. "He's a little...*wooden*, but I'm sure he'll come around by showtime."

"I'm sorry, babes, but he and Sergio are the only reliable tenors in town—I tried everyone but everyone out—and Sergio's too young for the part."

"I'm confident Phil will settle in." No, she wasn't sure at all, but that was her worry, not Donna Sue's.

"I hope so. What about Travis and Micaela?"

"I was never in the production that didn't have backstage hanky-panky going on, but to tell you the truth, Travis and Micaela make me uncomfortable, probably because I know Rocky."

"You can't do anything about it, babes. Travis—whom I absolutely adore—is digging his own grave. I'm five years older than Rocky, but she was in my little sister's grade so I knew her reputation—a good friend and a bad enemy. If Travis gives her much more grief—I'd *kill* Xavier if he played fast and loose with me—she might take a frying pan to him."

Moira smiled. "Not till after the show is over, I hope."

Donna Sue exercised her dimples and lowered her voice as if someone lurking behind a door might overhear her. "And how are things going with you and Rafe?"

Oh crap, she wasn't expecting that, but of course, Donna Sue would know she was sleeping with Rafe. Everyone else did.

* * *

Rafe folded up the proposal he was trying to proofread and put it away. It was impossible to concentrate on repurposing yet another old small-town high school as the town museum when Mervin had come by this morning to give him the latest news. The pathologist said the trajectory of the bullet that killed Beth was all wrong for celebratory gunfire.

"I'll need you to come down to the station next week," Mervin had said. "How about Monday morning—so I can get you on video about the weeks leading up to her death. We've had reports that y'all were quarreling and that Beth was going to leave you."

Rafe gave his cousin a hard stare and slapped the Baylor proposal down on his desk.

He and Beth were quarreling?

"That's Chub talking, and you know it. He's had it in for me ever since he married Alice Fuller. She's an echo of her mother."

Mervin massaged the back of his neck, like a hick sheriff, which he wasn't. "I know that and you know that, but we gotta get you on tape. I'm pursuing this case, Rafe, and when we find out what happened, I want to make sure it's airtight."

* * *

Moira held Ivanhoe back by the collar as she opened the door.

On the other side of the screen stood an eye-blinding vision in a leopard vest, purple shirt, and jeans with gold trim down the sides. Her fingernails were spotted like a leopard's paw print.

"Rocky! Wait a minute while I put Ivanhoe out."

"Sure thing, hon. That dog looks vicious. We don't have them on the ranch. They spook the cattle."

Moira expelled Ivanhoe to the backyard, then tracked back to open the screen for Rocky. Donna Sue yesterday and Rocky today—her social life had picked up.

Rocky walked in and gave her a quick hug.

"I was visiting with Bertie next door, and I thought I'd stop in and see how you're doing. Have a minute?"

"I've got all day, and sometimes it's a little lonely. Astrid is working all day now. Let's go on into the family room. It's cozier."

Rocky looked around as they passed through the house. "I like the way you arranged that furniture you got from Josie's—the desk, the armchairs, and the other stuff. Hon, you sure know how to make a place look good."

"Thanks. Make yourself comfortable, and I'll check the pantry for sugar cookies."

She walked back to the table. Rocky was looking around the room as if searching for the house she used to know. Moira felt a twinge of sympathy. It must be hard for her to deal with someone else living in her mother's house. She put the plate of cookies down in front of her as an offering of comfort and apology.

"Does it feel odd to be back here in your old home?"

Rocky shrugged and reached for a cookie. "Not really. I spent most of my time at Beth's or the C Bar M. Ma always said that this place was just a house we were passing through till we got to where we were meant to be." She gave Moira an impish grin. "And Ma was meant to be in Florida with her honey, and I was meant to be at the C Bar M."

Moira finished Rocky's sentence for her. "With Travis."

Rocky bit into the cookie. "Yeah, the C Bar M is in my blood." She glanced over at Moira and grinned, her eyes dancing. "Hey, hon, how are things going with *Gift of the Magi*? What about ol' Phil?"

Moira laughed. It was a good thing that Rocky had stopped by. She needed to vent, and she certainly wasn't going to let her hair down to anyone connected with the show. "He's driving me crazy. He has this wonderful voice, but can't seem to relate to…some of the cast."

No need to mention which particular member of the cast. Rocky and Travis were having a hard time right now without her throwing Micaela's name in her face.

Rocky laughed, a tinkling of bells. "Hon, Phil never could act. You should have seen him in our high school play. He looked like a wooden puppet. We called him Pinocchio all the rest of the year. It made him so mad." She laughed again, and her eyes danced. "And what's going on with Vashti? She's usually good for a chuckle."

"Vashti is crossing swords, muskets, and cannons with the

Fontaines every time I turn around. They're mostly at odds about one of Desdemona Benton's ballets."

"Hon, Vashti can be a real pill. And have you seen her house? I swear, hon, she's got more concrete in her front yard than Walmart's parking lot."

Moira laughed and claimed a cookie for herself. "It is overdone."

"And she's always wearing those long skirts and dripping with old-fashioned jewelry. And her hair—it looks like a fright wig an angry cat got hold of."

Moira laughed again. Rocky was so wicked. She could make a funeral sound funny.

"Let me tell you the whole story, hon. Vashti moved into town when Carmen and Micaela were little kids, bought that crazy house, got a job as organist at the biggest church in town, then started teaching music on the side." She laughed again. "This is the good part—she calls herself *Mrs.* Atherton, but as far as anyone can figure out, there is no *Mr.* Atherton." Rocky pursed her lips and shook her head slowly in mock disapproval. "She doesn't have a picture of him in that conglomeration on her hall wall, and she never talks about him. Probably never was a *Mr.* Atherton. Or maybe…"

Moira appreciated the pause for dramatic effect. She *had* to get Rocky involved in theater.

"Maybe there were two of them—two—uh—husbands." Rocky lifted her eyebrows and put a delicious disbelieving twist on the last word. "Carmen and Micaela look different as night and day. Micaela is dark—probably half something-or-other—and Carmen is so bleached out she looks like she got left in the laundry too long. And that isn't all. Carmen went off to some big music school up in New York, then showed up back home two years later with a baby boy, but no husband." Rocky laughed and rolled her eyes. "Like mother, like daughter."

Moira didn't know what to say. She'd never given a thought to Vashti's or Carmen's marital status. And not to Micaela's dark complexion either.

Rocky dusted cookie crumbs off her fingers. "By the way, hon, Ma called me this morning and said she doesn't want to push—Ma's like that—but she sure would like it, now that Rafe's buying the house back from her, if he paid her in a lump sum. Her guy needs to get started on his tour-boat business."

Boy, that came out of the blue. Moira stiffened. "You'll have to consult Rafe about that. He's never talked to me about his business dealings."

"Not even pillow talk?"

Moira could feel the heat rising in her face.

Rocky laughed. "Moira, hon. You can level with me. Remember, I live on the ranch and I know everything that happens there. I *see* everything that happens there." She closed one eye in a wicked wink.

"Everything."

Chapter Seventeen

Moira lay back against Rafe's chest as her breathing returned to normal. She hoped Rocky didn't see *everything* that went on at the ranch. Rafe had teased her into a climax so shattering that she'd screamed like a banshee.

He ran his hand down her arm. "What are you thinkin' about?"

"Rocky. She told me she sees everything that goes on here, and I was wondering if..."

His chest shook with suppressed laughter. "That's ol' Rocky—she's just messin' with you. No way she can see inside the house."

Moira gestured toward the window wall. "But I can see outside."

"I was in on the design of the house, remember? The angle is wrong for someone looking in, and she knows that."

Moira tilted her head up to look at him.

"There's something else that has to do with Rocky that's

bothering me, Rafe. When she came by the house the other day, I confided in her that I was having problems with Phil and Vashti, and she told me some stories about them that were really funny—at least the way she told them—but after she left, I had a sick feeling in the pit of my stomach. I like Phil and Vashti, and I'd hate for them to know I was laughing at them."

Rafe lifted a strand of her hair and let it fall back into place.

"Don't worry, darlin'. Rocky tells stories on all of us—we sort of expect it—but she's just playin'." His hand moved down to the scar on her arm, and he congratulated himself that she didn't react anymore when he touched it. "But what's Phil's problem? I haven't been around during his rehearsals much, but is he still actin' like a sanctimonious church music director instead of Micaela's husband?"

"You hit it. I've talked to him about his character until I'm blue in the face, but he's still holding back. He interacts with everyone else in the play—all the other characters—but he keeps Micaela at arm's length. There is absolutely no chemistry between them."

Rafe snorted. "I don't know if you can say anythin' to get ol' Phil in line, but as for the chemistry, maybe the problem is that Sammy and Desdemona are usin' it all up. It's not just to keep himself from gettin' pneumonia that Sammy's sittin' in that auditorium every night."

Moira snuggled into her pillow. "Do you think so? I've wondered if something was going on. They're always whispering back and forth, but Buck doesn't seem to mind—or even be aware of it. Maybe he's so confident of Desdemona that he doesn't see Sammy as a threat."

"Could be." He lifted another strand of her hair and curled it around his finger. "Anythin' I missed out on during the week? What about the kids' rehearsal?"

Moira yawned and turned over on her side. "The kids are just fine, but the adults are still sniping at each other. If I never hear another word about the tempo of Desdemona's ballet, I'll be happy.

"I had to call Vashti and Xandra over and lay down the law, that Vashti had to quit speeding up the tempo of the ballet, and that Xandra was not going to be getting a second reprise of 'Around the Christmas Tree' to accommodate yet another flower-girl dance."

And she wasn't going to say it, but the first "Christmas Tree" reprise wouldn't make it to opening night if Wendy Nixon kept mugging at the audience like she was doing now.

Rafe could hear the tiredness in her voice and reached for the bedside lamp. "Let's call it an evening then. Sweet dreams."

Moira bunched the pillow up under her head again, closed her eyes, and drifted into darkness.

Pitch-black darkness.

The darkness of silence.

The darkness of a tomb.

The leather collar chafed her neck, and the chain-link leash was so short that she couldn't lie down. She tried to scream—to scream to God because she knew the basement was sound-proofed—but a braid of her long, long hair had been wound across her mouth to hold her tongue down, and all she could do was gobble.

She sank back on her haunches. It was useless to try to es-

cape—she knew that from the times before. She had to wait, with every minute seeming like an eternity.

And no guarantee Master would return.

A hand touched her in the dark. Was it Master?

Was he back so soon? She hadn't heard him coming.

She struggled against her leash, eager to show him her gratitude.

Thank you for giving me another chance. I'll try harder this time. No more sad faces, only smiles. Anything you want me to do, I'll do.

Obedience—that was the important word. Cheery obedience.

Dear God, what was happening? There was light in the room and her master was disappearing into the receding darkness.

No! Don't leave me down here alone!

A soothing voice broke into her dream, and she opened her eyes.

"Moira. Moira, darlin', relax. Everything's okay. You're having a nightmare."

It was Rafe. Big Red. Rafe of the sparkling eyes. She was safe.

He cuddled her against his side, and she slept the rest of the night in his embrace.

* * *

Rafe ran up the fire escape faster than he'd known was possible, unlocked his office door, then stopped to catch his breath before walking out into Sissy's office to greet Moira.

He attempted a smile. "Sorry, I'm running late."

"That's okay. Is the reservation at the Bosque Club still good?"

"If we can get a move on."

He hustled Moira through his office and back down the fire escape. This was not the sort of lunch date he'd imagined. He'd thought they'd stroll into the club about an hour ago, and that he'd introduce her to whatever luminaries were present before they moved on to the dining room for a leisurely lunch.

Instead, his day got shot to hell. And by his very own cousin.

He got Moira in the car and revved up the engine.

She gave him a sidelong look. "What's going on? You seem upset."

It all poured out of him.

"Beth's case has been reopened, and Mervin called and asked me to come down to the police station for an interview." A muscle twitched in his jaw, and he slammed on his brakes at a stop sign. "I assumed it wouldn't take more than fifteen minutes, because I don't know anything other than what I've already told him, but it turned out to be a two-and-a-half-hour interrogation, just like on TV, with a video camera running the whole time!"

He slammed his hand against the steering wheel. "Damnit, I know from the true-crime shows that the husband was usually the one who did it, but I went to school with two of those guys, and another one of them worked for me on the ranch a couple of years ago. They all know what kind of person I am, but they were all looking at me like I might have killed...like I might be a murderer!"

Beth—how could they think he'd want Beth dead? She'd been his joy, his love, his happiness. She was the mother of his child. And having to talk about how she died tore his soul in two.

He glanced over at Moira. *Crap fuck!* This wasn't how he'd thought their dinner date would start off.

Turning the wheel harder than he needed to, he cut across traffic into a side street.

Two and a half hours. Two and a half goddamn hours!

God, if he had known anything that would help, he'd have stayed two and a half years, but he didn't. And that made him angry too. How could his wife be murdered, deliberately killed, and he didn't catch on?

And why did Mervin ask him all the personal questions? Whose business was it if he and Beth had sex the day she died? They'd had sex *all* the day. Beth's mother had claimed Delilah for the weekend and they were all alone in the house, celebrating the new baby by indulging in the very same activity that had created it.

Beth—the familiar wave of sorrow engulfed him. Why, why, why had she been taken from him? And by something as random as a bullet gone astray when someone was celebrating New Year's?

Moira adjusted her seat strap and turned to him. Her voice was a soothing balm. "Would you rather drop me off at my car and drive back to the ranch?"

Would he? No way. He needed her right now more than

ever. Which meant he'd better clean up his act. Just because he was feeling like shit didn't mean he had to unload it all on Moira.

C'mon, cowboy. Your mother raised you better than that, so put a smile on your face, take her arm, and act like a gentleman.

He jerked the truck to a stop in the Bosque Club parking lot, and lifted Moira onto the ground.

* * *

Moira picked up her menu and perused the fare. The Bosque Club was the sort of place where one *perused the fare* rather than seeing what was for lunch. Rafe had told her it would be a change from Six-Shooter Junction, and he was right. He'd rushed her through the rooms like they were trying to catch the red-eye, but she couldn't miss seeing the gold-toned bamboo wallpaper above the dark wainscoting, the squat, deep-cushioned couches and chairs upholstered in bold persimmon-and-saffron prints.

The Bosque Club was upper crust, and she was glad Rafe had suggested she dress up a little. She hoped her wrap-around silk shantung was up to snuff.

A waiter who looked more dignified than God poured water into their glasses from a silver carafe and asked about their drink orders.

Rafe closed his menu with a snap. "I'll take Jack Daniels on the rocks, and the lady…will have…?" He looked across at her expectantly.

"The lady will stick with water."

"Then I think we're ready to order our meals now too, just to give y'all a head start. Moira?"

"I'll have—"

A soft buzz interrupted her. Rafe pulled his cell phone out of his pocket and put it to his ear.

The waiter gave him a stern look. "Mr. McAllister, the Bosque Club's rules require you to turn off all—"

Rafe waved him silent and stood up from the table.

Moira tensed. Something was going on. Lots of "uh-hunhs" and then an "I'll be there in ten minutes."

Rafe laid a ten on the table in apology. "Moira, we've gotta go. Travis is in the hospital again."

They dashed out of the club as if they were absconding with the silver, and she barely had time to fasten her seat belt before he revved the engine and took off for the hospital. It was another wild ride. Rafe didn't actually run any red lights, but he did cut them close.

Once he swung into the hospital parking lot and they hit the pavement, it was a race to the waiting room.

Enid and Rocky were sitting on the pink couch again. Rocky scooted over to give Moira room, and Rafe pulled up a chair facing them.

Enid took her son's hands as if to draw strength from him. Her face was ashen, and her diamond eyes looked dull. "Rocky called me just before noon and said she was taking Travis back to the hospital."

Rocky nodded. "He was okay when I left the house to check on that out-of-season calf in the two-twenty-three, but when

I came home for lunch, he was doubled up and clutching his stomach."

Rafe's face morphed into the stern, stone-faced expression of his Indian forefather. "That does it. I'm getting him transferred down to Scott and White in Temple."

* * *

Rafe woke up before Moira for once. Friday night was always good, but last night had been spectacular, maybe because they'd both had a rough week. Travis was home now but they still hadn't received reports from the lab tests, so Moira had to hand his role over to Sergio, which altered the dynamics of the show.

He pulled on some jeans and went into the bathroom for a cup of water. When he got back, she had thrown off her sheet, but was still asleep.

God, she was beautiful. His eyes followed the graceful lines of her body. The thrust of her shoulder, the curve of her breasts, the dip of her waist and the swell of her hip, the round belly, the changing planes of her legs from thigh to knee to ankle, the graceful arch of her feet. He fetched the sketchbook from his office and moved a chair next to the bed.

First he blocked out the basics—circles and ovals—then returned to her head, lightly penciling in horizontals across the egg shape to indicate her features. After adding in a few strokes to indicate an ear and the fluff of her hair, he moved down her neck to delineate the slope of her shoulders.

He'd draw in her hands later. Right now he wanted to

record the rise of her breasts and the sweet roundness of her belly, the triangle of her legs—one outstretched and the other one bent at the knee.

Her softly shaded pubic mound was another triangle, and her puckered nipples were soft scallops. And every line he drew was a caress.

He looked at his tablet.

This sketch wasn't about art. It was about Moira. It was about, well—love.

My God, he was in love with Moira Farrar.

* * *

Moira wrapped the ruffled little dress in pink paper and tied it with a silver bow. It was time to drop by Donna Sue's again.

The weather had warmed up a little, and the winter sun was shining bright. Donna Sue welcomed her with her usual overwhelming enthusiasm, sat her down at the kitchen table, plied her with hot cocoa, and opened the baby gift.

"It's so darling—like a little ballet dress!" She looked up. "How's our Desdemona doing?"

"I think I've finally gotten Vashti to understand the tempo of the ballet *will* slow down."

"Vashti is a dear, but she's also a perfectionist and can be very stubborn." Donna Sue put the dress back in its box. "But now, tell me, babes—I'm dying to hear—what's the story you said you wanted to tell me about Pen Swaim and Judy Schoenfeldt?"

Moira grinned. "You know I've been concerned about Phil

all along because he's never warmed up to Micaela onstage. *Gift of the Magi* is a love story, and if the relationship between the leads doesn't work, the show is sunk."

Donna Sue blinked and shook her head as if to clear it. "But what—I'm missing something—does that have to do with Pen?"

"He came to the rehearsal last night and said we needed to change the location of the story from London to New York because of the song about John D. Rockefeller."

Donna Sue's eyes widened, and her mouth dropped open in horror. "Ooh! When I read the script last summer—I can be such a ditz—it passed right by me."

"I told him we'd work something out, but that I thought the playbills had already been printed. As it turned out I was wrong. Judy Schoenfeldt dropped by later in the evening to show me the mock-up, and she said it wouldn't be any trouble to replace the write-up of Victorian London with one of old-time New York. Then—and this is the best part—she stayed for the rest of the rehearsal to watch Phil."

Donna Sue's eyebrows drew together in confusion. "I don't get it, babes. What's the big deal about Judy—she used to do theater, by the way, and she was really good—seeing her husband act like a department store mannequin?"

"Because the second he finished his first scene, Judy went down front and talked to him. I couldn't hear a word, but her body language was expressive enough. And when Phil went onstage for his next scene, he was transformed. I mean, you'd never mistake him for Rudolph Valentino, but he looked at Micaela, he smiled at her, and he actually touched her hand without acting like she might give him the cooties."

"Two birds with one stone, Moira! You're super!"

Moira shook her head in denial. "I didn't have a thing to do with it. It was all Judy."

A wail came from down the hall, and Donna Sue got up. "Ginny's unhappy about something. I'd better go see what's going on."

"Take your time."

Moira took a sip of hot cocoa and looked at the picture of Donna Sue and her family over the wood-burning fireplace. Xavier was strikingly handsome. Was he into theater? Did he sing?

Donna came back into the room with Ginny in her arms. "I think she's hungry. Do you mind if I nurse?"

"Not at all."

Donna Sue opened her blouse, unsnapped the cup of her bra, and attached Ginny to her breast.

"So—how are things going with you and the Fontaines?"

"Beats me. I backed Xandra up on the tempo thing, but she still looks at me like I'm about to knife her in the back. I don't understand what's going on with those two." She sighed. "But what the heck—they're patient with the adults and sweet with the kids, even Wendy Nixon, who can be a pain."

Donna Sue shifted Ginny into a more comfortable position. "Give them a little time, babes—or maybe a lot—and they'll come around. The sisters Fontaine are nervous around new people."

Moira took another swallow of cocoa and sat back in the chair. "You know, with their love of children, I'm surprised they never married. I've seen their publicity photos from when they were younger, and they were both quite attractive. It's odd, though, that when you get past that black hair—which they must be dyeing in India ink—they look even less like sisters than Astrid and I do. And their body builds are totally different too—Xandra is tall and long limbed, and Fleurette looks like a lady wrestler."

Donna Sue switched Ginny to her other breast and gave her an amused smile.

"Oh, babes, did you really think Xandra and Fleurette are sisters? Let me tell you—my aunt worked voter registration and—at least according to the great state of Texas——they were not born Fontaines."

"I don't understand."

Donna Sue snapped her bra shut and closed her blouse. "Babes, no matter what they say, there's just one small—it's really minuscule—bedroom in that apartment over the studio." She shrugged. "We all play along because they keep to themselves, and—as you say—they're patient with adults and good with the children."

Moira blinked. "You mean..."

"They reinvented themselves—French names and all—so they could live together. You've got to understand the small-town mentality, babes. Everybody wants to know what's going on in everybody else's bedrooms—every juicy detail—but they aren't going to rock the boat."

The door opened, and Donna Sue's face lit up. "Xavier! I'm so glad you got back early! I want you to meet Moira!"

* * *

Moira had barely gotten home before there was a knock on the door. Her heart sank. She'd noticed Rocky's yellow Jeep parked in front of Mrs. Fuller's house when she drove in.

She wanted to avoid the laughing girl for a while, but after all, her feelings of guilt weren't Rocky's fault. If the stories about Phil and the Athertons had made her uncomfortable, she should have said so instead of laughing.

But Rocky wasn't laughing today. She wasn't even smiling. "I've got to talk to you, hon. It's about something really important."

Moira put Ivanhoe out, then opened the door and ushered Rocky into the family room. No sugar cookies this time.

Moira sat down on the couch and Rocky pulled up a chair. Moira had the impulse to put more distance between them, but made herself hold her ground.

"I don't know how to bring this up, hon, but you're my friend, and I don't want you to get hurt."

"What do you mean?" What sort of story was Rocky going to feed her now?

"From what I hear, Rafe's a sex bomb and a half, but, hon, you gotta be careful. Maybe you need to back off of him. A lot of folks around here are thinking he had something to do with Beth's death."

Rocky paused as if considering how to phrase bad news tactfully. "Now, I love Rafe to death, hon, but I've gotta tell you that a couple of days before she got killed, Beth told me she was going to up and leave him—take Delilah and go move in with her parents. She didn't like living on the ranch—the loneliness, all the noise when the calves and cows were separated for weaning, knowing that we castrate the little bulls at roundup, that sort of thing. And she said it was more important to leave right then because she was pregnant with a baby boy."

Moira bit her tongue. A month ago she would have swallowed every word of what Rocky was saying. Now she knew to take it with a grain of salt—or maybe one of those big blocks of salt that Rocky was always talking about.

Rocky's taffy-colored ringlets bounced like coiled springs. "It was so sad. I knew Beth and Rafe had been fighting a lot lately, but I didn't know how it would end up."

She laughed and threw her hands up as if releasing a bird into the air. "Of course, it's ridiculous, hon. Rafe had nothing to do with it. No way he could have arranged for one of those Mexican guys to kill Beth just by shooting his gun into the air. Even though Mervin Hruska has made two visits to Rafe's office lately and taken a deposition from Beth's brother, I'm sure that pathologist the city has hired isn't going to find anything."

Moira couldn't let this go on any longer.

"But Rafe loved Beth and—"

Rocky glanced at her watch and stood up. "Hey! I've got to get a hustle on! Cattle don't move themselves across the river! Sorry to talk and run." She laughed, reached down for her canvas bag that had a playful kitten painted on it, and headed for the door.

Moira watched out the window as Rocky hopped in her yellow Jeep and raced down the street way too fast for a family neighborhood.

What was that all about? Was Rocky trying to scare her off Rafe?

* * *

Thanksgiving day dawned bright, cold, and windy—just like the day Delilah had been born. She'd been almost a month early, Rafe remembered, and he'd prayed without ceasing all the way to the hospital.

After grabbing a quick breakfast, he retrieved the bouquet that he'd kept wet all night and drove to the cemetery.

It would be a full day, with Delilah's birthday falling on Thanksgiving this year. Hosting a combination Thanksgiving and birthday party was not in his field of expertise so Mom had moved back in to supervise the proceedings. At last count, there would be twenty-four adults and eleven children, including TexAnn and her family.

But before he did anything else, he had to visit Beth.

He parked on the church road and walked to her grave, then squatted down to put the Thanksgiving chrysanthemums in the vase and think things over. He thought about when he first saw her, the weekend she'd met his family, their two-year courtship, the day they got married, and their honeymoon in the foreman's cottage. They were so young, so infallible.

Their years at the University of Texas had been difficult, but somehow the hardships drew them even closer together, and when they graduated, the world had opened its arms to them. Beth was starring in Dallas productions, and he was an up-and-coming architect. Delilah had been the frosting on the cake.

Then Dad started having stomach trouble and he'd spent every other weekend in the Bosque Bend Hospital waiting room. And when the end came, he knew he had to move Beth and Delilah back to the ranch.

He'd been surprised at how quickly Beth had adjusted to the lifestyle. Oh God, they'd had so much together. They'd ride out every day, with Delilah on the saddle in front of him. And the week before Beth died, she'd told him she was pregnant.

He stood up. He would always love Beth, but she was slipping further away from him every day. And Moira was drawing closer and closer.

He bowed his head for a long minute, then stood up, tugged the gold band off his ring finger, and put it in his pocket.

Beth was the wife of his youth, but he wanted Moira to be the wife of his maturity.

Chapter Eighteen

Astrid turned around slowly so Moira could check her out from every angle.

"Do you think this sweater dress is okay? Is it too tight from the back? I can change into something else. There's still time."

Moira gave her a puzzled look. "You look great, your butt's just fine, and I like your nail color."

Something was going on with Astrid. Why was she acting so nervous? Not only was she concerned about what she was wearing, which had never before happened in the history of womankind, but instead of painting something like turkey drumsticks on her nails, she'd matched them to the deep mauve of her dress. What was different about today—aside from it being Thanksgiving, of course?

Moira sat down on the bed. "Are you sure you don't want to come to the C Bar M with me?"

Astrid shook her head, then made sure her chandelier earrings hadn't tangled themselves. "I told Dr. Sjoberg I'd come over to her house for Thanksgiving."

Ivanhoe barked as an automobile horn sounded outside, and Astrid's head whipped around. "Right on time!"

Moira went on big-sister alert. Why was Astrid so excited about going to her boss's Thanksgiving dinner, and why had the car horn sounded different than usual?

"Uh, who is picking you up?" This wasn't her sister's usual ride.

Astrid turned away and reached for her purse. Her voice was studiously casual. "Aaron."

"Aaron?"

"Aaron Sjoberg, Dr. Sjoberg's son. He's a veterinary student at Texas A&M, and he's been helping out at the office all week."

So that was it. Moira smiled. At last Astrid had found herself a guy with the potential of commanding a fifty-dog kennel.

* * *

Rafe took charge of Moira as soon she walked through the door. He'd been watching for her out the front window for the last half hour as he fended off aunts, uncles, and cousins who knew damn well what he was doing and seemed to get an unholy joy out of trying to distract him.

Moira was a Renoir come to life—the bright eyes, the red cheeks, the tendrils of baby hair escaping from under the fur-lined hood of her blue twill coat. It was all he could do not to whip out an art pencil and make a quick sketch of her.

She handed him an oblong box wrapped in a paper with a design of pink-and-blue balloons on it. "Could you hold this for me? It's an American Girl doll, and it's from Astrid too. She couldn't come." She looked around. "Where's Delilah?"

"She's upstairs in her playroom, workin' off her excess energy chasin' around after her cousins." He put Moira's package down on the wide window ledge next to the door and helped her out of her coat. "Cousin Sharon is runnin' the show."

Three of his mother's sisters, pretending they were casually passing through, drifted into the foyer. As he hung Moira's coat in the closet, he heard Aunt Clarice introduce herself and her sisters and, when he turned back, saw all three of them beaming at Moira as if she were pumpkin pie with whipped cream on it.

He'd known exactly how it would be. Today was a triple treat for the McAllister-Schuler clan—Thanksgiving dinner, Delilah's birthday, Moira Farrar.

The sisters all but congratulated him when he reclaimed Moira, told him how happy they were that she was joining them for Thanksgiving, then looked at one another as if transmitting a secret signal and moved on.

Moira didn't know it, but she'd passed her first test as far as the Schulers were concerned. Rafe put his arm around her waist and walked her into the living room, maneuvered her through a pack of teenagers too absorbed in each other to notice his guest, then walked her into the empty dining room to deposit Delilah's birthday gift on the overburdened buffet.

Moira glanced at the mixture of birthday and Thanksgiving decorations on the long table.

"What's the schedule of events?" she asked. The aroma wafting out the kitchen door reminded her that she'd skipped breakfast this morning.

"We all crowd around the table in about an hour and eat enough to last till Christmas. Then we'll watch Delilah open her presents and blow out her candles. Afterwards, while the aunts and uncles are sittin' in armchairs sleepin' off the tryptophan, TexAnn will herd the children upstairs to Delilah's playroom again."

"TexAnn—she's here?" She wasn't sure whether she wanted to meet Rafe's formidable sister or not.

Rafe nodded. "She's helpin' Mom and Granny Mac in the kitchen. My great-grandmother, is in there too."

He pushed the kitchen door open, and Enid came over to give Moira a quick hug.

"Happy Thanksgiving, Moira! Let me introduce you around! That's my grandmother, Oma Schuler, folding napkins at the table, and my mother-in-law, Granny Mac, is the one preparing the mushrooms. The one wielding the electric carving knife is Rafe's sister, TexAnn."

Moira eyed the serrated edge of the knife. Enid's daughter looked like a younger edition of her mother, but she also looked like someone who could command an army. It was obvious why TexAnn would run for senator, but Moira was surprised that she wasn't running for governor.

TexAnn laid an authoritative hand on her mother's shoulder. "Mom, everything's under control here, and Sharon will be bringing the kids down in about twenty minutes, so how about you getting rid of the apron and introducing Moira to the rest of the family? I think the Schulers have congregated in the family room. I can hear the piano."

In other words, TexAnn was ordering her mother to go enjoy herself.

Enid made a gesture of surrender and let Rafe put his arm around her and walk her out of the kitchen.

The front door swung open as they reached the foyer, and Rocky stepped inside, hauling what looked like a large cardboard box behind her. "Howdy, y'all! Can anyone help me with this thing? It's for Delilah."

As Rafe took the box from her and leaned it against the newel post, Moira finally made out what Rocky's gift was—the big, expensive flap-out playhouse Overton's had advertised in yesterday's *Retriever*.

Rocky put her hands on her hips and looked around. "Where's the birthday girl?"

"The kids are upstairs in the playroom," Enid answered.

"Well, I'm still a kid myself so that's where I'll be too!" Rocky declared with a melodic laugh. "Hey, Moira, how about you walking me up the stairs?"

Enid waved her hand. "You two girls go on up and see Delilah." She winked at Moira. "The Schulers can wait for another day."

Moira laughed and joined Rocky on the stairs. Maybe she could begin all over again with Rocky, now that she knew not to take her seriously.

"How's it going with Travis?" she ventured. Rocky's husband's health was a safe topic. No way it could evoke any funny stories that she'd feel ashamed of laughing at later.

Rocky laughed. "He's feeling sorta puny today and decided to stay home. He's saving himself for roundup tomorrow."

"Roundup?"

"Didn't Rafe tell you? The McAllisters always hold a roundup on the day after Thanksgiving. That's when they castrate the baby calves."

Moira refused to respond to her sidelong glance. Was Rocky trying to provoke her?

They reached the landing and followed the hullabaloo to Delilah's room, or rather, her suite. She had two rooms—one for sleeping, and one for playing—which could be separated by the same kind of sliding doors that guarded Rafe's bathroom, closet, and office The doors were open now, and the children were running back and forth, engaged in some sort of catch-me game, while Carmen Atherton and a redheaded woman looked on.

Moira glanced around. Delilah's sleeping area, which faced out over the front of the house, was sweet and simple—a single bed with a lamp on a table on one side of it and a wall of closets on the other side. Over her bed hung a pencil drawing in an oval frame.

Rocky noticed her interest. "That's Beth, but it doesn't look like her. She had a lantern jaw, and her hair was flat straight—not a bit of body in it."

Moira studied the sketch. The broad jaw was there, but somehow it worked with the rest of her features. Maybe love was blind, but it was also likely that Rafe was recording more than Beth's chin and hair. Even in the photo in Enid's collage,

Beth had a radiance about her, a glow, that Rafe had captured perfectly in his drawing.

Delilah, suddenly aware she was in the room, rushed over to embrace her, then took her by the hand to lead her into the midst of the children. "I want to 'troduce you to all my cousins."

Moira had just finished helping Delilah put all her My Little Ponies to bed when TexAnn came upstairs to call everyone to dinner. Rocky immediately stepped forward and exerted her auntie rights to walk the birthday girl downstairs, which left Moira and Carmen bringing up the rear.

Carmen gave her a warm smile as they walked to the landing. "You know, Enid really likes you. She's telling everybody how happy she is that Rafe's found someone he wants to bring home."

Well, that was a quite a conversation starter. "I like Enid too." What else could she say? What was the accepted way to acknowledge the approval of one's sexual partner's mother?

They started down the stairs. "Delilah's my goddaughter," Carmen continued. "Beth was my best friend all through school—and an even better friend then when I came back to Bosque Bend with my baby."

Beth was Carmen's best friend? But Rocky had said *she* was Beth's best friend.

* * *

Thanksgiving dinner had been cleared from the table, Delilah had opened her gifts and been serenaded by all present, Carmen and Rocky had left, the birthday girl was down for a well-deserved nap, and TexAnn was driving her grandmother and great-grandmother back to Waco.

Moira stayed to help Enid with the final cleanup, while Rafe went out to the barn to prepare for the roundup. Once the last counter had been wiped, Enid broke out a bottle of Pinot Noir and the two women sat down at the kitchen table.

Enid took a healthy swallow. "I've been meaning to thank you for rescuing Sammy. As many brothers and sisters as I have, I'm closer to some than to others, but I have a loyalty to all of them—and their kids. In fact, I'm writing a family memoir."

"With the size of your family, that's quite an undertaking."

"Oh, I've already covered the Schulers. Now I'm working on the McAllisters and the history of the ranch. It's one of those classic Old West stories, but it's more about relationships than cattle."

Moira sipped at her drink and activated her mental recorder. "That's the best kind."

"Back in the 1850s, Rocky's great-grandfather won the ranch in a poker game and started running cattle. But he didn't have a lick of business sense and would have lost every acre of it if Gilbert McAllister hadn't stepped in. They went half and half, but Colby resented sharing—it's always that way when the money person comes on the scene. Anyway, Colby thought he could win the ranch back if he played enough poker, but the cards went against him this time."

Moira nodded. So this was why Bertie Fuller had told Astrid that the C Bar M had been stolen from the Colbys.

"You'd think the animosity would have died down in this generation, but grudges last a long time in a small town. The Colbys have been grumbling ever since." Enid raised her glass to her lips. "I never took to Rocky's mother. She wasn't the sweetie she pretends to be. Rafe thinks Bertie Fuller—who is the most gullible person on the face of the earth—was the source of the rumors about the ranch and Beth's death, but I think it was Theda Eagan and that she repeated the big lie often enough that Bertie and Chub believed her."

Enid paused as if she were wondering whether to go on.

Moira didn't say a word, just looked expectant. Whatever the story was, she wanted to hear it all.

"Rocky made a play for Rafe early on, but he'd already met Beth, so then she went after Travis—he and Micaela were having problems at the time. I think Rocky told him she was pregnant because the next thing that his father and I knew was that they were married. Three months later, she said she'd had a miscarriage."

She finished off her glass with a flourish, then looked straight at Moira.

"Rocky's the sort of person that women catch on to, but men never figure out till it's too late. Rafe's father thought Rocky was a ministering angel because she sneaked 'real food' in for him when he was in the hospital." Enid poured herself another half glass and topped off Moira's glass, which wasn't anywhere near empty. "I wish he'd seen her face when she learned Rafe inherited everything, just like the oldest son always has."

Moira took a few more sips from her own glass. She wasn't

a drinker so it was heady stuff to her, but what Enid was telling her was even stronger.

Too many things were adding up against Rocky for her to ignore. Maybe she'd better steer clear of the laughing girl for a while. At least till she sorted everything out.

* * *

The Christmas season went into full swing the next day. Cars sprouted felt deer horns out their windows and cheerful plastic wreaths on their grills, cedars along the road wound themselves with tinsel garlands, Santa Clauses sat on rooftops, reindeer pranced on parched lawns, and a Salvation Army bell ringer had stationed himself in front of Walmart.

Rafe bought the biggest wreath he could find and dropped a twenty into the pot as he left. He'd have to remember to arrange for a couple of cast members to come sing carols around the kettle. It would be good publicity and bring in a few more bucks for the Salvation Army Christmas dinners.

Yesterday had been a good day. It was always a good day when the family got together, and Thanksgiving falling on Delilah's birthday this year made everything extra special.

But what was going on with Moira? She didn't have much to say when he got back to the house, just thanked him for inviting her, told Enid she'd enjoyed the dinner and meeting her family, then drove home. Maybe she was tired, maybe it was the turkey, or maybe it was the wine his mother had fed her. She and Mom had looked pretty chummy when he came in from the barn yesterday afternoon.

He drove home, hung the wreath on the front door, and walked inside as he and walked inside. An oven buzzer sounded, indicating that Mom, who'd stayed overnight again to prepare lunch for the roundup crew, was up and about.

They'd have about ten on the scene, as far as he knew—Rocky and Travis, Omar, Jimbo Crane, two Schuler uncles from Marlin, and a couple of ranchers to the west.

He snorted. Mervin and his oldest girl were coming too. Probably trying to mend fences after that damn jailhouse interrogation. Besides, Mervin would need his help when his ranch had a roundup.

That's the way it worked—his neighbors and kinfolk helped him with his roundups, and he helped them with theirs. And with that many people involved, they should be through about six o'clock.

He hung up his jacket and headed toward the kitchen.

He'd be tired afterward, he knew, but it would feel good, and he'd already made plans for the perfect way to spend the rest of the evening. He and Moira were going to Good Times to dine on pork ribs, drink Bud Light, and dance to songs about women who did cowboys wrong. Then they'd come back to the house, and she'd spend the weekend.

Tomorrow, they'd decorate the tree together, and who knew what else might happen?

He rubbed his ring finger. It felt strange—so bare. But if everything worked out, not for long.

* * *

Moira pursed her lips and glared at the rock band playing on the Good Times stage. Omar's ribs were tender, and the beer was—well—beer, but the would-be rockers didn't cut the mustard. The lead singer's vocals were on par, although his guitar licks must be attracting every stray cat within earshot, while the bass was just enough off beat to be annoying, and the drummer looked like he was asleep at the wheel.

To top it off, the feedback from the sound system was classic fingernails on a chalkboard.

She looked at Rafe across the table. He didn't even seem to be aware of the band. As far as she could tell, he'd been brooding all evening, and from the cryptic hints he'd given her, it was about something Mervin Hruska had told him at the roundup.

What now? Was his cousin going to haul him in for another interrogation?

The band started on "Yellow Submarine." Moira winced and took another sip of beer. "Does Omar hire rock bands very often?"

Rafe shook his head. "Only if they're related."

"They're Schulers?"

"No way, darlin'. His wife's side of the family."

She laughed and picked up a rib. "How's Travis doing?"

"He came to roundup, but left early. I wish we'd get the result of those damn lab tests."

He paused and looked into his mug as if making a decision, then raised his eyes.

"Gotta tell you somethin'. Mervin had his eyes open when he drove in today, and he wants to send someone out to look at the old tree house. He thinks the shooter could have been standing up there."

"You've got a tree house? Where?"

"In one of the big live oaks in front of the house. It's hard to see. I checked this morning and the boards my father nailed on the tree for Travis and me to use as a ladder are rotted off now, but they could have still been usable three years ago."

He took a long swallow of beer and glanced toward the stage. "That caterwauling is driving me crazy. Let's go back to the house. We'll have a better day tomorrow. I'll chop down a cedar in the morning, and we can decorate it, then spend the evening in front of the fire."

* * *

Moira watched with fascination as Rafe rubbed the inner layer of the cedar bark between his hands to shred it for tinder. She'd never seen anyone start a fire from scratch before.

They'd been together all day, and, just as he'd promised, he'd chopped down a nicely shaped tree for them to take back to the house. Then, after he'd finished up his ranch business this afternoon, he'd pulled out boxes of ornaments and strings of lights for them to hang on it—fragile glass balls, yards of white blinking lights, and an angel tree-topper.

And now, after a nourishing dinner of popcorn—something not even Rafe could screw up—she was lying on Enid's Navajo rug in front of the fireplace and waiting for the show to begin.

This was the thrilling moment, the birth of the universe—Rafe struck a piece of flint with a short length of steel.

The tinder flared for a second, then died, but he lit it again and blew gently on the flickers until they caught for sure, then added twigs from a canister on the hearth. As the fire grew, he fed its appetite with sticks. Finally, he added a couple of small logs on top of the grate to keep it happy.

Moira rolled over onto her stomach and watched as the flames snapped and flickered against the dark recess of the fireplace and orange and yellow arms fought each other, twisting and turning like whirling dervishes.

This is the very same fire the Neanderthals warmed their caves with, she mused, but it was a different fire—every fire was the same but different—and every fire was beautiful.

Rafe lifted two more logs from the elegant rack beside the fireplace and added them to the fire, but this time the greedy flames seemed to reach out for him. He stepped back quickly and put up the screen, then turned to Moira.

"This should take care of us for the evenin.'"

She rubbed her eyes, wondering if staring at a fire was as dangerous as staring at the sun. After all, they both burned. Maybe she should focus on Rafe, her own private Prometheus.

Who was pretty damn hot in his own right.

She sat up and looked at him. "I didn't know anyone could start a fire from flint and steel—I mean for real. I thought it was either rubbing two sticks together or turning on the gas."

She risked a quick glance at the fireplace. The fire was bigger now, fuller, and the embers under the grate glowed red as the flames above them reached up the chimney.

"Good grief, it sounds like a vacuum cleaner. I didn't realize fires made so much noise."

Rafe laughed and flipped off the overhead so that the only light in the room was from the fireplace and the Christmas tree situated beside it. "That's what you get for living in Pasadena."

Her own flame lit as he lay down beside her on the thick rug and looped an arm around her shoulder. Sex was in the air, and every nerve cell she possessed was reporting for active duty. There was something about being alone with Rafe in front of the blazing fire that brought out her inner cavewoman, and this woman was hungry, but not for popcorn.

His lips brushed her cheeks, and she turned over on her side to give him access to whatever he wanted, and he took possession of her mouth—a long, comfortable kiss that said he wasn't going to rush her.

Her mouth had gone dry and she was tingling all over. He backed off and ran his fingers through her hair. "You have beautiful hair, sort of a nimbus of light that never quite settles. It's like a halo."

"Thank you." Her voice sounded wobbly, but it was the best she could do right now.

The fire popped and crackled behind them.

"The heat is firing off the water pockets in the big logs," Rafe explained as his hand caressed her cheek.

God, a simple touch, and she went hot all over, all the way down to her toes.

He leaned over to nuzzle her face, settling on her mouth again, then drew back again. His hand moved up and down her arm, slowly, very slowly.

Oh God, she was about to explode, and they hadn't even gotten naked yet.

He smiled. "I like your mouth too. In fact, I like everything about you." He kissed her again, not giving her a chance to reply. She didn't know if she could have. She wrapped an arm around his shoulders to urge him on, but he shrugged it off. "Tonight is for you, Moira. Let me make you happy." His voice was a deep purr.

Moving in closer, he balanced on an arm while his hand moved under the sleeve of her shirt and continued stroking, coming nearer and nearer to her breast, then retreated and moved down the side of her thighs, up and down, slowly. Torturously slow.

She tossed her head and moaned, then began sliding her legs against each other, begging.

"Not yet," he whispered.

He kissed her lips, but when she tried to give him entrance to her mouth, he moved around to the side of her face and left a trail of quick, tiny kisses across her cheek. At the same time, the tips of his fingers moved gently up and down the side of her neck.

Wave after wave of sensation shot through her. Oh God, she was going to die before this night was over!

Finally, watching her face the whole time, he released the top button of her shirt, then he smiled, an angelic smile in an angelic face. But his eyes sparkled like a demon's.

Damn, he was teasing her, and she didn't like it. But she knew that her ultimate reward would be worth it.

He slipped the second button, then the third, revealing

her bra, then frowned and moved his legs to adjust himself. So—she wasn't the only one who was hungry.

His pace quickened now. There was a bit of desperation in the way he kissed her neck and the swell of her breasts, then unfastened her shirt all the way down.

She drew in a ragged breath and bent her head back as the heat suffused her like a warm blanket. He opened her shirt to unhook her bra, and deep growl erupted from his throat as he lifted off her bra and covered her breasts with his hands.

He rolled her nipples between his fingers, like he had in the museum lobby, and she closed her eyes to intensify the ecstasy. Then he then sucked at them, one after the other. The fire snapped and crackled as she moaned and arched in response.

He and he claimed her lips again and teased her mouth, then moved a hand down under the front of her jeans and palmed her mound.

She nearly came off the floor.

He unzipped her jeans and drew them off her legs, an inch at a time. Her arms felt heavy and weightless at the same time, and her brain clouded over as if she'd been drugged.

The fireplace flared suddenly, but she didn't care. She didn't care if the house burned down. All she wanted was Rafe, and she wanted him now.

She reached down to pull off her panties, but he grasped her wrist. "I'll do it, darlin'."

Hooking a thumb under the elastic, he lowered the flimsy nylon to the tops of her legs, then bent down, spread her petals, and sipped her nectar.

She couldn't breathe, she couldn't think. It was like he was worshipping her, giving her every pleasure he could, before he sought his own. All she could do was brace her hands on the floor as the rapture began to engulf her.

Then he stood up. "My turn."

Looking into her eyes, he stripped off his sweater and shirt, then his jeans—in slow motion again, like he was performing for her, the firelight highlighting his every move.

Then he knelt beside her on the floor and, still maintaining eye contact, moved her hand on the elastic band of his briefs. "Your turn."

But the second she touched him, he groaned, pushed her hand away, shoved down his briefs with one quick move, and straddled her.

His hand went straight down to her navel, then below. He slipped a finger inside her and she whimpered and moved against him. She must be wet as Niagara by now.

Parting her legs, he probed for entry and pushed past her barrier of flesh to sink into the female heart of her, then kissed her mouth and began a slow, controlled rhythm.

She closed her eyes and floated into another universe, where there was no tomorrow, as her body clutched at him and spasms of desire lifted her against him.

But she wanted more. She wanted all of him. Her hips met his every stroke, urging him to completion. *Fill me. Let me hold you within me while I can.*

The lights on the tree flickered in the background and Rafe's body gleamed slick with sweat.

Moira bucked up against him. Her climax was coming fast

and her breath was short. He'd built her up to a combustion point, and she'd erupt into flames any second.

A second later, her toes curled and she heard herself give out a long keening sound. She was a supernova exploding in the depths of space for what seemed to be forever. A supernova that floated back to earth to rest in Rafe's arms as the tender aftershocks shook her.

He kissed the tip of her nose.

"I like goin' to bed with you, darlin', and I like wakin' up with you." He kissed her nose again. "I love you, Moira."

All her alarm bells went off.

Love.

Exactly what she didn't want to hear.

She sat up and started scooting away from him.

"You can't love me. I won't let you!"

She grabbed for her shirt and tried to put it back on, but one of the arms wasn't working right. Oh God, this was the worst possible thing that could happen. She turned the sleeve right side out and fastened the top button, then reached for her panties.

"You said sex only, no commitments!"

The fire crackled its anger and Rafe's deep voice roared around the room.

"You mean, I'm good enough for Colin Sanger's wife to fuck, but not good enough for her to marry?"

Chapter Nineteen

Moira's mouth widened to a travesty of a smile that trembled like a mirage and then dissolved. She was scared, frightened, on the brink of tears, but when he tried to touch her, she crossed her arms across herself protectively and retreated even more.

He pulled on his jeans. Maybe she would deal with him better if he wasn't letting it all hang out.

Her voice was choking and weak. "It's—it's not like that at all." She started shivering and he offered her his sweater. She snatched it from his hand and tied in around her shoulders.

"Tell me." This better be a good story.

"You've—you've got it all wrong. You're ten times—a hundred times—better than Colin Sanger—a hundred times better than me." She looked around at the Christmas tree innocently twinkling in the corner, the fire burning brightly, the tall, handsome man—the *good* man—in front of her.

God, she'd hoped she'd never have to tell him this.

"I'm—I'm damaged goods, Rafe. I let Colin do horrible things to me, and he turned me into something awful."

"Tell me."

She drove her fingernails into her palms and closed her eyes tight. Rafe deserved an explanation, but there was no way she wanted to see his reaction.

Taking a deep breath, she focused her eyes on the crackling fire and began, "You know that Colin always played a good guy. The dashing hero, the debonair charmer, James Bond with an overlay of Indiana Jones. And he—he cooperated with the paparazzi and had a great reputation on the set. So when he started paying attention to a nobody like me, it was a fairy tale come true. The king of stage, screen, and television wanted to date *me*."

Rafe took a seat in one of the armchairs, but she stayed on the floor.

"But nobody knew the real Colin Sanger." She laughed, a brittle sound even to her own ears. "Colin was sick—not with a disease that made you feel sorry for him, but with a malignancy he imposed on others. He didn't love me. I wasn't courted—I was targeted. He needed someone who was naïve enough to believe in his image and easily controllable, and I fit the bill—a minor actress with a family to support. He needed…someone he could train to…obedience."

It took Rafe a second to catch on. "You mean…?"

She nodded. "In a black leather room in the basement of his mansion—shackles, St. Andrew's cross, the whole bit. I was his sex toy, and at first, it thrilled me that someone was interested in me as a woman rather than as a fast study."

She shivered. The fire was still burning hot, but she was cold as ice.

"He let me have a couple of months of marital bliss, then began showing me shots of glamorous women in provocative poses—women with their hands bound above their heads, women chained up with their legs spread, women posed as furniture, you name it—and told me how much fun it was. He said that no one got hurt, that it was only make-believe, and it helped him relax."

She lifted her eyes to the angel on top of the tree. It represented everything good, and there was nothing good about the story she was about to tell. "He flogged me, used a crop on me, put a dog collar on me, tied me up with ropes and chains and belts—whatever he wanted to do, then took photos and taped them on the wall to show me what I'd become. He called them games, but they weren't."

She risked a quick glance at Rafe. He was staring at her like he'd never seen her before—and in a way, he hadn't. Maybe she should shade the truth, but now that she'd started talking, she couldn't stop. She'd had everything bottled up far too long. "Do you know what the worst part of it was? I cooperated." Her mouth twisted. "Maybe if he'd forced me, I might have some self-respect, but I went along with everything at first, and then I was in too deep to get out."

"Why did you do it at all?"

She shrugged. "I loved him and wanted to make him happy.

And I thought he loved me." Her smile was bitter. "Even in real life, he was a great actor."

"I'm surprised you didn't leave him."

The fireplace flames leaped and crackled like evil sprites, but the tree lights, uncaring, blinked on an off in a regular pattern. "At first, because I thought that I could heal him. Later, I was too ashamed of what I had become. Toward the end, I was so dehumanized that I wouldn't have walked out the door even if it had been left open—which none of them ever were."

"I even liked it at first—pain and sexual arousal are first cousins, you know. It was forbidden fruit—sophisticated and naughty—and I was curious. There were other things going on too, of course. Obedience was very important to him and he made a list of rules I had to follow, like what I could and couldn't eat. And if I objected or didn't follow the rules to the letter—or if he just felt like it—he'd leash me up to a hitching post and wind my hair around my mouth so I couldn't scream—I had long hair then—then leave me alone in the black room with all the lights out for what seemed like days."

"The nightmare."

She nodded. "I never knew how long I'd be there, and I was so grateful when he'd come back and untie me that I'd do whatever he wanted."

The fire popped again, but she ignored it.

"Do you want to know why I got upset when you touched the scar on my arm? It's where I had a tattoo removed. Colin's signature of ownership—two crossed whips."

Her face twisted, and the tears rolled down her cheek. "It

was all so awful. That's why I don't want you to love me, why I can't marry you. I'm…dirty."

Rafe reached out and drew her into his arms. His jaw was as rigid and set as Quanah Parker's.

"No, Moira. You went through fire and came out steel. You are the strongest, bravest woman I've ever known, and I love you even more now that I know what you survived."

* * *

Moira woke up alone.

Rafe's side of the bed was empty, and the doors to his office, closet, and bathroom were open. He must be downstairs, trying to figure out how to dump her as tactfully—and quickly—as possible. He'd probably say something about how busy he was with the ranch and renovating the Hauco Theater.

She leaned back against her pillow and replayed every minute of the scene last night from the second Rafe had said he loved her to when they trailed upstairs to the bedroom and she finally fell asleep. It must have disgusted him to hear what she'd allowed Colin to do to her, to realize how—how *tainted* she was. He'd put on a good front, of course, and kept insisting that said he loved her even more because of what she'd been through, but in the bright light of day, he'd be having second thoughts.

She looked around at the room. She would never forget it—the white, white walls, the window wall, the balcony. And she'd always remember Rafe too—and how much, despite herself, she loved him.

Yes, she loved him. She could admit it now, but only to herself.

Maybe she should pack up and leave Bosque Bend right now, but where would she go—and how would she earn her daily bread? There weren't that many well-paying civic theater director jobs lying around, and the places she applied to would want to know why she skipped out on Bosque Bend. Leaving town right now would be hard on Astrid too. Dr. Sjoberg was talking to her about A&M's veterinary program, and she was spending her evenings with Aaron, who was home for holiday break.

She could hear Rafe coming down the hall.

It was going to be hard to make her farewell speech while she was lying naked in his bed, but she had to do it now, while she was still thinking rationally. And after she'd had her say, she'd wrap the sheet around herself and, with as much dignity as she could muster, walk across the room to the closet and slide the door shut to dress.

Rafe came into the room with a smile on his face and a tray in his hands.

"How about some breakfast? Eggs and toast, fresh from the skillet of Chef McAllister."

Moira's jaw muscles sagged.

"You want to *feed* me?"

His eyes glittered at her. "I want to do a lot more than that to you, darlin', but let's start with breakfast."

She gave him his cue. "Don't you want to tell me how busy you are and that you don't have time for a relationship right now?"

He put the tray on the bedside table and sat down beside

her. "Moira, I have all the time in the world for you, and what you told me last night made me love you even more." He kissed her fly-away hair.

She tried again. "You deserve someone so much better than I am. Someone fresh and clean."

He took her hand. "I'll bide my time, but you're the one I want." He gave her a lopsided grin. "Now, get your cute little fanny into some jeans and we'll take a ride. I want to be sure the panther isn't still hangin' around before we move the bulls in there."

* * *

Sarge exhaled a long, low snort as they skirted the edge of the river, and Rafe rested his hand on the stock of his shotgun.

Moira rode up beside him. "What's going on?"

"Sarge smells panther. We'll quarantine this pasture right now, and maybe Travis will feel well enough next week to help me go after him. That cat's a big boy, and I want backup with a big gun."

He shaded his eyes with his hand and looked toward the sun. "But we'd better be headin' back to the house now. It's about time for Delilah to get home."

His mother seemed to have accepted the relationship he had with Moira, but he wasn't ready to introduce Moira into his Delilah's everyday world yet. Delilah liked Moira, but he wouldn't want his daughter to fall in love with her like he had, then go through the same anguish he'd go through if Moira left him.

He glanced over at her. If Moira wanted to drive him off, she'd made a big mistake by telling him about Colin. Hearing what she'd survived had only intensified his feelings her. She was more than the delight of his heart—she was someone he admired and respected. There was no way he was going to cut and run.

* * *

Moira sat down beside Carmen, leaned her head back, and closed her eyes for a second of meditation as Vashti ran the chorus through "Love Triumphant."

She liked Carmen. She was easy to talk to. There was a sense of peace, a contentment, about her that she needed to tap into right now. Nine days till the show opened, and Billie Joe was still moving the wrong way in the mob scene, Rafe's police helmet had gotten lost in shipment, one of the flats had had to be redone, two children had dropped out with pinkeye, and the light crew couldn't get the spotlight to stay on track.

On the other hand, the second act was really shaping up well.

She nudged Carmen. "Hey, violin lady, how did you get off the hook? You've got a counterpoint on this song."

Carmen laughed. "I'm getting stale so Mother's gave me time off."

The song ended on an exultant note, the curtain was drawn on the chorus, and Rafe was left alone on the stage.

His final song was vital, not only to give the story closure, but to ensure each member of the audience walked out smiling. That was the attraction of musicals. People had way too many problems in their everyday lives, and plays like *Gift of the Magi* sent them out the door with a warm glow in their hearts and the hope that their own troubles would merely be the prelude to their own happy endings.

Like maybe hers would be. Rafe had insisted on visiting the jewelry shop under his office this afternoon. He wasn't pushing, but he was nudging.

"Rafe is perfect as the policeman," Carmen commented as Rafe began swinging his truncheon in his hand. "I'm glad you two are together. How are things at the C Bar M? I haven't been out there for ages."

"I love that ranch. Maybe I was a cowgirl in a past life."

She froze. *Oh crap, had she said the wrong thing?* Rocky had told her how much Beth hated the C Bar M, and here she was extolling it to Carmen, Beth's best friend. She tried for a quick save. "On the other hand, most women would want to live closer to town, especially if they have children. And then there's the weaning. And the roundups. I can understand why Beth didn't want to stay on the ranch."

Carmen eyes widened in shock and disbelief. "Moira, Beth stayed with her parents when the calves were weaned because their bawling upset her, but she understood that it was necessary, just like banding the little bulls. But she loved the ranch just like you do, and she loved Rafe too. If they were having problems, I would have heard about it." She gave Moira searching look. "Whoever told you she wanted to leave Rafe? Was it Rocky?"

Moira didn't answer—it would be telling—but Carmen

nodded her understanding. "Rocky and I used to be friends, but she dropped me when I wasn't of any more use to her. It hurt me at the time, but was a blessing in disguise. That woman is toxic."

Moira watched Rafe finish his song with four more thumps of the truncheon.

Even allowing for a bit of bias on Carmen's part—no one likes to be dropped—that was a strong indictment of the laughing girl. Maybe she'd better steer clear of Rocky for a while.

Not that she'd have much time for her right now. The final dress rehearsal was looming. Then would come opening night, and if Boyd Yancey didn't show up by curtain time, she was home free.

* * *

Moira wiggled herself into the most sophisticated dress she had in her wardrobe, a moss-green velveteen with fitted sleeves and a low-cut scalloped neckline, slipped on heels that lifted her to heights unknown, put Gram's long jade earrings through her earlobes, and sprayed herself with perfume. She knew how a director should present herself.

Her plan was to arrive at the museum an hour before the performance so she could make sure everything was in working order, then meet and greet every audience member she could. She was the public face of the Bosque Bend Theater Guild, and it was important that she be available and approachable—and besides, with this being opening night, she'd generated a major adrenaline rush she had to use up before she started running around, flapping her arms, and trying to fly.

The curtain went up at seven, but Moira drove in two hours early in case there were any last-minute developments she needed to take care of. It was anxious mother syndrome, she knew, but she couldn't help it. This was the first show she'd ever directed without a drama professor hanging over her. It was also the first show she'd ever directed that would have a general admission audience, not other theater majors or students looking for cheap entertainment.

And the first show she'd staked the rest of her life on.

Everything seemed to be going well so far. The final dress rehearsal had hit several small bumps and a mountain or two, but Billie Joe had finally figured out which was her right foot and which was her left, Rafe's police helmet had arrived yesterday, Sammy had jerry-rigged the injured flat, no one else had come down with pinkeye, and the spotlight was finally clamped tight enough that it wasn't slipping all over the stage.

Moira smiled as the driver in front of her put on his brake lights to slow down, then sped up when the traffic light changed. The red taillights and green traffic lights glowing in the dark looked like Christmas decorations. At this time of year, everything did.

She resumed speed and thought about what she was going to say to the cast before the play, when they would join hands in a circle in the traditional show of solidarity. Probably the same thing she'd heard from her directors—own your character, break a leg, and no matter what happens, keep on going with a smile on your face.

Keep a smile on your face.

Come to think of it, that was good advice for her too, especially since Arthur Sawyer would be interviewing her for the *Retriever* before the performance tonight.

A worm of panic slithered through her gut. Would Boyd Yancey accompany him? After all, if his editor wasn't interested in the story unless he could get it in before the play opened, this would be his last chance.

She turned into the museum parking lot and, for good luck, parked in the same spot she'd taken five weeks ago, when she'd first met the people who were now so important in her life—Pendleton Swaim, Vashti, Xandra and Fleurette, Travis…Rafe.

A BMW sedan honked at her and pulled in beside her. Sergio and Desdemona climbed out and accompanied her across the street.

This was as good a time as any to ask them about *Pirates of Penzance* and *Cinderella*.

"What are your plans for the spring, Sergio? I'm thinking of a Gilbert and Sullivan lead for you."

He avoided her eyes. "I'm thinking of leaving right after the show, so I probably won't be around. My uncle in New York wants to introduce me to a few big names up there, and a friend of mine and I may go up there right after the show and see what happens."

Clunk. Her ship hit the rocks. No way Phillip Schoenfeldt could pass for a twenty-one-year-old apprentice pirate.

"That's terrific! I wish you well!" She turned to his sister. "What about you, Desdemona? Are you hitching a ride with Sergio to the Big Apple?"

The ballerina shook her head. "Dancers are a dime a dozen in New York, and I don't want to do what I'd have to do to stand out from the crowd. I've decided to stick around Bosque Bend and sign up for the nursing program at the community college in Waco."

"Would you still have time to do theater?"

"Of course. It's my outlet."

Moira nodded. At least *Cinderella* was still an option.

* * *

Percy Washington was struggling to get into a dove-gray morning coat that was a shade too small for him as Rafe walked into the men's dressing room.

Percy shrugged his shoulders to ease the fit. "I hate to tell you, Rafe, but the Rockefeller Bank isn't holding together. It's failed."

"Clever, guy, but that flat is just plain too big." Rafe lifted his police uniform off the costume rack. "The balance board I put in should have taken care of it—unless someone hit up against it again backstage. I'll check it out after I get dressed."

"By the way, I saw Moira out in the hall when I was coming in. People were lined up to shake her hand, and, man, she's gone Hollywood on us. That dress—wow! It looked like it had been made for her to wear to the Oscars." Percy dusted off his homburg and twirled his cane. "I figure a lot of people came to the play just so they can say they've met Moira Farrar."

"She's doing us proud, Percy." Rafe took off his jacket and shirt and sat down at the makeup counter.

Moira usually dressed down, but not tonight. He'd caught a glimpse of her as he walked back to the dressing room. That dress fit her every inch along the way, and he'd bet she didn't have a bra on. If this were Friday, he'd be taking her home with him and finding out for sure.

He touched the ring box in his pocket just to be sure it was still there. She'd liked this set, he knew—had even tried them on—which he took to mean that she was coming around.

He opened a can of dark-toned pancake and smeared it on his face so the lights wouldn't wash him out, then darkened his eyebrows and picked up his handlebar mustache clip. Most of the guys in the cast had been issued mustaches. Not Sergio, of course. The Dreamer was a shadow figure, and besides, Sergio looked too young for a full mustache.

Percy took a final look at the mirror and twirled his cane. "I'm going off to guard the Rockefeller Bank before anyone knocks it over again."

"Give me a few more minutes and I'll be out there." Rafe zipped up his navy-blue pants and reached for his double-breasted jacket. Sammy, Sergio, and Buck came in as he was closing the Velcro strips.

Sammy told him the Rockefeller Bank had fallen on hard times, Sergio said it had gone broke, and Buck just stood there grinning.

Rafe rolled his eyes and reached for his truncheon, helmet, and big copper badge. He'd better prop up that damn flat before the whole world reported in.

* * *

Moira met Art Sawyer—who was unaccompanied—in a far corner of the auditorium behind the ropes. It was the most private place she could think of.

"Thank you for your time, Ms. Farrar. First of all I want to offer my condolences on the death of your late husband. I've seen every one of Colin Sanger's films, and the world will be a sadder place without him."

She gave him the usual sad smile and mumbled a thank you. Hopefully, having once expressed his condolences, Sawyer would never mention Colin's name again.

He took a small spiral notebook out of his breast pocket and poised a pen above it. "Now, tell me about Pendleton Swaim's play."

That she could do. Her smile was real this time. *Gift of the Magi* is a wonderfully heartwarming story, and it's so appropriate for Christmas, not just because of the subject matter but because of the theme—love."

Love...

Rafe had walked her through the jewelry store so many times the past week and a half that she knew all the clerks by their first names. If he was trying to wear her down, he was doing a good job of it.

But she didn't want to make a commitment until every second of Boyd Yancey's deadline had passed. For all she knew, he was out in the hall, ready to pounce when she emerged from the interview with Art. Pray God Yancey wouldn't show up and she'd be safe.

More important, Rafe was safe.

She posed next to a blow-up of the *Gift of the Magi* poster in the hall outside the auditorium for Sawyer's camera, then dared the devil by staying there till the ten-minute light blinked, talking to people she knew and people she didn't. If Yancey showed, he'd have to get in line like everyone else.

Once she entered the auditorium again, so many people on the aisle wanted to welcome her to Bosque Bend that it took her the full ten minutes to get down to her reserved seat. It was on the first row, at the end, as near to the stage steps as she could get, in case she needed to run backstage and save the day.

Astrid and Aaron, she knew, had prime seats in the tenth row beside Enid and a group from Floravista. Xandra and Fleurette, dressed in their usual black—did they ever wear any other color?—were on the front row at the other side of the stage, probably with the same motive she had.

The theater darkened, the audience hushed, and Vashti played the opening chords of the overture. Carmen lifted her bow and came in on the third measure.

The show had started and Yancey hadn't appeared. Relief flooded through her. Now she could sit back and enjoy the show.

The overture ended, paused, then started up again in a variation Moira had never heard before. Something was wrong. Vashti and Carmen were stalling.

Moira jerked as a loud thud sounded from behind the curtain, then another, followed by a muffled yell. There was a buzz of speculation in the seats around her.

The Athertons headed into a third version of the overture, this time with Carmen taking the lead and her mother playing an accompaniment

Moira fixed a smile on her face, and she half rose in her

chair, preparing herself to walk up onto the stage and make a long, rambling speech about how wonderful it was to work in community theater. She knew how to handle this situation—was it an unwritten rule that something always went wrong on opening night.

A thumbs-up came through the side of the curtain, and she sat down again.

Vashti nodded at Carmen and finished off the fourth run-through of the overture with a thundering chord.

The theater was silent with expectation.

Moira went cold. It was make-or-break time.

A New York copper strolled out in front of the curtain, slapping his truncheon into his hand four times to set the beat, and began singing. His unaccompanied voice filled the auditorium.

New York morning, clear and bright
Not a single cloud in sight
Ladies and gents are strolling the street
Talking with all the friends they meet
While children trundle their hoops along—
Everything's right, nothing is wrong.
Nothing is wrong, everything's right—
Try as you may
Try as you might,
Whatever you say
Life's a delight
You won't find anything wrong today,
Not on this beautiful New York day.

Moira let herself breathe. Rafe was good—even better than in rehearsal. Some people were like that. An audience brought it out in them. No wonder he was so popular.

Applause erupted at the end of the first verse, and Vashti waited for it to die down before playing the introduction to the street scene. The grand drape opened slowly on a frozen stage, a 1900s tableau of Christmas in New York.

Not a soul moved—not even Wendy Nixon, bless her.

As soon as Rafe walked back across the stage and launched into the second verse, the stage came to life in double-time. The bootblacks lined themselves up and shined shoes in rapid rhythm, the Loughlin girls trundled their hoops onto the scene, and the flower girls darted back and forth, alternately playing with each other and peddling limp violets to people hurrying along the street.

The tempo increased by the second as the stage bustled with activity approaching frenzy. As the chorus came in for the third verse. Rafe dropped down to a strong obbligato below them, and the activity evolved into a round dance with the children running in and out between the adults, tagging each other.

The pace slowed as Phil and Micaela entered the scene. And Moira's eyes wandered over to Rafe, standing on his mark at the side of the stage like a wooden Indian. Her heart warmed.

Boyd Yancey hadn't shown up. The monkey was off her back. She could accept Rafe's ring.

Chapter Twenty

Moira rushed backstage at intermission to congratulate everybody on a great first act and find out what had been the cause of the delay in opening the curtain.

"Percy knocked down the bank flat," Billie Joe explained. "And each time he tried to set it up, it fell down again."

Moira laughed with relief. She'd been half afraid Buck was going after Sammy for moving in on Desdemona.

The ten-minute warning blinked, and she hurried out the back door of the greenroom into the second-floor hall of the museum, planning to go up the stairs and make a grand entrance through the auditorium entrance.

Crap. What was the door to the docent's room doing hanging open? Moira felt around her purse for her key ring as she walked toward the door. She'd better go close it up. None of the museum rooms were supposed to be open after hours.

She stopped in her tracks. Was that someone talking or a vibration from the floor above or was someone in there? She slipped out of her shoes, approached the door, and peeked in.

The room was dark enough that she couldn't see exactly what was going on, but she recognized the people in the room—Buck and Sergio, and they had their arms around one another.

She backed up quietly, stepped back into her shoes, and headed for the stairs.

That explained a lot.

* * *

The curtain opened on the second act, and Moira watched as Micaela and Phil pushed through to their happy ending. Jim had lost his job and Della couldn't find work so they exchanged the useless comb and the useless watch fob on Christmas Eve, which made them realize how much they loved each other. After sinking into the depths of despair, Jim started writing short stories and Della finally got herself hired to mop the milliner's floor at night. Within a month, Della, who'd been playing with the hats when she was alone in the shop, had risen to head designer, and Jim had sold his first short story to the *McClure's Magazine*.

Simplistic, but it worked. Now for the last big scene.

The curtain opened on the tableau again, but this time, thanks to a clever light filter, snow was falling. The chorus sang about the snow and danced around a papier-mâché snowman, as Della and Jim walked down the avenue again. But this time, she had on a huge hat and the hem of her dress flipped up enough to show off her shiny spats, while Jim was not only wearing a cutaway jacket and striped trousers, but sported a big gold pocket watch.

The chorus moved in behind them to support the final number, and the curtain closed. Carmen lowered her violin, and Vashti folded her hands on her lap, then looked expectantly toward the stage.

Somebody in the audience started to clap, then stopped as Rafe marched out in front of the curtain and slapped the truncheon into his hand four times.

> *New York evening, New York night,*
> *Everyone is snuggled up tight*
> *Asleep in their beds, awake in their dreams*
> *Where nothing is really what it seems*
> *And problems are solved by love and a song*
> *Everything's right, nothing is wrong*
> *Nothing is wrong, everything's right,*
> *Try as you might,*
> *Try as you may*
> *You won't find anything*
> *Wrong to say*
> *About this wonderful New York night.*
> *Everything will be right tonight*

He slapped the truncheon four more times and walked offstage.

The audience sprang to its feet and exploded with applause that kept on coming, and Moira joined them, clapping her hands till they hurt.

* * *

As everyone lined up in the wings for curtain calls, Rafe tossed his truncheon a few extra times just for the joy of it. A standing ovation was pro forma in small-town Texas, but the multiple rolls of applause were voluntary. The show was socko—a success, a big success.

This was when he should approach Moira again. Not when they got to the truck or back to the house, but now, as soon as he went backstage to escort her to the lectern.

The curtain call line moved forward one by one, and he heard the audience roaring with applause, probably for Billie Joe, who was always a favorite. Next would come Sergio, after which he himself would march out, slap his palm with his truncheon, and join hands with the rest of the players as Micaela and Phil took their solo bows.

Then there'd be a pause as he fetched Moira from the wings so she could thank everyone involved and say a few words about the theater guild.

He checked the ring in his pocket.

That's when he'd strike.

* * *

Standing backstage, Moira analyzed each round of the applause as she watched the curtain call. Everyone cheered the chorus and children. Billie Joe was obviously popular. Sergio seemed to have a strong teenage following. And Rafe got yells as well as applause. Phil's audience appeal seemed a little weak, but Micaela's more than made up for it.

Oops. She'd better pay attention. Rafe had left the line and was coming over to escort her to the lectern.

But instead of taking her arm, he lifted her left hand and kissed her ring finger. His eyes sparkled at her.

"Are you ready?"

His voice was a deep-down whisper, and she knew he was asking her about more than walking onstage. She knew what her answer was too—the same as it had been when he asked her to join him for lunch and to go home with him on Halloween night.

"Yes."

Rafe reached into his pocket, and slipped a diamond-encrusted ring on her finger, then escorted her to the lectern and stepped back into the cast lineup.

The audience greeted her with light applause and listened politely as she expressed her appreciation of everyone involved in the production. Vashti and Pen received special citations, of course, and the Fontaine sisters were asked to stand in place. She ended by thanking the audience for coming, made a pitch for the theater guild, and invited everyone to the cast party in the boardroom across the hall.

Her role fulfilled, she turned to Rafe to be escorted off so the cast could take a final bow, but instead he walked up to the lectern and took her left hand in his.

She looked at him in surprise, then understood and smiled, not a closed-mouth widening of the lips, but a big, open smile that brought happiness to the world and joy to the universe.

He lifted her hand so everyone could see the ring, and the audience gave them a standing ovation.

A voice that sounded like Sammy Schuler's yelled from the curtain call lineup, "Kiss! Kiss!" The audience took up the chant, and Moira looked up at Rafe.

"Always let the paying customers have what they want," he said, taking her in his arms and giving her a lot more than a stage kiss.

* * *

The cast party was a madhouse, like every other opening night celebration Moira had ever been to. It seemed like the whole audience had accepted her invitation to come to the cast party, and every single one of them was also determined to offer her and Rafe congratulations, count the diamonds in her ring, and ask highly personal questions about their living arrangements.

Enid and Astrid joined the impromptu receiving line, of course, and Enid garnered almost as many congratulations as she and Rafe did. He stayed with her during the initial bombardment, then escaped to the dressing room to change clothes, wipe off his stage makeup, and ditch the handlebar mustache, so she had no defense when his Aunt Clarice cornered her with a long, very involved story about the family's first indication of Rafe's artistic talents.

After the first ten minutes, Donna Sue, who'd been standing nearby for moral support, flashed a dimpled smile and interrupted.

"Babes, let me borrow Moira for a few minutes, okay? She

hasn't had a thing to eat—not even a cracker—since breakfast, and we need to get some nourishment down her."

She took Moira's arm and walked her over to goodies table. The hot wings, skewered shrimp, and fajitas that the members of the city council had supplied had been pretty well picked over, and the doughnuts, kolaches, and sliced sheet cake from the Loughlin Bakery existed only in memory, but she was able to score a couple of decent-looking shrimp Donna Sue helped her extract a ginger ale from the ice tub under the table.

"How did you know I'd skipped lunch?" Moira asked as she popped the top off the bottle.

"I didn't, babes, but you needed rescuing."

Opening a Diet Coke, Donna Sue took a major swig of it, then stiffened as she looked behind Moira. She lowered her voice so Moira could barely make out what she was saying.

"Don't look now, but Buck's father—he's a total ass—is heading this way. I had a huge run-in with him—it was monumental—about casting a black guy as the mayor in *The Music Man*." She backed off as if she were searching for a last remaining doughnut. "Babes, you're on your own on this one."

Moira affixed the standard smile to her face as Dolph Overton Sr. introduced himself and his wife, complimented her on the play, told her how fortunate she was to be marrying Rafe, and that Buck had been seeing a Waco debutante so he and his wife were expecting a marriage in their family soon too.

Moira didn't know what to say so she nodded pleasantly and tried to start a light conversation with his wife, which didn't go anywhere. It was an awkward situation but Moira noticed that Stu Schlossnagel was fast approaching, and the load of kinfolk he had with him looked big enough to overpower the Overtons.

Stu was ruthless about claiming her attention.

"Hey, Moira, I want you to meet my dad and his wife! They're in town just for the show! And my sisters are here too! And my grandma!"

An elderly woman with well-trained blue-tinted hair clasped her hand. "Ooh La La thanks you for the full-page ad in the playbill, Ms. Farrar." She gave Moira's coiffure cut a critical look over. "Looks like you're due for a trim. We'd love to see you at the shop. I can guarantee a discount."

Stu looked embarrassed and tried to step in, which gave the Fontaines the opportunity to bring selected parents over to meet Moira.

Next came the Bentons, then Sammy's father, then Travis, and surprisingly Rocky.

She picked up Moira's hand, admired her ring, and laughed charmingly, like a bird greeting springtime.

"Well, that pretty much seals the deal, doesn't it? No turning back now."

Chapter Twenty-One

Moira smiled as she walked up the wide steps of the imposing yellow building. Her life had changed a lot since the first time she entered the portals of the Bosque Bend Museum. And it was all for the better.

Her costume had changed too. The weather was springtime-warm so she'd worn a short crimson dress with a stylishly flared skirt. No need for her safari dress or sensible shoes anymore. She was flying high. *Gift of the Magi* was a hit, and she was engaged to Red Rafe.

She walked on up to the third floor and circled around to the theater entrance. Directors often abandoned their casts after opening night, but she planned to attend every performance. The Fontaines and Vashti were huddled together in a corner of the entryway in what looked like an intense, but nonlethal conversation. What was that all about?

The women looked up. Three pairs of eyes focused on her like rifle barrels, and Vashti signaled her to come over.

Xandra's hiss carried in the empty hall. "Are you sure we should tell her?"

Moira went rigid. Had Desdemona sprained her ankle? Or Micaela developed laryngitis?

Vashti nodded once, like a puppet on a string. "Yes. She needs to know."

Moira walked over to them, telling herself to stay calm, but her apprehension was growing with every step.

"What do I need to know?"

Xandra pursed her lips. "Sister heard something." She nudged Fleurette to step forward. Moira gave the little woman what she hoped was an encouraging smile.

Fleurette looked at Xandra and took a sniffling breath.

"I—I stopped by G&G today for a sit-down lunch and heard someone talking about you in the booth behind me. It was that Rocky woman, the one who always dresses like she's a going to a rodeo—you can't mistake that laugh—and I think she was talking to that reporter who was in town a couple of weeks ago, the skinny one who looks like he's still in high school."

Moira's smile froze on her face. Boyd Yancey.

Xandra prompted her. "Tell Moira what Rocky said."

Fleurette swallowed hard. "The reporter kept asking her what you had told people about Colin Sanger, but all she wanted to talk about was how she's your best friend and she loves you to death and is really worried about you because the show is stressing you out and you're about to be fired—which I know isn't true in the least.

"She even had the nerve to tell him that you've been running after a rich rancher, and you two pretended to get engaged last night to boost ticket sales, but actually he's just using you—and we all know Rafe would never do anything like that." Fleurette's jaw trembled. "And she also said that you're all depressed and suicidal now."

Xandra jumped in. "Fleurette told me about it the second she came in, and I said we must consult Vashti to see about whether we should tell you or not. Sometimes it's best to let these things go, but that's your choice."

Moira could feel an anger rising within her, but that wouldn't help the situation. Right now she had to calm the Fontaines down. They had a show to put on, and while Vashti could probably play through a hurricane, Xandra and Fleurette were more high-strung and would transfer their anxiety to Desdemona and Sergio.

She maintained her smile. "Thank you for telling me about this, Fleurette. It's something I needed to know, and you can be assured that I will speak with Rocky about it."

* * *

Rafe turned into the ranch road and stole a glance at Moira to make sure she was still awake. She hadn't said a word since she got in the truck. Maybe she was having a second-night let-down. He parked the truck at the back of the house and reached for his door handle.

Moira jerked to attention, as if she'd just been awakened from a dream.

"Don't get out." Her voice was somber. "I need to tell you

something, and afterwards you may want to take me home."

What the hell? He pulled his door shut again, and the cab went dark.

"There's a Hollywood reporter in town. His name is Boyd Yancey, and Fleurette overheard Rocky telling him that that I'm…depressed and suicidal."

Rocky? That was carrying a joke too far.

Moira continued in a monotone. "I don't want things like that to get around, so I'm going to set up a meeting with Yancey and clear things up."

"Do you want me to come with you?" He'd fight off all her dragons if she'd let him.

She shook her head. "Thank you, Rafe, but I need to handle this by myself. Pressing her fingers to her temples, she breathed slowly in and out three times. "This interview may turn out to be about…a lot more than *Gift of the Magi*." Her voice became stronger, as if she were reaffirming a decision. "What Yancey may really want to interview me about is how Colin died, and if he asks, I've decided to tell him the truth."

She looked over at him. "But I want to tell you first. Maybe I should have told you before, but it didn't seem relevant."

She looked away again. "The official story is that Colin broke his neck by diving into the pool at night without realizing it had been half emptied during the day."

Her voice faltered. "Part of that was true. The pool was undergoing repairs, and that's where the police found Colin's body. But he hadn't ended up there on his own, and diving into it wasn't what killed him."

A chill ran down Rafe's spine, but he kept his voice steady.

"What *did* kill him?"

She looked out the window into the night. "You have to understand the situation. We had separate bedrooms. His had a lock on the inside, and mine had a lock on the outside. They were both released at precisely seven o'clock every morning—Colin did everything precisely—and I was expected to come out of my room dressed to the nines and wait for him, even if he was running late."

"Wait a minute—your bedroom door was locked from the outside?"

She gave him a quick glance. "Is it a surprise? Anyway, I waited for Colin for about an hour. He'd never been that late before, so I wandered around the dining room, not really trying to find Colin, just enjoying my freedom. Then I got bolder and started checking out all the forbidden rooms."

"Forbidden rooms?"

"All the other rooms in the house." She paused as if she was sorting through her memories. "I left Colin's bedroom till last, hoping he'd be gone."

She wiped her forehead. "I hadn't been in his bedroom since the first month we were married. It was large and beautifully decorated—French, with a lot of silk, curlicues, and gilt. As far as I could tell, everything was in perfect order. The pillows on the couch had been wedged against its arms just so, and his bed was made up so neatly it didn't look like it had ever been slept in."

He waited for her to continue.

"His closet door was open. I went down the rows of drawers and racks of clothes to the end, where the room turned a corner into small alcove. That's where I found him. Stone-cold, with a noose around his neck."

Rafe shuddered. May Colin Sanger burn in everlasting hell for what he had done to Moira in life and death.

"I got a knife from the kitchen, wrestled a Louis XV chair into the closet, and climbed up to cut him down. Then I wrapped him in a sheet and dragged him down to the pool." She gave Rafe a quick glance. He didn't look happy, but he hadn't shoved her out of the car so far.

"I tipped him in headfirst, hoping that it would look like he'd broken his neck in a diving accident. That was the only thing I could think of to do."

Now he looked confused. "But why did you try to hide the way he had died?"

"To protect his image. It was what he would have wanted."

"But…he'd committed suicide."

She shook her head. "You don't understand. It wasn't suicide—it was accidental. He was hanging from a clothes rod and…the rest was obvious."

"You mean…?"

She nodded. "Autoerotic asphyxiation, like David Carradine. I had him cremated, but the police knew. They'd seen that sort of thing before. And when the word started leaking out, the studio came down hard on them."

"I didn't know that could be done."

She shrugged. "With enough money, you can do anything, and Hollywood is a showbiz town." She exhaled a soft, jeering laugh. "You should have seen the funeral. It was a show, a performance. Anybody who was anybody was there, standing room only—like at the Academy Awards. I wore black, of course—a Balenciaga that the studio supplied—and stars who'd never given me the time of day before patted my hand and kissed my cheek and told me what a wonderful person Colin had been."

She went quiet for a few minutes, then turned to stare out the side window again. Rafe respected her silence, but he had the feeling she was building up to something else.

She removed the ring from her finger and held it out to him, meeting his eyes for the first time. "And if you want this ring back now, here it is."

Like hell! She wasn't going to get rid of him that easily!

He clenched his hand around hers, and his sparkling eyes hardened into shards of steel. "Moira, what I want is for this ring to go back on your finger and stay there. We're in this together. I love you, and I'll stand by you, no matter what!"

* * *

Moira walked into G&G Chicken and scanned the tables for someone who looked like a cub reporter.

She'd called Yancey the next morning, as soon as she located his card in the pocket of her new coat, and they'd agreed on G&G Chicken at two in the afternoon—a time when she knew the restaurant wouldn't have many customers. Discretion was the name of the game, and a fast-food restaurant on a lazy Saturday afternoon was about as discreet as one could get in Bosque Bend.

He rose from a front table when she came in, and she recognized him from Fleurette's description—skinny and boyish.

He recognized her too and greeted her with a big smile and a limp handshake, then insisted on buying her a chicken combo she knew she'd never be able to eat.

They picked up their orders at the counter and took a booth toward the back of the restaurant. Yancey put a pocket recorder on the table. "Thanks for giving me this interview, Ms. Farrar. I know you're really busy with the play right now. How's it going with the play?"

Boyd Yancey's voice was upbeat and his boyish face invited trust, but Moira knew better than to accept a showbiz reporter at face value. Instead, she manufactured a big smile of her own and added a boatload of enthusiasm for good measure.

"Really well! The story is wonderful! The author, Pendleton Swaim, was nominated for a Pulitzer for *Garner's Crossing*, you know—and the music is fantastic!"

"I've been talking around to people and heard a lot of great things about you—the newspaper editor, the mayor's wife…"

Yancey left the end of the sentence open, as if he wanted her to know he'd interviewed a third person who didn't say great things about her.

Rocky.

Moira dropped her smile and looked him straight in the eye. "My personal life is also great." She flashed her ring. "I'm engaged to a man who loves me, I'm not depressed, and I'm not suicidal, no matter what you've heard."

Yancey looked blank for a moment—she'd caught him by surprise. "That little woman who was in the booth behind Rocky McAllister and me, the one with the black hair who wouldn't talk to me the last time I was in town—she heard everything the cowgirl said. Right?"

Moira nodded.

His smile faded and his face looked ten years older.

"Look, Ms. Farrar. I'll level with you. I'm not interviewing you for an entertainment magazine or even a tabloid. I've been hired by Solid Gold Entertainment, the studio that's bought up the rights to *The Clancy Family* and also all of Colin Sanger's movies, starting from when he played the junior senator in *Learning the Ropes*."

He looked around, then hunched forward. "I've been sent here for two reasons. The first is that the studio wanted to be able to assure all of Nancy Clancy's and Colin Sanger's fans that you're okay, that you haven't overdosed or ended up in jail or a mental hospital. Solid Gold Entertainment is aimed at the family audience, and image is everything."

His voice turned hard. "The second reason I'm here is to find out what you're going to say about the way Colin died."

Moira's gut cramped. This was it.

She blinked her eyes as if she didn't understand. "What do you mean?"

"*The Clancy Family* is already eating up the airways, and the big guns are planning to offer Colin's movies one at a time for limited-run rerelease. They'll be a gold mine—he's got a rabid cult following, especially since he died at the height of his career." Yancey curled his lip, an ugly look on his choirboy face.

"If his fans had anything to do with it, he'd be elevated to sainthood."

Yancey looked around again, maybe to make sure Fleurette wasn't anywhere in sight.

"Hollywood is a small town, and word gets around. Everyone in showbiz knows how Colin really died, but the studio doesn't want the public to know. Solid Gold is protecting Colin like a mother tiger, but you're the joker in the deck. Colin Sanger had a pristine image, and Solid Gold wants to make sure it stays that way. It wants to be sure you won't talk about the black room—yes, we know about that—and that Colin will continue to have died by diving into that half-empty pool at night."

Moira took a long second to digest what he had said. Yancey knew. They all knew.

They knew what Colin had done to her and they knew that she'd cut him down from the closet rod and shoved him into the half-empty pool. And instead of exposing her, they wanted her to maintain her lie, the fiction of Colin's life and death.

Somehow, it wasn't right.

But what good would it do to shout out the truth? Would it help Arthur Sawyer to learn that his hero was a fake? Would it help her if the world knew what she'd endured in the black room?

Moira gave Yancey a look of wide-eyed innocence. "Black room? I don't know what you're talking about, Mr. Yancey. "My late husband was as heroic as all of the characters he brought to life, and I will always treasure my memories of our lives together."

He patted her hand and got up to leave. "Good girl. Eat your chicken. I gotta go make some phone calls." He indicated his shirt pocket. And by the way, I've got you on tape. Don't change your story."

Moira watched him go out the door, then exhaled and slumped against the back of the booth. Then she pulled her cell out of her purse to call Rafe and report in. Maybe they could go out to dinner before the show to celebrate.

* * *

Moira cleaned a mat of golden dog hair out of the lint filter and moved a load of heavy denims into the dryer. Astrid was off at another Sunday afternoon dog-training class, but this time she'd left Ivanhoe at home, and the poor dog was following her everywhere like an abandoned child.

She stared at the jeans jumbled together in the machine as if they were a conglomerate eight ball.

Why in the world had Rocky told Yancey she was suicidal? Sure, she hadn't made time to see Rocky much lately. Partially because the show was taking up so much of her time, but mostly because of what Enid and Carmen had told her. And maybe a little bit because she still felt guilty about laughing at Rocky's stories.

She closed the dryer door and turned it on. It heaved into action, groaning like one of Delilah's restroom elephants.

Now to toss a chunk of detergent into the washer and dump in her underwear. How strange—even with the evidence piling up, it was hard for her to let go of the image of Rocky as her friend. She had been so much fun, but she could also be mean—like when she told her and Astrid about Rafe and Travis's cow-pat war. And then there were the stories about Phil and Vashti—and even Carmen.

But, hey, maybe Fleurette had misunderstood. Maybe the laughing girl was just pulling the leg of the big-city reporter, seeing how far she could go. Maybe Rafe and Beth had had a few little spats, and Rocky had exaggerated them.

She closed the washer lid with a bang.

Whatever it was with Rocky, she didn't like it, and she'd call Rocky as soon as she finished the laundry. Maybe they could get together at Starbucks on Monday and hash this thing out. It was *not* funny.

Ivanhoe growled and pushed at her leg.

She reached down to pet him. "Don't worry, boy. The dryer always makes that groaning noise, remember? You should have gotten used to it by now."

Ivanhoe turned toward the door and barked. His ruff was up and his ears were peaked forward.

Moira sighed. This was all she needed—the dryer acting like it was in its death throes and the dog acting like she was under attack.

"Ivanhoe, sit! No one can come in the house. The doors are locked"

The mastiff obeyed, but he didn't want to.

A sixth sense told her to look up.

Rocky was standing just outside the door of the laundry room, a big smile on her face, a pistol in her hand. She lifted the gun and pointed it at Moira. Her fingernails were decorated with yellow daisies on a purple background.

"You made me do this. I really didn't want to, but I can't have you standing between me and the C Bar M."

Moira tried to think of something to say, something that would make Rocky put down that gun—was it for real?—but Ivanhoe took instant action.

Snarling out a great war cry, he leapt at Rocky's arm. The shot went wild and the gun dropped to the laundry room floor.

Moira peeked out the laundry room door as Rocky ran down the hall, with Ivanhoe, barking like an avenging angel, behind her. Then, with a steadying hand on the wall, she walked to the front door and called Ivanhoe in.

A glance told her that Rocky's Jeep was halfway down the street and traveling fast.

After giving one last triumphant bark to the world in general, Ivanhoe trotted back into the house, obviously very pleased with himself.

Moira closed the door and knelt down to love on the big dog and tell him how wonderful he was. He *should* be pleased with himself. He'd saved her life.

Oh God, he'd saved her life!

A shock wave hit her, and she staggered to the couch in the family room. *Rocky, her friend Rocky, had tried to kill her. Little Moira Farrar, who'd never harmed a person in her life. No one, not even Colin, had ever tried to kill her before.*

A siren traveled down the street and stopped abruptly in front of the house. Walking slowly, as if through water, Moira went to the living room window and looked out.

A uniformed policewoman was coming up the walk. Calling on every ounce of energy she had left in her, Moira put Ivanhoe outside and met the woman at the door.

"I'm Officer Joann Gerbig with the Bosque Bend Police Department." She produced an identity card. "May I come in?"

Moira stood aside and the woman walked into the hall. "Your neighbor reported hearing a gunshot from within your house."

Moira nodded. "It was Rocky—Rocky McAllister." Her words came out slowly. *Was that her own voice? It sounded strange to her ears—like she was speaking into an echo chamber.* "She tried to kill me. She said I made her do it because of the C Bar M. Ivanhoe knocked the gun out of her hand."

Officer Gerbig looked around. "Where's Ivanhoe? I'll need to interview him."

"He's a dog—the one making the ruckus in the backyard. The gun is still on the laundry room floor, if you want to see it."

"Have you moved it?"

Moira shuddered. "I didn't want to touch it."

The policewoman eyed a piece of pink paper on the floor on the floor of the hall.

"Where did that come from?"

"I think Rocky must have dropped it when she was leaving, but I didn't want to touch it either."

The officer picked up the page by a corner, glanced at it, then showed it to Moira. "Did you write this?"

Moira looked at it. The note was typed, but the signature was a reasonable facsimile of her own.

Please forgive me for killing myself. My life is empty and I can no longer stay on this earth without my beloved Colin.

Moira Miranda Farrar

She shook her head in denial.

"No, I didn't write it, but I gave Rocky an autograph for her mother on paper like this."

Officer Gerbig shook her head. "It would have been easy enough for her to wrap your hand around the grip, then run back across to the neighbor and say she found you that way."

Someone knocked at her door. The policewoman opened it cautiously, and Bertie Fuller rushed in to embrace Moira.

"Oh, Moira, I'm so glad you're okay, that you didn't do it after all! When Rocky left, she said she was going to drop in on you and try to get back the pistol she'd lent you because you were so depressed about the show and the way Rafe has treated you—that man should be hanged—that you would…I was so afraid that…that…"

Officer Gerbig finished Mrs. Fuller's sentence for her. "Bertie called 911 and said she thought you had killed yourself."

Mrs. Fuller looked around. "Where's Rocky?"

* * *

Rafe picked up a hat and started walking down to Travis's house to meet up with Mervin Hruska and open up Travis's house. He could have saddled up Sarge, but the winter sun was shining, Travis's house was less than a mile off, and on the way, he could enjoy seeing the new calves frolicking in the front pasture.

Mervin wouldn't tell him why he needed to get into the house—just said it was routine police business and he hadn't been able to locate Rocky.

He walked around to the front of the house and found Mervin, Jose Mercado and Terrence Craddock waiting for him on the porch steps. This must be more serious than Mervin had indicated. Joe and Terrence were his senior deputies.

He tipped back his hat. "What's goin' on?"

Mervin lifted himself off the step. "Criminal investigation, Rafe. We got a call from the Waco police department this morning. It turns out Travis's gastritis is arsenic poisoning. We need to search the house."

"Arsenic? We don't use any on the ranch."

"What about in the barn to kill the rats?"

"No way. We trap them. Couldn't be well water either because Travis is the only one who's sick. And we cleared out all the treated wood after construction."

"Then we've got to search the house."

"You're sayin'…"

Jose leaned back against the porch post and put in his two cents. "Maybe Rocky got tired of Travis sniffing after Micaela Atherton all the time and thought a good dose of arsenic would keep him at home."

Mervin shot his deputy a disapproving glare. "I'm not say-ing anything except that we need to search the house."

Rafe reached in his pocket for the keys. "Go to it. Mind if I stick around?"

Mervin unlocked the door and walked in. "We want you to. You own the property."

Rafe looked around the comfortable living room. He had good memories of this house. This was where he and Beth had begun their marriage. It had been an idyllic summer, a three-month honeymoon. He hoped Mervin would find some way Travis could have ingested the arsenic by mistake—maybe a mislabeled box.

Mervin sent Jose and Terrence into the bedrooms and started going through the kitchen himself. Rafe followed after him and watched as he unloaded the utility shelves beneath the sink.

Jose's suggestion that Rocky had deliberately poisoned Travis was preposterous. But this business of her telling the re-porter that Moira was suicidal was just as preposterous.

God, he'd known Rocky almost her whole life, but how well did he really know her? Maybe there was a reason Mom had never quite taken to her.

Mervin lifted something out from behind a solid row of cleaning supplies.

"Found it."

The box of arsenic was clearly labeled and had been opened.

Rafe went numb.

Terrence called from the front bedroom. "Chief, you'd bet-ter come see this."

Rafe followed Mervin into Rocky's bedroom. Terrence was standing by her rolltop desk, holding a piece of pink paper in his hand. "This might be interesting to you too, Rafe."

Rafe looked over Joe's shoulder and read a pink page signed several times by a poor rendition of Moira's handwriting.

"It's a damn suicide note, and it doesn't make any sense. That isn't Moira's writing."

Mervin's lips compressed to a thin line. "Looks like someone was practicing for a better version. We've got to get somebody over to Moira's house ASAP." He hit his shoulder mike. "Hruska here. Get a squad car to…Yeah…Yeah…Moira Farrar?…Yeah…Rocky McAllister?…Really?…Twenty minutes ago?…Which direction?…"

Mervin clicked off his mike. "Moira is safe. Rocky took a shot at her about half an hour ago, but her dog saved the day. Joann Gerbig is with her now."

Rafe sat down on the nearest chair he could find. Rocky had not only poisoned Travis, but also had tried to kill Moira? He buried his face in his hands, trying to comprehend, to understand.

Rocky, whom he had welcomed into his home and family, whom he had trusted to babysit his child, who had consoled him after Beth's death.

God in heaven, what sort of person was she? How could she feed Travis arsenic, then tend him like Florence Nightingale? How could she act so friendly to Moira, then try to kill her?

Rafe's brain rocketed back three years, and the specter of

Beth lying on the ground as if she were asleep, the back of her head matted with blood, rose up in front of him.

His gorge rose. Three years ago, the tree house ladder was still usable, and Rocky was a crack shot. Could she have killed Beth? No, that was unthinkable. Beth was her friend.

But Moira was supposed to be her friend too, and Travis was her husband, whom she had promised to love, honor, and cherish.

A car come up to the house, then burned rubber as it drove past. The fog on Rafe's his brain cleared in a flash. He knew the sound of that engine.

"That's Rocky! She must have seen the squad car!"

Mervin looked around at his deputies. "Terrence, you stay here in case she comes back, and call Dispatch for someone to get hold of her cousin in San Saba and see what he has to say. Jose, you come with Rafe and me."

Rafe had a clear view of Rocky as Mervin drove around the trees in front of the house, and he wasn't surprised to see her run into the corral, haul herself up on Bella's bare back, jump the fence, and take off down the road.

Mervin screeched the squad car to a halt beside the barn and got out, then just stood there in the middle of the road and watched as Rocky disappeared down the turn in the tarmac. Rafe knew exactly what Mervin was thinking—that she'd be over a fence in no time, and the car couldn't handle a pasture fast enough to catch up with her.

His temper erupted. Like hell he was going to let Rocky get away from them!

He shoved his door open and leapt out. "What are you waitin' for, guys? Let's saddle up and go after her!"

But she'd already disappeared from view and they didn't know which way she'd gone. There were more than a dozen pastures down the road to choose from.

Chapter Twenty-Two

The bulls were in the west pasture so Rafe headed north, Mervin went off to the east, and Jose went the south. They only had about three hours of daylight left, but that would be enough if Rocky were still on the ranch.

God, how could Rocky do it? Try to kill Travis and Moira, and maybe have killed Beth? He'd known her since they were kids, and he didn't know her at all.

By sunset, Rafe had checked out four pastures, but all he'd seen were cows.

He pushed back his hat. Rocky knew every inch of the ranch and could hole up in it for days. But more likely, she would go cross-country from pasture to pasture until she got somewhere no one would recognize her. Depending on the terrain, Bella was good for thirty miles a day, which meant Rocky could reach Waco cross-country in a few hours. Then all she'd have to do was set Bella loose and hook up with a friendly truck driver, and she'd be out of the state in no time.

Of course, friendly truck drivers weren't always safe, but he'd bet Rocky could take care of herself.

He glared into the western sun. It would be coming dark in half an hour, and horses don't come equipped with headlights. He might as well call it a day.

He pulled out his cell. "Merv. I'm in two-eighteen and haven't seen a damn thing. There's a big stand of trees across the river I want to check out, but that's it. Any luck on your end?"

"Nope. I'm in three-sixty, next door to you, and it's clear as far as I can tell. But we did hear from Rocky's cousin. Seems that the last time Rocky was in San Saba, she told his wife you were sweet on her, and she was gonna make sure the next C Bar M heir was half Colby, but she had to take care of a few problems first."

Rafe could feel the anger rising in him again. *Problems*—she meant Travis and Moira. But where the hell did Rocky get the idea that he had a thing for her? Crap—that extra attention he was giving her because Travis was trailing after Micaela.

"My God, Merv. That woman is puredee evil. She poisoned Travis and took a potshot at Moira because of the ranch?"

A horse screamed across the river.

"Merv! Did you hear that?"

"Hear it—damn near blew out my eardrums!"

"How soon can you get here?"

"Four minutes, tops. Can you pinpoint where the horse is?"

"Under a stand of live oaks below the cliffs on the other side of the river. You'll see it."

"I'm heading your way. Wait till I get there before you do anything."

"Be careful. There's a heavyweight panther around here somewhere."

Another scream rent the air as Rafe clicked off his phone. To hell with it. He was going over there on his own. That was Bella, and she sounded angry. He lifted his shotgun out of its scabbard and laid it across the saddle in front of him, just in case.

Mervin caught up with him at the river's edge. "Good, you've got that big ol' shotgun of yours. All I have is my regulation peashooter, and I have a feeling that's not gonna do the job."

Rafe nodded, shifted the shotgun across his arm, and urged Sarge forward into the water. Another scream, even louder, cut through the evening air. God, he didn't like that horse, but he wouldn't wish that kind of torment on anyone.

He cleared the river and edged forward, with Mervin right behind him. The horses were breathing hard. This was panther territory.

What's that—? Something was thrashing up ahead in the shadow, something white.

He narrowed his eyes.

It was Bella. Beautiful Bella.

Blood ran down her neck, her head whipped back and forth with rage, and her right front leg folded under her every time she tried to get up.

And on her back was the biggest panther he'd ever seen.

The cat opened his mouth and roared out his possession of the downed horse.

Rafe lifted his shotgun and took aim. The shot boomed

across the pasture, and the panther yowled and flew up into the air, twisted as if it were trying to land on its feet, and fell to the ground with a thump.

The pasture was silent for a second. Then Bella rolled her eyes and screamed again, flailing her broken leg.

Mervin dismounted to do what had to be done. Aiming carefully, he put her down with a single shot between the eyes. She collapsed onto the ground in mid-scream, her flowing mane matted with blood.

Mervin holstered his gun, looked around, and fastened his gaze on a bloody lump off to the side in the shadows.

Rafe recognized the purple shirt Rocky had been wearing when he'd seen her ride out to check nose flaps this morning. She'd been trampled into the dirt. The two men looked at each other. The glen stank of death. Mervin spat onto the ground and slapped his hat on his thigh.

"Far as I can see, the horse threw Rocky and killed her, breaking her own leg in the process. Then the cat dropped down on the horse—or something like that. We'll never know."

He put his hat back on his head and surveyed the scene again. "Crazy horse, crazy woman, hungry cat—that's a lethal combination."

* * *

Moira went backstage and gave out ten-dollar Starbucks gift cards to the cast as her Christmas present, then claimed the seat she'd reserved in the middle row, center.

This was the final performance, and tonight, for the first time, she felt free to doff her director cap and take in the show as a member of the audience, as someone who wanted to see a happily-ever-after musical that would warm her heart and send her home humming catchy tunes.

The lights went down, and Rafe marched across the stage, slapping his truncheon, and the audience exploded. He was a local hero now, the guy who had killed the panther.

Next came the street scene and the real action began. Moira absorbed the fantasy with a hungry heart. She needed it. She needed escape, to overwhelm the image of a charming, curly-haired imp with a pistol in her hand. To forget for a few hours that Waco had matched the bullet that killed Beth with one of the rifles Mervin had sent off to them. And that Mervin had been talking to Rafe about exhuming his father's body. And that Enid had told her Rocky's mother had requested that her daughter's belongings be shipped to her, then tried to guilt Rafe into giving her some kind of lump sum payment for the house.

Ninety minutes later, Jim and Della, dressed to the nines, were celebrating New Year's Eve by walking along the avenue again.

> *Love triumphant wins the day*
> *Now we are happy, happy and gay*
> *Happy New Year,*
> *Be of good cheer*
> *Times may be tough, times may be rough*
> *But there's always a way, always a way*

Always a way if you love enough
Be of good cheer
Happy New Year
Love triumphant wins the day

The audience applauded, and Moira repeated the words to herself. *Times may be tough, times may be rough, but there's always a way, always a way, always a way if you love enough.*

Rafe came out in front of the curtain and went through his routine again, ending with the usual four smacks of his truncheon. Then he added a new twist, throwing it into the air and catching it.

The auditorium vibrated with sound—applause, whistling, stomping of feet, then the obligatory standing ovation.

The curtain calls were even stronger than on opening night. She noticed. Everyone was getting thunderous applause, even Phil.

She also noticed that Sergio and Buck weren't part of the lineup.

Apparently when Sergio had said he and Buck might be leaving right after the show was over, he meant it. The theater guild would lose the Overton Department Store's two-page spread, but she wished Sergio well. New York musical theater was a hard nut to crack, but Sergio had the talent to do it.

* * *

Eight days later, Moira stood in the hall outside the auditorium and watched as Astrid, Carmen, and Donna Sue walked up onstage single file and took their places opposite Rafe's groomsmen.

She would never have guessed a formal wedding could be put together in less than a week, but Rafe had wanted them to be able to spend Christmas together as a family. And he knew the strings to pull to arrange it.

The piano medley of classic love songs came to an end and Vashti struck the opening chords of "Love Triumphant," then nodded in the white-robed *Gift of the Magi* chorus, which was standing on risers at the back of the stage.

That was her cue. Moira caught her breath. *Here I go.*

She took Johnny's arm, and they started their long walk down the aisle. She'd had qualms about asking Johnny Blue to give her away, but so far he'd stayed sober.

Her eyes focused on Rafe and Delilah waiting for her on-stage.

They'd talked over venues for a couple of days before finally deciding to rent out the museum auditorium. As Rafe explained, they needed someplace big enough to seat every Schuler and McAllister for miles around, the cast and crew of *Gift of the Magi*, and everyone else Rafe had ever known

Astrid, of course, was her only family member present. Gram and Gramp weren't comfortable flying anymore, and Kimiko hadn't responded to the invitation.

Her mind hearkened back to her first marriage. Colin had flown her off to Tahiti for a quickie wedding and a honeymoon spent touring the local nightspots. It was the first time they'd had sex, and he'd been almost too gentlemanly. In fact, she'd wondered if he was really that interested in her. Where was the passion that leapt out of the screen and sent every woman in his audiences into raptures?

Rafe, on the other hand, was marrying her in his hometown under the watchdog eye of the community. And she *knew* he was interested in her. Enid had taken Delilah for the weekend, and they'd burned up the bed last night.

Johnny walked her slowly up onto the stage, taking care that her long satin gown didn't snag on the corners of the steps.

She'd suggested to Rafe that a short dress might be more appropriate for a second marriage, but Rafe had opted for the full monty.

"It's gonna be a family reunion," he explained. "We gotta put on a good show."

The song swelled to its climax as Rafe stepped forward to claim her. She glanced across at his groomsman—Travis, Mervin, and Uncle Omar. Yes, it was a family reunion, and in a few minutes, she'd be part of that family.

Moira McAllister. It had a nice ring to it.

Rafe came over to her, holding Delilah by the hand, and Moira handed her flowers to Astrid so she could take Delilah's other hand. They wanted her to understand that she was part of the wedding too.

The minister stepped forward and recited the classic words: "Dearly Beloved, we are gathered here this day…"

Moira blanked out and didn't come back to consciousness until she heard the minister pronounce them husband and wife.

They exchanged a chaste kiss over Delilah's head, then turned to their audience.

She looked out over the friendly faces and realized she'd

committed herself not only to Rafe, but also to Bosque Bend. This would be her home from now on. Her friends would be here, and she'd raise her children here. It would be the center of her universe.

She smiled a real smile, a smile of appreciation, and blinked away the tears that were clouding her vision. Bosque Bend had given her more affirmation than she'd had in her whole so-called career. She loved this little town with its football mania, its Pumpkin Party, its Six-Shooter Junction. She loved the Athertons, the Fontaines, Pendleton Swaim, Donna Sue, Josie Apodaca, Billie Joe, Phil and Judy, Percy and Deborah, Travis, Enid, and everyone else she'd met.

But she loved Rafe McAllister most of all. She looked at her husband and squeezed his hand, and he gave her a smile that promised a lot more.

But first would come the party.

Rafe waved at the crowd.

"Y'all, thanks for comin'. We're gonna be leavin' tomorrow to spend Christmas with Moira's folks in Pasadena, but I gotta tell you, I sure will miss seein' ol' Omar dressed up as Santa Claus and singin' 'You Ain't Nothin' But a Hound Dog' again this year." The audience gave him a deep-voiced belly laugh. "But before you leave tonight, we want y'all to celebrate with us. There's a full spread in the boardroom across the hall—no champagne, but plenty of soda water, G&G chicken, and a great big ol' weddin' cake from the Loughlin Bakery. But I'd appreciate it if you'd let us get over there first."

As Vashti played the recessional, they walked off the stage, out of the auditorium, and crossed the hall.

* * *

The receiving line took forever, starting with Enid, who dabbed her eyes and told Moira she'd already added her picture to the collage. Next in line was TexAnn, who welcomed Moira to the family, then took Delilah off with her so "you and Rafe can have a one-night honeymoon." Following TexAnn were the Fontaines, who actually embraced her. Travis and Micaela were farther down the line.

"We're going to be setting out for Nashville after the New Year," Travis said. "I think Jimbo Crane can take over from me. He did a good job while I was down."

Rafe nodded. "Can't say I didn't see it comin', Trav. You know we wish both of you the best of luck. Keep in touch."

Every member of the *Gift of the Magi* cast was there, and Moira met enough Schulers to populate a small state plus a good number of McAllisters.

The line finally petered out, and she could relax her smile muscles. Maybe she could even snag a piece of that cake, if there was any left.

Rafe leaned down to whisper in her ear. "Ready to go? I think it's about time for our weddin' night."

All thought of food flew out of Moira's mind and she took his arm.

Big Red won out over cake any day of the week.

Laurel Harlow wants nothing more than to put her difficult past behind her and move on. But when Jase Redlander, the bad boy crush who left her heartbroken sixteen years ago, appears on her doorstep, she can't turn him away— especially when he needs her help…

Please see the next page for a preview of

What the Heart Wants.

Chapter One

Laurel held the long rope of pearls up to the brilliant mid-summer sunset shining in her bedroom window.

Here she was, sitting at her dressing table and wondering if pawning Gramma's necklace would provide enough money to pay the bills for the next couple of months. Her finances would straighten themselves out once she sold the house, but she'd had it on the market for almost seven weeks now, and not one soul had expressed interest in her six-thousand-square-foot white elephant.

She should have tried to sell it last fall, but managing her mother's funeral was all she could accomplish back then. Besides, she'd had another year to go on her teaching contract, and her work had become her life after Dave left her and Daddy died.

The past three years had been mind-numbing, one blow after another. Not that she really missed Dave. She'd married him because it was time for Bosque Bend's favorite daughter to march down the aisle, and he'd seemed like the logical choice. Too bad he'd ditched her when being married to Laurel Harlow became a liability rather than an asset.

The last blow came seven weeks ago, when her principal told her she wouldn't get another contract. She should have seen it coming, but she'd thought she was safe in the elementary school across the river, in Lynnwood, the new subdivision populated by new people who didn't know the protocols of old Bosque Bend, and who seemed to care more about her effectiveness as a teacher than her family history.

She'd driven home in a trance from the meeting with her principal, and as soon as she entered the safety of the house and locked the door, she'd whirled into a spate of activity to counteract the numbness that fogged her brain and made her feel like she was dragging around a fifty-pound weight. First she called the Realtor father of one of her students and put the house she'd lived in for most of her life on the market. Next she started contacting school districts in the Rio Grande Valley for jobs. Her days of servitude to Kinkaid House and her family legacy were over.

She rolled the pearls between her fingers. Living alone was the pits. Mrs. Bridges, across the street, employed a live-in maid, had a daughter who visited regularly, and was followed by a big, happy-looking dog everywhere she went. Laurel was her own maid, had no friends anymore, and Kinkaid House hadn't housed a dog since Mama's older sister died of rabies seventy-five years ago.

The doorbell chimed from downstairs. She sighed and nestled the rope of glowing beads back in its padded box. Who was it? Prince Charming magically appearing to rescue her from Bosque Bend?

She stood up and squared her shoulders. She didn't need Prince Charming. She'd make her own happy ending.

The bell rang again as she headed down the hall toward the stairs. Probably the ill-mannered paperboy come collecting, though it didn't seem time for him yet. He always peered behind her down the hall as she handed him the money, then ran as if all the demons in hell were chasing him.

Her overactive conscience, part and parcel of being a preacher's daughter, charged into action. Of course the paperboy was afraid. Who could blame him? This house was notorious. Everyone in town knew what had happened here.

She started down the wide stairway.

If she could just mail in her payment, like when she used to take the *Dallas Morning News*, but Art Sawyer, who put out the town's biweekly newspaper, had never met an innovation he didn't dislike. Thus the *Bosque Bend Retriever* was printed on the same press he'd been using for the last forty years and was still hand-delivered by an army of schoolboys on bikes.

The doorbell pealed a third time. She gritted her teeth.

Sorry, whoever you are. I'm not about to break into a gallop. I might not have anything else left, but I can still muster a shred of dignity.

Three generations of family portraits on the staircase wall watched in approval as she regally descended the steps. As a child, she'd sped past them as fast as she could go to avoid their see-all stares, but now she drew strength from them. She might have to sell the house out from under their gilded frames, but she'd do it with her head held high.

And she'd burn the house down to the ground before she'd let it go for taxes.

Think positively, Laurel Elizabeth. Maybe your caller is a prospective buyer that the Realtor has sent over to look at the house.

She opened the heavy oak door a few cautious inches. Just last week someone had lobbed a string of firecrackers at her when she was out in the yard, searching for her newspaper. Of course, it was right before the Fourth, but she doubted that those firecrackers were a patriotic salute.

Dear God in heaven, who was this on her doorstep?

Her caller was a giant, a big man darkly silhouetted against the red blaze of the high-summer Texas sunset. She couldn't make out his face because of the glare behind him, but he was built like a tank and stood maybe six four, six five. Definitely not Prince Charming. More like the Incredible Hulk. She glanced down to make sure the screen door was still locked.

"Laurel? Laurel Harlow?"

The voice seemed familiar. She couldn't quite place it, but her visitor sounded more surprised than dangerous. She pushed the door open wider, and the man's face came into focus as he moved forward to examine her through the wire mesh.

She stepped back a pace. He responded by taking off his dark glasses and smiling, a slight baring of his teeth.

"It's Jase Redlander, from old Bosque Bend High."

Her heart did a quick rabbit hop. Jase Redlander, of course.

His voice was deeper now, his shoulders broader, and he'd grown a good three inches in height, but it was definitely Jase.

Jase, whom she'd loved to distraction. Jase whom she thought she'd never see again. Jase, who sixteen years ago had been run out of town for having sex with his English teacher.

He folded his sunglasses and put them in his pocket. "Sorry to bother you, but I just drove in from Dallas and I've got sort of a…well, a family emergency that might end up in your lap." He grimaced and glanced behind himself at the evening traffic moving along Austin Avenue. "Can we talk inside?"

The noise got bad this time of day, with everyone driving home from work and out to play. Back in the 1880s, when Great-Grampa Erasmus built Kinkaid House on a narrow dirt road that headed toward the state capital, he never could have imagined that it would one day be widened to four lanes, with a central turn lane being proposed for next year.

Laurel tried to keep her hand from shaking as she unlocked the screen.

"Of course. Come in." Her voice got stuck somewhere in the back of her throat. "How nice to see you," she managed to murmur.

But, standing aside as he entered, she saw that this was a different Jase Redlander than the teenager she'd fallen in love with sixteen years ago. The cut of his coal-black hair, the up-scale Levi's and European-style polo shirt, the set of his shoulders—everything about him signaled money and power and confidence. Obviously he'd wrestled with life and won. She, on the other hand, had lost big-time. Could he tell?

Not if she could help it.

She relocked both outside doors, led him down the wide central hall, and unfolded the doors into the drawing room.

Three generations of her mother's people, Kinkaid women with money to burn, had managed to make the overlarge room, originally a double parlor, into a popular gathering place for Bosque Bend's moneyed elite in times past. Victorian sofas, heavy chairs, and grotesquely carved little tables, all flanked by potted greenery, formed intimate conversation groups, while fragile undercurtains, confections of snowy lace, filtered the harsh Texas sun coming in the front windows into fantastic arabesques on the oriental carpet.

Jase had always loved this room. Years ago, he'd told her that if he ever died and sneaked into heaven, God's front room would look like this.

She hoped he wouldn't notice that heaven was somewhat the worse for wear. The upholstery was threadbare, the drapes faded, and the windows dingy. She glanced uneasily at the dark rectangles on the far wall, where the more saleable paintings had hung, then at the entrance to Daddy's study, which looked positively naked since she'd sold the fig-leafed marble youths who'd guarded the doorway for as long as she could remember.

The antiquities man from Austin had almost salivated as he loaded them into his van, and the money had, fittingly, paid off the last of Daddy's obligations.

Claiming a spindly ribbon-back chair for herself, Laurel gestured Jase toward the same velvet-upholstered sofa on which the two of them would sit and talk while Jase was waiting for Daddy to emerge from his study and summon him for his weekly counseling session. At first they had discussed school events in stilted little conversations, but after a while, when he started coming half an hour early, they'd relaxed with each other and began talking about what was going on in their lives. Jase had shared her joy when she made straight As and was elected sophomore representative to student council, and he'd consoled her when Mama and Daddy said she couldn't have unchaperoned dates until her next birthday.

In turn, she tried not to look shocked as she learned about the way he lived. Everyone in Baptist-dry Bosque Bend knew that Jase's father was a bad-tempered bully who kept a rowdy tavern just over the county line, but Laurel had been horrified to learn that Growler Redlander was such a poor excuse for a parent that his son had been working odd jobs since he was nine to support himself.

Jase had shrugged off her concern. "Laurel, I was five six when I was in the fourth grade. By the time I hit middle school, I was five ten and could pass for an eighteen-year-old any day of the week. The car wash is easy, and it's only one night a week. The only problem with the yard work is hiding the mower from my father so he can't toss it in the river like he does everything else."

Laurel's fifteen-year-old heart had opened to him. He was so brave, so valiant—and so handsome, just like the heroes on the covers of the romances she borrowed from Mrs. Bridges's extensive collection of paperbacks.

But that was sixteen years ago. What had brought Jase back to Bosque Bend? What sort of "family emergency" could possibly involve her?

She watched him deposit himself carefully on the delicately carved sofa, as if afraid it would break under his weight. He focused his gaze on her, and she took a quick breath. She'd forgotten how dark his eyes were—so black that iris and pupil seemed to blend into one. But why was he staring at her like that? Was something wrong? She glanced down at her silky white blouse. None of the buttons had come undone, and the zipper of her gray slacks was still closed tight.

He blinked, waved his hand in apology, and shifted his gaze. "I'm sorry. It's just that you seem so much the same. Somehow I expected you to look, well, *older.*"

Suddenly nervous, she pushed a heavy sheaf of dark hair back behind her ear and gave a little laugh, flattered but disbelieving. She was thirty-one years old, had been through hell, and didn't doubt that every bit of it showed on her face.

Nothing to do but seize the conversational bull by the horns. "You said you have an emergency?"

He exhaled deeply and rubbed his fingers along the nap of the sofa. "It's my daughter. She ran away from home this morning and left a note saying she was going to Bosque Bend to find her roots. I think she might try to contact you."

His daughter? Jase had a *child*?

Through the years, Laurel's mind had frozen him at age sixteen, standing alone against the world, her tragic lost love. The idea that he would marry one day and have a family had never even entered her head. Jase Redlander hadn't seemed to be the type to settle down. Instead, she'd pictured him as an unshaven roughneck putting out oil fires—or maybe a steel-jawed hero fighting off a Mexican drug cartel. Year by year, he'd become a fantasy figure to her—a heroic dark knight. Certainly not a father.

He pulled a photo from his wallet. "Here's a picture of Lolly from last year. She looks a lot older than she is, but don't be fooled—she's only fifteen."

Using a thick-barreled pen, he scrawled something on the back of the picture before offering it to her. Laurel reached for it. Their fingers touched and a sizzle of awareness shot through her. The picture fell to the carpet.

Jase bent down to retrieve the photo and placed it on the rococo table beside her, his eyes catching hers for one long moment. "I'm at the old house," he said, his voice a bit deeper. "It's between renters right now." His gaze moved to her mouth, and his pitch dropped even lower. "You remember it. You were there...once."

Laurel picked the photograph up from the table, willing her hand not to tremble, and forced herself to study it. Jase was right. His daughter did look older than she had any right to, but that was how fifteen-year-old girls always looked, even when she herself was in high school. Probably back to caveman times. Lolly was lovely, just as pretty as Jase was handsome. Butter-yellow hair swooped down across her forehead, almost covering her right eye, while her pouting lips and lazy-lidded eyes were studiously sexy. Her eyebrows were long, like her father's—Hollywood eyebrows.

But did she have her father's smile? Jase didn't smile often in the old days, but when he did, it was like the sun coming out—a wide, brilliant, heartbreaking grin, perhaps more effective because it was so rare.

Well, from the looks of him, he had a lot more to smile about these days.

Laurel raised her eyes from the photo and held it out to him, this time careful to avoid all contact of the flesh. *He's married. Off limits.*

"If she does show up, I'll be sure to let you know."

Jase put up a refusing hand. "No, keep it. I wrote my number on the back. Show it to your parents too, in case she comes by when you're not here."

Laurel froze.

"Mama and Daddy are dead." She kept her voice steady as she placed the photo on the little table again. "I'm living here alone now, and I'm between jobs, so I spend most of my time at the house."

Jase's mouth opened and closed. She'd caught him by surprise. Apparently he hadn't kept up with the goings-on in his old home town. Who could blame him? He'd been all but ridden out on a rail.

"I'm sorry about that. I'd meant to come back here sometime to visit with your dad. Reverend Ed's support meant a lot to me. He's the only one who believed in me through that whole mess, you know. I guess I thought he was eternal."

Laurel shrugged. "Nothing lasts forever." And Daddy, her wonderful Daddy, had died in spirit long before his body finally gave out. She studied the philodendron in the wicker stand beside her guest. How long had it been since she'd watered the local vegetation? And why on earth had she focused on the stupid plant? Because she didn't want to think about Daddy.

Jase exhaled softly. "I thought maybe you were here visiting your parents, but you and Dave are living in this house now? Aunt Maxie said you two—"

"Dave Carson and I were divorced three years ago," she interrupted. "And we didn't have any children. I've been teaching music for the past six years at Lynnwood Elementary, a new school over on the east side of the river, but my contract wasn't renewed. I'm trying to sell the house so I can get a fresh start somewhere else."

He leaned forward to lay his big hand gently on hers. His voice was soft and comforting.

"I'm sorry for that too. It's hard to start over in a new place."

Her eyelids quivered. What was this man doing to her? She refused to let herself dissolve into tears just because Jase Redlander had gotten her libido going, then offered her sympathy when no one else had.

Withdrawing her hand, she directed the subject back to Jase's truant daughter. "What makes you think Lolly will come here?"

"Her history class did a unit on personal roots last semester, and she's been after me ever since, wanting to know about my family." He paused as if trying to decide what to say. "And her mother's."

His eyes avoided her questioning glance and wandered around the room.

Laurel held her breath. Had he noticed the Greek statues were gone? Daddy would have called it false pride, but she didn't want anyone to realize she was pawning jewelry and selling off family heirlooms to buy her bread and butter.

Having the FOR SALE sign in front of the house was different—the more people who knew she was planning to leave Bosque Bend, the better. Maybe then they'd get off her back.

She glanced at the baby grand in the corner next to Daddy's office. There was no way to take anything that large with her when she moved. She'd tried to sell it—discreetly, of course—but it turned out that old pianos were a drag on the market. Her hands flexed. The Steinway was so out of tune that she could hardly bear to play it anymore, but how could anyone not love a piano?

Jase began again. "I cleaned up my father's memory as much as possible for Girl Child, but had to do some pretty fast talking when it came to her mother. I tried to keep things vague, but she added two and two and came up with five."

"Five?"

"She left a note. She's come to Bosque Bend to find you. She—she thinks you're her mother."

Laurel's eyes widened and her jaw dropped open. What? Had she heard him right?

"Me? Why? Your wife—"

His gaze held steady. "I'm not married and never have been. Lolly's mother abandoned her at birth."

Laurel felt like she was treading water. "You're a—a single father?"

He nodded.

She reached for a lifeline. "But…usually the mother takes the baby."

"She wasn't the maternal type."

The tide was rising. "But I still don't understand. Why me? Why does your daughter think *I'm* her mother?"

Jase dropped his gaze and moved his hand as if trying to back off from the question.

"I…well…it just happened. It wasn't deliberate. I think she misinterpreted some of the stories Maxie told her from when we used to live here." He cleared his throat. "You remember Maxie, don't you? Maxine Hokinson, Swede Hokinson's daughter, my mother's oldest sister? She's the one who subbed at your friend Sarah Bridges's house that summer their regular housekeeper got swarmed by Africanized bees. Anyway, you don't need to get involved—just call me if Lolly shows up on your doorstep, and I'll come fetch her."

"All right." What else could she say? She was way out of her depth.

He glanced at his watch. "I've got to go now. It's getting late, and I don't want to be gone from the old house too long, in case Lolly shows up there."

Laurel stood up to walk him out. "I'm sure you'll find her soon."

She was sure of no such thing, but at least she hoped so. A fifteen-year-old could land herself in a lot of trouble in an unfamiliar town, no matter how small. *The Retriever* had reported that a group of rowdy teenagers had been gathering in the parking lot of old Bosque Bend High School every night this summer and disturbing residents nearby. Art Sawyer had accompanied the story with a blistering editorial about under-age drinking and promised more to come as the investigation continued.

Lord only knows how Art always got the inside scoop. Probably because his wife was a Hruska and her cousin's nephew was the new chief of police. That's how things worked in Bosque Bend. The old families, the ones that had been anchored there for generations, all knew each other, and—good, bad, or indifferent—the news got around.

Laurel unlocked the big front door, then held the screen open with one hand while offering the other to Jase in farewell. He enveloped it in his own for a single warm second and smiled at her—that dazzling, absolutely devastating smile that people saw so rarely, the smile that had sealed her to him for all eternity when she was just fifteen.

"Thank you, Laurel. You're kinder to me than I deserve."

Her heart thumped so loudly that he should have been able to hear it. She watched as he crossed the lawn to the long driveway on the south side of the house, waved once, and opened the door of his car—a big black Cadillac, just like Daddy used to drive.

* * *

Accustomed to Dallas's big-city traffic, Jase made his way through Bosque Bend's rush hour without even noticing it.

Where the hell was Lolly? Girl Child was quite a handful, but she'd never pulled a stunt like this before. A shiver shot through him as he glanced at the rapidly setting sun.

Relax, Jase. Everything's going to be all right. Lolly's a smart kid. She can take care of herself. In fact, she's probably sitting on the front porch of the old house right now, waiting for you to come

pick her up. Where else could she be? You needn't have bothered
Laurel by barging in on her like that.

He changed lanes, moving to the left.

Laurel…instead of working himself into a panic about
Lolly, he'd think about Reverend Ed's daughter, like he always
did when his life started going down the crapper. She was the
only girl he'd ever loved, and remembering her kindness—her
goodness—gave him peace and strength.

But this time, picturing Laurel Harlow in his mind's eye
made him feel even worse. His fingers tightened on the
leather-covered steering wheel. Sixteen years to learn better, and he'd still made a complete ass out of himself when
he tried to talk to her—but he'd never imagined she'd be
orphaned and divorced, all alone in that big, cavernous
house.

His mouth twisted. He should have figured out something
was going on when Information told him the Harlow number
was unlisted. That was quite a change from the old days, when
half the boys in Bosque Bend were on the horn to Reverend
Ed—or at least the "at-risk" half.

But how could anyone be stupid enough to let Laurel
Harlow get away? Driving into town earlier this afternoon,
he'd thought that ol' Dave was one man who went to bed
happy each night. As a teenager, Laurel had been sexy as
hell—tall, with a full-breasted woman's body, soft gray eyes
fringed with long black lashes, her lips sweet and tender—the princess of Bosque Bend. Now, in full woman-
hood, she was in her glory.

He stomped on his brake as a traffic signal that hadn't been there sixteen years ago went from amber to red in front of him. Time to switch on his headlights. The last of the radiant sunset had finally sunk below the horizon.

He'd better get a move on. His old neighborhood had always held a particularly prominent position on the Bosque Bend police blotter, and he didn't want Lolly out there alone after dark.

The signal turned green. He hit the accelerator and shot forward.

Crap! He'd missed his turn.

No wonder. The old Alamo Drive-in on the corner of Crocket Avenue had finally been torn down, and in its place was a Walmart, complete with a large, white marquee advertising a post–July Fourth sale in patriotic red-and-blue letters.

Which meant that Overton's Department Store, which had reigned supreme on the city square since before he was born, finally had some competition. Jase smiled grimly. At least Overton's blatant racism ended when Reverend Ed threatened Dolph Overton, this generation's CEO, with a congregational boycott. You didn't fuck around with the pastor of the biggest church in town.

Exiting at the next street, he circled back, driving through the crowded parking lot. A constant stream of customers entered the store through the sliding door on the right, slowing him down to a crawl. Another wellspring exited from the slider on the left, the adults carrying bags of merchandise and pushing grocery baskets while the children bounced red, white, and blue balloons on strings. He maneuvered carefully around a little boy dashing about in the near dark with a blue balloon tied to his wrist, U-turned, and eased out onto Crocket again.

How much time had he lost? The streetlights were glimmering now. Night was falling fast.